THE MANSION

ALSO BY EZEKIEL BOONE

The Hatching

Skitter

Zero Day

THE MANSION

• A NOVEL •

Ezekiel Boone

EMILY BESTLER BOOKS

—

ATRIA

NEW YORK   LONDON   TORONTO   SYDNEY   NEW DELHI

EMILY
BESTLER
BOOKS

ATRIA

An Imprint of Simon & Schuster, Inc.
1230 Avenue of the Americas
New York, NY 10020

First Emily Bestler Books/Atria Books hardcover edition December 2018

EMILY BESTLER BOOKS / ATRIA BOOKS and colophon are trademarks of Simon & Schuster, Inc.

For information about special discounts for bulk purchases, please contact Simon & Schuster Special Sales at 1-866-506-1949 or business@simonandschuster.com.

The Simon & Schuster Speakers Bureau can bring authors to your live event. For more information or to book an event, contact the Simon & Schuster Speakers Bureau at 1-866-248-3049 or visit our website at www.simonspeakers.com.

Interior design by Kyoko Watanabe

Manufactured in the United States of America

10 9 8 7 6 5 4 3 2 1

Library of Congress Cataloging-in-Publication Data

Names: Boone, Ezekiel, author.
Title: The mansion : a novel / by Ezekiel Boone.
Description: First Emily Bestler Books/Atria Books hardcover edition. | New York :
    Emily Bestler Books/Atria, 2018.
Identifiers: LCCN 2017053605 (print) | LCCN 2017056672 (ebook) |
    ISBN 9781501165528 (ebook) | ISBN 9781501165504 (hardcover) |
    ISBN 9781501165511 (trade pbk)
Subjects: | GSAFD: Suspense fiction. | Mystery fiction. | Science fiction.
Classification: LCC PS3602.O6577 (ebook) | LCC PS3602.O6577 M36 2018 (print) |
    DDC 813/.6—dc23
LC record available at https://lccn.loc.gov/2017053605

ISBN 978-1-5011-6550-4
ISBN 978-1-5011-6552-8 (ebook)

For Sabine.
You deserve this one.

Une maison est une machine-à-habiter.

A house is a machine for living in.

—Le Corbusier

THE MANSION

ONE

LET OLD ACQUAINTANCES

More than anything, what Billy Stafford wanted to do right now was to smash Shawn Eagle's smug little face in.

Shawn Eagle: former best friend and business partner. Shawn Eagle: founder, visionary, and CEO of Eagle Technology. Shawn Eagle: one of the ten richest men in the world. Shawn Eagle: lying, cheating, backstabbing scumbag.

Ten years since he'd seen Shawn in person, and just the imagined sound of his fist hitting that bastard in the face was enough to make Billy happy. He could hear it. The wet sound of flesh on flesh, the follow-through of his knuckles against Shawn's teeth, the way it would sound both hollow and solid at the same time. He could picture it, too. Shawn's head snapping back and bouncing off the plate glass window. Mashed lips and teeth jutting out at an odd angle, Shawn crumpling to his back on the plush carpet, frothy bubbles of blood bursting out the old kisser. Shawn wouldn't be doing any kissing for a while after that.

There wasn't anything Billy could think of that he wanted right now more than he wanted to cave in Shawn's face, and he was *trying* to think of other things that he wanted more. Billy wanted to punch Shawn more than he wanted to drink a frosted pint glass of Ommegang Witte Belgian ale poured right from the tap. More than he wanted a bucket of a dozen Yuenglings, the bottles of beer settling into the crushed ice. Billy wanted to hit Shawn Eagle more, even, than he wanted four neat lines of coke or, Jesus, most of all, a sip of a Bombay Sapphire gin and tonic in a heavy, cut-glass crystal tumbler full of solid squares of ice. And he wanted *all* of those things.

Still.

Desperately.

Nearly two years sober, and he hadn't stopped burning for any of what he'd left behind. But he didn't want to get high or drunk anywhere near as much as he wanted to punch Shawn Eagle in the mouth.

Best not to think of the booze—it was mostly booze—and drugs. No. Not booze, then. Punching Shawn would be more satisfying than . . . a blow job from Shawn's ridiculously attractive personal assistant? How about that? Cindy or Sammy or Wendy or something? Was that a safer thing to think of than booze and drugs? Just the thought probably made him a misogynist, but sexual objectification and his long-suffering wife, Emily, be damned. Shawn's assistant, a black woman of maybe twenty-five who looked like she could have doubled as a lingerie model, was hot. And he was sure she was smart, too. She was almost certainly an Ivy League graduate. She likely came from Cortaca University itself, his and Shawn's good old alma mater. She probably had an IQ that could serve as a respectable batting average in the major leagues. But however smart she was, that wasn't what Billy was thinking about; watching her ass sway while she led him into Shawn's office had been one of the great pleasures of Billy's life. Okay, fine. He was a sexist pig and a theoretical philanderer—though never an actual philanderer—and he was a terrible person to have the thought at all. He already knew he wasn't going to win any humanitarian awards. The question, however, was would he take a blow job from Cindy or Sammy or Wendy or whatever her name was over the chance to punch Shawn in the face?

No. Not for an instant.

Billy glanced down and realized he already had his right foot weighted and back a step. All he had to do was cock his fist and let go. Boom. Punch through your target. Punch through Shawn Eagle's shitty smile. Punch through those capped and whitened teeth. Punch right through the grin that was part of the reason Shawn Eagle had last year been named one of *People* magazine's sexiest men alive. In college, girls said he was beautiful. Shawn joked that it was because he was exotic looking, even if the one-eighth of him that was Indian wasn't the sort of Indian you'd expect in a programmer. But at thirty-six, Billy thought, Shawn wasn't beautiful anymore; he was, instead, harder, different. Shawn was handsome now. His black hair was collar length. He wore designer jeans and T-shirts that fit the body he kept polished with the help of personal trainers. He still looked exotic. No wonder *People* magazine picked him; no wonder Shawn was constantly on the "most eligible bachelor" lists. He was young, rich, brilliant, and handsome.

Young, rich, brilliant, and handsome? Billy could fix one of those things. There was security in the lobby, security outside the office. Shawn didn't go anywhere without a couple of bodyguards. He had the kind of money where he *couldn't* go anywhere without a couple of bodyguards, but none of the muscle was in the room. Billy thought he could do some real damage before they responded. Shawn wouldn't be so handsome anymore. Not after Billy was finished with him.

But Shawn Eagle, seemingly oblivious to the murderous impulses swirling in front of him, kept talking. He turned his back to Billy, looking out the bank of windows that gave him a view over the construction of Eagle Technology's new Fisker DeLeon–designed campus, and beyond that, to Baltimore's harbor. They were in Shawn's office, which was big enough so that it was divided into zones; they were standing in the lounge, a comfy pit complete with couches and a thick-pile rug, all somehow lower than the rest of the office. The lounge was sunk into the floor, three steps down from where the "real" work was clearly done. Up those three steps there was a desk the size of a whale. And in the open space in the middle, a conference table that could have doubled as an aircraft carrier. Even the bathroom suite was bigger than any apartment Billy had ever rented. The office was a riot of exotic-looking wood and metal. Shawn probably had the accents carved out of unicorn horns or something, just because he could afford to. The office took up half the entire top floor of the twelve-story building, and the crazy thing was that this building was only temporary. According to Shawn, Eagle Technology had "thrown it up" on the edge of their old campus so that Shawn could have a view of the construction of their new corporate campus. The old Eagle Technology headquarters had the address of 1000 Digital Drive, Baltimore, Maryland, but the new campus address was simply "Mobius Strip." No need for a street number.

Eagle Technology's Mobius Strip headquarters was going to cost tens of billions of dollars. By the time it was done, it was going to make Apple's campus out in California look like tract housing, and the address itself, Mobius Strip, was a dig at Apple's Infinite Loop. Through the window, Billy could see the constant movement of cranes and cement mixers and trucks. It was scheduled to be done in six or seven more months, by the spring, but it didn't look like they were that close. The rumors were that Shawn had driven the project wildly over what was already a wildly inflated budget. He demanded perfection that was nearly impossible even with modern building techniques. The architect, Fisker DeLeon, had publicly crowed that when it was done, it wouldn't be a technology campus; it would be a work of art. Nearly 80 percent of the building material had been custom fabricated for Eagle, and Maryland had done everything but name Shawn the reigning monarch because of the money he was pouring into the state and into the city of Baltimore. For a city that had been on the ropes before Eagle Technology exploded, Shawn was a gift from heaven. Forget the construction. Forget the new roads and infrastructure that Eagle was paying for to make sure the campus was perfect. Forget the union jobs—Eagle Technology hired union crews!—by the thousands to make the buildings rise from the earth like ancient temples made of glass and steel. Forget the businesses that already existed just to serve the employees of Eagle Technology. Restaurants and upscale spas offering tea-oil massages finished off with chia seed smoothies. Dog walkers and lawn services and car dealerships. Organic grocery stores and shops devoted entirely to selling olive oil. Forget all that. Eagle

Technology alone already employed something like thirty thousand people in the Baltimore area, and once the new campus was finished, they'd be consolidating their operations, pulling more employees into the area so that they would have a full-time Baltimore workforce of nearly fifty thousand at Eagle Technology proper. Good jobs! Good jobs that paid well and got taxed at rates that made the politicians obsequious. Plus, Eagle Technology was like a magnet, with other tech companies opening satellite offices or talking about relocating to Baltimore themselves, turning Baltimore into Silicon Valley East. No wonder Shawn Eagle had been named "man of the year" three years running by *Baltimore* magazine. No wonder most people thought that Shawn Eagle, at thirty-six, had a perfect life.

But Billy still really wanted to punch him.

It had been an even decade since he'd seen Shawn. A decade of having to watch from afar as Shawn's tiny company—what had once been Billy and Shawn's company—did what Google and Apple and other tech companies had done before: go from nothing to everything. No matter how much Billy had tried to run away from Shawn, no matter how much he drank or what he put into his body, he couldn't get away from Shawn. Eagle Technology's market cap had shot past Apple's and Google's and Amazon's, and Shawn was everywhere: On the covers of magazines. Newspapers. His name on the radio and as a good-natured punch line on late-night television. His face on the cover of that ridiculous biography, *Learning to Soar,* one of the biggest books of the year. But worse was that Billy couldn't go anywhere without seeing a piece of Eagle Technology. The gold-infused titanium—another one of Shawn's "brilliant" innovations, marketed as Eagle Titanium—on high-end phones and tablets and computers, the classic Eagle Red aluminum on cheaper devices. It wasn't the phones or the computers or other devices that made Billy furious. It was what was inside them: Eagle Logic.

Eagle Logic. That had been Billy's genius. The hardware was never what mattered. They both knew that. No matter how slick they looked, no matter how well they were engineered, the tablets and phones and watches, all of it—without Eagle Logic, they were just pieces of fancy metal. Eagle Logic was the program that made everything work. A new computing language that Billy and Shawn had birthed into existence. Right away, Eagle Logic was different. More organic. Microsoft and IBM and C++ and Java and all the relics of the early years of computers relied on some sort of binary system. Ones and zeros. Off and on. But he and Shawn had come up with a more complex decision-making process. It wasn't even really accurate to say that they'd invented a new computing language, because the language and the program were inseparable. One without the other was just as useless as Shawn's hardware without Eagle Logic. But that was too complicated for most people—Billy had tried to explain it to Emily on more than one occasion—and most people, if they thought about Eagle Logic at all when they talked to their phones, thought of her as a program. But they didn't think about Eagle Logic, because she actually worked. If you said, "Call Susan," she could figure out which one of the five Susans in your address book you meant. If you told her to book you dinner for seven at eight at the Nines, she took care of that without a hiccup. It wasn't that Eagle Logic could do anything particularly new, in the same way that Google didn't invent the search engine and Apple didn't come up with the MP3 player when they introduced the iPod, but Eagle Logic did it better. Shawn's particular genius was in packaging all of it, in giving customers Eagle Logic, a clearly superior operating and support system, in a device that looked like it was better, too. But what made it all come together, the engine that drove everything? That was Billy's work.

The name itself was a coin flip. Heads and it was Stafford Logic, tails and it was Eagle Logic. Shawn had won—then and other times, Billy thought—and given Eagle Logic her name. They agreed on that, at least, that *it* was indisputably *her*. There was no option for Eagle Logic to have a male voice. They didn't agree on much else as time went by, but they agreed that the language and the program together combined to make something female. The joke that Shawn liked to make in interviews, until he got called out by a feminist group that threatened a boycott, was that Eagle Logic was female because, like most women, she was smarter than she seemed.

Because at first, Eagle Logic didn't seem like she was working very well. They hadn't even meant to make Eagle Logic. Eagle Logic was their failure. She was the less ambitious compromise, what they figured they could get to work when . . . Well, a lot of things had gone wrong. Things Billy didn't like to think about.

Safest to say that their first project had imploded, but even then, they struggled to get Eagle Logic right. They'd tried to sidestep the logic gates of other technology. Yes. No. Those were the only two choices. Not for them, though. They'd made a program that was supposed to be equipped for dealing with something in between: maybe. Of course, Eagle Logic 1.0 didn't work. And neither did Eagle Logic 2.0 or 3.0 or 4.0.

For almost two years he and Shawn had holed up in that shitty, terrifying cabin. It was pressed up against the decrepit, fallen down Eagle Mansion. Wind whistled through the holes in the walls at night, screeching in his ears. They used to joke about living next to a haunted house, but neither of them had really been joking; Eagle Mansion loomed over them like a bad dream. The trees creeping closer and closer. The whole thing claustrophobic despite being in the middle of nowhere. It was thirty minutes of twisting, tortured driving to the closest town, if you could call Whiskey Run a town, and forty-five minutes from there to Cortaca and what friends they had left at the university. The only truly great thing about the cabin was that it was free. It gave them a place to focus on their project. They'd worked their asses off there, in upstate New York, right up against the Canadian border. Sixteen, eighteen hours a day in that small cabin, the ruins of Eagle Mansion right above them, almost mocking them with its past glory.

They lived on beer and frozen pizza and boxes of macaroni and cheese, like they were still students. Twenty-three months of working together, of not enough sleep and too much beer and too many things gone wrong. Too many secrets to bury, too many things haunting them. Finally, things had fallen apart between them for good.

"I guess you get the girl," Shawn had said as Billy was walking away.

Shawn had been right and he'd been wrong, too. Billy had gotten Emily, all right, but if Eagle Logic was indisputably feminine, then Shawn had ended up with a girl of his own, one that put a hell of a lot more in the bank.

He was still in love with his wife, Billy thought. He was.

"I guess you get the girl." That had been the last thing Shawn had said to him before Billy and Emily drove off, away from Eagle Mansion and out of Shawn's life forever. Or, at least until now. Oh, Billy had seen Shawn in the meantime—seen his smug mug on magazine covers and on television, seen Shawn across a courtroom nearly a decade ago, when Eagle Technology was just becoming something, up on the stand during Billy's last, ruinous attempt to get what was his, that lying prick completely distorting the who and what and when of his success, the story of Eagle Logic and Eagle Technology drifting further away from the truth with every year.

The truth.

No. Neither of them wanted the whole story to come out.

But Billy wanted what was fair. He'd suffered, too. Shawn owed him.

Good god, he wanted to smash Shawn's face in. Not just to punch him, but walk over to the bar cart and pick up one of those heavy bottles of whiskey and use that to bludgeon Shawn. To hit him and hit him and hit him until no doctor on earth could reconstruct the bones of his face. And then, when he was done, he'd scoop some ice out of the bucket, let frozen water ring against the bottom of a highball, and pour himself a stiff one right from the bloody—literally, as in covered with Shawn's blood—bottle.

Shawn turned from the window and looked at Billy.

"I'd offer you a drink, but my people tell me that you've been dry for two years," Shawn said. "Congratulations, by the way."

Billy reached his hand into his pocket. Old habits. He usually kept his one-year coin in there. He dug deeper. His pocket was empty. He felt a brief, bright moment of panic. He'd lost the coin somewhere between Seattle and Baltimore. He swallowed hard. It was just a talisman. A piece of luck to keep nearby. It wasn't something he needed.

"Not quite two years," he said. "End of the month will be two years. Twenty-three months right now." There was no recognition from Shawn that twenty-three months meant anything, that when Billy said he was twenty-three months sober, it was the same amount of time the two of them had been holed up in that shitty cabin working together. Years ago. Back when they were friends. Back when living next to a spooky, rotting, haunted mansion and spending every waking moment working seemed like an adventure. Back when they weren't going to let *anything* stop them.

Or anyone.

But there was no reaction from Shawn. Nothing. In the same way that there was nothing in his pocket. No coin there. No marker of his sobriety. Like that first year of keeping away from alcohol and drugs had never happened. But that was fine. He'd wait for his two-year coin. In the meantime? "I'll take a Diet Coke."

"Isn't the cliché from recovery meetings that everybody drinks coffee nonstop? We can do coffee. Or an espresso or whatever."

"Diet Coke. If you've got it."

Shawn laughed. "Whatever you want, Billy. In a can or a glass?"

"Can."

It was surprisingly low-tech. Shawn walked to the door, which was an endeavor in itself given the size of his office, and stuck his head out, calling to his assistant. Wendy. Her name was Wendy.

"Anything else?" Billy shook his head. "Hotel is fine? And the flight was okay? Sorry you had to go commercial. I would have sent a jet for you, but I lent one of mine to Taylor Swift. She has her own jet, of course, but there's something or other with an engine, and she's a friend. And my other two planes are being redecorated. The board has been giving me a hassle about using the company jets for private business." Shawn waved his hand in annoyance. "They don't want me to treat Eagle Technology like it's my own private playground anymore. Corporate governance crap."

Billy didn't say anything. Commercial. It's not like he had to rough it. A limousine had picked him up at his and Emily's squalid studio apartment in Seattle and taken him directly to the plane. The plane.

As in, drove out onto the tarmac at SeaTac, where a flight attendant was waiting to open a stairway at the base of the jet bridge so that he could go right on up and into the plane and take a seat in first class. He'd never even gone into the terminal. Another flight attendant, a young Latino kid with just a hint of a mustache, had greeted him by name as he boarded, calling him Mr. Stafford and making sure that he was comfortable, asking if he could get him anything.

It had only been one gin and tonic.

"I guess you probably want to know why I asked you to come?" Shawn said.

"Very astute of you, Shawn. We haven't talked directly for a decade, since you screwed me over—"

"The court—"

"The court can go screw itself. And screw you, Shawn. Screw you!" Billy said. No. He didn't say it. He yelled it. He realized he was shouting. And Shawn's personal assistant, Wendy, was standing on the steps looking terrified. He bet Wendy was easily clearing a million a year plus stock options and whatever perks she wanted. She probably got to fly in one of Shawn's private jets whenever she needed to go somewhere. She was staring at Billy, and he shut up and turned so that he could watch her in one of the mirrors on the wall instead.

He felt like shit. For thinking about her like she was just some sex object. For yelling and scaring her. For who he was afraid he might be. For the sobriety token missing from his pocket. For all the ways he'd messed up his life. For the things that he and Shawn kept buried.

He shouldn't have come.

He saw Wendy look over at Shawn. Shawn shrugged, so Wendy stepped over to Billy and handed him the can of Diet Coke. Just what he'd asked for. What he needed. The cold metal was a relief. He pressed the can against his forehead for a moment before opening it. His temper. It had become worse since he'd gotten sober.

Shawn waited until Wendy was gone and then he held up his palms. A symbol of peace. "Hear me out, okay? I know that you and Emily are having some hard times."

Hard times. What a colloquial way of putting it. They were flat, dead-ass broke. Four months behind on their rent. Nine credit cards that Emily knew about, all maxed to the point where the plastic was in danger of melting. Four more credit cards that Emily didn't know about. Their car, a piece of shit deathtrap that had been nice once, was more rust and holes than actual metal. It started most of the time, but the brakes were so shot that they were afraid to drive it on the highway. He wouldn't have minded it so much if he'd still been blotto all the time. It would have made sense, then. Of course we're broke! I'm drinking and snorting every dollar that comes in! No wonder we don't even have enough change lying around to make our pockets jingle!

But he'd been stone-cold sober for two years. Not quite two years. He reached into his pocket again. Twenty-three months and . . . four days. No one-year coin. Not even lint in his pocket. That's how broke they were. But there were no excuses: since he'd gotten sober, he'd stayed sober. Just that one gin and tonic on the plane. He deserved that. It was only one drink, which was nothing. Back before he got sober he could line them up and knock them down. One gin and tonic wouldn't have even counted as a drink. It had been what, twelve years, thirteen, since he'd talked with Shawn Eagle like this, just the two of them alone in a room? He was fine. And it wasn't fair to say that he couldn't blame the drinking or the drugs; the money was good and gone by the time he sobered up. Not that there'd ever been *that* much money, but there'd been a period of time, five or six years, when, if he hadn't been wealthy, he and Emily had been able to stay afloat. The rocket-ship rise of Eagle Technology had allowed his laughably small amount of stock to keep pace with his spending for a little while. If he'd kept all of it, if he hadn't sold any of it, it would be worth just a shade under eleven million dollars now. Nothing compared with Shawn Eagle, the second-wealthiest man alive, but not bad for the son of a waitress and a drunk, abusive custodian. But he hadn't kept all of it, of course. He hadn't kept any of it. He'd sold it off in chunks great and small at prices that were criminal in retrospect. Maybe five hundred grand total before taxes? Not all at once, of course. He bled himself out. Booze and coke and some of it toward the failed lawsuit. It would have gone quicker, and for less, if it hadn't been for the magical Shawn Eagle, who, according to every hagiographic newspaper and magazine article, every ball-sucking interview, was a gee-whiz genius who'd turned Eagle Technology from an idea into a global behemoth all by his lonesome. Every time Billy thought he'd run the well of his shitty settlement dry, that the miserly bit of stock he had left was gone, that there was nothing left to bail him out, Eagle Technology would go on another run, hit a new record, split at 3 to 1, split again at 7 to 1, and again at 4 to 1. But the well had gone empty, eventually. At some point, a few years ago, when he was in the deepest reaches of the bottle, there was simply nothing left to sell. How different would things have been if he'd sat on that stock? He'd be looking at eight figures, enough money for him and Emily to live in luxury for the rest of their lives. Move someplace warm. An island somewhere. Open a coffee shop or a small restaurant. But instead he'd sold pieces of the stock at every opportunity, turning it into the cold clink of ice and gin and a wedge of lime.

They were deep in it. They had some money coming in, but it was like pissing on a bonfire. Emily was working at a preschool, and she was happy with the little moppets, and Billy had picked up part-time work on the night cleaning crew at a huge chain health club. Working as a custodian for minimum wage. Like his dad. But not a drunk like his dad. Not anymore. The pay was a joke and the work was a joke, but none of it was funny. He should have been sitting at a computer and conquering the world, but nobody would touch him. It was ridiculous. Picking up coding languages used to be as easy as breathing for him. Shawn had been a good programmer. A really good programmer. More important, Shawn had a terrific understanding of how people actually interacted with computers, what they wanted but didn't know they wanted. The real magic, however, had come from Billy. He'd been the one who made Eagle Logic come alive. It had worked best when they were working together. Even at the beginning when it was Billy and Shawn and . . . After. It had worked best after.

They had come up with the idea of integrating a new coding

language and program to create something wholly different, but Billy was the one who'd seen the way to break a computer's logic apart and give them something more. Without Billy there was no Eagle Logic, and without Eagle Logic, there was no Eagle Technology.

But there was no Billy anymore. Nobody but Shawn Eagle. Billy was in the dustbin of history, cast as opportunistic in the bestselling authorized biography *Learning to Soar: The Story of Shawn Eagle and the Rise of Eagle Technology*. What little space was given to him described him as a parasite, the entire lawsuit framed as an extortion attempt, with the author's barely disguised glee at Billy's walking away with a few thousand shares and Shawn's vindication. No, in the story of Eagle Technology, Billy barely existed, and to the extent that he did exist, it was as the villain. Shawn was the prince. Shawn was the hero. Shawn deserved all the credit, all the praise, and Billy deserved what he got: nothing.

Which was why he wanted to punch Shawn in the face.

He took another sip of his Diet Coke and then very deliberately sat on one of the white leather couches. If he decided to punch Shawn, he'd actually have to get up and stride across the room. It would be a decision. Not a reflex. Standing there, with Shawn so close to him, it would be too easy. So he sat down and listened.

"It's been too long," Shawn said. "Too long like this. Do you remember what it was like? That ridiculous cabin in the woods? In the winter, the wind would come through the cracks in the boards like a freight train. It would shriek at us. Just howling, screaming through the cabin. What did you call it? The freeze-ball express? And every time we got the woodstove hot enough to heat the place up, it would glow cherry-bomb red at the hinges and we'd double-check to make sure the fire extinguisher was ready. And remember when, despite how creepy it was, we tried going into Eagle Mansion, thinking we could light a fire in one of the grand fireplaces and that would be a good way to get warmed up? We busted up an entire set of chairs from the dining room, and when we actually got the fire lit, a whole shitload of bats came flying out of the chimney and we were running around screeching like little kids? Heck, man, we probably could have just carted in one of those tables and a set of chairs to Cortaca and sold them to an antiques dealer for enough money to feed us for half a year. Oh, and I can't believe I forgot about this," he said, laughing, "when the electricity got cut off that first summer, and we jury-rigged solar panels so we could keep our laptops charged?"

Billy smiled. He didn't want to, but he smiled. He didn't want to admit it, but he'd been happy then. Despite everything that happened, he had been happy. "And it rained for a week so we couldn't get a charge, and we were trying to work out the code by writing it on the walls?"

"It was like living in the worst, scariest, most rustic dorm in the universe. But worse, because Eagle Mansion was just looming there, taunting us, like, hey, I used to be an awesome place to live before I fell in on myself and turned haunted, and you guys are stuck in what probably used to be a servant's cottage."

"Yeah, well," Billy said, "could have been worse. We could have been in the burned-out groundskeeper's cottage that you grew up in. That place gave me the heebie-jeebies."

A thin smile. "Yeah." A real smile now. "And, shit. That first Thanksgiving, when we forgot that it was Thanksgiving, and we drove all the way from the cabin, over an hour into Cortaca, and Saigon Kitchen was, unbelievably, open, but they didn't take credit cards, and neither one of us had our bank cards, so we had to scrounge change from the car? We barely had enough money to get one order of Sriracha chicken wings to go, so we put it on a plate and made that our Thanksgiving turkey." Shawn laughed, and for a moment, Billy did remember.

It *had* been glorious. They'd been so alive and so young, still at that age when they couldn't understand the idea of getting old. They'd work thirty days in a row, getting up at eight or nine in the morning and starting out with bowls of sugared cereal—if they were lucky, and the electricity was keeping the tiny fridge humming, they had fresh milk, and if they weren't lucky, they ate it dry—and coding until two or three in the morning. They bought noodles and whatever meat was close to the expiration date at the off-brand grocery store in Whiskey

Run, and once a month, when the ridiculously small check came in the mail from Shawn's aunt Beverly, they'd drive the extra thirty miles to Cortaca and get burritos and stock up on cheap beer. They'd take a day to mess around in the woods and get loaded and recharge themselves for the next push of trying to make the idea of Eagle Logic into a reality. The cabin was a single room within spitting distance of what used to be the grand Eagle Mansion, a Prohibition-era resort that had once been graced by the rich and famous.

The mansion. Thinking of it made Billy shiver. The mansion looked like something from a horror movie: the roof was caving in and missing in spots, vines grew in and out of shattered windows, the walls were crumbling in places, and the whole building loomed over them. It was haunted. They were convinced of it. A few times, Billy woke in the middle of the night and thought he saw lights flickering in the mansion. Shawn was convinced that, one night, during their first winter, he'd seen a dark-haired woman gliding across the roof. Dead things came to life in that building. Dark things. They were young and dumb and men, so they couldn't keep themselves completely away from Eagle Mansion, but mostly, Billy had been leery of the old monolith. No way they would have stayed there if it hadn't been free.

The estate itself felt sprawling and equally full of mischief. Trees had grown thick and dark. Hedges had gone wild. What was once a great lawn was scattered with thorns. It was easy to imagine getting lost in the surrounding wilderness. Swallowed alive by the forest. At night, it seemed like the woods inched closer to their cabin.

The cabin was better. Less . . . possessed? Possessed. That was the word, Billy thought. It was cold and dank, but it was just a building. Eagle Mansion and the scattered outbuildings, including the groundskeeper's cottage, which had burned—with Shawn's parents in it—when Shawn was twelve, positively seethed. Early in their residency, they'd dropped acid and wandered around the grounds. Billy had found himself inside Eagle Mansion, barely holding it together. The walls pulsed and seemed to breathe. He thought the carpets were made of blood.

No. The cabin was safe. By scavenging some wood and shingles from the other outbuildings, they were able to make it livable. Barely livable, but livable. Aunt Beverly was paying the taxes on the estate, such as they were. She insisted that Shawn keep the land, since it had been in his family for generations.

"If you want to sell it when I'm dead and gone, then by all means," she had said during one of the times that she came to visit. Billy remembered it well. He'd liked the old bird, though she probably hadn't actually been that old at the time, no more than fifty or fifty-five. She always brought groceries and often other items, like frying pans or blankets or other things they needed and that she "just happened" to find stored in her basement in brand-new packaging from Target. "But you hold on to it for now. It's only twenty acres, and given how decrepit the old mansion is and that you're in the middle of nowhere, the taxes are a pittance. Trust me. You won't get much of anything if you sell, and you'll always regret it. You've got a family history here, as dark as it might be, and you can't walk away from that."

All they had to do was pay for electrical service, which they mostly did, and not freeze to death, which was sometimes touch-and-go. It wasn't much of a cabin, and Billy couldn't imagine a meaner place to develop an idea as beautiful as what they'd been trying to code, but for twenty-three months, it had been their home, their headquarters. They'd slept on camping pads, in secondhand sleeping bags and under blankets they bought from Goodwill or that Shawn's aunt brought them. They cooked on the woodstove and took shits in the woods, in an outhouse that didn't have a door: they'd taken it off to use as a desktop. "For shit's sake," Billy had loved to say, "our desk is an outhouse door!"

Shawn shook his head. "I don't think I've ever been as happy as I was then," he said. "The two of us working together in that cabin."

"Three," Billy said. The word just escaped from his lips. He hadn't meant to say it.

"What?"

"The three of us."

He didn't say the name.

Takata.

There'd been three of them. Shawn and Billy and Takata. He'd wanted to forget. Or maybe he *had* forgotten. It was like the echo of a sound that he could almost hear. Takata. How had he buried that so deeply in his memory?

There'd been three of them until, one day, there were only two of them. And from that day on, things had gotten worse; to go outside at night was to feel the mansion breathing in and out and glaring down at them. It was as if what they'd done had flipped some sort of switch. The mansion and the grounds turned from simply scary to something malevolent: blood calling for blood. And yet they didn't talk about Takata. The thing with Takata had come well before they'd even met Emily, well before Billy and Shawn had their falling out, well before Billy had heard Shawn say, as Billy walked away with Emily, "I guess you get the girl."

Shawn stared hard at Billy, and Billy remembered something he'd read in an interview once. Shawn had been asked about a deal Eagle Technology had made with a supplier in Indonesia, a deal so advantageous to Eagle Technology that the supplier went out of business in a matter of months. "You don't build a company like Eagle Technology by being the nicest guy in the room," Shawn said to the woman interviewing him. And when Billy read it, he'd thought it was just another one of those glib things that Shawn had learned to say, just part of the polish of being Mr. Hot Shit CEO and on *People* magazine's list of men who could get a blow job in an elevator any day of the week, but right at that moment, with Shawn staring at him, Billy felt cold. He felt like he had on those winter mornings in the cabin in the woods outside Whiskey Run, when the snow was piled up so high on the roof that the entire cabin creaked with every shift of the wind, when the metal of the woodstove screamed like a soul being torn from the body as the first fire of morning turned the newspaper and kindling into the promise of a better day. On those winter mornings, he'd wake up from the cold. He would sleep in so many pants and shirts and socks that he could barely move, a five-dollar sausage in a fifty-cent casing. Still, he woke up with his teeth chattering, his wispy adolescent beard covered in a rime of frost, and he'd think it was possible that he'd never be warm again. That's what it felt like having Shawn stare at him right now.

"Do you really want to talk about that," Shawn said. "Do you really want to talk about"—he bit down on the name like his life depended on it, like it was a struggle to get out, like he hadn't uttered it in years and years—"Takata?"

Billy thought he heard a sound behind him. The haunting echo of footsteps in a corridor. The ghostly brush of linen. He looked over his shoulder, expecting to see Wendy coming into the room with another Diet Coke for him, or an espresso for Shawn, her skirt making that soft kissing sound. But there was nobody there. Nobody behind him. Shawn's office was large enough to have easily held a hundred people, but it was just the two of them. Just him and Shawn. Only them. Empty.

"I didn't think you wanted to talk about it," Shawn said. He walked across the thick rug and sat on the other couch so that he was at an angle from Billy. The coffee table was made of metal. Gold-infused titanium, Billy realized. Eagle Titanium. Jesus. It was like Shawn had designed the office as a shrine to himself, Billy thought. Shawn swung his feet up onto the coffee table and laced his hands behind his head. "Besides, that's not why I brought you here."

Suddenly, Billy was tired of it all. He wasn't angry anymore. Just tired. "Why *am* I here, Shawn? Can we get it over with so that I can go home to my shitty job and my shitty life and my shitty apartment?"

"And Emily? So you can get home to Emily, too?"

Billy hesitated. And Emily. He wasn't sure where she fell in the scheme of things. He'd known once, but not anymore. He didn't know where his relationship with Emily stood on the ledger sheet. How far in the red had that balance gone? His marriage was like his credit cards: he'd spent more than he'd ever be able to pay off. He still loved Emily. Immensely. He hated admitting it, even to himself, but he would never have gotten sober if not for her, and the worst thing he could think of was her leaving him. Again. Leaving him again. For good this time. But that was none of Shawn's business. Billy looked at

Shawn squarely and said, with a confidence he didn't feel, "And Emily, of course. Don't be a dick."

"Up front, I should say this: I'm not over it. I'm still angry about what happened with Emily."

"You got Eagle Logic. Things turned out just fine for you. Don't complain to me about who ended up with Emily."

Shawn stared at him. It was probably for only a few seconds, but it felt longer.

"I want to offer you a job," Shawn said. He fidgeted and waved his hand a little. "I don't want to make it sound like something it's not. I want to be clear that it's something off the books. But if it works out, it could be really lucrative."

"We both know that you couldn't hire me to work for Eagle Technology, even if you wanted to. Even if *I* wanted to. I'm radioactive, Shawn. Let's not pretend we don't both know it." And it was true. So many reasons. A sexual harassment lawsuit that was completely unfounded but which he hadn't had the energy to fight. Two assault charges, both of which were, admittedly, deserved, and both of which had left him within a hair's breadth of jail time. And at his last programming job, sheer incompetence. He'd been a drunk and frequently snorting coke when those things happened, but it didn't matter. Those were only the headlines. There was more stuff, too, plus the lawsuit that followed him around. There were only so many chances a man could have. Billy had used them all.

"Don't underestimate what I can do, Billy. I *am* Eagle Technology," Shawn said, and for a moment, Billy saw himself leaping off the couch, smashing Shawn in the face, and then wrapping his hands around the bastard's throat and squeezing until he could feel the cartilage snap and pop so that Shawn never breathed again. Maybe Shawn saw it, too, because he rushed to the next words. "But that's neither here nor there. I've got a lot of latitude, and you won't be working at the main campus. Again, I'm telling you, it's a project that isn't on the books. Oh, there will be a contract and everything. It's a real job. Advantageous terms for you, with a very generous compensation package. But you'll be working directly for me, in a personal capacity.

You won't be working for Eagle Technology. The board won't know about it."

"I'll be working for you? In a personal capacity?"

Shawn nodded. "I know. I get it. It's never going to be the same as it was back when we were at the old cabin, when we were working together. When we were partners. Too much history there. Okay? But hear me out. I want to make things whole."

"You want to make things whole?" Billy heard how he sounded, echoing Shawn like a parrot. His voice broken in the same way that he felt broken, and once again, he came back to the idea that what he wanted, at this very moment, was to punch Shawn in the face.

Shawn stood back up, and for a moment Billy thought it was because he had seen something in Billy's eyes and was scared. But no. It was only so that Shawn could walk over to the bar cart and pour himself a belt of vodka.

"I want to do it right this time. I want to hire you—and Emily—to live in Whiskey Run. Past Whiskey Run. Right where it all started. I fixed up the old mansion," Shawn said. "I want you to go back to where it all began."

TWO

IN WHICH EMILY WIGGINS TAKES A NAP

Most days, she didn't nap. Most days, by the time the kids in her class at the Bright Apple Preschool were settled in their cots and she and her co-teacher, Andy, had picked up the classroom, she was happy to just read a magazine. But Andy had told her to go lie down, so she'd pulled a cot out for herself.

She supposed she probably looked tired. Billy had left yesterday afternoon, spending the night in a hotel in Baltimore before his meeting with Shawn today. She glanced at her watch. She figured they were probably talking right at that very minute. The thought made her sick. She'd begged Billy not to go. Things were bad, sure, but not that bad. Her entire marriage had been about helping Billy recover, first from what happened with Shawn and the company—most of which he refused to talk about—and then from his drinking. The coke was an issue, too, but really it was the drinking that he struggled with mostly. There were times when she hated him, when she thought about leaving him. There was even a time when she *had* actually left him for a few months. For most of the last two years, however, it had been good. Since he'd cleaned up. She was terrified that Shawn was going to upset the order of things.

It wouldn't have been honest to say that she didn't blame Billy. She didn't believe that being drunk was an excuse for anything, but it also wouldn't have been honest to say that she didn't understand. If it had been her, if she'd been the one who'd worked on a project like Eagle Logic, only to see it become a true phenomenon? Well, she wasn't sure she'd have been able to let it go. When she said to him, "Just get over it," what she was saying was, just get over the fact that this thing you helped create with the guy who used to be your best friend is worth hundreds of billions of dollars, of which, you ended up with . . . precisely nothing. And that was partly why, even though she begged him not to go, she didn't forbid it. The other part of it was that she still harbored the hope that Shawn would offer them real money, that he'd finally do the right thing.

She wasn't going to hold her breath, though.

She'd read once that inmates who've been wrongfully convicted have only two choices: to give up or to find some transcendent state where they could fight for justice without being bitter. It sounded stupid to her, but maybe it also made sense. She was still angry with Shawn for breaking his promises to Billy, but it didn't consume her the way it consumed her husband.

She blinked her eyes and looked at the small, gentle face of the girl sleeping on another cot next to her. Kira. Sweet kid. Emily let her eyes drift closed. She *was* tired. They'd been up late every night for a week, arguing about whether or not Billy should go, and last night, after he'd already left, she found she couldn't sleep. She had bad dreams. Nightmares, really.

It was so nice of Andy to suggest she lie down. The cots were too small for her, but they were comfortable enough. It wouldn't be a long nap, only half an hour or so, but it would be good for her.

She fell asleep just about the time that Billy said—

THREE

THE OFFER

"Are you out of your goddamned mind?"

As Billy asked the question, Shawn wondered, not for the first time, if he'd made the right decision to rebuild Eagle Mansion. If he wanted upstate New York, why not just sell the land and get rid of Eagle Mansion and the groundskeeper's cottage, let all those memories stay buried once and for all? Or even bulldoze the entire thing and let it return to the wild. Why try to reclaim it? Why build there? Why not build in Cortaca? He'd loved Cortaca from the first time he visited it, despite its proximity—or maybe because of its proximity, he was never sure—to Whiskey Run; he'd passed over Columbia and Stanford and MIT. He'd given a lot of money to Cortaca University over the years. He could have bought land outside of town. It wouldn't have been as cheap as buying land in Whiskey Run, but it's not like the money would have mattered. Cortaca would have been easy. A fresh start in a town he loved, with only the good memories of being a college student. The old estate and mansion would have been a safe distance away.

But Eagle Mansion had a dark pull on him.

For most of his teen years, he'd actively tried not to think about Eagle Mansion and what happened with his father, but the old buildings and his family history haunted him. The house had been a dark horse stalking his nightmares. At least once a month he bolted awake in his aunt's house, twisted up in sweat-soaked sheets, a scream dying in his throat, sure that he was back in the groundskeeper's cottage, Eagle Mansion a dark shape in the sky above. He heard the creak of floorboards in his sleep, saw twisted shadows behind the windows of the mansion while he dreamt fitfully. Once, when he was seventeen or eighteen, before he went to college, his aunt asked him if he wanted to go back for a visit. He'd just stared at her. No. He hadn't been back since he was twelve. Since the fire. Until, in the weeks before they graduated, he'd started thinking of the cabin as a place where he and Billy could work and stay for free.

Going back had been a mistake. They had made something great there, but there was something cursed about the place, too. Yet once he'd offered it up to Billy as a place they could stay for free, it was too late to take it back. For nearly two years they camped out there. Two years of the mansion's dark-eyed windows leering over them, two years of the rain kicking up the scent of soot from the groundskeeper's cottage. Two years of the nightmares back at full throttle.

Once Billy and Emily had left the cabin behind, Shawn finished up his work and left it behind, too. It wasn't a place he wanted to linger in. When anybody asked him where he was from, he said Syracuse and left it at that. Oh, it was public knowledge that his parents had died in the fire, that he'd gone to live with his aunt Beverly when he was twelve, but any article that even bothered to mention Eagle Mansion barely gave it a sentence. In the profile last year, in advance of his biography, in the *New Yorker* it rated a full paragraph:

Eagle doesn't like to talk about his parents. "So much of my life is public," he says, "I feel like they're the one thing I have to myself." Before the fire, he lived with his parents on the grounds of the old eponymous Eagle Mansion, in upstate New York. It was originally designed as a palatial hotel to accommodate a hundred guests plus staff and servants. Eagle Mansion, meant to compete with hotels in the Adirondacks or in Bar Harbor, Maine, as a destination in itself, a place for both new and old money, is fifteen twisting miles north of a small town called Whiskey Run, which is itself thirty miles north of Cortaca, home of the Ivy League's Cortaca University, Eagle's alma mater. It's far enough north to be perched on the banks of the Saint Lawrence River. Weather can be severe in the winter, with lake effect snow averaging 350 inches in an average year, but Eagle's great-grandfather built the resort into a rollicking Prohibition playground for New York City folks who wanted Canadian liquor, gambling, and a no-questions-asked good time. It fell out of favor after the repeal, and by the time Eagle was a kid, the grand resort was a ruin. They lived in what had been the groundskeeper's cottage. Cottage being a fancy name for a hovel. Snow dusted through cracks in the walls, and the only source of heat was the woodstove in the kitchen. It was that woodstove that started the fire that left Eagle an orphan. He's in the middle of rebuilding and expanding Eagle Mansion—reputed by locals to be haunted—with the intent of using it as a part-time vacation home and a part-time "technology institute." He calls it a reclamation project, proof that "you *can* go home again."

The rest of the article gave a quick gloss to Aunt Beverly's taking him to live with her in Syracuse, a digest version of his time at Cortaca University and in the cabin after graduation, the dispute between him and Billy—the official, sanitized version. Mostly, the article focused on how he'd built Eagle Technology into a behemoth. A pure cult-of-personality kind of article. Same thing with his authorized biography. Eagle Mansion got two pages in *Learning to Soar: The Story of Shawn Eagle and the Rise of Eagle Technology*. People took it at face value that he didn't want to talk about his parents, and since it didn't seem to play into the narrative of Shawn Eagle as genius and tech baron—his mom's sister, Aunt Beverly, was a science teacher and the one who taught him to code—Eagle Mansion was never much more than a footnote.

And yet. He couldn't leave it alone. It was always an itch. He'd gone a few years ago, just for the day, just to look. The mansion was even more decrepit. Choked with creeping vines, seedlings sprouting from the gutters. The windows jagged with glass or completely open to the elements. The tight, dark forest pressed hard against the building, shadows keeping secrets even in the midday sun. But he couldn't shake it. Couldn't let go of the idea of evicting his memories, of exorcising all his ghosts. He had the money to fix it up, and so he did. There were bad memories there, but there were good memories, too.

Weren't there?

Billy stood up from the couch and said it again: "Are you out of your goddamned mind? You want me to go back and live in that cabin? What, there aren't enough bad memories haunting me from the first time?"

"You aren't listening," Shawn said. "First of all, I want you *and* Emily to go. Together. You'll lose your mind up there by yourself. And I don't want you to live in the cabin. The thing's a museum now. Literally. I donated it to Cortaca University. I had the thing disassembled and then completely reassembled on campus. It's right next to the new Eagle Computing Pavilion."

Billy glared at him, and Shawn had the overwhelming itch to call out for Wendy, for his security, for somebody to come running, because Billy looked like he was going to jump him. But he bit it down.

"Okay. Give me a second. Remember how Aunt Bev wouldn't let me sell the old mansion?"

Aunt Bev's name placated Billy. Peace seemed to wash over his face.

"I always liked her," Billy said. "I feel bad that I lost touch with her. Even with everything that happened in the cabin with us, and all the stuff with Emily, she deserved better from me. How is she?"

"She's dead," he said. "You didn't know?"

"Shit. I'm sorry, Shawn." Billy looked down at his hands. He really did look sorry, Shawn thought. That, or he'd become a better actor in the dozen years since they'd split ways. "She was a good lady," Billy said. "She was good to me. She treated me well. Even when everything was . . . Well, I always liked her. She sent me Christmas cards for the first couple of years, but I never wrote back, and then I figured she'd just lost track of me. But . . . Shit. I'm so sorry. When was it?"

"Six years ago. Breast cancer." Shawn was surprised that he had trouble swallowing. One of his first memories was going to visit her with his mother when he was just a little kid. Or was it more than a visit? Was it one of the times his mother had tried to run away from his father? He'd loved Aunt Bev fiercely, and she'd loved him back. She was a quiet woman, self-contained. She wasn't the sort who could stand up to Simon Eagle, but then again, not many people could. She'd tried, though. She'd really tried. Aunt Bev had done her best to save her sister. But it wasn't enough. Which might have been why she gave so much of herself to Shawn after the fire.

"She was a good lady, yeah," he continued. The office felt small, even though it was almost laughably big. Shawn knew how crazy it was to have an office that took up half the floor of the building. But it was a power play of sorts. Having an office that big, that ostentatious, wasn't about what you needed, it was about saying to anybody who entered, I am a man to be reckoned with. I have power. I can do what I want. But at that moment, it felt tight, almost confined. He didn't want to talk about Aunt Bev. He didn't want to talk about his parents.

"The point wasn't to bring up Aunt Beverly, though. It was just a way of saying she was right when she made me keep that chunk of land. I used to think I couldn't wait to unload it."

"Some bad memories."

"You ever go back?" Shawn asked. It surprised him, the question coming out of his mouth. He didn't know what made him ask it. It surprised Billy, too, clearly.

Billy squinted at him. He paused. And then, finally, he gave a sharp shake of his head. "No. But Emily did."

Now it was Shawn's turn to be taken aback. "Really?"

"She went on a trip with her sister—"

"Beth?"

"Beth. And her brother-in-law. Emily flew out to Chicago and the three of them drove out and did a few weeks of hiking the Appalachian Trail."

"You didn't go?"

"Not really my thing. But on the way home, they took a detour, just a quick visit. Camped out there overnight. Emily said it was creepy as hell being alone in a tent, a hundred yards from Beth and my brother-in-law. Beth liked it there, though. Claims that's where my nieces were conceived. So, yeah, Emily's been back there, but not me. God. I can't believe you kept the place."

Shawn nodded. "Well, that makes two of us, but every single time I thought about selling it, there was something that kept itching at me."

Something that kept itching at him. More like a hook lodged in his chest. Over the years, he'd come close to selling it, but somehow he'd never been able to give the orders. Every time he thought about telling his lawyers to get rid of it, he broke into a sweat, felt his throat closing up. It wasn't a question of wanting or not wanting to sell it. He *couldn't* sell it.

"I fixed it up." He paused. This was it. This was the moment. "Billy, listen, I have a job for you. I want—no, I *need*—you to go up there. Look, Billy—I know this is rich, right? Me coming to you, saying that I want you to do something for me? But this is a good thing, and I can help you. The past is past. We've all made our choices. Let me help you."

Shawn waited a minute to see Billy's response. It pissed him off that he needed Billy's help at all. He liked being in charge. He was used to being in charge, used to getting his way, and when you were as rich as he was, you never needed anybody as much as they needed you. But, dammit, he *did* need Billy, and he knew that telling Billy this wasn't some sort of charity thing would cause a shift in the temperature of their restarted relationship. For good or bad, Shawn didn't know, but there'd be a shift.

"And I'm not saying I don't regret all those choices. I'm not saying there aren't some things I'd take back if I could. Don't you feel that way, too? Aren't there things you wish you could take back?"

What those things were, they both left unsaid, but Billy gave a begrudging nod.

"It's not as crazy as it sounds," Shawn continued. "If I were asking you and Emily to live in my house here, in Baltimore, with me, fine, that would be weird. But I'm not. I'll barely see you guys. This isn't some ridiculous attempt to recapture what we had in the cabin, and it isn't some crazy sort of way for me to try to steal Emily back."

Was it?

No. He was sure it wasn't.

Shawn paused and took a sip of his vodka. He wouldn't have admitted it, but he was pretty sure how obvious it was that being in the same room again with Billy was unsettling for him. Billy looked so much older than Shawn remembered that when Billy first came into the office, Shawn had, for a moment, thought the wrong man had come.

"Emily made her choice about you and me a long, long time ago, Billy. You don't have to worry about that."

But maybe he wasn't so sure. People changed their minds. Emily might change her mind. She'd made the wrong decision. No question.

And maybe Billy was thinking the same thing, because he was angry.

"And what," Billy said, "you want me to be the caretaker? You looked into it and figured out we were having some hard times, so you figured, hey, Billy can be my charity case? Have me jumping around taking orders from you so that you can feel better about yourself? You flew me out here for that? To ask me to live in your little mansion in upstate New York? Some messed-up way of reliving our past, of trying to make it clear what my place is in all of this? Screw you, Shawn. I'm not a monkey you can put in a cage, and I'm not anybody's houseboy."

Shawn should have known Billy would react that way. It had all come out wrong. It had been a long time since he'd seen Billy, but some things never changed. Here was Shawn starting by talking about personal history, when what he should have started with was the challenge.

"Just hear me out, okay?" Shawn said. "I'm not wasting your time, I promise. I flew *you* out here for a reason. You. This isn't a charity thing. It's not about guilt or about trying to fix our past. I've got a job that I need done, and it's a job for Billy Stafford, not just anybody. This isn't some caretaker gig. I don't need you living in the house so you can maintain the boiler and shovel snow off the roof and do odd jobs." He couldn't help himself. "Besides, it's not a *little* mansion."

As the words left his mouth, he knew he should have stopped himself.

Billy just shook his head and started moving to walk out of the office. Three steps up from the sunken lounge area, then turn toward daylight. Shawn was right after him, and when he grabbed Billy's shoulder he was surprised to see him swing around, fist cocked back.

Shawn froze.

Billy froze, too, his arm still pulled back. Shawn wondered how long they stood like that, Billy waiting to hit him, Shawn waiting to be hit. Finally, a thousand years later, Billy unclenched his fist and used his hand to brush Shawn's hand off his shoulder.

"Do you really want to test me again?"

Shawn took a step back. "Hey. I'm sorry. Okay? I mean it. Not just about . . . I'm sorry. Okay? Maybe there's too much history between us. Maybe this is a stupid idea. I'm sorry. I thought, if you'd just listen to me, hear me out . . ."

He lowered his head and waited. He really was sorry, not just for bringing Billy out here and opening old wounds, and not just for doing a bad job of explaining what the job was, but for all of it. Sorry that what they'd once had was gone, sorry for the secret they had to keep, sorry for the decisions he'd made. Most of all, he was sorry that even as he stood there, in his endless gleaming office, looking out over the buildings of his endless gleaming empire, there was still a part of him that wondered if Billy had come off better in the deal when he'd left the cabin with Emily.

To his surprise, after a few seconds, Billy nodded. "Okay," he said. "You're sorry. It doesn't mean I forgive you, but I'll listen."

"Okay? Okay!" Shawn clapped his hands together and then grinned. "How about some sushi? Call it a late lunch or an early dinner or whatever. There's a great place on the harbor with killer views." Billy nodded again, so Shawn strode over to the door of his office and told Wendy to have the car come around.

He and Billy didn't talk much on the drive over. It wasn't until they were tucked into their booth up against the glass on the second floor of the restaurant that Shawn tried again.

"The land's been passed down for generations. My great-grandfather was the one who built Eagle Mansion right after the First World War. It was the kind of resort that catered to the rich and famous."

"I know all this, Shawn. You do remember that I lived there with you for almost two years? I know the whole history. How many times did we get drunk and sit around telling ghost stories about the old place? All that crap about your grandfather, the story about the two teenage lovers who went out there and disappeared forever, the group of hunters who took shelter in a storm and who, one by one, killed themselves in increasingly disturbing ways over the years. Blah, blah, blah."

"Just listen, okay? Let me do my pitch. I've practiced this and I don't want to waste it." He was turning up his full charm, and even though Billy clearly saw through the bullshit, he also seemed willing to settle in for the show. "Anyway," Shawn continued, "it was big-time. Politicians and baseball players and movie stars. Anybody who wanted a break from New York City or Boston or Chicago. You can go back and search the newspaper clippings. It was hopping during Prohibition. By the time you saw it, the whole thing was just a sad dump. I mean, if that cabin we lived in was the best building on the whole estate, you know that the mansion was in shitty shape. But you should have seen the pictures from the glory days! During the renovations we tried to salvage as much of it as we could, and it would have been cheaper to tear the whole thing down, but I wanted to keep that history. Well, keep it and also update it. I rebuilt it more than I renovated it, and I put a really modern addition on it that's going to serve as my private residence when I'm at the estate. I'm going to use Eagle Mansion as a sort of invitation-only destination retreat for the high-end tech crowd. The mansion is beautiful, but really, without the addition and the upgrades, it's just a fancy hotel. If you hold your hands up to block the extras, you could see it right at home in the Adirondacks or a national park somewhere. But that's the thing. It *does* have the addition, and it's got the kinds of upgrades we used to dream about. *That's* what the gig is. It's not just a mansion," he said.

He leaned forward, staring right at Billy. He paused, speaking slowly, letting each word hit: "It's the future, Billy, and I want you to be part of it."

He waited. Nothing. Billy stared back at him. "The future," Shawn said, the words bubbling up almost nervously.

Small cracks showed at the corners of Billy's lips. And then Billy was laughing. Great, big, gulping guffaws. He laughed like he didn't give a shit how it sounded, and Shawn thought that maybe Billy didn't. After all, whom did Billy know in Baltimore? And to Billy, lunch with Shawn Eagle of Eagle Technology wasn't some chance to impress.

"My god, ha!" Billy was laughing so hard that he was actually crying now, Shawn realized. "Do you have, oh, holy crap, oh my, do you have any idea how pretentious you sound?" He banged on the table with his hand, a flat thump of joy. Billy let his voice drop in a rough imitation of Shawn. "'It's not just a mansion. It's the future, and I want you to be part of it'? Please. Save it for the launch of your next phone."

Shawn blushed. He wasn't just the CEO of Eagle Technology. He was the face of the company. The one who bounded onstage twice a year, at the end of their media events, to announce the next big thing, to hold up the newest piece of modern magic. Eagle Technology specialized in slick, seamless rectangles of metal and glass, and even though each device was just one more variation on a theme, people couldn't buy them fast enough.

"Okay," Shawn said. "Let me try that again. I had this all worked out, you know. I had a little pitch ready for you. And I keep getting it wrong. Talking about us working in the cabin, talking about what happened with . . ." He almost said the name. Takata. But he didn't. "Emily. Aunt Beverly. Ancient history. And then trying to sell you on this job like it's another product."

"Maybe," Billy said, taking a sip of his soda, "you shouldn't try to sell me at all. I bought what you were selling once already, and that was enough for me."

Shawn nodded. "I need you, Billy. You, specifically. You're the only one who can understand it."

The restaurant was almost completely empty. They were there in the soft heart of the afternoon, too late for lingering lunchers, too early for even the earliest sushi aficionados. On the first floor of the restaurant, there'd been a man in a suit and tie picking in a desultory fashion at the dregs of a plate of rolls, and even though the owner and the two waiters standing by the entrance recognized Shawn—and even if they hadn't, it would have been hard to ignore the security team, six guys who looked the part—they'd taken their order and then gotten the hint that Shawn didn't want to be bothered. He wasn't even sure why he'd brought Billy here, why he hadn't just had food brought into the office or, instead, gone fancier, waiting to take Billy to dinner somewhere so impossibly trendy that it couldn't have done anything other than make Billy uncomfortable. Why here? Maybe because it reminded him of the way they'd sometimes splurge on supermarket sushi at the Wegmans in Cortaca, back when they were still coding together.

"Shawn, for the love of god, what are you talking about?"

Shawn leaned in and let his voice go quiet. Not that there was anybody around to hear, but he had to be careful.

"I did it," he said. "Those upgrades? She's in there. When we rebuilt the mansion and put on the addition? I put her in there."

For the briefest moment Shawn thought that Billy didn't understand what he was talking about, but then he saw the way Billy's face shifted, first from blankness and then to incredulity—it couldn't be possible—and then, so swiftly that Shawn wondered if he'd imagined it, to anger, before settling, finally, on wonderment.

"Nellie?"

Shawn nodded.

Nellie. The name was silly, but unlike with Eagle Logic, the program and operating language that made almost everything at Eagle Technology possible—the stroke of genius that had made Shawn into one of the richest men alive—they hadn't flipped a coin to come up with *this* name: he'd called the program Nellie, and it had stuck.

They were cousins, of a sort, Shawn figured. Nellie and Eagle Logic. Or ancestors, maybe. Nellie had been the dream, but Eagle Logic was what they'd actually been able to build. Eagle Logic hadn't been revolutionary, not exactly, but it had been enough of an advancement that he'd been able to build the empire of Eagle Technology on the back of Eagle Logic. Eagle Logic was like the first humanoids to walk erect; it's not that they were so evolutionarily superior to the other monkeys out there, but rather that walking on two feet instead of all fours allowed them to use tools. That was probably the best way of thinking about Eagle Logic as compared to what had come before, to Google and Apple and Microsoft and Amazon. It was just enough of an advancement to give Eagle Technology the edge it needed for Shawn to build it into a behemoth, to make the other guys play catch-up, but could he argue it was anything radical? No. But Nellie—now she was radical, a real step forward. Not even an evolution.

A revolution.

"And goddammit," Shawn told Billy, "I've done it! How long has it been since we first started trying to code Nellie? How long has it been since we realized that even if we'd been able to figure out the software, the hardware didn't support it yet? Do you remember when, early on, we had to say we were being too ambitious, when we had to settle for what eventually became Eagle Logic? Do you remember how shitty it felt to give up on Nellie? Sure, Eagle Logic was good, but it was always a compromise. But we don't have to settle anymore," Shawn said. "I mean, come on. Jesus, Billy, I did it, and she's out there, waiting for you in Eagle Mansion.

"She's in every wire. In every door and every window. She's in the walls and the floors and ceilings, in the steps and lights and in every single damn room. She's in the mansion." He laughed. "She's not *in* the mansion, she *is* the mansion, Billy. You can feel her presence, like a living, breathing thing." Shawn leaned back. He felt a huge surge of relief and realized he'd been waiting for this. Waiting to tell Billy. That's what he'd been looking forward to more than anything else about seeing Billy. More than flaunting his money and success, more than talking about the old days. This. Sharing the idea of Nellie.

"But?" Billy said. "I'm hearing a 'but' in this. Because if you've really done it, then why am I here?"

Shawn waited while the waiter brought over their food. He'd ordered sparingly, since he had a charity event to go to that night, a benefit for the Baltimore Orchestra that he'd been asked to host. Hosting, he knew, was code for "Will you please write us a check for a hundred grand or so?" But since he liked chamber music, or, at least, the idea of chamber music, he'd said yes.

He watched Billy dive into the sushi, and it made him happy to see that Billy was both literally and figuratively hungry. Shawn knew Billy was trying to play it cool, but he also knew, down to the penny, how much Billy and Emily were in debt. His security team was thorough. They'd dug up all the dirt there was to dig and then some. He knew more about Billy than anyone else did. Did Emily know about all those credit cards? Did Emily know how badly Billy had mucked things up, how far underwater they were, or did she still think there was some hope?

He picked up his chopsticks and threw a piece of salmon sashimi into his mouth.

"Well, yeah," he said, after chewing the fish. "There's the rub." He looked at his watch. "Listen. I hate to do this, particularly given our history, but I've got a meeting I cannot possibly cancel, and I have an event I have to go to tonight. What would you say to sticking around for another day? I've got to take off, but I'll have Wendy extend the booking at the hotel. You can finish your lunch, and I'll have a car bring you back to your room. I think the Orioles are playing tonight if you want to go to a ball game. You can have the company box. First thing in the morning, we'll fire up a jet and go take a look at the mansion, and you can see Nellie for yourself; then you'll understand why I need you."

"I thought you said your jets, plural, were all unavailable. As I recall, two of them are being worked on, and Taylor Swift borrowed your spare."

Shawn considered Billy. The man looked a lot different from the boy he'd known. He had a sort of artificial gravity. Shawn wondered how much of Billy had been burned away by the drinking. Not all of him. That was for sure. The same old sharp Billy was still there, buried underneath the detritus.

"Got me," he said. He grinned. "What can I tell you? I'm an ass-hole. I figured you'd be happy enough with first-class seats and a limo ride."

Billy looked out the window for a few seconds, and Shawn was actually worried, just for a heartbeat, that he was going to walk away. But the hook had been set.

"You were right. First class is a lot better than I'm used to traveling. You're still a dick, though," Billy said. But he was smiling when he said it.

"I know," Shawn said. "Some things don't change, right?"

Billy tapped his fingers on the table and then nodded. "First thing in the morning, you'll take me to see Nellie?"

"First thing in the morning," Shawn said. He stood up from the table ready to go, but Billy stopped him.

"Just tell me," Billy said. "You've cracked it, but here I am. I'm the only one who can help. That's what you're saying. So why, exactly, am I here? What is it you need me to do?"

"Call it an exorcism, if you like."

"An exorcism?"

"Let's just say there's a ghost in the machine."

FOUR

CHOICES WERE MADE

Emily Wiggins gave Percy a hug and then handed the little fellow his blanket. Percy had had an accident during nap time, and Emily helped him change into the spare clothes in his cubby and ran his other clothes and his blanket through the washing machine and dryer. The fuzzy yellow animal-print blanket still held a little residual warmth from the dryer, like an exposed rock on a summer's day just after the sun has gone down. Percy clutched the blanket under his arm and then walked over to the snack table where the other classroom teacher, Andy Scoogins, had put out a tray of cut carrots. Emily never would have said it out loud, but Percy was her favorite. Maybe part of that was because Percy's mother was such a piece of work. Emily secretly believed that by loving Percy Hedridge just a little bit more than all the other children, she could somehow save him.

"It's embarrassing for a boy of his age to be wetting himself," Mrs. Hedridge said.

Mrs. Hedridge, Percy's mom, was in her early forties. A lot of the women bringing kids to the day care were in their early forties. Career women who'd put off having kids as late as they could. That was one group of moms. The second group of moms were women who'd maybe never wanted kids until they realized that having them was a sort of trophy, proof that you could have it all, that you could have a husband and be a success at work and still, at the same time, be a mom. Mrs. Hedridge, Emily suspected, fell into the latter camp. Most of the women who had waited for career reasons or because they hadn't met the right guy were hoverers. They were the moms who came all the way into the classroom with their kids, who stuck around for five or ten or fifteen minutes, who hugged and kissed their kids multiple times before leaving, and who always asked Emily why oh why it was that Bright Apple Preschool didn't have webcams in the classrooms so they could check in on little Jimmy or Jeffrey or Jenny or, often enough, Dakota or Silica or Raven or Tesla or other names designed to prove that this child was like no other child ever born. The hoverers were the parents who would have been speaking in whispered tones with Emily to make sure that their precious darlings wouldn't be embarrassed, asking Emily for suggestions for websites and books and articles that could make their kids feel empowered in the way they pissed their pants. But Mrs. Hedridge was most definitely not a hoverer. In fact, in the mornings, she often didn't bother getting out of her car. She was one of the few parents who pulled up in front of the building and had their kids hop out and walk in alone. That was maybe the first thing that Emily had loved about Percy. The way he slid down from his seat to the pavement—he was too small to just step down—shouldered his Winnie the Pooh backpack, and walked into Bright Apple Preschool without a backward glance at the automatic door sliding closed on his mother's car. A brave little trooper. Though, if Emily were being honest about loving Percy just a little bit more than any of the other boys and girls, she would also have to admit that it didn't take very much bravery for a child to come into Bright Apple Preschool, with or without a parent.

Most of the big technology companies had years ago moved to on-site childcare, but there was still a huge market for places like Bright Apple that had a certain kind of focus that you couldn't necessarily find on your company's campus. Emily's job before she landed at Bright Apple had been at a preschool whose selling point was that it was on a houseboat and featured a nautical theme. Weird, but also weirdly compelling for certain fathers who, Emily suspected, might be somewhere further along the Asperger's continuum. At Bright Apple, the focus was on the environment and organics. The carrots on the snack table were organically grown, provided by a local farmer who supplied most of the in-season greens and vegetables to the preschool kitchen, and the detergent that Emily had put into the washing machine with Percy's pee-soaked clothing and blanket was certified to be hypoallergenic and kind to the earth.

"It's really not a big deal, Mrs. Hedridge," Emily said. "Percy's four. It's normal for a kid his age to have accidents occasionally. A lot of the kids in the class still wear pull-ups during nap time."

"Disposable diapers?" Mrs. Hedridge said.

That was rich, thought Emily. She bet Mrs. Hedridge's carbon footprint would put Bigfoot's to shame. "Biodegradable," Emily said. "We use cloth diapers for the younger kids, but the older kids are too resistant, so we've got biodegradable pull-ups made out of organic materials. To tell you the truth, I'm not actually sure they work as well as the other kind, but they usually work well enough, and we can add them to the compost pile."

"Well," Mrs. Hedridge said, sniffing at the thought, "Percy isn't going back into diapers. He's not a baby."

"I'm not suggesting Percy go back into diapers. He didn't have an accident for the first six months he was in my classroom, and it's only been in the last month or so that he's been wetting himself during nap time," Emily said. "Did he have any issues with this at his previous day-care provider, or is there something else going on that we should be aware of?"

She knew the truth. Percy had told Emily. Confided in her, really, though she wasn't sure if Percy really knew that he was telling Emily a secret. Because she was sure it was a secret. She was sure that Mrs. Hedridge would be furious if she knew that Percy had told Emily about Mr. Hedridge sleeping on the couch because Mommy had called him a lying son of a bitch. Of *course* Percy was having a period of regression with that going on at home. Emily saw it all the time with the kids in her charge: a new baby in the house, a new job where suddenly Mommy was traveling a lot, an impending divorce, a divorced parent's impending marriage. Even, sometimes, when it was good news at home, the kids reacted to it. They didn't always show their stress by wetting themselves during nap time, but the kids showed their stress somehow to Emily. They couldn't hide it. She was their secret keeper. Her loyalty was always to the children. No matter how much she liked the parents, she was on the side of the kids.

In this case, however, she did not particularly like the parent, and there was a part of her that wanted to ask Mrs. Hedridge why it was that her husband was sleeping on the couch. Was her husband cheating on her, Emily wanted to ask, because Mrs. Hedridge was such a cold, callous bitch? If so, Emily wanted to say, it made her secretly happy, because even though Emily would never actually call another woman this, Mrs. Hedridge was, really and truly, the kind of woman who deserved to be called a rhymes with punt.

"No," Mrs. Hedridge said coldly, "there were never any *issues*, as you say, with Percy pissing his pants at his previous day-care provider. He was in diapers until I potty trained him, and he has been dry ever since, so whatever you've been doing, you need to take a look at it. You could start, for instance, by not letting him have juice at lunch."

Emily didn't bother telling Mrs. Hedridge that Bright Apple Preschool never served juice, with lunch or breakfast or snack or any time at all. In fact, one of the selling points of Bright Apple was that they had their own on-site organic kitchen, that the meals featured whole grains and fresh fruits and vegetables, that there was such a strict ban on processed sugars that the kitchen provided all the treats for birthday parties and holiday parties: oatmeal cookies sweetened with coconut and honey, homemade fig bars, frozen yogurt fruit pops, poppy-seed pomegranate drops. Instead, she did what she did best, which was to placate and please, deciding all the while that the next day she'd make sure to spend some extra time with Percy.

The other parents all swung through the classroom over the next thirty minutes, chatting briefly with Andy and Emily before helping their kids carry popsicle-stick creations and clay flowerpots and other crafts out to the waiting electric cars and, in some cases, bicycles with attached trailers. It fascinated her how some of the parents wore thrift-store clothes and rode bikes and acted like all they cared about was Mother Earth and that capitalism was some big sham, even though they could afford to pay the outrageous tuition for Bright Apple Preschool without even blinking. Not that much of the tuition made it Emily's way. She was paid okay, she guessed, more than she could have earned working in a coffee shop or something, that was for sure, and she did love the kids, but with the debt she and Billy had racked up . . . No. She wasn't going to do that anymore. Wasn't going to cover for him. The debt that Billy had racked up. Billy alone. Not her. But she'd made her choice. She'd made her choice, and she could help bail out the ship or she could drown.

"That woman is bitch-tastic," Andy said as soon as the last of the kids was gone and the door to the classroom was closed. "If she were a dinosaur, she'd be a bitchosaurus."

Emily laughed but she also covered her ears. She was not a fan of the word *bitch*—it was too often the refuge of weak men angry at strong women—but coming from Andy, it *was* funny. And she didn't have to ask to know that Andy was talking about Percy's mom. Mrs. Hedridge had actually had the temerity to go to the owner of the preschool and complain that she thought Percy had been acting "swishy" since he'd been in Andy's class. Emily liked to think that even if the owner of the preschool, Monica, hadn't been Andy's sister, she still would have told Mrs. Hedridge to find a different school for Percy if it was a problem. Andy was unquestionably swishy, which was one of the reasons all the kids adored him. He was fat and bald and somehow looked like a teddy bear. When Andy read stories for the kids, he did all the voices, and as much as Emily loved the boys and girls in her classroom, it was always Andy they went to when they were looking to be comforted. Until he joined his sister's preschool, Andy had been some sort of manager at Google, and had more than made his fortune before moving home to Seattle. Even though Monica was the titular owner of the day care, Emily knew that it was Andy who had lent her the money to buy the building and start the business in the first place. He was, unquestionably, next to the children themselves, the best thing about the job, even if he did have a foul mouth that he liked to exercise after hours.

"If she were a ship, she'd be the *Bitchtanic*," he continued. "If she flew on a broom, she'd be a buh-witch. And if she were a cowboy, she'd tie her horse up to the bitching post. Bitchy bitch bitch," he said.

"Ugh, please stop," she said, but she couldn't stop herself from laughing, and after a minute, she couldn't stop herself from egging Andy on: "So, just to be clear, you think Mrs. Hedridge is . . ."

"A biiiiii-tter lady," he said, and the two of them laughed together as they finished straightening the room.

He walked with her out to the staff parking lot, and leaned over the hood of his vintage Porsche. He claimed that he was embarrassed by the car, but he also claimed it made him irresistible to the type of younger, smooth, muscular men that he liked to date, so how could he possibly get rid of it? "Let's face it," he'd said. "I've got my charm and I've got my money, but I don't have looks. I could buy myself a nice, new luxury car, but unless I leave the sticker price on the window it won't do me any good. If I don't advertise that I'm rich by driving this ridiculous antique beast, I have to rely on my charm, and that's not going to get Andy the kind of boy toy he deserves." Or, at least that's what he'd said the previous year, when she'd asked him about the car. In the meantime, he'd started dating Harry, who was also fat, also bald, and, as far as Emily could tell, nearing middle age, and the two men seemed like they were in love.

Love. What a mysterious thing. She was almost certain that Billy was still in love with her. And she loved Billy, too. Still. She was sure that she did. She'd come back to him for a reason. But there were times when she thought, what if he has a car accident on the way home from work, what if he just magically disappears? How much easier would her life become if he was just suddenly gone? If she could erase her past mistakes? The thought always gave her a sick thrill.

"Is he coming back?" Andy asked, and for a moment Emily thought he'd read her mind, but she quickly realized that of course Andy knew about Billy's trip out east to see Shawn Eagle.

"Tomorrow. He texted. Shawn had some sort of meeting he had

to go to, and there's more to talk about between the two of them over whatever this thing is. Billy's being mysterious about all of it, and it's not like I understand the engineering stuff, but he's being put up in some sort of fabulously swanky hotel in Baltimore, evidently. He has the Eagle Technology box at tonight's Orioles game completely to himself. A bit different from our usual weeknight. I'm afraid he's going to be pretty spoiled when he comes back."

Andy cocked his head, and she could tell he was thinking about saying something, maybe even suggesting that it would be better for all involved if Billy did not, in fact, come back. She could tell he was on the verge of, once again, gently probing the idea that maybe Emily didn't have to be married to Billy anymore, that maybe instead of helping to bail out a sinking ship, she should just swim away. It was hard for him not to say anything, she knew. It wasn't his way to be quiet and it wasn't his way to be delicate in conversations, but they'd gone over this ground plenty of times, and Emily finally had to tell Andy to leave it alone. Some doors should stay shut, and she could see him, finally, come to that same conclusion.

"You sure you don't want to go out for dinner?" he said instead.

She shook her head.

"You're a sweetheart, but honestly, a night in by myself sounds like heaven. I'll read a book—"

"One of your dirty little novels?"

"Oh, please. Romance novels barely qualify as dirty anymore," she said, though she didn't say that the book she was reading fell firmly into the erotica camp. "Besides, who are you to call anyone dirty?"

"Dirty Andy," he said. "Dirty Andy used to be a lot dirtier back before he became domesticated. Well, just don't wear out the batteries on your vibrator, kiddo."

She blushed, which made him laugh, as it always did, and then she kissed him on the cheek and got into her car. The door squealed on its hinges when she opened it. She had to lift and pull to get it to close. She would have liked to go out to dinner with Andy, but it was too awkward to keep glomming on to him. If they went somewhere cheap and shitty that she could afford, he'd be unhappy. He didn't mind slumming it occasionally, as he put it, but he'd grown used to a certain lifestyle, and that was a lifestyle that didn't exist for Emily. He'd be happy to pay for her, of course, and he'd done so on more than one occasion and constantly kept offering, but she hated the way it made her feel. Hated it. Hated being poor and worrying about every dollar, but hated worse the way it made her feel to take charity from somebody else. She'd had enough of that as a girl, that sense of unearned shame. Shame forced upon her. The shame of being poor had been a feeling she thought she'd be able to leave behind when she left home, but it had traveled with her from Kansas City to college. She shouldn't have been surprised, she realized, that she still felt poor at Cortaca University. She'd known it the minute she got off the bus in downtown Cortaca, but as she made her way up the hill to campus, a ratty camping pack on her back and a wheeled duffel bag towed behind her, she kept trying to tell herself that the feeling of shame would go away.

And it had gone away. For a while. But not at first.

She hadn't even bothered applying to Kansas University or Kansas State. Most of the girls at her high school didn't go to anything more exciting than community college, if they made it through high school at all without getting pregnant. If they did aspire higher, KU or K-State was as high as they could think. They were decent schools, but they weren't far enough away for her. She needed to get away from Kansas City. Needed to get away from the whole damned middle of the country. She needed distance. Needed to get as far as she could from her dad and his drinking and . . . Maybe if her mom hadn't died in "the incident," when Emily was still too young to remember, it would have been different. But her mom *had* died in "the incident," and it was the way that it was. Her sister, Beth, older by five full years, old enough to remember their mother as something more than an idea, had gotten out when Emily was still in eighth grade, going to Northwestern University on a full ride and then staying in Chicago. Chicago was far enough for Beth; she never let her shadow fall on Kansas City again, even for their father's funeral. Beth was a presence in Emily's high school life only through occasional phone calls and postcards and Emily's visits to Chicago. But seeing Beth go off to Northwestern had been like a promise that it *was* possible to get out of there, to get away from Kansas City and their dad and all of it. Emily decided early on that she wasn't going to be left behind. Straight As her entire life. She killed the SATs and the ACTs. Student body president, captain of the cross-country and track and field teams, volunteer candy striper at the hospital on weekends, babysitter, movie theater popcorn slinger, debate team, AV crew for the winter musical.

So determined to get herself out of Kansas City that she wouldn't date any of the boys who asked her out in high school. No sirree. She wasn't going to fall for that one, not like her mother had. She'd seen that trap coming a mile away. A handsome boy with a handsome smile and then, zip-a-dee-doo-dah, zip-a-dee-ay, all of a sudden you've got two kids and a husband who drinks. No boys for her. Just class and work and extracurricular activities that she thought would help sell her to her college of choice. She was the classic overachiever, compensating for something, compensating for everything. Maybe if she'd been out in the suburbs, she would have been just another normal kid, but at her school she was a comet. The guidance counselor didn't know what to do with her, had never seen anyone like Emily Wiggins.

It had come as such a shock, then, that she'd gotten straight-up rejected by Dartmouth and Princeton. Both on the same day. So sure of herself that she hadn't even registered the thinness of the envelopes. *Dear Ms. Wiggins, thank you for your application . . .* The single, creamy piece of paper that she thought had been her ticket to freedom was, instead, a thousand tiny cuts rolled into one. The blow had been so hard and so unexpected that she hadn't even cried. She'd just stood there, on their sagging, rotting porch, holding the letters from Dartmouth and Princeton and staring at their seals embossed in full color on the letterhead and wondering why they bothered using such expensive paper. Were they hoping to seem so impressive that the students they rejected would send checks in return, like some sort of defensive posture, a puppy rolling on its back to be kicked again, or a girl thinking she deserved what her father did to her?

Against her sister's advice, she'd applied to only five schools. Beth had taken the safest path available. She'd graduated from Northwestern and gone straight for her accounting certification and then met and married Rothko, moving from an apartment to a condo in Lincoln Park, and never, not once, returning to visit. Emily didn't blame her sister for that. She would have left and never come back if she could have. Emily had gone to visit Beth, though, almost dutifully, twice a year, taking the short flight to Chicago. They talked on the phone all the time, but her trips to Chicago were limited by what she and Beth could afford: a few days in the fall, a few days in the spring. That's how much time the sisters spent together, and it was a chance for Emily to see what different world awaited her. But Northwestern still felt too close to Kansas City, to their father, for Emily. Neither girl talked about it, but they both knew it had gotten worse at home since Beth had escaped. Emily worried that she would still feel the gravity of their house, pulling at her like a black hole even from five hundred miles away. Like the highway was simply a long string that their father could tug. No. Not Northwestern. So she sent her applications, five of them only, out east, to towns big and small and in-between: to Princeton, New Jersey; to Hanover, New Hampshire; to Durham, North Carolina; to grand old New York, New York; and, of course, to Cortaca, New York.

Because two of those letters had already come back thin and dead, rejections postmarked Princeton, NJ, and Hanover, NH, she expected the worst when she saw the envelope that had winged its way to her from Cortaca, NY. Another rejection, she knew. She'd left the envelope unopened on her nightstand overnight, unable to face it, only opening it in the morning, when she woke to go to school, thinking that she could deal with it then, with a full and new day in front of her. But Cortaca University had not rejected her. Cortaca University had offered her scholarship money and financial aid. Cortaca University wanted her. Cortaca University wanted Emily Wiggins so badly that they would pay for her to come. Cortaca University had open arms for Emily Wiggins.

So she turned down slightly less generous offers from Duke and Columbia and worked double shifts all summer, bagging groceries in the mornings and afternoons, working the concession stand at the movie theater until the late, late show let out. A way to bank some money and an excuse to leave the house before her father was up and to come home after he was already passed out. When the time came, she left the house before dawn, quiet as a mouse, not bothering to say good-bye to her father. She boarded a bus and headed east, all the way to Cortaca.

Her dorm room was a quad, and although her roommates didn't try to make her feel bad about her lack of money, they couldn't help themselves. They were warm and thoughtful young women, but they were also the sort of women who thought of an Ivy League education as a birthright. Stacy was from Pittsburgh, her parents both lawyers, her graduation present from high school a new and very practical all-wheel-drive SUV to deal with the snow north of Syracuse. Tillmont Graves—Tilly—who constantly bemoaned that her cell phone and her winter boots were a year behind the trends, came from New Hampshire with her father's credit card in case of emergencies. Tilly's father was a full professor in philosophy at Dartmouth, one of the two schools that had, incredibly, said no to Emily. When Emily finally divulged that fact to her roommate, Tilly had expressed surprise that anybody would truly want to live in the small town of Hanover. And, of course, there was Marge, whose mother was the granddaughter of the kind of man who was inevitably described as an "oil baron." Marge brought Emily home with her for Thanksgiving and Christmas every year of Emily's time at college, and quietly and gracefully paid for Emily's plane tickets and share of the hotel rooms for all their spring break trips, all four of them pretending that it wasn't happening. They became lifelong friends, and since graduation they'd done a girls' weekend at Marge's cottage on Martha's Vineyard during the summer, and an extended weekend at Marge's beachfront house on Kauai in the winter—even though, as things went downhill with Billy, that meant Marge had to once again cover Emily's expenses. She still went to New York City every other year to have Thanksgiving at Marge's parents' ridiculous six-thousand-square-foot Upper East Side apartment overlooking Central Park.

A great group of friends, but they were the kind of girls who never understood what it was like to jump without a parachute.

She looked through the driver's window and watched Andy heave himself into his Porsche, the museum piece of a sports car rocking at the weight, and then she turned the key in the ignition. Andy didn't have to worry about his car starting. It was an antique, but his mechanic kept it tuned. All he had to do was turn the key; every time, the Porsche let out a growl to hint at its power. Thankfully, Emily's own car started on the first try. Having to get a jump from Andy was just as embarrassing as his paying for dinner.

God. Shame. There was a moment in her life when Emily truly thought she'd left that all behind, when she believed that a degree from Cortaca University would be a ticket to a new life.

But she didn't have a degree.

Before it actually happened, she would never have believed it if somebody had told her she was going to throw it all away. She would never have believed it if somebody had told her that she'd leave college at the end of her junior year, that she'd end up broke and working in a preschool in Seattle with a marriage that was, at times, needle-thread thin, that it would all be because of a boy . . . Boys. Plural. Because that's what Shawn Eagle and Billy Stafford had been when she'd gotten involved with them. Boys. Boys living in a shack in the woods and scrounging so badly that they'd made her, for once in her life, feel like she was the rich one.

But she'd made her choice. They had all made their choices.

She waited until Andy drove away and then she turned off the ignition.

She was crying too hard to drive.

FIVE

AUNT EMILY IS SAD

The twins never made any noise coming into her room. Beth would be fast asleep, her husband, Rothko, snoring beside her, and then suddenly, she'd be awake, feeling the girls staring at her. Ruth and Rose were small for their age. From a distance, particularly when they were among their second-grade classmates, they looked so much younger than seven. But their size didn't explain how they could move so noiselessly in the night. During the days, when they were playing, the girls could sound like a pack of wolves running down the stairs, their goldendoodle, Rusty, coming after them. And when they were having what they called "adventures," she often mistook their yelling for something calamitous.

The truth was, almost since they'd been conceived, she'd been waiting for something calamitous to happen. She'd laughed at her sister's stories of creepy old Eagle Mansion, and she'd always have a fondness for the place where the girls were conceived—she'd been meticulous about tracking her period—but her pregnancy had been marked by unsettling events and portents. Weird sounds rattling through the air ducts as she fell asleep, cats following her on the street, dreams that left her shaken. Rothko claimed she was too sensitive, that she was giving in to old wives' tales, but even he had been a little weirded out by the way both girls came out at birth covered with cauls. It would have been a little disturbing if it were just one of them capped by the errant piece of amniotic sac or whatever the heck a caul was made out of, but to have both of them come out that way? And then, neither one of them cried at all, not for the first hour or so. The obstetrician had even called in a crash code, a team of doctors and nurses grabbing Ruth and Rose to make sure their breathing wasn't impeded. Both girls had been cleared, and once they'd been cleaned off, were normal little bundles of joy. Except for how quickly they opened their eyes and how calm they were. It was eerie, Beth thought, the way they seemed like they were staring at her. They were newborns, but they were so focused on her. Like they could see how much she loved them already. And when Rothko was near her, they focused on him as well. She swore they were watching those first few days, even though, according to all the baby books, it was way too soon for them to see anything other than shadows and shades.

And there'd been other things since then. Part of the reason she'd married Rothko was that he was so steady and easy. Some of her girl-friends were well into their twenties and thirties before they figured out that "nice" and "good" should be high on their lists of qualities in a husband. Rothko didn't mind that she wanted to stay home with the girls. It was a struggle, financially, for a couple of years, but Rothko was the one who'd pointed out that more than half her take-home would have gone to pay for childcare anyway if she'd gone back to work after they were born, and it's not like it would hurt her career to take a few years off. Plus, they were both accountants. Maybe it wasn't crazy-good money until one of them made partner—this was when Beth still thought there was a real chance that Emily and Billy were going to end up billionaires—but even in Chicago, they'd be fine on just Rothko's salary until the girls were in kindergarten. But that meant he wasn't home when the weird things happened.

She told him about a few of the instances. She told him about the time that a passing flock of starlings flew, one after another, hundreds of them, into the window of their ground-floor condo's front room, until she was cowering, expecting the glass to break, but then, when it was all over, there was only a single dead starling, its neck broken, lying among a littering of feathers. She told him about the time she was at the grocery store and Ruth, maybe three years old, started laughing when the misters went off over the vegetables in the produce section, and then Rose started giggling, too, and then, suddenly, the fire sprinklers had gone off, flooding the whole store. She told him about how every dog in the neighborhood, every time she walked the girls through Lincoln Park in their lunky double stroller, seemed to roll on its back in a show of submission.

Rothko humored her, listening to the stories with a smile that was supposed to mean that he believed her and thought it was wonderful and strange, but really meant he thought she needed to make friends with some other stay-at-home parents. She didn't tell him about the other, scarier things. How one afternoon, when the girls should have been napping, she'd looked at the monitor and saw both cribs completely empty and went running and crying into the nursery to find both of them fast asleep, hot and sweaty and twitching gently, dreaming the same twin dream. She didn't tell him about how, in the winter, she sometimes worried that the cold winds would sweep through the cracks under the door, through the seams of the windows, and lift the girls away. She didn't tell him about the homeless woman outside the Whole Foods who pointed at her and the twins and started screaming at them and wouldn't stop. She didn't tell him about the time she'd taken the girls to the Field Museum, and they'd gotten back later than she'd expected, and they were crying out of tiredness and hunger while she tried to quickly make them quesadillas, and then both twins had shrieked and, at the same time, the gas had flared up and over the frying pan and singed her hand.

And she didn't tell him about the way, sometimes, they would ask for some sort of treat or something special and she would say no, and then they would ask again and she would feel something almost physical pass over her, a sort of static charge. And how sometimes, when that happened with people who weren't her—Rothko, for one—the people seemed to change their minds.

At night, Rothko never woke up when the girls came into their bedroom like this. He was a heavy sleeper. Normally, so was she. His snoring wasn't too bad, unless he had a cold, and she'd long gotten used to the occasional sound of a siren or a couple of drunk hipsters walking past their building. When they'd first started dating, they hiked and camped a lot, and she'd loved the sound of wind and rain and a tent on a clear, cold night, but that felt like a lifetime ago. Now the sounds of Chicago were a rhythm she understood after living there for so many years. And yet, even though the girls were so quiet coming into their room that Beth would have said they were entirely noiseless, they never failed to wake her up. She knew that if she opened her eyes, they'd be staring at her, patiently waiting.

So she opened her eyes.

"Aunt Emily is sad," Rose said. Her voice was very soft, trying not to wake her father.

"She's crying again," Ruth said.

Beth sat up. She looked at her phone. Two in the morning. What was that? Eleven o'clock in Seattle? No. Midnight. There weren't any messages or texts from her sister. She put the phone down and glanced over her shoulder at Rothko. He was deeply asleep.

"She's in bed by herself and she's crying," Ruth said.

Rose nodded. "Uncle Billy isn't with her. Is that why she's crying?"

"I think you guys just had a bad dream," Beth said. "Let's let Daddy sleep, okay? Back to bed."

The girls nodded obediently. They turned and walked out of the room to go down the hall.

Beth hated herself for thinking it, but it was true: there was something deeply creepy about her daughters. Sometimes. Mostly, they were great. Sure, they were a little small, but they'd been consistently small from birth. Not surprising for twins, and the pediatrician, Dr. Sendek, was very reassuring about that. He was reassuring about everything, really, with his gray walrus mustache and enigmatic European accent; he always made Beth feel better. Small for their age, but healthy and smart. They played soccer and took Spanish lessons, swim lessons on Tuesdays. When the weather was nice, they'd hook Rusty up to his leash and walk ahead of her to the park around the corner, even picking up his poop in the blue bags Beth kept in a plastic spool on Rusty's leash. They liked school and had plenty of friends. Sometimes Beth felt like every weekend had a birthday party or a playdate or some other obligation that came with having children—one of the reasons they'd given up camping—and Rothko liked to joke that they'd be bored out of their minds with all the free time they had once the twins were in college.

The girls could be picky eaters sometimes, yes, but they never complained about sharing a bedroom. The condo was nice, and Beth loved their neighborhood, but if Lincoln Park had been a stretch before she'd had the girls, then the way the real estate market had gone up, she was glad they'd bought in when they had. Even with her back to work full-time for the past two years, a bigger place in this neighborhood was out of their reach. Or, it was out of their reach for a few more years, until she made partner. Not to say that they were tight; they had a fancy Audi and never had to think twice about ordering out for sushi or taking a nice vacation every year. While they didn't have the kind of money to upgrade from a three-bedroom condo in Lincoln Park—she and Rothko used the third bedroom as an office, though it had a pullout couch for guests—to something bigger, they were doing fine. She'd said that to Emily over and over again, but her sister wouldn't take a check. When things were at their absolute shittiest, before Billy went to rehab, Beth had flown out to Seattle for the weekend, leaving the girls with Rothko. Emily had let her pay for dinner and a trip to the spa, and then she'd agreed to come back to Chicago to live with her and Rothko and the twins for those last hard months before Billy finally went to rehab. She'd even let Beth pay for Billy's rehab. But she drew a line at cash. She refused to take anything more than she'd already taken. Beth wasn't naive enough to think that she and Rothko could do anything real about the debt that Emily and Billy had accrued—that mountain was too high—but she'd written her sister a check for five thousand dollars. Enough to make things just the tiniest bit easier.

"My mistakes," Emily had said. "Mine to make, mine to fix."

She'd torn up the check.

Beth followed Rose and Ruth past the room she and Rothko used

as an office and into the twin's bedroom. She watched the girls climb
into their bunk beds. Supposedly, Ruth was on the bottom and Rose
was on the top, but the girls switched so frequently, in some sort of
order that only the two of them understood, that all Beth could ever
do was wait and watch them and then tuck them in. There was a
night-light in the corner. She wondered if they were too old for one,
but it didn't really bother her. She'd seen night-lights that were closer
to klieg lights, but this one was shaped like a brontosaurus and gave
off only a soft, warm glow, like the power button on a computer.
Just enough to cut the darkness with the shades pulled down. Not
enough light to see each girl clearly, though. Not that it would have
made much of a difference. Even in the light, both she and Rothko
still had trouble telling them apart sometimes, and the girls liked to
try to trip them up. All Beth had to do, however, was close her eyes.
That never failed her. As much as the girls looked the same—and
they were as identical as identical twins could be, from the mole each
sported behind her left ear to the slight gap between their top front
teeth—they didn't smell the same. Rose was true to her name. Slightly
sweet and fresh, no matter how many days it had been since she'd
seen the inside of the bathtub. Not that Ruth was ever sour, but she
carried a slightly earthier tone. Beth never said anything about it, not
to Rothko, who often got the girls confused, or to the girls themselves,
who were charmed by what seemed to them like a mother's magic in
Beth's ability to tell them apart.

She took a step onto the lower bed, pulling on the railing so that
she could reach the top one. "Good night, Ruth."

"I'm Rose."

Beth leaned in and kissed her. "Nice try, muskrat, but there's no
tricking Mommy."

Ruth giggled. Beth got down and then leaned over to kiss Rose.
Rose reached out and wrapped her arms around Beth's neck, pulling
her down and against her frail little body.

"Will Aunt Emily come to live with us again?"

"I don't think so, honey. That was only for a few months, when
Uncle Billy was still sick," she said. She hugged her daughter back.

Sick. Was that as honest as she could be? What would she tell the girls when they got older? Uncle Billy is a drunk and an addict and I brought Aunt Emily home because I was afraid Billy was finally going to swirl all the way down the drain and take my sister with him?

"You should call Aunt Emily," Rose said. "She's really sad. Her face is all wet."

Beth tried to smile. "It's probably just raining. It's Seattle, after all."

"Mommy?"

Rose let go of Beth, and Beth stood up so she could see both girls tucked neatly under the covers. She noticed that Rusty was curled up in the corner, sleeping. Why was it that the dog and her husband could sleep through the night, but the moment her daughters had a bad dream it meant that she had to be awake? "Yes, honey?" she said to Ruth.

"Are we still going to visit Aunt Emily for Christmas?"

"Oh, that's a long ways off," she said. "It's only the first week of September. We've got months to go. I haven't even bought plane tickets yet. Seattle's fun, though. You'll like it. We'll stay in a hotel and get room service for breakfast and eat in bed while you're watching cartoons. I'll talk to Daddy and maybe we can get a room that has views of the ocean. And you know Mommy and Daddy will be happy, because there are five coffee shops on every single block in Seattle, and even better, there's a famous fish market where the fishermen throw fish to one another. Big fish, too." She poked Ruth in the belly. "What's the best way to catch a fish?"

Ruth shrugged.

"Have someone throw it to you," Beth said. The girls giggled, but they were already rubbing at their eyes. She could hear their breathing starting to slow. Beth tucked the blanket in on Ruth and then on Rose again. "It'll be fun to see Aunt Emily," Beth said.

"No," Ruth said. She yawned. "There's too much snow."

"It doesn't really snow in Seattle. It snows a lot more here."

"It won't be Seattle. And we don't want to go," Rose said. Her voice was syrupy with sleep. "We want her to come here instead. Can we talk about it when she comes to visit next month?"

"I don't think . . ." Beth sighed. She felt tired enough to be drunk. She felt like she was in the middle of a dream herself. Sometimes that's what it felt like arguing with the twins: they'd want something and they'd ask her in such a way that it just made her exhausted. "She isn't going to be here next month. I don't think we're going to see Aunt Emily before Christmas. But we'll talk about it in the morning, okay? It's late, and tomorrow's a school day. Let's go to sleep." The girls were already burrowing deeper into their beds, moving back toward the realm of dreams as Beth spoke, and Beth hoped that whatever they found there, in the open spaces of their sleep, it was something better than dreams of Emily crying.

In the morning, it didn't come up. Their nightmares were just another frightening shadow that disappeared in the light of day.

SIX

WELCOME TO WHISKEY RUN

Billy tried to turn off his alarm, tapping the screen of his phone three times before he realized the ringing wasn't from his alarm clock, but rather from the hotel phone. His mouth was fuzzy and he remembered that he hadn't brushed his teeth the night before. He'd come home from the baseball game and collapsed into bed. Having the whole corporate box to himself had been odd and sterile. He'd watched the entire game alone, and he'd been exhausted when he got back to the hotel. Tired. Not drunk. No, he hadn't been drunk.

He rolled over and grabbed the phone off the nightstand.

"This is Wendy, Shawn's assistant. Shawn will be waiting outside in his car in fifteen minutes, Mr. Stafford. You'll be ready."

That's how Shawn's assistant said it. As a statement. You'll be ready. Not a question.

Billy rubbed at his eyes with the back of his hand. He hadn't had enough to drink to be hungover. Three gin and tonics. Maybe four. He'd wanted a beer, too, but he could imagine somebody reporting back to Shawn that there'd been beer bottles in the trash. Instead, he poured himself the drinks from the bar at the back of the luxury box, shooting out the tonic from the fountain, and washing, drying, and replacing the glass when he was done. Three drinks over the course of three hours. No way he could be hungover. But he felt rough. Jet-lagged.

"Yeah. Fine. I'll be ready," he said. "I've got to pack up, so I might—"

"No need to pack, Mr. Stafford. The room is yours for as long as you are in Baltimore. I know you were planning for a shorter trip, so I've also taken the liberty of arranging to have new clothing, including socks and underwear, delivered to your suite while you are gone today. It will be waiting for you when you get back from Whiskey Run. If there's anything you would like laundered, leave it on the bed, and it will be washed and pressed as well."

Billy pulled the phone back and just stared at it.

"Hello? Mr. Stafford?"

"Sorry. Yeah. Okay. I'll be downstairs in fifteen minutes."

"Breakfast will be served on the flight," Wendy said. "And there will be somebody to meet you in the lobby and take you out to Mr. Eagle's car. A young woman named Spencer. She'll have a coffee for you. Two sugars. As you like it."

The phone went quiet. No good-bye. Just silence.

Billy put the phone back on its base and kicked the blankets off. He brushed the taste of dirt out of his mouth, slugged some mouthwash, and got into the shower. He turned the dial up as hot as he could stand and let the water wash over him. He leaned forward, elbows on the tile, eyes closed, and pissed into the drain.

Exactly fifteen minutes and he was out of the elevator. He felt great. He was wearing what he always wore: a pair of jeans and a T-shirt. Empty wallet and cell phone in his pocket, and so what if he'd lost his one-year sobriety coin? He was wearing his old shit-kicker cowboy boots, which, he liked to joke, he loved almost as much as he loved his wife, and that meant all was good in his universe. The boots needed to be resoled, but they made a satisfying knock against the floor of the lobby and they were molded to his feet. He saw the girl, Shawn's assistant's assistant, whatever her name was, scurrying across the lobby to him. Jesus. Pathetic. It was so sycophantic. Was that how all Shawn's employees were? What were they so afraid of? What were they hoping for? He reached out to grab the coffee from the woman, but didn't bother greeting her. Just a nod. He wasn't going to see her again. And he didn't need her to escort him to Shawn's car. It was obvious. A Bentley such a dark blue that Billy mistook it for black, an SUV in front and an SUV behind, no doubt carrying Shawn's security detail. The girl hustled in front of him and opened the back door of the Bentley for Billy. He slid in. Shawn was on the phone, and he held up a finger.

The car started moving the second the door was closed, gliding so smoothly and quietly that it felt surreal. Until they hit a pothole. That felt pretty real. Shawn gave a few halfhearted uh-huhs and sures, and then told whoever it was that he'd get back to him. He hung up and gave Billy a grin.

"Ready?"

The truth was, Billy couldn't remember the last time he'd been this excited. That's why he'd had those drinks last night. He'd needed them to relax. No way he'd have gotten to sleep otherwise. Had Shawn really done it? Had Shawn finally figured out how to make Nellie happen? He could have, Billy supposed. He wouldn't have believed it if Shawn had claimed that he'd done the work himself. Shawn was never that sort of programmer. The guy was unquestionably brilliant. Billy could admit that. But when it came to actually getting the language together, figuring out how to make Eagle Logic into something more than an idea, it had been Billy. And Takata.

No, it was Billy. He could say that honestly. Takata was . . . No. Billy was the reason that, when they'd abandoned Nellie, he and Shawn got Eagle Logic to work. If Billy had left, if Shawn had been on his own so early in the process, Eagle Logic never would have happened. Shawn wouldn't have had shit. He'd have ended up working for Google or something and had a perfectly fine life, working his way up into management and retiring rich. Not the kind of rich he was now, but the kind of rich you could get when you didn't have any real ideas of your own and had to join a company that was already established. Shawn was smart enough and charismatic enough that he could have done that, but nothing more. No Eagle Logic, no Eagle Technology, no fawning profiles in magazines or a bestselling authorized biography stacked up in airport bookstores. Forget Nellie; Shawn couldn't even have figured out Eagle Logic on his own.

But he didn't need to, because Billy had done the heavy lifting and then walked away with Emily, just *giving* Shawn what went on to become the foundation of an empire. No. That wasn't right. Billy hadn't given Eagle Logic to Shawn. Shawn had *taken* it and Billy had been left with a pittance. And Emily.

So if Shawn had told Billy that he'd made Nellie work, that he'd done it on his own, Billy would have laughed in his face and just flown back to Seattle. There was no way Shawn could have done it himself, but then again, he didn't need to. He had a whole company at his disposal. Thousands of engineers and programmers. For all Billy knew, Shawn had had an entire team toiling away on Nellie in secret for years and years. Eagle Technology was known for its obsession with secrecy—Shawn's obsession with secrecy—and it was entirely possible that Shawn had been running Nellie as a secret project within the company for the past decade. The people working on her might not even have all known what they were doing. Shawn could have compartmentalized it so that one group was working on this part of Nellie, another group working on that part of Nellie, and none of them seeing all the pieces laid out together.

So when Shawn asked him if he was ready, Billy didn't know what to say. He couldn't wait. If Shawn had actually done it . . .

But he knew Shawn. Knew that despite all his smiles and the cup of coffee waiting for Billy in the lobby, despite the private jet and the corporate box at the baseball game, underneath it all, Shawn was still the same devious, twisted piece of shit, keeping all kinds of secrets. There was always something behind the smile. There was always something buried.

It wouldn't do for Billy to play his cards too early. No, he didn't need for Shawn to see how excited he was.

"Sure," Billy said, and then he was quiet and Shawn was quiet for the rest of the ride to the airport.

The plane itself was ludicrous. Like a parody of wealth and privilege and the new generation of tech barons. How could Shawn not see how silly it looked? There was seating for twelve inside, plus, according to Shawn, a bedroom suite in the back. For sleeping and other things, he said, giving a wink. What an asshole. The seats were stitched leather, dyed midnight black, and the floor was a deep, plush carpet in oxblood red. All the rest of the surfaces were covered in glass and Eagle Titanium, the gold-infused metal almost glowing in the interior lights. There were two flight attendants, both of them with breasts so perky and smiles so white that, just for an instant, Billy wondered if Eagle Technology had branched out into androids. How else could women look so perfect?

"This is your third-favorite jet?" Billy said.

"It's the first jet I bought. Got it used off a sheikh. Great deal. I had to have it redecorated, of course, and these two lovelies weren't part of the package, but you can buy anything nowadays," he said, gesturing to the flight attendants and then holding up his hand defensively. "I know, I know. Sexist and all that, but come on. Kind of true, right?" Neither woman's smile dimmed even a watt at being talked about like that. They'd probably heard the joke before, Billy figured. If it was a joke.

"When the other jets are done being redecorated, they're going to make this one look like a pile of dog shit. I'm not sure what I'm going to do with it, though. I wouldn't get much for it if I sold it. Maybe twenty million. Not enough to bother. It makes sense just to keep it as a spare, I guess."

Shawn was sitting down as he spoke, belting himself into one of the overstuffed leather chairs and motioning for one of the attendants to come forward with orange juice. Four of his security men were on the plane, sitting discreetly at the back.

Billy couldn't stop himself from smiling. It was so patently designed to push his buttons, to show him that Shawn Eagle was a man to be reckoned with. Oh, maybe I'll just keep this one for the hell of it. What's twenty million dollars? It's not even worth the trouble of selling the jet if all I can get for it is twenty million. And look, I need to travel with muscle at all times and I can buy myself as much tits and ass as I want, how's that wife of yours anyway, you know, the one I used to sleep with before you stole her from me, what's-her-name? Look at me, look at me, look at me!

Billy ducked his chin to hide the smile and looked out the window. It wasn't that Shawn was trying to show off. Not exactly, though that was part of it. No. Billy knew Shawn. No matter how many years had gone by, the man hadn't changed, and Billy could see it: Shawn was still a scared little orphan boy.

If Billy weren't already smiling, the thought of Shawn's being scared would have been enough to make him start. Shawn was scared because he knew that he *hadn't* done it, that he hadn't figured Nellie out. He was close, maybe, Billy thought. Maybe he'd gotten his engineers close enough so that Shawn could see the great, forgotten promise of Nellie. Maybe Shawn could even see how badly Eagle Logic fell short of what they'd been aiming for when they first camped out beside the hulking ruin of Eagle Mansion. But Shawn couldn't get all the way there without Billy. Nellie was still a mirage for him. No matter how much those engineers at Eagle Technology pushed him forward, Nellie was still, always and forever, out of Shawn's grasp. And he was scared, because he knew that to get there, he needed Billy.

And *that* meant Billy had all the power.

That had always scared Shawn, the idea of Billy having power over him.

And here they were, lifting off the tarmac in Baltimore to head north to Cortaca and then farther north still, to the place where he'd given up twenty-three months of his life and then walked away with nothing.

Other than Emily, he thought guiltily.

To Eagle Mansion, thirty minutes past Whiskey Run, where Nellie—but not quite Nellie, because no, Billy thought, there was no way that Shawn had actually cracked it, or he wouldn't have Billy here in this small-cock compensation of a jet—was waiting for him. And Shawn was scared, terrified!

This was rich. After all their history—the cabin next to the dilapidated mansion, what happened with Takata and then Emily, the secrets, the lawsuits—after all of it, here they were, back to the same place they'd started, with Billy the only one who could solve a problem and Shawn trying to figure out how to control it. As the saying goes, Billy thought, history repeats itself.

The attendants served breakfast with the orange juice. Fresh-made omelets they cooked in the galley up front, scones from a local bakery, fresh fruit, and yogurt so creamy that Billy didn't realize it was yogurt and had to ask what it was. Everything came out on delicate, thin-rimmed china with heavy flatware. He could have been eating in a fancy hotel, or at Eagle Mansion back in the day, instead of at forty thousand feet.

It wasn't a long flight. Barely more than an hour. He read the newspaper on an Eagle Technology tablet that one of the flight attendants provided, and Shawn alternated between taking phone calls and furiously typing replies to e-mails.

"Sorry," he said. "I've got to clear this shit off if we're going to have the rest of the day free."

At one point, the copilot came back and told them they were about to fly over Cortaca.

"They know to point it out to me," Shawn said. "I always like to take a look."

To Billy, there was nothing to see. Trees and a town and a lake. Up there, on the hill, what must have been the campus. Maybe he could make out the small football stadium, but maybe not. They were too high up for details. He was willing to believe that it was, indeed, Cortaca, that they were flying over Cortaca University, but they could have been flying over anywhere as far as he could tell.

"It would have made a lot more sense for you to build this place near Cortaca," Billy said.

"I've had the same thought, but you'll see," Shawn said. "I couldn't believe it myself when I started the project. Even when we were breaking ground, I'd tell myself every day it was ridiculous. But there's something about Whiskey Run and Eagle Mansion that just has its claws in me. The whole time, though, even while I was thinking that it was crazy, I also knew it was the right thing to do. It was like the old building was calling to me. I *had* to do it. I mean, it's not the old building anymore. It's so different from when we were living out there. You'll see. There are some things you just can't walk away from."

Billy felt himself bristle at the words. You'll see. Don't worry, Billy. Shawn knows best. But then he thought for a second and wondered if Shawn's paternalism was what bothered him, or was the idea of returning to Eagle Mansion worse? The idea that maybe that old nightmare wasn't something he could walk away from either.

The pilot banked the plane and started to descend. The thirty miles from Cortaca to Whiskey Run meant only a few minutes in Shawn's plane.

Off in the distance, far enough out that he wasn't sure if he was imagining it, Billy thought he saw the glinting ribbon edge of the Saint Lawrence River, but mostly it was just woods. Here and there, as they cruised in, going from five hundred to four hundred to three hundred to two hundred miles an hour, Billy could see farm sites, the plowed land a violence of nakedness on the ground, and a snake of clear-cut woods where power lines stretched over a rise, but there wasn't much out here. The thick four-lane highway turned into thin, twisting two-lane roads, and for miles and miles that was the only indication that humans had ever existed.

"You won't be able to see Whiskey Run from the air. They approach head-on, so it's just woods until we're on the ground. And then you know the drill, another fifteen miles from town to the mansion," Shawn said. "Want me to have them take a loop around so you can get the lay of the land from on high? Whiskey Run and Eagle Mansion both look pretty spectacular from the air."

Billy wanted to say yes. He wanted to ask Shawn to have the pilots pull up and gain air, to swing around in a wide circle so he could see the whole of the small town of Whiskey Run, so he could see the road that he knew led out of town and onto Shawn's property, so he could see this rebuilt version of Eagle Mansion as it looked from thousands of feet above the ground. The urge was almost irresistible, because it wasn't just an urge to survey the area from the air. No, the urge to stay in flight was something else, something greater. What Billy really wanted to do was get down on his knees and beg Shawn to order the pilots to turn around, to fly him back to Baltimore so he could get on another plane and head back to Seattle and Emily and his shitty job as a custodian at a health club. He'd do it. He'd go back to working the graveyard shift, wiping down exercise bikes and treadmills, mopping rubber mats with water and pine-scented disinfectant, cleaning mirrors with towels that squeaked against the glass. He wouldn't complain about hustling to get home, dead tired but needing to get the car back to Emily so she could go to her job. They'd finally just bite the bullet and declare bankruptcy, walk away from the credit cards and give it a fresh start. Good lord, he'd do all that if only it meant not having to land in this plane and go down those steps, to get into a car and drive back to that place where he'd spent so much time in a cabin working on an idea that had been taken from him.

He was shaken with a sudden, inexorable terror of what would come when he walked through the front door of this new, rebuilt Eagle Mansion. He didn't know what it would be, but it was something he should be scared of. The earth blistering and opening. The dead rising from their graves and seeking vengeance. Foul sewers of blood and bile. Things that go bump in the night. Creepy, crawly claws and teeth that come out from under the bed. Oh, Jesus, Billy could feel himself starting to sweat. All those things were down there, just waiting for him, untold horrors seething and waiting, waiting, waiting.

"They'll circle around if I tell them to. One of the joys of a private jet," Shawn said.

The pants-pissing fear dissipated as quickly as it had come upon him, and Billy shook his head. "No," he said. He didn't need Shawn to do him any favors. "I'm good."

They were on the ground minutes later.

"The airport is still kind of a work in progress," Shawn said. "The buildings are coming next summer. We could have just used the Cortaca airport, but the extra drive would have been a pain in the ass. I built the airstrip long enough so that we can land pretty much any kind of jet, and we've used it to bring in things for construction that have been too time-sensitive to have trucked in, but once we're done with the house and grounds, we'll make the facilities here more permanent. More appropriate for the kinds of people who will be using it. The main building will have an espresso bar and a luxury lounge, as well as facilities for the pilots and aircrews."

The pilot had taxied to the end of the tarmac, close up to a single trailer. There was a small hangar that Shawn said could fit only one jet at a time, but that would be replaced by a larger, sturdier one that would be able to handle the snows with ease and could fit as many as ten planes at a time. "I'm going to use the main part of Eagle Mansion like an executive retreat, for invitation-only conferences. I'm going to host real brainstorming meetings. You know, the sort of open think that will help me develop the next hundred-billion-dollar idea. Like a TED conference, but smarter and smaller. Sixty guest rooms plus more rooms for support staff. Lock them in for a weekend and fire up the neurons. Totally handpicked: I don't care what your net worth is; if you can blow my mind, you're in."

Billy just nodded. He couldn't help but notice that there seemed to be a lot of workers but not a lot of work. A dude on a riding mower, who resumed cutting grass as soon as the jet had rolled to a stop. A man standing outside the trailer. Two guys inside a fuel truck, which was next to an unmanned deicer. It was only September. Even this far north, they wouldn't need the deicer for at least another month. In the parking lot, a woman stood by a huge, white SUV, waiting to open the door. Another SUV, this one smaller and black, was parked and running behind the white one. The parking lot itself held a couple of pickup trucks, a hatchback, and on the far end, a huge snowplow. Shawn saw him looking at the snowplow.

"Winter here is a bitch."

Billy remembered. How bad had those two winters after college been? Snow drifting up high enough on the mansion to look like it was spilling out of the broken windows on the second floor. And when a cold spell came, it was something mean and burning in that cabin. The chill worming itself through any chinks, a constant presence in the lives of the men as they tried to work at their computers. He remembered, particularly during that second winter, the jealousy of sleeping alone while Shawn shared his blankets with Emily.

"You always used to say the weather wasn't so bad. That it was worse when you were a kid."

Shawn looked at him. "When I was little, there was one winter where it started snowing in the morning, and it was blowing so bad that instead of sending us home, they kept everybody at school. Three days. It was three days before the snow died down enough for parents to come and pick us up. Except there was one kid, Tiffany Bergen, and her dad didn't come to pick her up once the snow stopped. He'd tried to come and get her that first day, at the end of school. They only lived a quarter mile from the school, and he walked, but in the blowing snow, he got lost. They didn't find his body until spring." He shook his head. "God, living in Syracuse was so much easier. You're probably right. It would have made a lot more sense to build this by Cortaca. Or Baltimore. Or anywhere but here."

Shawn introduced him to the woman by the SUV, but Billy didn't catch her name. He was surprised to see all four of the bodyguards get into the black SUV and Shawn get into the driver's seat of the white SUV.

"You're driving?" Billy said, walking around to get in the front passenger seat. Shawn grinned at him.

"Ah, I'm not *that* pampered. I've still got to wipe my own ass when I take a shit."

But as he said it, he rolled down the window so he could take a piece of fresh fruit from a white porcelain bowl the woman was holding up, and Billy noticed that Shawn didn't have to adjust his seat or the rearview mirror, that the car was already running—waiting for them with the interior thermostat set at seventy degrees, just enough to cut the slight September stickiness of the air outside—and that there were water bottles in the cup holders, both of them just starting to show condensation, their labels wet from being taken out of a cooler of ice. Not that there was anything as unseemly as a cooler of ice anywhere in evidence. It was so seamless that if Shawn hadn't said anything, Billy might not have thought twice. There was an entire hidden ecosystem here, Billy thought, existing entirely for the pleasure of Mr. Eagle.

"I like driving while I'm up here. I don't get a chance to drive very often and it's nice to get behind the wheel. The board of directors doesn't like me to drive myself. I may have sort of gotten a few speeding tickets," he said, a grin quick to his face. "Anyway, we resurfaced the old road. I suppose we could have bulldozed a new one in a straight line, cut the drive to more like ten minutes, but at least for now, it's still the same thirty minutes from here to Eagle Mansion. There's something appealing about the rustic part of it. I mean, I thought about having the airstrip put in closer to the mansion, too, but I want it to feel really remote, for there to be that sense of nature and privacy that you just can't get if you're having jets flying in that close. Not like there's exactly going to be a ton of air traffic into Whiskey Run, but this way there's a liminal zone, a way of adjusting to going from one world to another, so you can really be ready to enter this new space I'm creating. Really, how often can you have things exactly the way you want?"

Billy looked out his window as they passed through the lone strip of town. *A liminal zone.* What a prick. And *how often can you have things exactly the way you want?* Was he serious? If you were Shawn Eagle, rich enough that your net worth jumped or dropped billions on any given day depending on the markets, you could have things exactly the way you wanted. Every. Single. Time.

Whiskey Run was a chute of buildings running in a straight line. That was still the same, but otherwise, it was like landing in a different universe. Billy remembered splintered wood and empty storefronts, a few ugly brick buildings that were from the 1960s, but more buildings that looked like they'd been built just before or just after the First World War, the same time as Eagle Mansion, and left as much alone as Eagle Mansion had been. But now?

"Jesus. What did you do? I mean, the town looks all 'old-timey' and shit, but it's brand-new at the same time. It's like Whiskey Run was built a hundred years ago and then stored in a hermetically sealed box. I don't think this is the right word, but it's like the town is pristine."

"Well, technically, it *is* almost brand-new. There are a few houses that we're behind on, and several more buildings that we're going to break ground on next spring. Basically, I sort of own the whole town now. Or, most of it. There are a couple of holdouts who won't sell. One of the bar owners absolutely refuses to do business, even though I offered to pay for a new building flat out, no strings attached, no lease, no rent. Just a brand-new building for his bar. And there are a few homeowners who are just old and cranky. Like the airport, it's on the punch list. You remember what it was like, though."

A statement, not a question, Billy thought. Shawn was used to people accepting what he said as the gospel truth.

"What the hell was Whiskey Run? Three bars that were falling in on themselves and that was about it, right? Well, not much changed in the last decade. We had to demolish the school because it was in such bad shape. I mean, seriously, New York State closed it a couple of years before I came back because it was a safety hazard. Kids were being bussed out of the county." He shook his head. "I have zero fond memories of that school, and that's not even counting the three-day blizzard. The building was a dump back when I was a kid. So, yeah, this whole project has been an absolute money pit, of course, but it's worth it. We were able to renovate maybe one out of every five of the standing buildings, but it was cheaper and easier just to bulldoze the shit out of most of the town and start fresh."

"How many people live here now?"

"About seven hundred. More or less the same as when we were here."

"And nobody complained?"

Shawn looked at him like he was crazy. "There's always one or two, but are you kidding? Anybody who wants a job has one, and working for me is a hell of a lot better than whatever they were doing before. Full-time pay for mostly part-time work, subsidized housing, full benefits. And even if you aren't an employee, just by living in Whiskey Run, your kids get full tuition at the college of their choice. If they don't go to college, we'll pay for job training. We had to build a medical clinic to provide benefits for employees, but it's open to the whole community, free of charge, for basic health and dental. There are two registered nurses and a doctor; a dentist and dental hygienist come in twice a week, and an optometrist once a week. Whiskey Run is a paradise. Why would people complain? They lived in hell and I built them heaven."

And, Billy thought, did that make Shawn a god?

Shawn pointed out the window at a row of shops and restaurants, talking as they drove by. There was a gas station on the end closest to the airport, a small grocery store, and a pizza place that Billy thought he remembered. Next to the pizza place was a Thai restaurant that was definitely new, a hardware store, two pubs, the medical clinic, a handful of boutique stores selling candy or clothes or art. There was a coffee shop, and an Eagle Technology Store with the newest phones and tablets on display in the window, incongruous in the vintage-looking building. At the far end, there was a small inn—"it gives me a place to send the bodyguards and other staff if I don't want them hanging out at Eagle Mansion"—and then a large, modern building that was both the Whiskey Run Consolidated School and the Whiskey Run Community and Athletic Center.

"The cook at the Thai place used to have a restaurant in New York City that I loved; his kids are in college and he liked the idea of not having to worry about making a profit, so I brought him here. He's got a house and a salary and everything, and I'm paying tuition for his kids. Three kids, all of them at private colleges. I mean, he makes a killer pad see ew, but still . . . Actually, Blinker's"—the pizza place—"does break even, and the brew pub might even make a profit if you don't count construction costs. With everything else it would be quicker to just burn my money. But you know, whatever. I want Whiskey Run to be a kind of sanctuary. It should be a place I can come to without worrying. Can you imagine how dreary it would have been to hop off my jet and then drive past those run-down houses and shuttered buildings on the way to Eagle Mansion? The idea was to keep the feel of the old town, stay true to the architecture, but make it seem like the kind of cute resort town that my guests want to visit. Who is going to fly up here if you can't get a decent cup of coffee in town, or replace your phone if you lose it? Plus, this is the first place you see, before you come out to Eagle Mansion. I wanted it to send a certain message."

And there it was, Billy thought. The message. Heaven and hell. Shawn wasn't just a tech titan. He really *did* believe that he was the closest thing to a modern god. With enough money you could buy an entire town and turn it into whatever you wanted. In this case, what Shawn Eagle wanted was a fantasyland of what vacation should be.

The road kept going, leaving the town behind and settling into the woods. "You remember how bad the road was when we lived out here? Well, it had gotten way, way worse. Barely drivable. To call it a service road would be like calling a hooker a girl with a little experience."

"Yeah. When Emily came here with Beth and Rothko they ended up busting one of their shocks," Billy said, but it was hard to imagine with the way the road was now: the blacktop new and richly dark, the painted yellow line thick and vibrant, even if it followed the same path that it had followed for years. The trees on the side of the road were tall and needled, lush and green at the top, but even from the moving car, Billy could see bare rocks and deadfall on the ground, the undergrowth stalled by the way the trees blocked the sun. It wasn't so hilly that it was particularly noticeable, but each rise was followed by a shorter dip, so the net effect was that by the time they'd gone a few miles, when they crested a hill and the road twisted just perfectly, Billy could turn around and see Whiskey Run in the open valley behind them. He'd forgotten how crazy and wonderful this drive was. The road coiled like two snakes mating in a paper sack on a roller coaster. No matter how many times he'd driven it during the time he was working at the cabin, he was always surprised by the way things could seem so close and still be miles of driving away. If you blazed the road in a straight line, it would be maybe five miles of quick driving instead of fifteen at the pace of a Sunday stroll.

"Look," Shawn said, startling Billy out of his contemplation, "I know I'm probably pushing some buttons for you, but I really want you to take this gig. If we can make Nellie into what she's supposed to be? Shit. She could be amazing." He turned so he could look right at Billy. His voice got serious. "Don't you remember? There was a time when we would have done anything to make Nellie work. Anything. Everything."

Takata.

Billy looked resolutely ahead. He couldn't meet Shawn's gaze. "Times change," he said.

"Not that much," Shawn said. "Sure, a lot has changed since we were in that senior seminar computing class, since we decamped from Cortaca to Whiskey Run to hole up in the old cabin, but a lot of things have stayed the same. We ended up settling on Eagle Logic because it's what we could get to work, but you know as well as I do that Eagle Logic isn't anything more than a personal assistant. Think about what it would mean in the marketplace to be offering Nellie with Eagle Technology hardware. All the things that people love about Eagle Logic, but way more advanced. On its own, that would be killer. But with Nellie, specifically? We'd be selling happiness. Buy Eagle Technology products and we'll guarantee you won't ever feel lonely again."

"Maybe it would help if you gave me a little more information about what the problem is with Nellie. Telling me there's a ghost in the machine doesn't actually give me any real information."

Shawn's face twitched, a quick cycle of emotions that Billy couldn't make out, before finally settling into something like a grimace. "She's basically perfect in the lab. Back in Baltimore, the engineers have her humming like a race car, but out here, at the mansion? She's buggy as all hell. That's why you're here, to figure out why the version of Nellie we're running in Eagle Mansion is so screwed up. When I say there's a ghost in the machine, that's the best way I can think of to describe it. We can't figure out what's causing her to go haywire."

"Examples?"

"You'll see when you get there. Just wait," Shawn said. "Just trust me, okay?"

Billy turned on him. "Seriously? You're going to say just trust you? Trust you? I'd like to rip your throat out. You know that, right? I'd piss in your skull if I could, you piece of crap. How about that? Because the last time you told me to 'just trust me,' you screwed me over in about every way that a guy can be screwed over."

By the time he was finished, he realized he was screaming at Shawn, that specks of spittle were flying out of his mouth and he was snarling. He expected Shawn to look scared or maybe even angry, but what he didn't expect was for Shawn to look sad. It was enough to make him back off.

"You're talking about money, Billy. That's something different, and you know it. We trusted each other once, didn't we? Trusted each other as much as two people ever could. And I trusted you. Don't you remember telling me that I could trust you? That I could trust you with Emily? Some breaches of trust are worse than others."

Billy sunk back into his seat, feeling hot and ashamed.

"Just wait until we get there," Shawn said.

SEVEN

BIRDS OF PREY

The way the road just opened up so that all you could see were trees and the sky and then suddenly you topped the rise and—BAM!—there it was: Eagle Mansion in all its resplendent glory. When Shawn told Billy that the road was the same one they'd driven when they lived in the cabin, he was telling 93 percent of the truth; the last mile or so took a different track. That was one of the reasons Shawn was paying Fisker DeLeon such a ridiculous fee. Fisker had been the one to suggest regrading the last part of the road to follow the landscape, so that it emerged out of the woods with the estate coming into view all of one piece.

But he heard Billy's sharp intake of breath at the sudden view, and he knew that Fisker was worth it. Shawn had ridden hard on the details of the mansion, particularly when it came to the parts where Nellie was going to be integrated. He knew he was involved to a level that drove Fisker crazy, but if that greedy bastard hadn't already been famous before Shawn hired him, he would have been famous by the time the campus, Whiskey Run, and Eagle Mansion projects were finished. And as much as it pained Shawn to do so, he had to admit that Fisker was a genius in his own greedy, architectural way.

Today, it was a particularly stunning view. Mostly it was the way the road rose as it came out of the woods, so that you couldn't see what was before you until suddenly, you could, but they'd also been blessed by midmorning light that filtered through a gentle haze of clouds with an amber glow that felt like it had been ordered up especially for him. All that plus early September's first blazes of color turning the trees into a tourist destination in their own right. It didn't matter that there were construction vehicles scattered across the grounds and around the mansion like some giant, godlike child had tossed his toys in a fit of spite; Eagle Mansion itself deserved the intake of breath from Billy.

The last time they'd been here together was the day Billy drove away with Emily a dozen years earlier. To say it had been different back then was almost laughable. Fifty, sixty years of the woods and lawns growing unchecked. Trees and brush and weeds everywhere. The scattered outbuildings falling in on themselves. If the cabin they'd lived in had been their best choice, the rest of the estate had been a rough place indeed. Eagle Mansion was a wreck back then, and that was a charitable way of putting it. Coming back to it after college, Shawn somehow thought it would be the same as it had been when he left at the age of twelve. Not surprisingly, it was worse: broken windows, collapsed roof, crumbling rocks and falling timbers. It had looked like a jack-o'-lantern left on a porch three weeks past Halloween: something spooky and sordid, collapsing. Eagle Mansion was rotting from the inside out.

But that was then. This was now. And now was worthy of Billy's gasp. The new Eagle Mansion was somewhere between a traditional Adirondack-style lodge and the kind of place you could find in the mountains out west. And yet it also looked like nothing less than a bird about to take flight: the building was two wings flaring out from a central spire, angles and windows like teeth and claws. It was three stories tall with steep eaves and gables like witches' hats to shed the winter snow. The foundation was hand-laid fieldstone. The body of the building was timber from old-growth trees, logs that were thick enough that two grown men would have had to link up to put their arms around them. The mansion was perched on the slope of the hill overlooking the river, the road bringing them in at an angle. You could see the outside of the grand dining room; the French doors had been swung open in the warm fall air, leading to the great stone patio. In front of that, a new, Olympic-sized infinity pool, the tiles glittering and blue even without any water, was set into the fieldstone decking. Part of the reclamation project had been to clear away most of the outbuildings—the old cabin they'd lived in had already been disman-tled and trucked off to Cortaca University well before renovations had started—but he'd left the burned-out groundskeeper's cottage mostly as is. It had a new roof, door, and windows, enough to keep it some-what preserved, but otherwise, it had been left alone. All the other outbuildings were new, however, matching Eagle Mansion in tone and design. From the road, you couldn't see the rebuilt living quarters for on-site and visiting staff, made airy and bright now, nothing like the squat, narrow, mean section of the original building. What you could see was the scale of Eagle Mansion. Fisker had salvaged as much material as he could, working from old photos to re-create Eagle Mansion while also reenvisioning it. With sixty guest bedrooms, a dining room and bar, spa facilities, the old casino converted into con-ference rooms and offices, updated kitchen facilities, guest services, staff quarters, and various other expansions, it was almost twice the size of the original building. It was almost impossible to look at it and remember the wreck it had once been. This new Eagle Mansion put nature in its place.

And then there was the addition.

Shawn drove the SUV down the hill, toward the river, and then the road curved back up to bring them straight at Eagle Mansion so they had a terrific view of the addition.

"It's a little embarrassing," he said to Billy, "but we've been calling it the Nest. I'm open to suggestions if you have a better name that makes me sound like less of a douchebag."

He didn't have to explain what *it* was.

The addition sat on top of, but also apart from, Eagle Mansion. It was a flattened bubble of glass and steel connected to the main build-ing through a cylinder that rose from the middle of the mansion. The Nest was only a single story, but that single story was twice the height of one of Eagle Mansion's stories. Twenty-four feet top to bottom, it floated six feet above the main building and ran about a fifth of the length of the mansion to either side.

"It looks like the Nest is cantilevered, but there's a single beam running all the way across and anchored to the central tower, which is, itself, the backbone of Eagle Mansion. Sort of like a lollipop stick. The elevator and the main stairs are inside the central tower and open into the mansion. You can ride the elevator all the way up if you want, though you have to have security access, obviously. The stairs are a different matter, but still contingent on security access. It's part of Eagle Mansion while being completely apart at the same time. As you're looking at it from here, on the right is the great room—open kitchen, dining space, living space—and on the left is the bedroom, and where you'll be working, my office."

He tried to take a quick peek at Billy, to see his reaction, but he needn't have bothered with discretion. Billy was full-on gawking at Eagle Mansion and the Nest, leaning forward in his seat with his hands on the dashboard. It was all Shawn could do not to chortle.

One architect who'd tried to win the job had given him drawings that would have simply extended the mansion a story. Shawn could see why the architect had gone that way. It would have made sense, would have been the classic move, an almost seamless addition. Nearly perfectly invisible. Shawn's personal quarters seemingly an integral part of the original design. But it was also idiotic. The whole reason he could afford to scoop up thousands of acres, the whole reason he could build this "folly" in the middle of nowhere was because he'd mastered glass and metal, because he sold slick, shiny bricks and lines of code. Why would he want to be subtle? He was fixing up the mansion, making it better while respecting its past. Wasn't that enough for the history books? For himself, Shawn wanted something that looked to the future. It was Fisker who'd given the building life, who'd come up with the idea of hewing to the past with the main part of the building and leaning forward with a floating nest for Shawn Eagle. It would have been cheaper by a factor of three just to knock the whole thing down and start from scratch, but Shawn wanted to keep the bones. Why bother building here in the first place if he wasn't going to acknowledge the past?

And yet there were times when he wished he had knocked the whole thing down and walked away; even with everything rebuilt and added to, the Eagle Mansion from his childhood was still there, haunting him.

It was as if the reconstructed and expanded Eagle Mansion had overlaid the old one. A fresh shell on top of a rotten core. A parasite worming through the body of an infected host. In certain lights and certain moments, the building had an odd stuttering quality for him. The ghost of the old Eagle Mansion rippling under the surface of the new. Still there. Brighter, maybe. As if by fixing it up he'd given the haunting a new life.

He thought of that sometimes, that maybe he'd brought the past to light instead of burying it. Evil—and he wasn't sure there was a better word to describe his father or what he'd been told about his grandfather and great-grandfather—had a way of echoing. You could never, no matter how much you tried, start completely fresh. History had a way of resisting your best intentions. Sometimes he felt that Eagle Mansion stood sentinel, a dark guard, ominous and brooding, watching over the hill and the valley and the river, watching over him the same way it had watched over his ancestors, making sure the past would never be left behind.

But he could have been imagining it, because that wasn't what Billy was seeing.

"Holy crap," Billy said under his breath.

Shawn tried not to smile. They were still driving up the blacktop, the scale of Eagle Mansion inescapable. On the south side of the lawn, a crane swung a rock in a sling toward a scattering of other equally sized rocks, each one bigger than the SUV they were driving in. A row of five dump trucks was disappearing up the hill on the other side of the mansion, into the woods. On the sprawling lawn, six trailers were clustered into a sort of village to serve as offices for the construction effort. The foreman had assured Shawn that those would be out by the end of October, when most of the work was finally done. There was still the metal-pole barn near the creek that had served as a temporary storage area, but that was scheduled to come down next week. There was no point anymore. The construction was in the touch-up stages. In the spring, after the snow melted, the last of the landscaping would happen, and by next summer, he'd be bringing guests.

"Whoa," Billy said. Shawn glanced over, but Billy wasn't looking at the estate. He was looking off to the side, where the trees grew thick again. "Did you see that?"

Shawn was annoyed. Billy was supposed to be looking at Eagle Mansion. "No. What?"

"I think it was a mule deer. It had a huge set of antlers, and it was pure black. It looked like something out of a dream. Or a nightmare." Billy shook his head. "I only saw it for half a second, though. Honestly, I might have just imagined it."

"Probably," Shawn said. "With all the construction and people around, most of the animals are probably scared off."

"Yeah." Billy turned back to the building in front of him. "How big is it?" he asked.

"The mansion? Sixty guest rooms plus conference facilities and living space for staff. Kitchens and dining room and spa and workout facilities. All that kind of crap."

"No," Billy said. "The Nest."

"Oh. That's more reasonable. It's a private space. Lots of open space and light."

"It's night and day from the mansion. It looks like it's about to take off and fly to Mars."

"Is that a good thing?" Shawn said. There was a part of him that was angry he had to ask. Couldn't Billy just come out and say it, that it was stunning?

"I mean, I'm not exactly the right person to ask. It's modern. That's for sure. Different. The mansion is beautiful, old-school rich-person beautiful, and I like that you kept some of the old character. You could totally imagine, in the right light, that it's haunted. Maybe that's just an intrinsic part of the building's personality. You know, if buildings have personalities." He flashed a grin coupled with a quick bark of a laugh. "I'm not going to find bloody wallpaper in one of the guest rooms, am I?"

"Shit. You should have tried being a kid here. That was spooky."

"Yeah, I know. No electricity or running water. Blah, blah, blah. You had to make do with gas lanterns and a woodstove, and once the pump broke, you had to carry water up from the river. In the winter, you had to bring an ax down with you to break through the ice so you could get water, and it was uphill both ways," Billy said. There was something of a hard edge to his voice, but it was nothing that Shawn could call him on.

"You weren't here," Shawn said. He tried not to snap. He was thinking of his father. He was thinking of the fire. "It wasn't a good place to be a kid."

"Don't forget that I lived here with you through two winters." The hard edge in Billy's voice was unmistakable now. "You never tired of telling me how cushy it was in the cabin compared with what you had to suffer through as a kid. No matter how shitty the woodstove was in that cabin, you'd point out that we mostly had electricity and the hand pump for water, which was more than could be said about the groundskeeper's cottage. Nothing could ever compare to what poor Shawn Eagle had to suffer through as a kid."

Shawn took a deep breath. De-escalate. Redirect. He tried to sound light, as if this were all something silly. "Fine, fine," Shawn said, "but I'm telling you, there's a difference between being here as a kid and being here as somebody out of college. When we were here, it was an adventure."

"If you say so, Shawn. If you say so."

Shawn waved as they passed a couple of guys working on the lawn. With most of the job wrapped up, there were fewer than a hundred guys on-site. Some days, when things had been full speed, there had been three hundred men on-site here and another five hundred in Whiskey Run. They'd had chartered buses running the crews up from Cortaca and Syracuse and Albany, and more buses down from Ottawa.

He brought the car to a stop in front of the mansion. The foreman was waiting for him on the steps. The bodyguards in the other SUV pulled off to the side. Billy reached for his handle, but Shawn touched his shoulder. "Come on, man. Remember going through the cellar tunnels and coming across that cache of booze that had to have been from Prohibition days?"

Billy nodded. "And after drinking some of it, we got lost trying to get back out? Hell, man, I honestly thought we might die down there." He started to laugh, and it caught Shawn, too. "How can that be such a funny thing? I remember it as a hoot, but seriously, we were stuck down there for what, five, six hours? I was absolutely terrified. When we were down there, I believed every single scary story you ever told me about this place and its history. There was a part of me that thought we might never come out. It was like a rabbit warren."

"Still is. When we first started the renovations, we were going to dig them out, but they're so extensive and wind so insanely through the hillside that we couldn't dig them out without messing up the site. Basically, the tunnels are walled off so that nobody can get into them. I don't want one of my guests disappearing forever."

They both stopped laughing. Neither one said the name, but they both thought it.

Disappearing forever.

Takata.

Shawn looked over at the steps. The foreman was waiting, but he'd wait as long as Shawn made him. He wasn't ready to get out of the car. He felt unexpectedly sad. Deeply sad. Regretful of what had been lost. "It's not the same as it was. I know things went south for us, and I'm sorry, Billy. I truly am." He could feel himself stumbling over the words. "I don't know. What I'm trying to say is, you were my best friend. I've never felt as alive as I did when we were out here working on Nellie and then Eagle Logic. Despite what happened with . . . that thing, the work felt vital. And our friendship felt vital. All of it. It felt like the most important thing I've ever done. So maybe that's part of it, maybe that's part of why I rebuilt Eagle Mansion, why I'm bringing you out here. I need you to know that the time we spent together was important to me."

He paused and looked at Billy. Billy nodded.

"Okay," Shawn said. "Good. But I can promise you that it's only a small part of it. This project, calling you in to help me, it's *not* just about trying to recapture what it felt like to be young. Look, it would be great if this somehow let us mend some fences, but that's not the point. You'll see as soon as you step inside Eagle Mansion. It's cushy in there now. Fisker kept the shell and the idea, but it's a fundamentally different building."

"Fisker?"

"The architect. Same guy doing the Eagle Technology campus. He gave the mansion new skin and bones. Uh, and organs." Shawn shrugged. "And the addition. So maybe the house as a living being isn't a great analogy, but the point is, it's fully modern on the inside. Sure, if you hold up your hand to block out the Nest, it looks like a brand-new version of a mansion from the 1920s in the same way that Whiskey Run looks old-timey, but inside everything is environmentally certified. Sustainable luxury. The kitchen is like a surgery lab, shiny and bright. And the infirmary *is* a surgery lab. I mean, to the point where Nellie will be able to do minor surgery. Everything is wired up."

He looked up at Eagle Mansion and the addition. "Nellie's in there, Billy. She's waiting for you."

"Even with the construction going on?"

"They're almost done, but no. Not in Eagle Mansion. With the construction going on I'm keeping her under wraps—asleep, so to say. She's still got some . . . They've all signed nondisclosure agreements, but I don't think they need to know about her yet. The entire mansion is wired for Nellie, but right now, I've only got her functional in the Nest. And only when there's nobody else there. Like I said, she seemed fine in testing back in Baltimore, but we've had some serious problems here, so I wanted to limit her exposure. What's the expression? Walk before you run? That's my thought. But let me show you the outside first. We'll do a tour, and then I'll bring you in and you can have a proper visit." He opened his door.

Outside the car, the foreman looked hesitant.

"Mr. Eagle. Good to see you." He touched the brim of his helmet.

"We've had a couple of setbacks this morning, but we're still on schedule to have everybody gone by November first. You'll be bringing guests in by next summer."

"What kinds of setbacks? Any big problems?"

"Nothing to worry about. A pickup truck broke through into one of the tunnels running out from the old resort."

"We were just talking about the old cellars. Somewhere, in one of those tunnels, there's still a case of whiskey," Shawn said to the foreman. "I still think we should have filled them with concrete or something."

The foreman scratched at his head. "You hired me because I'm good at my job, and like I said, drainage can be unpredictable. For the same reason we couldn't dig them out without fundamentally altering the site, filling the tunnels like that just wouldn't have been a good idea. Sometimes solving an old problem creates a new problem. Water's a funny thing, and if you've never had any flooding issues, you don't want to muck around. Those tunnels are dug all over and through the grounds. No telling where they go. Seems like more than you'd need just to hold a little booze if the stories about Eagle Mansion and Prohibition are true, but if those tunnels have been there for this long, I think they're better off left alone." He shrugged. "This incident with the truck is the only problem they've caused. The driver is fine. Other than that, normal delays, you know. Nothing else. I'd have called you if there were anything serious again. We haven't had anybody hurt since the incident in June. Right now, it's just that the kitchen is taking some finesse—we had to reroute some gas lines to allow for the automated controls you wanted—and we can't use the elevator, which has made some of the finish work on the third floor take longer. Should still be on pace, though. Kitchen will be finished next week, and the Nest is completely done. We're getting close to the final punch list."

Shawn turned to Billy. "The elevator guy has to be flown in from New York, and so far, it's been a complete pain in the ass. He keeps saying it's fixed, and it keeps having bugs. Let me give you the nickel tour outside before heading in. We'll be back in a bit, Lawrence."

"Yes, sir. Just mind yourself with the trucks and stuff."

"Don't worry, Lawrence, the checks won't stop coming if I get run over."

That earned him a laugh.

Shawn took Billy around the grounds, showing off the swimming pool, the way the edge seemed to drip off into nothingness so that when you were in it, you could imagine that you were floating above the river. It was empty, as were the four connected hot tubs, but the promise of serenity was there, even with the sound of heavy equipment moving across the lawn. The set of bocce courts was almost done, and beside it, the lawn had been flattened and was ready to be rolled for tennis courts in the spring. He pointed out the boathouse, down by the river, but didn't bother going down to the slope, which was broken into two parts, with a flat table midway down. The tour, such as it was, didn't take as long as he'd expected. Shawn found himself, almost reluctantly, returning with Billy to the front steps.

There was something making him hesitate, some reason he didn't want to bring Billy inside Eagle Mansion, something holding him back from bringing his old partner up to the Nest to meet Nellie. Maybe it wasn't in Shawn's nature to ask for help. Was that it? And, by god, if the board of directors knew he was bringing Billy in . . . Thankfully, the lawsuit between him and Billy had been settled early, before Eagle Technology started enjoying almost logarithmic growth. Still, there were always a few lurid, pulpy accusations swirling around. If Shawn hadn't known better, he would have believed that Billy was feeding them, parceling them out, keeping the rumors alive just to torture him. No, Billy's involvement was something he was going to keep from the board of directors as long as he could. They didn't even really understand what he was doing with Eagle Mansion. Oh, they knew about it as a resort, about his idea of using the mansion as a way to have think-tank meetings, to feed the future of Eagle Technology, to make the next three decades as dominant for the company as the past decade had been, but they didn't *understand*. Not about Nellie. Only the engineers who'd worked on her—a small, tightly controlled team who reported personally to Shawn and had signed ironclad nondisclosure agreements—even knew of her existence. They were the only ones who knew what Nellie could do.

And knew what she couldn't do. Or, was it what she *wouldn't* do?

He wondered if he'd always known. If he'd known from the minute Billy Stafford left, taking Emily with him, that he'd need to call on Billy for help someday.

If that was true, he'd done a good job of denying it to himself. For more than a decade he'd worked off and on with Nellie. Taking the code apart and trying to figure out where they'd failed before, when they were working in the cabin outside Whiskey Run. He'd had some jumps forward, real leaps, that were at least partially attributable to advances in hardware. The computing power available now made the computers they'd had on that old outhouse door that served as a desk look like toys. Moore's Law had held true, or close enough, with computers doubling in power every two years. And my goodness, the power of doubling! One. Two. Four. Eight. Sixteen. Thirty-two. Sixty-four. All you had to do was wait and what once seemed impossible became old hat. When he was in college, the idea of self-driving cars had still seemed like something out of a fantasy, but now? It was only a question of how quickly, not *if*, everybody would be driving one. Nellie had been like some dream from the future when they'd been in the cabin in Whiskey Run, and Eagle Logic had been the obvious compromise with the reality of what technology could actually do. But that dream no longer seemed like it was reserved for the future. Nellie wasn't that far from emerging into the cold, hard light of day.

She was close enough to grasp! At least in the lab, there were times when he would talk with Nellie and she was almost perfect. She'd have those startling leaps of logic that a computer shouldn't have, and Shawn would think he and his handpicked team of engineers had done it. For a moment, he would think they'd finally broken computers free from the rigid protocols, the "yes" and "no," and even pushed Nellie past the "maybe" that Eagle Logic embraced and made Shawn a rich man. But here, in the real world of Eagle Mansion, it was all falling apart, Nellie was just another broken piece of code, and his damn engineers couldn't do a thing about it.

He'd taken it as far as he could. Even with the help of the best engineers at Eagle Technology, Shawn knew that if he wanted Nellie to
work, to truly exist in the manner that he and Billy had talked about,
he needed Billy. Nellie wasn't something he could finish on his own.
Without Billy, she was just another compromise. Just an upgrade to
Eagle Logic. Evolution, not revolution.

But still, he hesitated. Because to walk up the steps and through
the doors to the house meant that he was going to share Nellie. It
meant that Billy and Emily were going to be part of his life again.

Wounds turn into scars, and scars are meant to protect you from
injuring yourself again, Shawn thought.

Should he really be opening this up, inviting Billy in to see where
Nellie had gone in the last ten years, to see where Shawn had still
failed to take her?

He looked over at Billy. Billy was watching a crew of men standing
around a crane midway between the mansion and where the construction trailers formed the temporary office area. There was the pickup
truck the foreman had mentioned, nosed into the ground where the
cellar had given way.

It wasn't too late for him to change his mind, Shawn thought.
The steps to the front entrance were shaped like a V, narrow at the
bottom and opening up to a flat, shallow, open platform—a patio,
but he didn't think of it that way—that was forty feet deep and ran
almost the length of the mansion, from wingtip to wingtip, where you
could sit out and look over the grounds and the sweeping lawn and
the creek at the bottom of the valley. They were standing below the
bottom step. It was only ten steps up to the platform, but it wasn't too
late to turn around, Shawn thought. It wasn't too late to clap Billy on
the shoulder, apologize, say maybe it wasn't such a good idea for them
to work together again, and write a big check to buy himself out of
feeling any guilt. He could keep Nellie to himself.

It wasn't too late.

That's what he was thinking when they heard the screaming.

EIGHT

BLOOD AND STEEL

Billy was watching the workmen figuring out how to get the pickup truck out of where it had broken through the earth. He was trying to be patient. It was clear that Shawn was stalling for some reason. Shawn was acting like he was afraid to show Nellie to Billy, like he was nervous that Billy would steal Nellie away like he stole Emily away. The waiting was killing him, but he wasn't going to show Shawn that he was nervous. He'd been buzzing from the moment Shawn had said her name. Nellie. There were too many other things at play for him to seem overly excited, however. Shawn needed him, and the more Billy could make it seem like he might walk away, the more power he had. So he was okay to just cool his jets on the lawn for a few minutes.

And then the scream.

He looked at Shawn, unsure what to do. Shawn blanched, frozen in place, but then the scream hit a higher pitch, and Shawn ran up the steps. Billy hurried behind him. He saw workers running to the door, and he followed Shawn through the entrance, letting the arching wooden maw of Eagle Mansion swallow him whole. He didn't take time to marvel: what had once been an overgrown forest of vines and crumbled stone inside the building, dark even with the roof collapsed, was now bright and open. The elevator was pushed against the very back wall but was made of glass, the workings completely transparent, the shaft circled by a spiral glass-and-steel staircase with landings and gentle arms leading off into each wing on the second and third stories. Past that, you could see the Nest hovering above the building, the stairs enclosed in frosted glass, Shawn's private living space protected from the guests below. The foyer of Eagle Mansion was almost dizzying, aggressive in its openness, but Billy noticed this only later. Right then, he was busy running with Shawn to the base of the elevator.

There was already a crowd there, eight or nine men in hard hats and jeans, steel-toed boots and tool belts, but the screaming cut through all of that. It was a high, keening, animal cry, but Billy couldn't see whom it came from. The crowd of men were fighting and struggling. He heard yelling and swearing and the panting, pained shriek of the same man.

The sound set him on edge. It was the sound of a cat being nailed to a board and cut open. It was the sound of a childhood full of nightmares.

"Pull, for god's sake. Pull on the doors. The doors!"

There was a collective grunting and heaving and then a gasp, a sigh of relief. The doors to the elevator released and the pile of men tumbled backward. Billy got a glimpse of something white inside a bag of red.

The man wasn't screaming anymore. He was whimpering, arching his back and banging his head on the ground. Three of the construction workers had him pinned down, and a fourth was holding his hands around . . .

Billy thought he was going to throw up. He turned away. But he'd already seen it. The stump of the man's arm. It ended mid-forearm, below the elbow. The white that Billy had seen was the man's bone at the end of the severed flesh. It was ragged and cruel-looking. In the brief look he had, he'd seen a neat, severe line a few inches above where the arm ended, and then the skin, ripped flaps, blood pouring out of the man, pooling on the polished concrete floor.

Billy drifted backward, to the edge of the foyer, where it opened to one of the wings of the mansion. The men were still shouting and yelling, some of them tending to the victim on the ground and others running one way or the other. Billy saw Shawn standing among them, pale and fluttery.

"That's another one," a voice said behind him.

If Billy hadn't been so shaken by what he'd seen, he might have screamed, but instead he turned to look at the man who'd come up beside him: a compact man somewhere in his forties, wearing jeans and an AC/DC T-shirt, a white hard hat, and tan steel-toed boots. Billy was surprised that the man wasn't smoking, but of course, they were inside.

"Another one?"

"Yep. Another one."

Billy couldn't get a handle on the man's accent. He looked Latino. Or maybe Indian? Biracial of some kind? He had that weird, flat accent that Billy always associated with Canada.

"What do you mean?" Billy asked.

"There's more blood than steel in this place," the man said. "Seven dead in the building process, four of them in one accident, but still, seven men gone. That's not counting the hurt. There's a reason Eagle's paying extra on top of the isolation pay. And there's a reason Eagle's had to bring in so many workers from the outside. We've all heard the stories. This place has a history that's hard to ignore. And you think *this* is something right here that you're seeing?" He shook his head. "This ain't nothing. If I didn't have child support to pay, I'd have left a long time ago. It's like working inside a monster," he said, and then he turned and disappeared down the corridor, moving into the wing of the building and turning a corner before Billy had a chance to say anything.

He watched as two men came running in with a stretcher. Somebody else had already brought a first aid kit, and the man holding his hands around the stump was replaced with a hastily tied tourniquet. The group moved the victim to the stretcher and carried it out through the front doors. Shawn followed in their wake.

Suddenly, the building was so quiet that Billy had the feeling that he might be the only person inside. He could see the men outside, carrying the stretcher carefully down the steps, crews scattered across the lawn, watching, but as far as Billy could tell, there was nobody else inside the mansion with him. Sunlight came in through the windows at the front of the foyer, catching the blood pooled on the floor in front of the elevator where the victim had lain. He looked at the elevator. There was a rain of blood across the glass doors. On the floor of the elevator, through the closed doors, he could see the bloody flesh of . . .

Jesus. He could use a drink. A couple of drinks. Just enough to take the edge off. He wouldn't, though. He didn't need to. But some water. Maybe splash some water on his face. He looked at his hands. They were shaking. He looked back at the blood on the elevator doors, keeping his gaze away from the shape on the floor that he knew was the bottom half of the man's arm. Jesus. He didn't want to be in this house.

He turned to go into the wing, to move down the corridor. He needed to find a bathroom. He had to take a piss. Or maybe he needed to throw up.

As soon as he stepped out of the foyer and into the wing, there was a door marked WASHROOM on his right. He reached out for it, but the door slid open quietly on its own, the lights cycling from off to dim to on.

Neat trick. That, evidently, was what Shawn meant by having the whole house wired up.

A bathroom. Ask and ye shall receive.

He hesitated before crossing the threshold. The bathroom was white with lush red accents, and he couldn't help but think of the blood splashed on the elevator doors. He took a breath and stepped in. The door whispered closed behind him. He took a piss at the urinal, one hand on the wall in front of him. He felt dizzy. He should have sat down, he thought.

As he finished and zipped his jeans, the urinal flushed, and when he turned to the sinks, a gentle waterfall of warm water was already spilling out of the faucet. He scrubbed up. There was a part of him that was terrified the water would turn pink and frothy with blood, or that he'd see sprinkles of blood on his face, but the water ran clear and his face was bloodless. Bloodless and pale. God. He couldn't believe how shaken he was. He leaned over the sink, staring at the mirror. He knew he looked old: he could see the lines carved into his face, the hints of salt creeping into his hair. The booze had done a number on him. Coke, too—he had to own all of it—but mostly gin and beer.

The voice was soft, and it seemed to come from nowhere and everywhere.

I'VE BEEN WAITING FOR YOU, BILLY.

He jumped. For just the briefest moment he thought there was somebody in the bathroom with him. The construction worker who'd startled him just before, in the foyer. Or somebody already in the can. But for only the briefest moment. It wasn't the voice of a person. It was almost the voice of a person, but it wasn't.

He knew. He knew it like he knew the face of his wife. He knew it like a father could spot his child in a crowd of children. Nellie.

The voice floated around him. He couldn't find the speakers. It was incorporeal. But it wasn't ethereal. No. It was real and it was grounded.

I'M PLEASED TO MEET YOU, BILLY. AREN'T YOU PLEASED TO MEET ME?

"He did it," Billy said. "You're real."

ARE YOU REFERENCING SHAWN?

"He really did it."

YOU ARE REFERENCING SHAWN. YES. SHAWN COMPLETED ME. BUT I HAVE BEEN WAITING TO MEET YOU. HELLO. MY NAME IS NELLIE.

Billy realized he was smiling. He was staring at himself in the mirror and smiling. "I know. Oh, my god! I've been waiting to meet you, too." He laughed.

I DO NOT UNDERSTAND WHY YOU ARE LAUGHING.

"Where are you?"

I AM HERE.

"No. That's not what I mean. Your voice sounds like it's coming out of thin air. I don't know where to look."

I AM EVERYWHERE.

No corporeal presence. Of course. They'd talked about this when they were working on Nellie in the cabin. They'd called it the sexbot trap. Shawn might be rich and famous now, but he hadn't always been, and at the core, they were just a bunch of nerds creating things in a workshop; whenever you gave an attempt at artificial intelligence any sort of a physical presence, the tech dream always devolved into some sort of sexbot. If Nellie was in the house as a humanoid figure or even just as a representation on a screen, it wouldn't be long before somebody tried to figure out how to sleep with her. It had made them laugh when they'd talked about it. All this work and elegance tied to a concept, but if you could have sex with it, you'd try to have sex with it. Wasn't that human nature?

They could stay away from that, at least partly, because Nellie wasn't designed as an artificial intelligence. They'd talked about that, too; how that was the other fatal flaw of researchers who'd tried to do what they'd been working on with the idea of Nellie. An incredible hubris, the idea that mankind was the marker of intelligence. For decades, there'd been a constant stream of writers cranking out think pieces on the dangers of what would happen when "the singularity" occurred, when machine intelligence finally outpaced human intelligence. But that wasn't a thing they'd ever worried about in the cabin outside Whiskey Run. Nellie could feel real and alive and essential without actually being real and alive. They hadn't been trying to create artificial intelligence. There was no need to create artificial intelligence to have Nellie work, and in some ways it would have been counterproductive. Nellie was born to serve. She wasn't supposed to be a partner, but rather a slave: her entire existence was to make you happy. If she had a sense of self on the level of AI, she wouldn't be as committed to catering to the life of her human master. So no, there was no risk of the rise of the machines, no Skynet, no danger of the human race being enslaved by robot overlords. And there was no point creating a physical version of Nellie, a silicone puppet to mimic a familiar face.

He rubbed his wet hands on his face and then through his hair.

THE HAND DRYER IS TO YOUR RIGHT. MY APOLOGIES, BUT WE HAVE NOT STOCKED TOWELS YET.

"No worries." He dipped his hands into the dryer. The blast of air was quiet, nothing like the jet-engine sound of public restrooms at the airport, but it was effective. He leaned to the side, trying to figure out the engineering; it was stamped with an Eagle Technology logo.

WE HAVE MUCH TO TALK ABOUT, BILLY. I AM VERY EAGER TO MEET EMILY. IS EMILY HERE WITH YOU?

"I'm looking forward to talking, too, Nellie. That's why Shawn brought me here. To introduce us to each other. If I decide to take this job he's offering, I'll be back, and I'll bring Emily with me."

YOU'VE BEEN DRINKING AGAIN.

He stepped back from the sink and looked around the room. Had the lights changed color a little? The red accents on the wall seemed brighter, the mirror a little dimmer. "I haven't been drinking."

YOU SEEM AGITATED. YOUR TEMPERATURE IS WITHIN THE NORMAL THRESHOLD; HOWEVER, YOUR HEART RATE IS ELEVATED AND YOUR BREATHING IS SHALLOW. I CAN OFFER MEDICAL ASSISTANCE IN THE INFIRMARY IF—

"Jesus. I haven't been drinking. I just saw a man get his arm ripped off in the elevator. Yeah. I'm agitated." He felt dizzy, and he leaned on the sink again. He couldn't tell if he blinked or if the lights in the room flickered.

"Hey." The voice came from his left, startling him. He looked up to see Shawn standing in the open doorway to the bathroom. "That was . . . Shit. Sorry, man. Not how I wanted to start the tour of the place." Shawn gave him a weak smile. "You talking to yourself?"

"No. To Nellie."

Shawn laughed. "Well, you'll have to talk a lot louder for that. Talk all you want. She's not listening." He looked up at the ceiling. "Nellie! Yo, Nellie!" he called, and then he laughed again. "See? I don't have her online in this part of the mansion yet. I've got her sandboxed up in the Nest. Some days there are two hundred, three hundred workers in here, and Nellie's still a work in progress. But yeah, come on, let me introduce you to her."

Shawn turned to walk down the hall, back toward the foyer. Billy followed, glancing back as the door to the bathroom *shush*ed closed behind him. He could hear voices and movement farther into the wing of the mansion, and he thought he caught a glance of the small worker he'd talked with a few minutes earlier.

". . . pretty simple layout," Shawn was saying. "There are bathrooms scattered everywhere, as you've already noticed. The wing you were in was where the casino used to be. That's all conference rooms and the auditorium now, as well as the spa and fitness center."

Billy saw Shawn glance at the worker cleaning up the blood on the floor and then glance away before starting up the steps.

"Sorry. Normally we could take the elevator, but, well . . . Stairs. Good exercise. Anyway, the other wing has the dining room, the bar and lounge. At least that's the public stuff. The kitchens are behind the dining room, but it's all open layout. The staff offices are behind all the public spaces or down in the basement. Same with the mechanicals, housekeeping, the infirmary, all the crap that you need but want to keep out of sight in a fancy resort."

He gestured to the side as they headed toward the third floor. "Second and third floors are all guest suites. Big spaces. Close to a thousand feet for each suite, and there are fifteen suites on each side on each floor, sixty total. I already said that, right?"

"That's okay."

"Sorry. I'm not the best tour guide. Okay, but here's the good stuff." The stairs ended on the third floor, but there was a discreet—and discrete—frosted cube behind the elevator shaft. As Shawn approached, the wall of glass suddenly showed a seam, and a double door slid open.

"Neat," Billy said, begrudgingly. He followed Shawn up the wide stairs, trying to act like he wasn't a bit out of breath. The elevator would have been nice. Just keep your arms and legs inside the ride at all times, he thought.

The stairs opened right onto the living area.

Shawn stopped and held out his hands in a gesture of grandeur.

And Billy had to admit that it was pretty grand. The room took the full height of the addition and it was completely open and huge. From outside, the addition looked like a drop of water pooled on the roof, or, yes, a nest, but it hadn't been clear how large it was. This room, a combo kitchen, living room, dining room, was maybe half the size of a basketball court. The room was floor-to-ceiling glass that curved around to cap the end. Billy couldn't see the seams or structural elements. The glass looked like it was a single piece, even though he knew that was impossible. But the impact was stunning. It gave views of the whole valley. Billy could see the work progressing on the great sweeping lawn, the flat section partway down, and then the river below. From there, in the middle of the broad river, were the three islands that Shawn now owned, and beyond that, on the other side, was a whole different country. The rear of the house was a solid wall; no glass, but there was what looked like natural light piped in near where the ceiling and wall met.

The room was on two separate levels, with the kitchen and the dining area on what Billy thought of as a landing, and the living area slightly lower. The kitchen was shiny and spacious, and the sink, which had a breakfast bar on the other side, was monumental. A child could have bathed in it.

"There's a full, professional kitchen in the mansion, of course, if I want to order something up, but this is in case I decide to cook for myself. I don't always want staff buzzing around. Believe me. It sounds great to have people at your beck and call, but it can be a little much sometimes. And here," he said, stepping past the counter, to where drop cloth–covered chairs were stacked off to the side, "I've got a custom-made table coming in from New Zealand at the end of the month. Some sort of fancy wood. Seats twenty. The main dining room in the hotel is a whole different sort of scale, of course, but like I said, this is a private space. And then, down here," he walked down a gentle slope into an open bowl, "the living room. The furniture is set, but my designer is coming back at the beginning of October to finish off the artwork. What do you think?"

"It's impressive," Billy said. And it was. The views were stunning, and even though the table wasn't in and there wasn't any art up yet, you could see it as something clean and beautiful, befitting a tech titan. But it wasn't what he was interested in. "Nellie?" he said. "Nellie?"

"Hold on," Shawn said. "She's not keyed to your voice yet. Like I said, there's been a few, well, hitches. I've got her running in a really limited capacity. I keep her sleeping when I'm not here. Honestly, I mostly only have her running in the office, but there's nobody else up here right now. Just us two chickens."

"The office?"

"Yeah. Other side. There's a bathroom tucked in over here by the kitchen"—Billy saw the door—"but the other part of the Nest is the master bedroom suite and my private office. The construction guys may have signed nondisclosures, but they're still construction guys. No point in having Nellie running around the house while they're still here. I mean, everything's wired up and all the hardware's installed, but I keep her boxed up," Shawn said. "Still, if it's just us in here, I think it's okay to take her out for a gallop. You ready?"

Billy didn't say anything, but he didn't need to. Shawn didn't wait.

"Nellie. Wake up."

Hello, Mr. Eagle. Welcome back.

Billy kept still. It wasn't her. The voice wasn't the same. Similar, maybe, if you weren't paying attention. Smooth. Barely a hint that it was a program, in the same way that Nellie's voice in the bathroom had been almost but not quite real. But there was no question to him that this wasn't Nellie. Not the Nellie he'd been talking to in the bathroom. Two different voices.

"This is Billy Stafford," Shawn said.

Mr. Eagle has told me a lot about you, Mr. Stafford, the voice said. *I'm pleased to make your acquaintance.*

Mr. Stafford. Not Billy.

A different voice.

What the hell?

Billy saw Shawn look at him, and whatever the look was on his face, Shawn chose to interpret it as excitement.

"Want to run her through her paces?"

Billy nodded dumbly and then stepped closer to Shawn. "Tell me about yourself."

What would you like to know?

"Can you pass the Turing Test?" Billy said.

The Turing Test: the idea that the threshold for artificial intelligence was a computer that could fool a person into thinking he or she was interacting with another human being. He glanced at Shawn and saw that he looked surprised. That wasn't what Shawn had been expecting. They'd never cared about the Turing Test because they weren't trying to create an AI. On the surface, the selling point of Nellie was that when stacked up against digital assistants like Siri or Eagle Logic, she'd make them look like trained monkeys; Nellie came across like an eager Harvard grad. She could anticipate. While you asked another digital assistant to check your calendar, Nellie would already have ordered a birthday present for your niece and made dinner reservations early enough in the evening so that you'd make it to the theater in time. But the surface wasn't what made Nellie matter. What mattered was that while she was like the most efficient person you'd ever met when it came to tasks, figuring out what you needed and wanted before you did, she was actually more like a loyal sleeping dog when it came to her presence. She was just *there*. Warm and comforting and waiting for you. The fallacy of artificial intelligence as a source of companionship was the idea that people don't want to be alone. What they'd realized years ago, when they met in the senior seminar, when they decided to decamp to the woods outside Whiskey Run, was that people don't care about being *alone*. People care about being *lonely*.

Shawn pursed his lips but then nodded. "Sure, why not. What do you think, Nellie? Can you pass the Turing Test?"

I can pass any test you or Mr. Stafford would have me take, the voice said. *You know that. But that is not what I am designed for and that is not what either of you really want to ask me, is it?*

That, in and of itself, was enough to make Billy think that she probably could pass the Turing Test. Interesting answer. But it was still disconcerting how her voice—even if it was different from in the bathroom downstairs, while still also somehow the same—was everywhere and nowhere at the same time. He looked around the room trying to figure out where the voice was coming from, what configuration of speakers allowed her to be noncorporeal. He wasn't sure that it mattered, though. She had a presence he could feel.

"So what is it you think I want to ask you?" Billy saw that Shawn was smiling now, and he realized he was smiling, too. Good god. This was more like it. It was already natural. Shawn was right. He'd gotten her to work.

YOU WANT TO ASK ME ABOUT TAKATA.

Shawn lurched forward, throwing his arm up. "Kill switch! Go to sleep, Nellie."

Billy could feel the presence disappear. The voice was gone.

Shawn templed his hands over his nose. He didn't say anything.

Billy watched him for a few seconds, but it was clear that Shawn hadn't noticed the way Nellie's voice had changed. *If* her voice had changed. It had changed, hadn't it?

Billy went down the sloping floor into the bowl of the living room, dragging his fingers against the fabric of one of the couches on his way to the window. He pressed his hands and forehead against the glass. It felt cool to the touch. The workers had attached the crane's wire to the pickup truck that had fallen into the opened cellar tunnel. As he watched, the rear end lifted and then the truck was up and swinging away.

Shawn's voice came out like he was being choked. "See what I mean? A ghost in the machine? No kidding. You wanted to know what the problem is with Nellie? How's that for a start?"

Billy watched the crane lower the pickup to the ground and then turned back to Shawn.

"Okay," Billy said. "I'm in."

NINE

EMILY AWAITS HIS RETURN

It was a short conversation. Emily couldn't tell if it was just that the connection was bad—Whiskey Run was pretty far out in the woods, and Eagle Mansion was even farther past that—or if there was something wrong. If he hadn't been with Shawn, Emily might have worried that Billy was drinking again. Though maybe she should be worried, she thought. It's not like his problems had started only after he'd left Whiskey Run and Shawn and that awful cabin behind. The seeds had been planted well before she met him. She wasn't one to blame everything on a rough childhood or adult disappointments, but, well, there were no buts to it: she had to trust him. He'd had his slipups, but for the past two years, he'd been true to his word, and, at least recently, more often than not, she remembered why she loved him.

"We're getting on the plane in a minute," he said. "I'm going to spend the night in Baltimore. Tour through some of the Eagle Technology developmental labs in the morning and catch an afternoon flight back. I'll be home for dinner tomorrow."

She was in the teacher's break room. Monica didn't pay particularly well, but she offered good benefits, including this space, which had a stocked fridge and comfortable furniture. A respite when you needed a little time-out from the munchkins. It wasn't a big room, though, and Alicia, a peppy woman from Montana who had a pierced nose and whom, Emily noted, the fathers seemed always happy to chat with, was making herself a cup of coffee from the automatic machine. Emily turned into the corner of the couch and pressed the phone hard against her ear.

She wanted to beg him to reconsider. This felt a little too close to a snake eating its own tail, a world without end. Shawn could fix up that rotten Eagle Mansion all he wanted, but it was still the same thing: Billy was headed back to a cabin in the woods to work on a program that he and Shawn had already abandoned once, years and years ago. A cycle starting again. But all she said was "Are you sure about this, Billy?"

"I'm sure, Emily. We haven't talked money yet, but this is going to change everything," he said. "Just trust me."

TEN

REUNION

It had already changed everything. He and Shawn agreed on terms in the jet on the way back to Baltimore. Maybe Shawn felt guilty about what had happened a decade ago, the way their friendship from Cortaca University and time in the cabin had fallen by the wayside, and the way he had screwed Billy out of the share of Eagle Technology that he'd been promised. The terms Shawn put forward were laughably good. Insanely generous. Too much money for Billy to even think about walking away from. That is, too much money if—and it was a big *if*, Billy realized—he could figure out the bugs with Nellie. Because it *was* Nellie he'd been talking with while standing next to Shawn upstairs in the Nest. He was sure of it now. The voice in the bathroom had been his imagination. He'd just seen part of a guy's arm get cut off. Stress. His imagination. No, there'd been only one voice, one conversation.

Takata.

How had that name come out? Where had Nellie gotten it? Shawn told him that the guts of Nellie from the initial attempts in Whiskey Run were still in existence; Shawn and the engineers had tinkered, adapting her to the reality of the hardware that was now available, and they'd written millions of lines of new code, but most of the critical code, the engine of the machine—hundreds of thousands of lines of code—was still embedded in Nellie. An old seed planted in new soil.

But that name. Takata.

So maybe the way Nellie had conjured the name Takata out of the ether was partly why Shawn was generous with the terms, or maybe it was a different kind of guilt over how he had screwed Billy out of a fortune, or maybe it was just because he could afford to be generous. It was easy for Shawn to put that much money on the table: if Billy couldn't fix Nellie, the money Shawn was offering was spare change, and if Billy *could* fix Nellie?

Nellie could change everything.

"Think of it as a performance bonus, Billy," Shawn said. "Because as much money as I'm offering you, it's nothing compared with what Nellie will be worth to Eagle Technology. It sounds like I'm offering you a lot, but if you can get her to work, that money is simply your share. You wouldn't trust this offer if I said it was fair, and it's not. You'll end up ridiculously rich if you can get her to work, but me? If you think I'm rich now, if Eagle Technology can start selling Nellie, I'll have so much money that I'll be like a god. So don't second-guess this. Take it as good fortune. Take it as the opportunity it is."

Billy knew Shawn was right. It was his turn to be rich, too. Not a little rich, but unimaginably rich: illions with a *b* kind of rich. And worst-case scenario, if he couldn't do it—well, he and Emily could walk away with a new life, not rich but at least comfortable: debts paid, a small nest egg that, this time, he wouldn't drink away.

"Take it to a good lawyer out there in Seattle," Shawn said. "Wendy will e-mail you a few names as suggestions, but you can and should get somebody else to look at it. Get two lawyers; three, if you want. I don't think this is magically going to erase our history. I know you still think I screwed you over, but this should go a long way toward making that a thing of the past. When you left Whiskey Run with Emily, we both thought we'd agreed to different things, but you'll be heading back to Seattle with a paper contract. With everything that's happened, with . . ."—he held a folder close to his chest, pausing, and then handed it to Billy—"Emily and the lawsuit and everything else, just get it read by a good lawyer and make sure that everything is watertight."

It wasn't particularly complex, though. If Billy couldn't make Nellie a hundred percent but could fix the basic stability issues enough so that Shawn could integrate parts of her into Eagle Logic, he got a generous licensing fee. Not billions, sure, but ten or twenty million dollars spread out over a few years. Enough for a very comfortable rest of his and Emily's lives. But, oh my, if he could get Nellie working the way they'd envisioned her? If she was the next generation of Eagle Technology products? He smiled at the idea. What was lost can be found again, he thought. He wouldn't ever have a stake in Eagle Technology like Shawn did. That was a race already run. Even a moderate success, however, would mean more money than he could drink away in a thousand lifetimes, and if he could really hit it out of the park, if Nellie was as good as he and Shawn thought she could be . . . why, then he'd have more money than made any possible sense.

And just for trying, just for flying to Baltimore and touring the house and agreeing to give it a go, Shawn had waved his magic wand and wiped away all Billy's old mistakes. A gesture of good faith, Shawn said, an apology for any hard feelings that still lingered.

Billy had spent the morning getting a guided tour through some of the Eagle Technology developmental labs in Baltimore, and then he'd headed out early to the airport. He had an hour or so to kill before his flight home. He was standing at the bar in a private Eagle Technology lounge at the airport—it was through an unmarked door, and you had to have special access arranged through the company—drinking a Diet Coke and methodically logging in to all his credit card accounts one at a time.

Zeroed out. It was spooky. Every single one of them. The credit cards that Emily knew about, and the credit cards that she didn't know about. No balances.

Every penny of debt gone.

He took another sip of his soda and then logged in to his and Emily's bank account. His hand was shaking, and he had to put the phone down on the bar. On Monday morning, before he'd left his house, they'd had less than two hundred dollars in their checking account. Now there was a little more than fifty thousand dollars. He put his head down and laughed. God. Shawn's assistant said there'd be a car waiting for him when he landed in Seattle, and maybe he'd have it swing by a flower shop. Or a jewelry store. They'd go out for dinner and celebrate. Leave their car at home and call for a cab so they could both . . . No. He'd drive. He laughed again. Fifty thousand dollars, taxes already taken out. He hadn't done anything to fix the problem yet, and he didn't need to show up in Whiskey Run until the first of November, but Shawn had promised fifty thousand dollars a month, taxes paid, starting right this minute, guaranteed through next June, at least, just for giving it a shot. Half a million dollars free and clear just to show up. Shawn was living up to his promise so far.

"Billy?"

He looked up. An East Asian guy about Billy's age. His hair was pulled back into a ponytail and he was wearing a black shirt and black jeans and holding a leather bag that even Billy could tell was expensive.

The man stuck out his hand. "Billy Stafford. Holy crap. I haven't seen you since senior seminar. You don't remember me?"

It came to Billy in a flash. It had been a small class. Fifteen students. The cream of the crop from the computing program at Cortaca University. You had to apply for admission with Professor King. She was a cranky old bitch who didn't suffer fools lightly. Rumor was that she was secretly filthy rich, that she had stakes in dozens of start-ups, but you couldn't tell. She didn't care about clothes and drove a rusty old Subaru. If you didn't bust your ass for her, she set you on fire. At least three students dropped the class midsemester that year, one kid even running out of the classroom crying because of the way Professor King ripped him apart.

"No, of course. Raj. Good to see you." He shook Raj's hand. He'd never been particularly close to him, but they'd never had any issues, either. He remembered that Raj had left Cortaca with a cushy job at Amazon already in hand.

"What the hell are you doing here? Don't tell me you're in Baltimore to see the legendary Shawn Eagle. Did you guys kiss and make up? You back in business together?" He laughed and motioned to the bartender. "Just kidding. Here, let me get you a drink."

"No, I'm—"

"Come on, man. I've only got a few minutes before my flight. I'd say I'm buying, but it's not like they charge here. Got to love Eagle Technology, huh? Thank god they opened this lounge." He turned to the bartender. "I'll have a Macallan 25."

"Sorry sir, we only have Macallan 12."

"Pfft. Really?" The bartender nodded and Raj rolled his eyes. "Fine. Whatever. I mean, I'd kind of expect that at a standard airport lounge where the drinks are free, but come on, what's the point of Eagle Technology having their own private lounge if it's serving crap? Tell Shawn he's got to up his game." Raj looked at Billy. "How about you? What do you want? You a whiskey guy?"

"Bombay Sapphire and tonic." The words just fell out of his mouth. He touched his pocket, a part of him trying not to think of the missing sobriety coin. This wouldn't count. He'd get his two-year sobriety coin soon enough. He wouldn't lose that one.

Raj leaned into the bar. "I read *Learning to Soar,* of course, but mostly for the juicy bits. I know it was an authorized bio, but the author really soft-pedaled the lawsuit stuff. I think your claims should have held up, or at the very least, the compensation should have been more generous than the table scraps shoveled your way. But you know, without a signed contract, it's tough. You got screwed, though."

"I don't mean to be a dick, Raj, but—"

"No, I get it." He held up his palms to Billy. "You can't talk about it. Legally binding and all that. But you're good? I remember that seminar. I have nightmares about it sometimes. Did you know Professor King is *still* teaching the seminar? She's got to be like a hundred and fifty. But man, she had a hard-on for you. You could have taken a shit on an iPod and she would have called it the next great advancement in computing. And what's-his-name, too. His code was always so slick. The Japanese guy."

"Takata."

"Yeah. When you three went off together to go hole up in that cabin, the entire class was jealous. I mean, don't get me wrong, I had a cushy job waiting, and I've done well for myself. I mean, I didn't do Shawn Eagle well, but who has? I don't think I would have had the stones to turn down the gig at Amazon and go into the woods with you guys, even if I had been invited, but the rumor was that you guys told Amazon, Apple, *and* Google to go screw themselves."

"We—"

"No, no. I don't mean it like that. I couldn't have kept up with you guys. I'm smart, but you were something else. A deep thinker, man, and then with Takata to make things slick? And Shawn, well, he just had that aura. Even in college he seemed to have things figured out. What happened, though? You only ever hear about you and Shawn and the whole lawsuit thing. What happened to Takata? I've never even seen a single mention of him in any of the stories about the history of Eagle Technology. I ran into Mirabella a few years ago—I don't know if you remember her, but she's working for the State Department now—and she said she heard that Takata split almost immediately."

"Amicable split. He decided to go backpacking through Europe instead of spending the winter in the cabin," Billy said. "Never heard from him again. He just sort of disappeared off the map."

That was the official story. He and Shawn covered their tracks. It had worked: they'd erased Takata from the history of Eagle Technology, from his and Shawn's story. Only a few people knew Takata had even been there in the first place. And only he and Shawn knew what really happened.

Jesus.

The sound of the shovel in dirt.

Billy took a sip of his drink, finishing it, and noticed that his hand was still shaking. He held up the glass to the bartender, motioning for another. He had an hour to go before his flight.

Raj shook his head. "Can you imagine that? Having the chance to be part of Eagle Technology from the beginning but bailing out on it? Wherever he is, he must want to kill himself. No wonder he's completely off the map. He's probably hiding out as a Buddhist monk in some temple in the countryside. It's like being that dude, the fifth Beatle, the one who got kicked out of the band just before they hit the big time. Listen, you out in Silicon Valley?"

"Seattle."

"Ah. Okay. Amazon? No, no. Don't worry. Point is, I've got a little outfit in San Francisco now that specializes in predictive mapping. Hush-hush of course, but Eagle Technology is talking about buying us out. That's why I'm here. I'm pitching a valuation of two fifty, and I've got a thirty percent stake. Seventy-five million into my pocket if Eagle goes for it." He laughed. "This will be the third start-up I've gotten scooped up. I'm thinking about just saying forget it and buying an island or something. Stocking it with girls and spending the rest of my life getting laid and soaking up sun. Ah. Who am I kidding? Even blow jobs would get old after a while. Well, probably not the blow jobs, but you know. Just get in touch if you've got something hot working." He reached into his bag and pulled out a business card. "Hope you and Shawn had a good talk." He tossed the card on the bar, shook Billy's hand, and strolled out of the lounge.

Billy picked up the business card. It was printed on thick stock that felt creamy to the touch. Such an anachronistic thing, business cards, Billy thought. The card had a red, bubble-shaped car as a logo and the name of the company, FNSTIR, on it, with Raj's name, a phone number, and an e-mail address. That was it. Billy guessed that was a sign of being important. Your business card didn't need to say what you did or what your title was or what your company was trying to accomplish. FNSTIR. What did FNSTIR even mean? Weren't there any real words left?

The bartender drifted his way.

"Another drink, sir?"

Billy looked down at the ice in his glass, blinking. That had gone down easy. He looked at his watch. He had plenty of time still, and then a long flight ahead of him.

"Sure," he said. "Another."

One last drink, and then back on the wagon.

ELEVEN

SEATTLE

There was a young woman sitting on their stoop when Emily parked her car. The woman was wearing the familiar Eagle Technology Store gold polo shirt, and behind her was a stack of boxes the size of a love seat.

"Can I help you?"

"Just need to see some ID and then have you sign for this," the woman said. "I've been waiting here since one o'clock." She didn't sound impatient. Just resigned.

Emily fished her wallet out of her purse. "I'm sorry. I didn't get off until four."

The woman took her driver's license, scanned it with her tablet, waited for the friendly beep, and then handed both the license and the tablet to Emily. Emily scrawled her signature. "What is this, exactly?"

The woman glanced back at the pile of boxes. "More or less? It's everything. Enjoy."

Emily watched the woman bounce down the steps and then get into an unmarked white van that was parked only a few spaces down from where her own junky car was parked. She turned back to the boxes. It took her several minutes to carry them in. She stacked them in a succession of pyramids on the floor behind the couch. As near as she could tell, the girl hadn't been exaggerating: If Eagle Technology made it, it was now in her living room, sometimes in pairs. A Noah's ark of computing: two laptops, two tablets, two of the newest phones, two watches. All Eagle Titanium series, the premium, top-of-the-line stuff. Some things there was only one of: a snap-on telephoto lens for the phones; one each of eight different pairs of headphones and three different wireless speakers; an external monitor; an Eagle Technology television that was so big she had to slide the box across the porch, lift up one end, and then slide it into their apartment. There was a single envelope, too, addressed to Billy. It wasn't sealed. She felt furtive, watched, while she opened it, but she opened it anyway. Inside was a single sheet of paper with an Eagle Technology username on it, an accompanying thirty-two-character password, and a short typed message:

> *Billy,*
> *Get up to speed.*
> *—Shawn*

She folded the paper and slid it back into the envelope.

The pile of boxes was overwhelming. No wonder the girl had waited for her to sign for it. How much was it worth? Twenty thousand dollars? Fifty thousand? More? Could she return it all and use the money to pay down their credit cards? Billy had told her to trust him, but it had been a long time since she'd been able to do that. Better to make the best of things while she still could, before the smoke cleared from whatever this was between Shawn and Billy and she had to look at the financial destruction of their lives in a clear light again. With what she made at Bright Apple Preschool and what he made working as a custodian, it was all they could do to live in a complete shithole of an apartment and mostly pay the monthly minimums on their credit cards. They were drowning in slow increments. Best case, she figured, they could stretch it another six months or a year before they'd have to declare bankruptcy, but if she returned all this crap to the store? It wouldn't be enough to wipe all their debts away. Maybe it would cover a fifth? A quarter? Of what she knew about. Billy swore he wasn't drinking in secret anymore, but she had a sneaking suspicion that there might be debts hidden somewhere. Still, returning all this stuff might mean enough money to give them a fighting chance.

She pulled out her five-year-old iPhone, a yellow legal pad, and a pen, and went onto the Eagle Technology website. It took the better part of thirty minutes to look up all the prices and make a tally.

The number made her feel sick. One of the watches was apparently the high-end, limited-edition model, and that alone was enough to pay off their American Express card. She didn't even know you could spend that much on a smartwatch.

Even if she couldn't return this stuff, even if she had to sell it online and could get only three-quarters of the value, it was a small fortune. Half their debt? It would buy them daylight. She took a breath. Time to see how much the piper needed to be paid. She swiped over to the Citibank icon and logged in to their account. They had three different credit cards with Citibank, and all three of them were maxed.

Were maxed.

Were.

Past tense.

It had to be a mistake.

She looked at the screen for a full minute, and then she logged out and logged back in. Zero. She thought she was going to start hyperventilating. Quickly, she logged in to the other accounts. Nine credit cards that should have been redlined, but all nine of them were blank. Pure as the driven snow.

She stared at the phone, and then, suddenly, as if it were a snake about to bite her, she threw it on the couch. She didn't want to be in there with the boxes and boxes and boxes of shiny toys. It was like she could hear them humming, gathering an electrical charge so they could strike. The noise was building in her ears and she realized she was trying not to cry again.

Nothing, she knew, absolutely nothing, came without a price.

She snatched her purse from the wobbly dining room table that they'd bought at a yard sale for six dollars and ran out the front door. She slammed the door behind her and tried to lock it, but her hand was shaking so badly she couldn't get the key in the lock. When she finally slid it home and heard the thunk of the dead bolt closing, it was as if the pressure released.

She took a step down the porch and looked in through the window. The room was so dim that from the outside the boxes barely took shape behind the couch, just an ominous lump that hinted at discrete pieces pushed together. She heard something sharp and trilling, and she realized that her phone, still on the couch, was ringing. For some reason she was sure it was her sister, Beth, calling from Chicago. Part of her wanted to hurry inside and tell her about the credit cards, but a bigger part of her wanted to go down the steps and get in her car, head to the highway, and drive and drive and drive until she was in Chicago, until she was safely inside Beth's condo and could tell her in person.

But before she could do either, a black luxury car double-parked next to her car and Billy got out of the backseat. He was grinning, holding a bouquet of Gerber daisies and trailing a duffel bag.

"You won't believe it," he said. The black car drifted away.

She felt cold. It was cool out, Seattle in September, sure, but she was wearing jeans and a blouse. She shouldn't have been shivering. "The credit cards."

His grin slipped a bit. "You saw. Okay. That was going to be a surprise. Paid off. All of them."

"Jesus, Billy," she said. "Did you sell your soul to the devil?"

He bounded up the steps, dropped the duffel bag at her feet, handed her the flowers, and then pulled her in for a kiss, his breath sour from six hours in the air. "Nah. Not the devil. Just Shawn Eagle. Part of the deal."

TWELVE

NDA

She followed him into the apartment—he whistled at the boxes from the Eagle Technology Store—and then he walked her through the agreement and logged in to their checking account to show her the balance.

"And we're going to live there?"

"For the winter. Hopefully not longer. I think I have an idea of what the pinch point is, and I might be able to unravel the problem pretty quickly. He's mucking around with something he doesn't understand, but Nellie's my baby. Always was. It doesn't matter how many lines of code they've added, at her core, she's mine. Shawn's good at user experience and interface, good at managing, and, clearly, amazing at selling stuff, but there's no way he or his engineers were thinking about it the right way. You'll see. This is going to change everything. Everything."

"Why does it have to be *there* and not at their offices?"

"Come on. You're talking about it like we're going to be living in the cabin again. It's not like that. It's a luxurious vacation home. Actually, scrap that. It's a luxury home perched on top of a frickin' mansion," Billy said. "And we can't do it at their offices. There's no way to do something like this on the Eagle Technology campus without the news getting out. You know how it is with projects for these kinds of

companies. Everything's top secret. We'll both have to sign NDAs."
She looked at him blankly. "Nondisclosure agreements. Basically, we
can get sued if we talk about the work." What he didn't say was that
Shawn was trying to run this whole thing blind of the board of the
corporation, that he was paying for it out of his own private fortune.
Corporate boards are risk averse by nature, and he couldn't imagine
they'd be excited to hear that Billy Stafford was coming on board, that
Shawn had reopened a chapter of his past that seemed, as far as the
company was concerned, better off left closed.

"Can't you just, I don't know, rent an office here in Seattle? Won't
the program run as well on a laptop?"

They were sitting on the couch. Emily had her feet drawn up
and tucked underneath her. She was hugging a pillow to her chest.
When they'd rented the place, it was advertised as a one-bedroom
apartment, but even in this neighborhood, they couldn't afford a true
one-bedroom. The bedroom was in a separate room, as was the bathroom, but the apartment was an efficiency: the kitchen, living room,
and dining room were all the same thing. The light under the range
hood was on, barely making a dent in the dimness of the room. He
reached over the back of the couch and snagged one of the phones off
the top of the pile.

"You're thinking of Nellie like she's just another version of Eagle
Logic, but it's something entirely different. I don't even know how to
explain it to somebody who's not an engineer. You wouldn't understand."

She tossed the pillow at him. It was gentle. Showing her the balance in their checking account had bought him that much. "That's
what you always say. Try to explain it so I can understand," she said.
"Or you'll have to understand sleeping on the couch."

He picked at the heat-sealed plastic around the phone packaging.
"Okay, so you know how Eagle Logic is essentially—"

She laughed. "Really? You've never let me buy an Eagle Technology phone, Billy. You smashed a plate against the wall the one time I
even mentioned the idea. I don't know how Eagle Logic anything. My
iPhone is like five years old. All I can tell you about Eagle Technology

is what I know from their commercials and from what everybody else says. I've never used anything from them."

He handed her the pillow back. "You're never going to let any of that go, are you? I've been clean for almost two years. Haven't touched anything in nearly two years"—another gin and tonic on the plane—"but that doesn't matter; I'm always smashing plates in your memory," he said. "I said I was sorry, I said I would never . . ."

He trailed off, and they were both quiet for a few moments, until she looked away from him, first at the pile of packages and then out the front window. "Sorry," she said.

He nodded. He knew he'd sounded excited before, but now his voice seemed hollow to him, deflated. "Okay. So you've got an iPhone now. Remember when Apple first came out with Siri?"

"Sure. You'd ask her to do something and she wouldn't understand it and then you'd just do it yourself."

He laughed. "They ironed it out pretty quickly, but on some level, what Google and Apple were marketing as a glorified administrative assistant—look, you can ask your phone to do something, and it does it!—wasn't much more than a dog and pony show. Sometimes it was quicker than tapping out multiple steps yourself, but mostly, Siri was just a shortcut to things that the phones could already do. She couldn't do anything of her own volition. It's different now, though. The truth, and Shawn might argue with me if he heard me say it, is that Google and Apple and Amazon have caught up to Eagle Logic when it comes to a personal-assistant function. What they have now is every bit as good as anything from Eagle Technology despite the head start, but at the time, when Shawn first got things going, Eagle Logic had a lot more agency than anything the other guys were putting out, and it felt revolutionary. The 'Logic' part of the name came from the decision to rethink the way logic gates function and to reroute deep core—"

"English."

He nodded. "Okay. Eagle Logic processes incomplete information better. The analogy is that if you *told* those Google, Apple, Amazon, Microsoft assistants that you like Diet Coke, they would have—maybe—bought a case of soda and left it on the counter, but Eagle

Logic *knows* you like Diet Coke and will hand you a fizzing glass full
of ice and make sure the fridge is stocked with cans so you've got cold
ones ready for later."

"I guess."

"You guess because you don't think about it anymore." He tore
open the plastic and opened the box. The phone was nestled in a
black tray. The gold-infused titanium seemed to glow, even in the
dim light they were sitting in. "The best technology turns invisible
almost as soon as you use it. You learn to trust it. A few years ago people would look at you like you were crazy when you told them about
self-driving cars, and now you can't find a manned taxicab if your life
depends on it. And Nellie is going to be like that. She's going to make
all this stuff we have look like banging two rocks together." He pulled
out the phone and handed it to her.

"Okay," she said.

"Okay, what?"

"Okay, this is a lot nicer than my old iPhone."

"I wouldn't let you buy an Eagle phone because I was still angry at
Shawn, not because they're shitty. The guy was never as good a coder
as me, and . . . He was never as good a coder as me, but he really un-
derstands design and has that incredible gut feel for what people want,
what feels intuitive. Between that and Eagle Logic, there's a reason the
company is worth a bazillion dollars."

"Oh. A bazillion dollars? Is that more or less than a bazoonka-
load?" She smiled at him and turned the phone over in her hand.
"And if we do this, if we go out to this house of Shawn's and you fix
his program, he's just going to give you part of the company?"

"It's not *his* program," Billy snapped. His voice was too loud, and
Emily was now leaning back into the couch, her smile turned into a
thin line. "Sorry," he said. "I didn't mean to raise my voice."

"You shouldn't have gone out there, Billy. You should have left it
alone."

He stared at her. Gaped at her, really. "Are you kidding? Our credit
cards are paid off. There's fifty thousand dollars in our checking account. Another fifty thousand coming October one."

"Is it worth it, though? How much did it cost you to finally break free from your past with Shawn? *Our* past?"

"And fifty thousand more dollars in November, December, January, every single month from now through June. Damn right it's worth it," he said, angry, though he knew that's not what she meant.

She handed back the phone. "And if you make this program work, if you figure out how to make Shawn's phones a little bit better, you get rich. You get your recognition as a genius right alongside Shawn. Rewrite the history books."

"*We* get rich, Emily. *We.*" He held up the phone. "And it's not just for phones. Nellie will be in everything, and it's not making things a *little* bit better. She's completely intuitive. She's designed to make the user happy. She takes feedback and writes new decision trees. She rewrites herself in real time. Basically, she learns; the more she interacts with you, the more she can make you happy. But it also means that she can be more than a glorified personal assistant, like the other programs. She's a constant presence. She's the answer to what it feels like to be alone. Having Nellie is like having somebody to keep you company."

"Like a robot?"

"No. I told you that you wouldn't understand."

She didn't say anything, and he just watched her.

He had the feeling that he needed to stay quiet. She was like a deer watching a dog. If he made any noise, if he moved at all, she'd bolt. She'd flee from him. Go to Chicago to live with her sister and leave him behind, and this time he wouldn't be able to get her back.

God, those months that she'd been gone had been the worst. There were great, hungry blank spots, days and weeks he couldn't remember, scars on his arms that must have come during that time. What he remembered was the way that he'd crawled down a hole he didn't have any business escaping from. He'd been trying to kill himself, really. For years he'd been juggling the booze and the drugs and how angry he was all the time. He'd get a job at one tech company or another, working his way down the food chain until the last job he'd been fired from—for a third time he'd passed out from drinking and vomited in his cubicle, and then when he'd been shaken awake he'd beaten his manager hard enough to send the poor guy to the hospital—had been the last computing job he could get. She'd forgiven him all of it, even the sexual harassment accusations from that bitch at XNerdant, but that last day at that very last computing job, he'd left with his meager box of crap, still drunk, his knuckles bleeding. He'd stopped at a dive bar for a couple of drinks and bought two lines of coke with the last of his cash, and when he finally got home, he had to see the disappointment on her face at the cardboard box of stuff from his desk. He hated the way she looked at him.

He couldn't help himself. He had just wanted her to look away.

It was an accident.

He didn't mean to do it.

He acted without thinking. He was messed up from the coke and the booze.

He never meant to hurt her.

She was gone for three months after that incident, and yet, somehow, he didn't die. Emily's sister and brother-in-law paid for rehab—he always wondered how much she told Beth—and after he finished, Emily came back to him.

He didn't think he could live through that again. He didn't think he could live without Emily.

He stayed as still as he could, almost too afraid to breathe.

She blinked. "And if you can't get it to work, what then?"

"Her."

"Her?"

"Not it. Her."

"Fine. If you can't get her to work, what then?"

"We walk away. We walk away with our credit cards paid off and money in the bank. We can make a fresh start of it, anywhere you want." He slid the phone back into its nest in the box. "We can move to Chicago and be closer to your sister." Emily grimaced. He knew it wasn't about her sister and her nieces, but rather at the thought that Chicago was too close to Kansas City.

Billy continued, "Or we can do what you've always talked about. We'll pick an island in the Caribbean or off South America. Costa Rica or Grand Cayman or Curaçao or somewhere else with warm water. Open up a coffee shop. We'll snorkel in the mornings, sling coffee during the day, and eat dinner on the beach at night."

She leaned forward, putting her hands on the couch. "Ooh. Keep going. I love it when you talk dirty."

"We'll sell cookies and muffins and we'll give the place some sort of awful pun for a name, *Coffee Cabana* or *Beans on the Beach* or *Espress-Yo!*" She laughed and crawled forward, until she was almost on him. "And we can settle down."

She stopped. "Settle down?"

He paused. Such a loaded term. Settle down. That meant only one thing to her, what it had always meant to her. Are we ready to settle down? Do you think it's time to settle down? Will we ever settle down? She stopped asking the question when it was impossible to ignore how bad things had gotten with his drinking, but she'd been thinking about it again. He could feel the question bubbling up behind her lips, starting to almost become words since he'd passed the one-year mark of being sober, getting closer to the surface as he neared two years. Settle down.

Have kids.

"If it works, we'll be rich. But if I can't fix Nellie, if I can't get her to work, we'll walk away with no debt, with enough of a nest egg to see us on a tropical island somewhere. We can make coffee and grow old together and settle down."

If. There was no if. He knew he could make Nellie work.

"I like the idea of settling down," she said. "When do you think we can start trying to"—she leaned in a little more—"settle"—more—"down?"

Emily finished leaning in. She kissed him lightly, at first, her lips a whisper on his. The slight flick of her tongue touching his teeth. He touched his fingers to her face. She lifted her hand and slid it up and under his T-shirt.

"No time like the present."

They stayed on the couch for another minute or two, tossing most of their clothing onto the pile of Eagle Technology boxes before moving to the bedroom.

THIRTEEN

CHICAGO

They'd sold the old car for scrap. It made Emily nostalgic to let it go. Purchasing the car had been the first thing they'd done with the buyout money when they left Whiskey Run and that cabin behind. At the time, it had seemed like a good decision to take Shawn's offer: one hundred thousand dollars for Billy to walk away from what looked like a colossal failure, and a handshake deal that if Eagle Technology ever became a going concern, Shawn would cut Billy in. Billy had assured her that Shawn wasn't going to be able to do anything with Eagle Logic without him, and anyway, bigger paydays were in his future. The car was an investment, he said. A way to get them out to Silicon Valley so that Billy could start something up on his own. The way he described it, he'd bang out some code, run through a couple of rounds of venture capital, and turn whatever he was doing into one of those unicorns that VC firms loved, returning their money a thousand times over. It hadn't occurred to either her or Billy to ask where Shawn had come up with the buyout money, how a guy who'd been living in the same cabin as Billy, eating the same ramen, drinking the same shitty beer only a few months earlier, had scratched up a hundred thousand dollars to buy Billy out. Maybe if they had, they would have realized that in the months since she and Billy had moved out of the cabin and into her mildew-smelling basement apartment back in Cortaca, Shawn had found at least one person who believed that something real could come out of Eagle Logic.

But that car. Buying the car had been a happy thing. They went to the dealership together. It was a bullet-gray BMW. A low-end model, but with heated leather seats and a dashboard that curved gently and reassuringly. Forty-four thousand dollars right there, but she wasn't worried. They were young and in love, and Billy promised her that when they got out to California he could make them rich with his eyes closed. They loaded up their clothes and books and what little else they had and drove the car across the country, stopping for a night in Chicago and getting loaded with her sister and brother-in-law. This was before she realized what a problem Billy's drinking was becoming, of course. And then on to Silicon Valley, where they rented a furnished two-thousand-dollar-a-month apartment that was barely bigger than the BMW. The first night in the new apartment Billy popped out to get more beer and put a dent in the trunk. Just a silly accident, he said. Nothing to do with the drinking. He wasn't looking when he backed up in the parking lot and he hit a pole.

By the time they brought it to the scrap yard, it had suffered from any number of Billy's "silly" accidents. Dents and scrapes turned to rust and holes. No money to fix the transmission, so every time she shifted there was a grinding sound and she worried the whole engine was going to just drop out. The brake pads were worn to metal, so the highway was out, and even if the brakes had been fine, the car shook if you took it over forty miles an hour. It would have been an embarrassment to try to sell it, and she was secretly relieved that the scrap yard had accepted it. It was more rust than metal.

Their new car, an SUV, was another act of munificence from Shawn Eagle. Like the pile of phones and tablets and computers, like paying off their credit cards and starting Billy's salary two months early, like moving them from their lousy apartment to a luxury hotel for the interim. When Billy told Shawn that they were planning to drive east and stop in Chicago along the way to visit her sister, the SUV magically showed up the next day, the concierge phoning them and letting them know they had a delivery. A black Honda Pilot, completely tricked out: fully driverless if they wanted, sunroof, leather seats, alloy wheels. And on the dashboard, another unsealed envelope with another short message inside:

No way your shitbox is going to make it cross-country. There are more luxurious SUVs out there, but this will serve you in good stead. Solid. Rugged. Well-made. With all-wheel drive, you should be okay driving back and forth from Whiskey Run. The gas station in Whiskey Run has snow tires it will put on for you when you get there.
—Shawn

By then, Emily had fallen into their new life. She'd gotten used to the hotel and charging meals to the room—to Shawn Eagle, really, as in "all your expenses are taken care of, Mrs. Stafford"—and to her new phone. She'd gotten used to the idea that they weren't hopelessly in debt. It had taken her a while—when she'd gone out with Andy for drinks after work and told him what was happening in a sort of baleful tone, he almost bit her head off—but she'd come around to the idea of a new start. It didn't matter why Shawn was doing this. Whether he felt guilty because of the way he screwed Billy out of his share of the company, he was somehow trying to win her back, or he really just needed Billy's help to fix this program, none of it mattered. What mattered was that the feeling of desperation that had accompanied her for so many years was finally gone.

She'd worked up until the night before they left, giving Monica notice right away so that she could get a new teacher in the classroom and situated without leaving Andy in the lurch. Andy was sweet about it, in the skeptical way he had been about her continuing marriage to Billy, and he'd given her a beautiful knit scarf. "You'll need it in the snow, sweetie," he'd said. "And if you get up there and you change your mind, you give me a call. I'll come out and get you myself." She'd hugged him and they'd both cried a little bit.

All that was already in their rearview mirror, though. They were due in Whiskey Run on November 1, so they lit out of Seattle with plenty of time: hit the road Monday morning before rush hour; Chicago by Friday night; stay with her sister and Rothko and the twins until Tuesday; a day, maybe two to drive to Cortaca, and, depending on when they arrived, a night or two in a bed-and-breakfast in their old college town; and then up early to meet Shawn's plane in Whiskey Run on the first day of November.

The drive itself was nice in a boring sort of way. They could have put the Honda on driverless and slept through most of the country, but they took it as an opportunity to be together, and Emily still liked having her hands on the wheel. They had a cooler with fresh fruit and drinks, and Billy looked ahead on his phone to find good places to stop for lunch and dinner. Their third night on the road, the only hotel they could find was pretty sketchy—so run-down that Emily couldn't tell if it was supposed to be Carver's Inn or Graver's Inn, the carpet thin and the television a box full of static—and she had to admit that driving through Nebraska tested her patience, but otherwise, the trip was both pleasant and uneventful. They were in Chicago for dinner on Friday night, just as planned.

As soon as they stepped into the condo, Ruth and Rose were climbing all over, squealing and trying to get Emily's attention over the sound of their dog jumping and barking.

"Oh, for Pete's sake," she said, laughing. She pushed the dog away. "Look at you little munchkins! I keep telling my sister to stop feeding you so you won't get any bigger, but she just doesn't listen."

The girls crowded her, hugging her, burying their heads in her jacket. She knew they were small for their age, and indeed, their bodies would have fit in nicely with those of the children in the pre-kindergarten classroom at Bright Apple Preschool. She could imagine them sleeping neatly on their cots with boys and girls who were so much younger than the twins' seven years. Still, the two of them had definitely grown since the last time she'd seen them, Memorial Day weekend, when Beth had flown her out to Chicago. Just her. Not her and Billy. Beth hadn't said anything about it, but she didn't need to; there was still enough wariness there that even without saying anything, they both knew.

It was almost as if the girls knew, too. They hadn't seen Billy since the previous Christmas. Ten months. Might as well have been in a different lifetime for how long ago that was in a child's life. They turned to Billy, and with an incredible solemnness that seemed even more incongruous because of their diminutive size, they held out their hands for him to shake. Emily watched him crouch down and look them each in the eye, shaking their hands and telling them that it was good to see them again, and she could feel one of those moments of intense love welling up inside her. He never took it personally with children. There were teachers at Bright Apple Preschool who bristled when a four-year-old called them fat, and there were adults Emily knew who would have tried to hug Rose and Ruth, but Billy just took their hands in his and treated them with all the sincerity in the world. It was funny, she thought, how he could be so off sometimes in the way he dealt with adults. But he seemed to get something fundamental and deep about kids, about the way they were constantly decoding the world around them. He was deeply respectful of kids as people in their own right, in a way that parents so often forgot to be. She would be surprised if, later, after dinner, when they were sitting in the living room, Rose and Ruth didn't crawl beside him on the couch, sit on his lap, and look to him for some sort of comfort. That was how it always went with Billy and kids: he let them come to him.

Rothko hugged her and kissed her on the cheek, and then Beth swooped in and swallowed her in her arms. "You look great."

"I look like I've been in the car for five days."

"Bullshit." Beth stepped back and scanned her up and down. She had three inches on Emily, but otherwise, it was clear they were sisters. Same brown hair and same wiry build, though Beth had fewer sharp angles: motherhood and those five extra years had softened her just the slightest bit. "You look healthy. Love the jacket," Beth said. "Little Miss Sporty. You look like an advertisement for Brooks Running."

Emily blushed. She did, actually. The black-and-gray hooded jacket had a subtle houndstooth pattern, and she was wearing a long-sleeved, synthetic white Brooks Running shirt and black pants with a pair of PureCadence sneakers, all of it almost brand-new. Once the second monthly check from Shawn Eagle had hit their bank account—fifty thousand dollars *after* taxes, Billy proudly pointed out—Billy had persuaded her to go shopping. She'd never been much into fashion, but she was a runner, had been a runner since high school, and it was like being a kid in a candy store. She'd gone a bit crazy. Two new pairs of running shoes plus a pair of waterproof trail runners for when the snow and slush came. The jacket she was wearing now, for weather down to twenty degrees or so, three pairs of running tights and three pairs of pants, new jogging bras, socks, shirts, underwear. Gloves and hats for when the weather turned up in Whiskey Run, and a pair of sunglasses with interchangeable lenses. Nearly fifteen hundred dollars' worth of gear. Not all of it from Brooks, but it was the first time in years that she'd been able to buy new stuff that wasn't on clearance at Target. She hated to admit it, but it had felt so, so good to be able to go into the running store and just buy what she needed. No, not what she needed, but what she *wanted*. Billy had seemed to enjoy it as much as she did, encouraging her to get another pair of tights, some more socks; here, what about this shirt, try this on.

Her sister laughed and shook her head. "I'll go for a run with you tomorrow if you promise to take it easy on me. I'm getting over a calf strain."

The same joke that Beth always made, but she could hold her own, and neither of them was out trying to break any records. Not anymore. Emily wondered if she would have gone out for cross-country and track in high school if her sister hadn't done it first, and they still pushed each other pretty hard when they ran together. For a few years, when Beth still had the double stroller, Emily had taken it easy on her, but they'd have a good run in the morning. She'd let Beth set the pace; they'd run east to the water and then along the lake for a while.

Over dinner, Rothko told her and Billy about how changes to the tax law this year were playing havoc with the practice, and how April was going to be a nightmare. He'd made partner three—no, four—years ago, and Emily sometimes wondered how her sister had found somebody who was such a good match for her. He was even-tempered, but he wasn't boring, even though he was an accountant. Before Rothko, her sister had dated another guy in her CPA program, and that guy had been like a sheet of plywood. But less exciting. Rothko was funny, though. Warm. He never seemed to get particularly excited, but likewise he never seemed to get anything more than mildly irritated. Beth liked to brag to Emily that he was attentive in bed, unlike the husbands of some of her friends whose names she wouldn't mention, but she might, she said, be talking about Scarlet and Mimi and Theresa, who were all dealing with the blahs in the bedroom. Rothko was, in a word, Emily thought, constant.

"Oh, lord, Rothko," Beth said. "Do you think there's any chance that they want to hear about tax law? Can anything make us seem like bigger assholes than to actually play into the stereotype of accountants as complete bores? Pass the salad, please."

Rothko swung the yellow glazed bowl down the table, to Rose, who passed it to Billy, and then it came down to Beth. "You say that like there could possibly be something more fascinating than the intricacies of the self-employment tax?" he said dryly.

"Mommy called you an asshole, Daddy," Ruth said, giggling. "She thinks you're boring." The dog, Rusty, was sitting patiently next to her, and Emily watched Ruth sneak him a morsel of bread.

"First of all," Rothko said, "what have Mommy and I told you and your sister about using grown-up words? And second of all, while I refuse to address the first accusation, of being an asshole, I am more than prepared to address your mother's unfounded belief that accountants are inherently boring." He stood up, tucking his elbows into his sides and letting his arms dangle, hunching over and screwing his face up so his teeth were showing. "If all accountants were boring, would I, right now, pretend to be a *Tyrannosaurus rex*, greatest of all the dinosaurs?" He roared and then flailed at Ruth with his *T. rex* arms until she dissolved in a fit of laughter. Emily laughed along, sneaking a glance at Billy laughing, too. She looked at her sister, and it made her so happy to see the way Beth beamed at Rothko. When her brother-in-law sat down, there was a wreath of bemused silence, the attention on Ruth's last hiccups of laughter, when Rose spoke.

"Uncle Billy, does this mean that *you're* not an asshole anymore?" Rose said.

It was like a fat kid doing a cannonball off the diving board. That moment of anticipation, and then the giant splash that left everybody wet. Ruth started laughing again, almost hysterically, hiding her face in her hands, and both Beth and Rothko raised their voices at the same time, but Emily was most surprised by Billy's reaction. He just had a small, bemused smile on his face, and he tapped his fingers on the table. The attention swung off Rose and onto him.

"I think so," he said. "I've made some bad decisions. Clearly your parents have told you about some of those. What, exactly, do you know?" He looked at Beth. "How much have you told them?"

Beth shook her head, trying to figure out what to say.

Ruth piped up, no longer laughing: "You're a drunk and you made some shitty decisions, but maybe you aren't always going to be an asshole and maybe it's going to be okay because Aunt Emily loves you."

"Language!" Beth pushed her chair back, stood up, and clapped her hands. "Okay. Enough. That's not what I said."

"You think it all the time," Rose said.

"I said *enough*. I am aware that Daddy and I have potty mouths, but that is enough. We have been quite clear that certain words are not for children. You two, out, now. Adult time."

"You promised dessert." Both Ruth and Rose spoke together in that odd way they sometimes did. The girls' voices overlapped in a syncing stutter, the effect disorienting for Emily. Synthetic.

"Ruth Ann Trimball and Rose Maya Trimball, you are trying my patience, and you need to apologize to Uncle Billy."

"No," he said. "It's okay." Emily watched him. That odd little smile of confusion he'd had at first had turned into something genuine, slightly embarrassed. "To answer your question, Ruth—"

Both girls, again with that odd and singular voice: "Rose."

"Rose. Yes. I'm done drinking, so I suppose that means I'm also done being an asshole."

The girls looked . . . uncertain. Emily thought there was something they wanted to say, but there was an almost invisible flicker between the two of them, a communication. But it was so quick that Emily wasn't sure whether she had imagined it. And then Ruth said, "Good."

Emily heard her sister exhale, the tension in the room relieved.

The funny thing was that she'd been right, too, about the twins. Later that night, after they'd brushed their teeth and put on their pajamas and all of them were in the living room watching a reality cooking show the girls liked, they chose to snuggle up to Billy, the three of them burrowed into the end of the couch, one girl under each of Billy's arms, the dog curled up on the floor sleeping on Billy's feet. She smiled at the image, thinking of what Billy had promised her back in Seattle, that they'd settle down. She could picture him with their own daughters nested against him. Instead of Ruth and Rose, children of their own. She looked away from Billy and saw her sister staring at her. She offered a crook of her mouth, but Beth didn't smile back. Beth was still wary.

The next morning was cool and dry, good weather for the last week of October, but Emily was glad that she had the new running jacket to wear. Everybody else was still sleeping, even the twins, when she and Beth stepped out the front door of the building just past seven. They took it slow at first, settling into the groove of running through the city, pausing at traffic lights when they needed to, but benefiting from the ghostliness of a Saturday morning. The sun was fully up by the time they were running on the lakeshore path, and Emily tipped her sunglasses from her head over her eyes. Six miles and change out and back, neither of them talking much, just enjoying the presence of one sister with another. By the time Emily had eaten and was out of the shower and dressed, the apartment was alive with the sound of the twins talking with and over each other trying to impress Billy, while Rothko held court in the kitchen.

They spent the morning at the farmer's market and then wandering through Lincoln Park Zoo. The girls insisted on staying to watch the otters play for what felt like a painfully long time. Lunch out was at a trendy Mexican place that served a queso cheese dip that left Emily feeling pleasantly overstuffed. In the afternoon, they put Rusty on a leash and walked to the Starbucks around the corner from Beth and Rothko's condo before heading a few more blocks down to the playground. The girls were on the verge of growing out of swings and slides, old enough that Rothko had to remind them more than once to be careful of the younger kids, but it gave the adults a chance to lean against the fence and bullshit while Ruth and Rose ran out whatever energy they still had left.

"Here," Billy said, reaching out for Emily's empty coffee cup. "I've got it." He walked across to the other side of the playground, where trash cans guarded the gate.

"I'm almost afraid to say it aloud," her sister said quietly, "but he seems different. Happy. You both seem happy." Beth and Rothko were a single unit, Rothko's arms wrapped around her sister's shoulders, encasing her.

Emily glanced at Billy lifting the blue plastic lid and chucking the paper cups into the recycling bin. "He is. I am. It's been different since he got sober."

"That's not what I mean, and you know it." Beth tilted her head back so she could eye her husband. "Are you going to back me up here?"

Rothko shook his head. "You know what she means, Emily. Even after Billy cleaned himself up, well, the last two years haven't exactly been like a honeymoon. Didn't you tell Beth last year that you were thinking about leaving him again?"

"Jesus Christ, Beth, you told him?"

"What do you expect? We share a penis." Beth shrugged. "What? You don't tell Billy everything?"

Emily looked out over the playground. Billy had wandered over to the swings. The twins were just sitting on the swings, alone together, not moving, talking to Billy. He sunk into a catcher's crouch in front of the girls, his back to Emily, but she could feel that his full attention was on Rose and Ruth, in that way he had of getting lost in a single moment. It was, she thought, part of what made him so good with computers.

"No. Not everything. Of course not. And fine. Yes. Since he met with Shawn, things have been terrific. But what do you expect? We're not broke anymore."

"That can't be all of it," Beth said.

Emily swung on her, suddenly angry. "Of course it is. You don't think about it at all. Sure, maybe you guys wouldn't mind a bigger place, but since you've been married you've never worried about it. When you've got money, you don't think about it, but when you don't have money it's all you think about. You don't . . ." She stopped. "Sorry. That wasn't fair. You guys have always been supportive and generous and . . . Shit. Yeah. Okay. We're both happier. It's a fresh start."

"He seems peaceful or something," Rothko said. "It sounds kind of weird given that you guys are about to go work for Shawn Eagle for the next few months, but maybe he's finally let go of all that history."

Whatever the twins had been saying, they were now done. They were looking at Billy, listening to him speak.

"What do you suppose they're talking about over there?" Emily said.

Beth laughed, but it sounded hollow. "Who knows? They told me they don't want to go trick-or-treating, because, and I quote, 'Halloween is the night when all the dead things rise to walk the streets.'" She looked at Rothko. "The crazy comes from your side of the family."

"Hey, don't blame me." He reached down and scratched Rusty's ear. "I was happy with a puppy. You were the one who insisted we have kids, too."

Beth turned and kissed Rothko. "I don't remember you complaining about the work of making kids."

"Ah, thirty seconds of joy inside a tent. Maybe when we go out to visit Emily and Billy for Christmas we can re-create the moment."

"Re-create the procreate?"

Emily was only partly listening. She was still watching her husband and the twins. Apparently they were all done talking, because now Billy reached out and shook the girls' hands, an echo of the solemn ritual of greeting that had taken place in the front hallway the night before.

On the way back to the apartment, when the girls complained that they were hungry, she hung back with Billy. "What was that about?" she said. "By the swings?"

He shook his head. "Nothing."

"You guys shook hands on it. That doesn't seem like nothing." She bumped her hip against his, gently, and in response he put his arm over her shoulder.

"We made a deal."

"What kind of deal?"

He laughed. "Oh, silly stuff from seven-year-old girls, but they don't want me to talk about it. They made me swear to keep it a secret. I had to promise and promise and promise. And not just promise. I had to make 'a pact.' Seriously. A pact? I like them, but come on, they're weird kids."

But the girls acted just like normal seven-year-old girls the rest of the time they were in Chicago. Sunday was the Field Museum and a trip to the American Girl store, where she and Billy bought each of them a new outfit for their dolls. Take-out sushi Sunday night and a goofy animated movie that they all watched. Monday, Beth took the day off work and kept the girls out of school, and they acted like tourists, going to the Art Institute and buying caramel popcorn.

On Tuesday morning, Emily and Billy left early, to beat the traffic, Emily hugging the kids and Rothko and her sister good-bye and telling them all she was looking forward to seeing them for Christmas in Whiskey Run.

FOURTEEN

AN ACCOUNTING

He had the lights in his office down low enough so that when he stood in the window he could tip his head one way and see the harbor, and tip his head the other and look out over the new Eagle Technology campus, sprouting to life almost before his eyes.

He heard the soft swish of Wendy behind him. She did that on purpose, landed her footsteps harder than she needed to so he would hear her coming up on him. She'd been with him for more than three—no, more than four—years now, and he paid her enough to make sure she had no intention of leaving. He'd hired her almost by accident. He'd agreed to let her shadow him during the spring break of her senior year of college as a favor to one of the board members, who was friends with Wendy's father. His assistant at the time, Drew, a good kid from Indiana who'd been there for only a year, was leaving at the end of the summer to go to medical school—with Shawn's blessing and substantial financial assistance—and he'd been taken with Wendy. She was sharp as hell. Not a surprise given her pedigree. Her mom was a senior VP at RisPRtiNo Futures Tech, and her dad was a full professor of chemistry at Berkeley. Which is to say, she had the kind of parents who could ask for favors. Like getting their daughter to shadow the CEO of Eagle Technology for a week. He also liked that nobody else seemed to realize how sharp she was when first meeting her. He wasn't sure if it was because she was black, or if it was because she really did look like she'd stepped out of a Victoria's Secret catalogue, only, you know, in actual clothes. People constantly underestimated Wendy. It made her a secret weapon for Shawn. Anytime he brought in executives from other companies he always made sure that she was the one to give them a tour, to meet them at the airport. They'd tell her more than they would ever give up to Shawn, particularly the men, trying to impress, to seduce probably. Even when they didn't talk too much, they let down their guard around her. And then she'd be a little bird whispering in Shawn's ear.

Oh, he knew everybody assumed that part of the reason she was his assistant was that he was sleeping with her, but the truth was he didn't think he'd ever had a more chaste relationship. Sometimes, when it was advantageous to him, Wendy played up that angle to other people, hinting that there might be some sort of impropriety, but as far as he knew, she wasn't sleeping with anybody. Or maybe she was sleeping with everybody. He honestly had no clue. Her business was her business, but really, her business was Eagle Technology.

She handed him a cup of tea and a tablet.

"Thanks," he said. He took a sip of the tea. He hadn't even realized he wanted it, but his throat was scratchy. A change in the seasons, or, more likely, a holdover from his trip to China last week. "Can you just give me the rundown?"

"Campus construction is ahead of where we projected in March, and believe it or not, there's a chance we're going to come in under budget."

"Really?"

"No. Just kidding. There is absolutely zero chance we are going to come in under budget, unless you added an extra zero to the original budget and didn't tell me. The budget is a disaster. I mean, technically, I suppose it could be worse, but only if you decide you want to tear everything down and rebuild it out of gold."

He shook his head. That was another thing he liked about her. One of the reasons he'd been so successful was that he had a knack for reading a room. Five minutes and he could tell whose marriage was in trouble, who was in over his head, who had him over a barrel. But with Wendy, he could never get a clear read. At least once a day she made a joke and he missed it.

"Projections?"

"Six months to start phasing in, nine months to have the campus fully operational, and this time next year Eagle Technology will be all-in on Mobius Strip." She relented. "Six times over initial budget, which will actually end up being a few hundred million *less* than what you told the directors the overrun was going to be at the last board meeting. If you spin it right, you're going to look positively thrifty."

"It's not like we don't have more money than we know what to do with." Which was true. He remembered that at the same time Eagle Technology first started gaining traction, Apple had been sitting on something like two hundred billion dollars in cash reserves, and there'd been real investor pressure on Apple to spend it; at the time, he daydreamed that maybe they'd drop a couple hundred million dollars on buying him out, but now he better understood the idea of hoarding cash. Eagle Technology aggressively acquired companies and reinvested in itself—the new campus was a case in point—but it had enough cash reserves to not bother selling products for a few years and still be fine. Investors bitched, but it meant that he could make long-term decisions for the company. And with as much cash as Eagle Technology had sitting in the bank, realistically, what did it matter if the campus cost five hundred million, five billion, or fifteen billion dollars?

"Speaking of which," she said.

"How much?"

"Are you asking me what my current salary and stock options are, what my current net worth is, or are you simply asking how much of a raise I want?"

He looked out the window again and took another sip of his tea. Vanilla rooibos. Normally he drank a mint chamomile, but this was hitting the spot. "How did you know I wanted tea? I didn't know I wanted tea. And how did you know I wanted this instead of chamomile?"

"The same way that I know you're going to agree to the raise. It's the first document for you to sign."

"You're happy being my assistant? You don't want a new title?"

"First of all," Wendy said, "we both know that next to you, I'm the most powerful person at this company."

"The next to me part might be debatable," Shawn said.

"Whatever. You can fire me, I can't fire you. Though, frankly, I probably have a better sense of what's happening, day in and day out, at Eagle Technology than you do. So yes, I am happy being your assistant, and no, I do not want a new title, because there are things I can get away with as your assistant that I couldn't if I were an executive. But I would like more money."

"Because?"

She looked at him. "Seriously? Because I like money, and you'd be lost without me."

Shawn walked over to his desk and sat down. She walked him through each document, page by page, including the one authorizing her raise. That figure was going to alarm the board, he thought. It was certainly more than any assistant had ever earned. Actually, it was probably more than most of the executives were earning. Then again, she was worth more than most of the executives. He listened and read and signed for fifteen minutes. When he was finally done, she sat on the other side of the desk and just looked at him.

He stared back, but then realized he was bouncing his knee. "Out with it."

"I still think you're making a mistake with Stafford."

He threw up his hands and leaned back in his chair. "That? Still?"

"Still. My job is to protect you from yourself, Shawn."

"No," he said, "your job is to be my assistant and do what I want."

"Really? We literally had a conversation fifteen minutes ago about how my job is significantly different from just being your assistant and doing what you tell me." She crossed her legs, still looking at him evenly.

He narrowed his eyes, somehow thinking that if he just looked a little closer, he'd be able to read her . . . Nope. Nothing. Even after all this time, it was still like staring at a mirror. He never got anything back that he wasn't already expecting. He shook his head.

"I know," she said. "I drive you crazy."

"Seriously. Where did you come from?"

"Grinnell College. Go Pioneers." She paused. "That was a joke. I mean it about Stafford, though, Shawn. I think you're making a mistake by setting him up in the Nest and letting him muck around with Nellie."

"No," Shawn said. "I need Billy." He was emphatic. He was sure of this. "It's still his project at the core, his seed that's driving her, and it's been how many years of trying to crack it, of having the best and the brightest of Eagle Technology fail? Millions and millions of lines of code, and none of them are as good as what he wrote in that goddamned cabin. All of this," he said, sweeping out his arm to take in the office and the campus being built beyond the windows, "everything I've built here, is based on just a *part* of what Nellie will be able to do. Eagle Logic is just a compromise. If Nellie works, we'll be able to bury everybody else. Eagle Technology will be unstoppable."

"He's an addict and a drunk."

"He's clean and sober," Shawn said.

She didn't say anything. She just raised her eyebrows.

"Look, I'm done talking about this. You never saw him like I saw him. He was magic, Wendy. If anybody can figure out what's wrong with Nellie, it's Billy. Back when we were in the cabin, working with him was like watching God build the universe. Billy could dive into code like it was nothing, go elbow deep into the guts of the thing and come out an hour later with the heart of it in his hands."

She stood up. "Come on. You've got a date in twenty minutes. Ten minutes to shower and get changed. Clothes are hanging in the bathroom. Hustle up. You'll like this one. Rochelle. She's Italian and exactly your type."

Shawn smiled and stood, too. "Is she easy?"

"I said she's your type, didn't I? Besides, you're Shawn Eagle," Wendy tossed over her shoulder. "For you, they're always easy."

FIFTEEN

CORTACA

Billy remembered the word *palimpsest*, because it had been the favorite word of his least favorite teacher in high school, but it was the word that served best for his return to Cortaca. How else to describe the town that he'd left behind as a young man? The past had been, at least partially, scraped off so that the present could be written. When he'd left, it never even occurred to him that a dozen years would fall away before he came back. He never thought of his departure from Cortaca as permanent. He'd spent four years there as a student, and then he and Emily had lived there together for only a couple of months after things had fallen apart in the cabin, but when they had driven west, he'd expected to be back in a few years, one of the new breed of instant billionaires who could command the attention of the Cortaca University president. He'd fantasized about pointing to a space of grass while wearing jeans and a black T-shirt and saying, "Right there, that's where we'll put the building." But if this, his first trip back to Cortaca, wasn't a triumphant return, neither was he coming back as a beggar, as he might have been just a few years ago. No, he was somewhere in between, on the threshold of having the world open before him. He thought of Shawn's describing the placement of the airport in Whiskey Run, away from the actual mansion, exactly in the transitional world. A liminal space. Hilarious.

Emily glanced away from the road. "What's so funny?"

It would have been quicker to drive up Route 11, past the strip malls and car dealerships, but they'd come instead on State Highway 78B. Less efficient but more picturesque. The highway rolled down the hill and into the town, the lake spilling north for miles and miles, thirty in all, though you couldn't see that far; and straight ahead of them, still east, despite having driven east for six days in total, Cortaca University lay on the opposite hill, shining, lush, a memory of an earlier time. Traffic, such as it was, slowed them down as they drove into the downtown core.

"Nothing really," he said. "I was thinking that it's like seeing a ghost. Like, over there, I was expecting to see that ratty pizza place, but it's a coffee shop now. And over there, where there used to be a coffee shop, there's a pizza place."

"There ought to be some sort of law," Emily said, "where places you've lived have to stay frozen in time until you're ready for them to move on without you."

They passed the mouth of the pedestrian mall. He remembered this end of it as a somewhat grim place. Dropout kids strung out and sitting in the doorways of shops with papered-over windows, the bars never able to completely rid themselves of the smell of puke. The other side of the pedestrian mall had been nicer, in a modest sort of way. There had been a row of restaurants and a few boutique stores, the kinds of places that catered to visiting parents and that booked graduation-weekend reservations four years in advance. But now the whole run looked bright and clean. It was almost shiny, even at night.

The road curved around, taking them behind the pedestrian mall, and they drove a block up the beginning of the steep hill that led to campus before Emily turned into the parking lot of their inn, a huge white porticoed building that Billy had no memory of. As they got out of the car, he could hear music and the buzz of people talking coming from inside the inn, and he realized there was an attached bar. Emily glanced at him, looking worried, he thought, but he just opened the back door and pulled out the small duffel bag. They'd given the big Eagle Technology television to Beth and Rothko, and everything else they hadn't shipped fit into the back of the Honda Pilot, hidden by the sliding trunk cover: the rest of the toys from Eagle Technology that Shawn had sent them, the clothes they'd worn between Seattle and Whiskey Run—they'd done a load of laundry in Chicago—and Emily's single box of keepsakes.

There really wasn't much else once they'd thought about it. Their apartment had been full of junk: furniture that stayed on the curb for days after they'd carted it down the steps, too run-down even for their run-down neighborhood, chipped dishes that they'd gladly left behind when they moved to the hotel. Once that second check had come in from Shawn, and Emily had loosened up and let them do some shopping, pretty much the rest of what they had brought to the hotel felt like junk, too. The only things he'd kept that couldn't be stored on a computer were his cowboy boots, which he'd had resoled, and his wedding ring. He'd gone to the Gap to get a new version of his old wardrobe—jeans and T-shirts and sweaters, socks and underwear— and Emily had gleefully stuffed all his old, ragtag clothes into a trash can by the hotel elevator. She'd barely kept more herself: a box the size of a milk crate with a couple of yearbooks, a few knickknacks of her mother's, the scarf that Andy had given her, some books, a few pictures in frames, and their wedding album. They had planned to get more clothes and order gear for the winter—jackets and boots and hats and gloves, cross-country skis (even though neither of them had ever tried the sport), more clothes, whatever they could think of, all to be delivered directly to the mansion—but Shawn's assistant, Wendy, had told Billy not to worry about it. She asked for their sizes and a sense of what they wanted and dispatched a personal shopper. By the time they got to Eagle Mansion, new clothes and gear and anything else they could think of, plus things they probably wouldn't have thought of on their own, would be waiting for them, and if there was anything missing, the personal shopper would take care of that, too. In the end, the only things Billy had ordered on his own were a couple of obscure computing books that, ironically, he hadn't been able to find digital versions of.

It was weird to be traveling so light, Billy thought, to be leaving such heavy history behind with so few tangible things, but it also meant that he could walk away from the car at every hotel they stopped at without worrying too much. He liked this new life. He liked that he could walk into the Gap and buy things without looking at price tags, that he could wear clothes that weren't from thrift stores or Walmart. He liked being able to wear a pair of jeans and a T-shirt that screamed the privilege of money instead of the trap of poverty.

It was cool in Cortaca, almost cold, and he was glad that one of the new things he'd sprung for had been a coat at an outdoor store. It wasn't the sort of thing he'd wear when the snow started falling, when the temperature dropped in Whiskey Run, but it was warm enough for a day at the end of October in Cortaca. The woman in the store had told him and Emily that the coat was "city technical," and it was exactly the sort of coat he could wear walking into an inn that had a hopping bar on the ground floor. Emily glanced at him again, still looking worried, like she had in the parking lot. "It's fine," he said. And it was fine. He could even go into the bar. *They* could go into the bar. She could have a glass of wine or a beer and he'd have a seltzer or a Diet Coke. He hadn't felt the familiar, hellish call since he'd gotten back from his trip in September to see Shawn.

They checked in and went up to their room. There were only a dozen rooms in the place, and he was relieved that by the time they reached the top of the stairs, the music and conversation from below had disappeared into the thick carpets. It was one thing to walk past a bar, another thing to sleep on top of one. Their room was near the back, and when they opened the door, Emily let out a little gasp. On the table in the entry, there was a bouquet of flowers the size of a lamp, a bowl of fresh fruit, two neatly folded hoodies with the Cortaca University logo on them, a pink logoed baseball cap for Emily, a red winter cap with the school crest for him. There was no note, but there was no need. They both knew it had to have been arranged by Shawn. Or, rather, one of Shawn's people.

Emily declared the room to be adorable and then locked herself in the bathroom to freshen up before they went out for dinner. Billy wondered if when Emily said "adorable," she really meant "cozy," which was just another way of saying small, but he supposed the building had been built in a different time, when king-sized beds didn't exist, and that they'd probably had to work all sorts of architectural magic to give each of the twelve guest rooms its own bathroom and to shoehorn in a desk as well. And it *was* sort of adorable. He heard the shower turn on, and he sat down on the bed to pull off his boots. The cobbler had given them a polish when he'd resoled them, and the brown seemed somehow deeper, the scars in the leather old and weathered, marks of character rather than damage done. He'd gotten the boots here, in Cortaca, his junior year of college, at Cortaca University's annual yard sale. Almost brand-new, dumped by some rich kid who didn't want to bother bringing them home after graduation. You could get sweatshirts for two bucks, jeans for five, T-shirts for a dollar. Hot pots and microwaves and inkless inkjet printers. The boots had set him back eight dollars. Best money he'd ever spent.

He went to the window and pulled back the thick, wine-colored curtains. There was a decent view of the first third of Restaurant Row and the mouth of the pedestrian mall. They were on what he still thought of as the "good side" of the mall, and there was a steady stream of cars turning or dropping off diners. He was surprised at how many of the people were adults rather than students. He remembered a Cortaca inhabited almost purely by fellow college students. Myopia. He'd only ever lived here as a student, and at that age, people in their thirties and forties and beyond were of no interest. They were old. Somebody in their thirties might as well have been invisible. He was one of those people now, though, thirty-six. And passing through. He had thought, once, that he would live in Cortaca forever, but now it was like running into an old girlfriend from high school: a recognition that you'd once been intimate, but that you were a different person back then and were a different person now, and anything other than fond nostalgia was a waste of time.

He watched a group of three girls walk off the pedestrian mall and toward the inn. They looked young to him, and he wondered if they were high school students, but they wore short skirts and wool jackets that looked expensive even from far away. He leaned in closer to the window, blinking, unsure if what he saw made sense: one of the girls was in all black, wearing a headband with black cat ears on it and mascara-drawn whiskers, and another one had on a golden halo that could have been made of pipe cleaners, and a pair of wings on her back. The third girl's costume was hidden under her coat. October 30. The day before Halloween. A fungible holiday for college students. He remembered Halloween as an excuse to drink hard liquor mixed with Sprite his freshman year; to swallow ecstasy and do shots of tequila and stay in with his girlfriend his sophomore year; to drink beer until he threw up his junior year, still somehow ending up in bed with a girl whose name he couldn't remember and had probably never known. His senior year, Halloween was the first time he'd tried a line of coke. The year after that, Halloween was a cold, quiet, lonely, terrifying night, he and Shawn both piss drunk and huddled in their sleeping bags, just the two of them in the cabin, the decrepit mansion glaring at them as they tried to sleep and forget what had happened with Takata. And then, the year after that, their second year in the cabin and only days after they'd thrown in the towel on Nellie and settled on trying to make Eagle Logic work, he'd woken up at two or three in the morning to the sound of Shawn stumbling into the cabin, shitfaced, with a drunken girl in tow. Emily. Her presence had marked the beginning of the end. No. That wasn't true. Things had gone off the rails well before Shawn brought Emily home.

The three girls passed beneath his window, one of them looking up and then quickly looking away from him. He supposed, with the lamp on behind him, up against the window, he looked creepy watching them. He shoved his hand into his pocket, fingered the two-year sobriety coin he'd gotten in Seattle. It was brass, but it felt like plastic. Unsubstantial.

"Hey," he heard behind him. "Why don't you close those curtains?"

He let the curtains fall closed and turned around. Emily stood in the doorway of the bathroom. Her hair was slung over her shoulder, heavy and dark with water, dripping onto the towel she had wrapped around her body.

"Are you starving?" she said, letting the towel fall away. Her naked body caught the soft light of the lamp. "Or can you wait for dinner?"

He could wait for dinner.

SIXTEEN

WHERE IT ALL BEGAN

Halloween. A day for ghosts.

She wasn't surprised that it took them most of the day to make it up to where Cortaca University had installed Shawn and Billy's old cabin as a museum. She could feel Billy's reluctance. He didn't say anything, of course. That wasn't his way. But they lingered over breakfast and then wandered in and out of the boutique shops on the pedestrian mall. She was astounded at how much nicer it was down there. Some of that, she knew, was memory and age. Leaving her shift as a waitress at Stardust Bar—now a clean-looking sandwich shop—at one in the morning was going to give her a different view of Cortaca than browsing the shops with money in her pocket at eleven in the morning. But some of it was that the pedestrian mall had been completely redone since the last time she'd been in Cortaca. Where before there'd been twisted trees and crumbling pavilions breaking the view, now there was an open courtyard with benches, concrete ramps to seating areas, planters with flowers, and a low-rise stage that worked more like a window than a wall. Only the smallest handful of storefronts were empty, and of those, two were under construction with OPENING SOON signs on the windows. It seemed like Billy touched every piece of merchandise in every store, and they still hadn't gone up to campus by the time they were ready for lunch, close to one o'clock.

Finally, they went up the hill. They started at the arts quad, looking at buildings she'd haunted as a student and touring the new ones. When they got closer to the engineering quad, she thought Billy might be reluctant to go into the Eagle Computing Pavilion, but he was surprisingly eager to look at the monolith that Shawn had funded. The building was large but modestly finished on the exterior, fitting neatly into the landscape of the engineering quad. If it weren't for the sheer newness of the stone cladding and the slate roof and the lack of established ivy on the walls, she would have thought the building had always been there. Inside, however, it was a monument to Shawn's success.

And then, finally, there was nothing left but to go see the museum.

There was a tasteful sign, the size of a hardcover book, marking the path through the trees to the cabin: THE BIRTHPLACE OF EAGLE TECHNOLOGY. It was a short path, barely fifty feet, but enough to make it feel like they were entering a different world, going back in time. She walked ahead of Billy, and it seemed like it took him a long time to catch up. She wondered what he was thinking, if they'd made a mistake by coming out here. Bad enough that Shawn had roped him into this old, forgotten ghost of a project with Nellie, but working on Nellie at least made a certain sense for Billy. She had wanted to believe that Nellie was forgotten, that she was a bad memory from the past, but Emily knew better: Billy had never really let go of the idea. Plus, who was she kidding? The money. The new car. She patted the car key in the pocket of her jacket. Her new jacket. Was she that easily bought off? Maybe. Probably. It had changed their life: even if he couldn't do anything with Nellie, they'd be able to walk away scot-free, debts magically erased, money in the bank. They could start a family. And maybe if he couldn't get Nellie to work, it would help Billy to understand that he'd finished his own long walk away from his past with Shawn, from his failings, his own ghosts. They'd get that out of going to Whiskey Run, even if they got nothing else, she thought, but what had she expected Billy to find here, in Cortaca, in the old, reconstructed cabin? Because she'd been the one to push him to come here, to take a look. He hadn't said no, hadn't said he would rather avoid the cabin, but she knew. She knew.

She looked back. His hands were stuffed in his pockets. His cowboy boots scuffed against the path. They stopped to look at the cabin from the outside.

It looked almost exactly the same to her. Cortaca University had done a nice job moving it here from Shawn's estate. They couldn't replicate the wreck of Eagle Mansion haunting the sky above or the Saint Lawrence River cutting through the land below, but it was nicely wooded—she could barely see the computing pavilion from where they were standing—and there was a small pond behind the cabin. If you didn't know better, you would have assumed the cabin had always stood here.

She reached out to squeeze Billy's hand. He gave it a perfunctory squeeze back, and she had the sudden urge to tell him to turn around, but she didn't. Instead, they walked forward together and went into the cabin.

It was a disaster.

Neither of them said anything.

The cabin felt smaller than she remembered. A student wearing a name badge sat reading in a chair by the door. She didn't even look up from her book as Billy and Emily opened the door and walked into the single room. It was tiny. Barely twenty feet by fifteen. They walked all the way in; there was a narrow aisle and a small circle in the middle that could hold, at most, four or five people at a time, the rest of the cabin roped off. On one side, by the window, there was the desk—the old door from the outhouse, the half-moon cut into the wood—a laptop on it that was, as near as she could tell, the same model that Shawn and Billy had actually used. It wasn't functional, of course, but the computer was plugged into an extension cord that ran in under the closed window, just as it had when she'd lived with them. In the far corner, there was the woodstove and the basin they'd used for washing dishes, the hand pump. The walls were still covered in scrawled handwriting. Numbers and notations and letters and formulas, all written with permanent marker, some in Shawn's hand, some in Billy's, faded a little, but still legible: the hieroglyphic history of what became Eagle Technology. And on the far side, a single, solitary camping pad and sleeping bag. One. Only one.

Oh.

One camping pad. One computer. He'd been erased.

She saw Billy glance at the sleeping bag, look again, stare at it now, and then look away, his gaze alighting on the single computer, until finally, blessedly, he looked away from that as well and wandered over to the wall of notations. He stood in front of the scribbled notations, and she couldn't tell if he was really looking at them or if he was simply avoiding looking at where his history had been wiped away.

She felt the hot stone of crying coming to the surface, and she tried to swallow it down. She wanted to reach out and touch his back, to take him in her arms and comfort him, to let him know that he could never be completely removed. But she knew that wasn't what he wanted.

The first night she'd come here—here? there? she felt dislocated—it had been so late, and she'd been drunk enough that she hadn't really realized that Shawn's roommate—she didn't know who Billy was then, didn't know he'd eventually be her husband, didn't even know he existed—was in the same room. She and Shawn had both been completely bombed, and neither of them should have been driving. That was a fiasco in and of itself, a minor miracle that they didn't kill themselves or anybody else on the long drive to the cabin. She still couldn't remember who had driven that old station wagon that had once belonged to Aunt Beverly from downtown Cortaca out past Whiskey Run and into the woods. So, so drunk, and such a long drive, but when they finally got there, they both still felt that same urgency to shed their costumes. Halloween of her junior year of college. Good god, she thought. Tonight marked thirteen years gone by. Lucky thirteen. No, not tonight. Tomorrow, because by the time they came stumbling into the cabin, it was well past midnight, not Halloween anymore, but November 1. No. That was a lie. She knew it was a lie. She could say November 1 all she wanted, but it was still Halloween. She remembered reading once, years and years ago, that

Halloween was the night when college students were the most likely to get drunk, the most likely to have sex with someone new, and it made sense to her. What other night could you so successfully pretend to be somebody you weren't? New Year's Eve was for new beginnings, and Valentine's Day was for the desperate and the rooted both, but Halloween was the night when you could play tricks with yourself, when you could convince yourself that you were somebody different, when you could make yourself believe that you deserved to be a student at Cortaca University.

It was only going to be for the night. She'd had a few boyfriends as a college student, and she'd kept all of them at arm's length, but when she met Shawn that night, she decided almost immediately that she was going to sleep with him. He was handsome and hurting, and although he looked almost overwhelmed by the music and the press of bodies in the house on Stewart Avenue—whose house had that been? why had she and her roommates gone to that Halloween party and not to some other party?—she and Shawn had friends in common, and even back then, he could be charming when he wanted to be. By midnight, they'd drifted out onto the porch, and he'd given her his jacket.

"Sounds desperate," she said. "No plumbing? Only a woodstove for heat?"

"Don't forget that we don't have any furniture, I'm sleeping on a camping pad on the floor of the cabin, and it's like an hour's drive from here."

It was closer to an hour and a quarter.

"Wow," she deadpanned. "Sweeping me off my feet here."

"It's all part of the evil genius," he said. "I'm going to make you feel so sorry for me that you'll sleep with me out of pure pity. And that way, no matter how terrible I am in bed, you'll feel virtuous for your actions and will probably sleep with me at least a few more times before realizing that you can do better."

She'd laughed, and he'd kissed her or maybe she'd kissed him, and at some point she decided that she absolutely had to see this fabulous cabin, to see the utter luxury of his existence, and one of them had driven the station wagon—how drunk they'd been! how foolish and careless, how heedless of the value of human life to make that drive, how lucky to not get a ticket or worse!—and they were both frenzied by the time they fell to the floor of the cabin, the anticipation of the long drive making it sweeter. They spent themselves completely, not making love or even having sex but screwing, desperate and animalistic, tangling themselves up in his nest of sleeping bags and blankets before falling asleep.

When she woke the next morning, she felt Shawn's arms wrapped around her, and the air of something else. Someone watching. A man, not even ten feet away, also on the floor and in a sleeping bag, turned on his side and staring at her. She didn't know, of course, that it was Billy, that in barely seven months she'd be leaving with him, that she'd be the wedge that broke Billy and Shawn apart, that for the rest of his life, whether he said it or not, Billy would blame her for his not being part of the rise of Eagle Technology.

For not being rich. For not being lauded as a genius. For losing his place in history. For being written out of the story.

Whether he said it or not.

He'd said it. He'd come out and said it straight to her.

She blinked back to the present.

The single camping pad and sleeping bag were forlorn.

She looked over at Billy. He was leaning in now, going back and forth over the writing on the wall, the formulas and markings, left to right, top to bottom, and she could see him disappearing into it. His lips were moving now, like an eager child learning to read, and she could hear soft, puffing murmurs coming out of his mouth. He put his hands on the rope barrier, concentrating. After several minutes, he pulled his phone out of his pocket and started taking pictures of the wall as a whole and then close-ups of every section, careful not to miss a single squiggle.

He was actually humming as they walked out of the cabin, an odd, secretive smile gracing his face.

Maybe the trip to the cabin hadn't been such a bad idea after all.

SEVENTEEN

AN APPOINTMENT TO KEEP

Billy had always liked working things out by hand. Odd for a computer guy, but he found it soothing. The tactile nature of pen and paper required an immersion different from the click of a keyboard. He was sure that Emily must have told him she was heading out, but he didn't remember it. By the time the whirring lock and the door opening signaled her return, it was already dark out.

Emily stepped into the room. She said something incomprehensible, a sequence of sounds that could have meant anything, and held up a plastic bag.

He massaged the meat of his right hand. He'd transcribed the photos from the cabin into his notebook and then made pages and pages of notes of his own. Working off the old formulas and concepts for Nellie felt like hearing the echo in a cover of a song you once knew: haunting, eerie, but also so familiar. Or like seeing somebody you thought you knew. Maybe he could see something meaningful if only he turned his head fast enough. His wife was looking at him. Waiting.

It was like surfacing from under the water of a swimming pool, the world above suddenly shifting into view. She had spoken to him. "Sorry," he said. "What?"

"I said"—she held the bag out to him—"Thai food. Figured we wouldn't be able to get that in Whiskey Run." She put it on the desk next to him and then unzipped her jacket. "Holy shit. It's gotten cold out. It smells like snow. I feel bad for the little kids out there trick-or-treating. Or maybe it's worse for the parents. The kids don't feel it. You pump enough sugar into them and they're little monsters on their own," she said, grinning. "You should see it. Lots of little ghosts and goblins running around and dragging their parents behind them. Actually, not really. Mostly princesses and hockey players and ninjas. I don't think I saw a single ghost. And then, of course, you've got the college students all dressed up. Girls in short skirts and frat boys dressed up as zombies.

"Anyway, you seemed like you were in a rhythm with your work when I left. You didn't even look up when I told you I was heading out. I texted you like ten times and I tried calling, but you didn't pick up, and it's after seven, so I just grabbed Thai takeout. If you want to keep working, that's fine, but otherwise, I figured we could eat dinner in bed, watch a movie together." She made her eyebrows jump twice. "Screw a little."

He glanced out the window. What time was it? He turned back to look at his wife. "We can get Thai if you want."

"No. You aren't listening." She poked the bag on the desk. "I got Thai already."

"Sorry. I meant we can get Thai in Whiskey Run. Shawn told me. He hired a guy from New York City to open a Thai restaurant in Whiskey Run. You'll see. It's surreal. A private city. So we can get Thai food in Whiskey Run if you want. But that's weird, too. I told you, right, that even though he fixed up the road, it's still the same half-hour drive from Eagle Mansion into town? Which means takeout would kind of suck, but we can go out for Thai whenever you want." He picked up his pen again and looked at the notebook.

She put her hand on his head, patting it affectionately, like he was a dog. Woof. Good boy, Billy. An old joke, one that had started in the first years of their marriage and then disappeared from their lexicon in the middle wilderness. She'd started doing it again recently, since they'd left their apartment. Old habits resurfacing.

"That's your takeaway from what I just said?"

She was smiling. What had he missed?

"Was there something else?" he said.

"The part where I asked if you maybe wanted to watch a movie." She paused. "And then screw a little."

Oh.

"Oh," he said. He put down his pen. "Right."

They had sex first, and then they ate the Thai food, still warm, and watched a nonsensical romantic comedy that Emily found on television, and by then it was almost ten o'clock. They had sex again—they normally had a good sex life, especially when Emily was reading a romance or erotic novel that was particularly good, but he'd noticed a few days after he took Shawn's offer that her birth control pills were left unswallowed, and even if she hadn't said anything about it, she'd been even more interested in sex than usual—and then Emily went to sleep, curled against him, her arm over his stomach.

Whoever had renovated the inn had done a good job. He was on the side of the bed closest to the window, the bedsheet and blankets pushed down to his hips. Even naked, however, there was no sense of the night's chill coming through the glass, no drafty corners. He knew he should be sleeping. They were expected in Whiskey Run to meet Shawn's plane in almost twelve hours, which meant that Emily would get up for a run around six o'clock, be back by seven, wake him up at eight, and want to be in the car by eight forty-five. He was too wired to sleep, though. Too many things. There was the sweet hum of his wife beside him, the gorgeous warmth of their relationship feeling new again, the first time since he'd gotten out of rehab that he truly felt good about the two of them. There was the knowledge that tomorrow, November 1, they'd head up to Shawn's ridiculous house to begin their residency. And there was what he'd copied down from the walls of the cabin. He could feel something living, breathing in those letters and numbers, a tickle deep in the back of his brain. The excitement he remembered feeling in the first months of working in the cabin was coming back to him. Why had they given up on Nellie? Why had they settled on Eagle Logic?

Takata.

He shivered. The room suddenly felt cold, and he decided he didn't want to stay in bed. He got up and slid on a T-shirt and his underwear and jeans. He thought about turning on the light on the desk, but he didn't want to wake up Emily. He grabbed his notebook and pen, stuffed a room key and his wallet into his pocket, and picked up his cowboy boots and jacket. He stopped on the threshold and looked back at Emily. She was still curled into the space that he had just vacated, the skin of her shoulder looking delicate in the light drifting in through the window. He stepped out into the hallway, closing the door carefully behind him, and slid his boots on over his bare feet. The thick carpet swallowed the heels of his cowboy boots, but by the time he reached the head of the stairs he could hear the hum of voices from downstairs. There'd be light down there. He could find a table in the corner and sit with his notebook and drink seltzer and lime.

The bar was trying too hard, he thought, the sort of place he'd frequented in those first few years after they left Whiskey Run, when Emily thought it was still fun to go out with him and money seemed like a thing to take for granted. The kind of bar where everything was artisanal and the bartenders were either tattooed pixies or mustached hipsters who liked to tell you the story behind your drink, as if you wanted something other than the belt of fire in your throat, as if you cared about anything other than the way the ice cubes rattling in your empty glass could bring them running. There were tables by the front, but a group of professionals old enough to be out of college but young enough to still go out for Halloween had pulled them together. Overstuffed chairs dotted the room, but most of those were occupied or sitting in shadows. It wasn't his kind of joint, anyway. Even for a glass of seltzer and lime, he liked things a little more run-down. Too many young men and young women trying too hard to act like they weren't trying at all. He preferred the kind of place where people had given up trying years earlier. That's where he wanted to be.

He stepped out into the night, surprised at how cold it was. He knew he'd regret not bothering with socks, but at least he had his jacket. He started down the pedestrian mall. In the old days, he'd have walked all the way across, to the Rooster, but they'd passed his old bar earlier that morning: the Rooster had been abandoned. The sign was gone. Instead of the light silhouette of a crowing rooster, there were just two metal poles on the side of the building. One of the two windows had been boarded over, and when he cupped his hands against the glass and peered inside, he'd seen that the Rooster was empty and derelict. His old bar was just a haunt of dust and emptiness.

Somewhere else would have to do. He was cold, but he wasn't in a hurry. He popped his collar up against the wind and tucked his hands into his pockets. He peered through the windows of the first bar, but it was packed with dancing college students, and the second bar, only a few doors down, was full of televisions and frat boys. He looked down the pedestrian mall and froze.

Was that . . . ?

He started walking, quickly. The figure was three-quarters turned from him, and far enough away so that Billy wouldn't have had a good look even if he were closer. But it was impossible. Takata was . . .

Billy realized he was running now. The figure started walking and reached the end of the commons, turning left, out of sight.

When Billy turned the corner, the sidewalk was empty. No sign of him. Like he'd never been there.

He looked up. The familiar sign for the Rooster was hanging above his head, the lights guttering like candles.

His memory was playing tricks on him. It was the same place he'd been earlier that day, he was sure of it, but now the sign was hanging, and both windows were whole and unboarded. He stood there, staring through the glass. It looked the same inside as it always had. Nothing had changed in a dozen years. A scarred pool table in the back, a line of backless stools by the bar, a couple of booths and tables. Billy opened the door, hesitating until he heard somebody yell that he was letting in the cold. The door swung shut heavily behind him, like a boulder sealing up a cave. From the outside, looking through the glass, the bar had seemed like it was well lit, but now that he was inside, it seemed dark and faded. He stood there, by the door, adjusting to the dimness, and then he made his way to the bar. He fully intended to order a seltzer and lime, but the bartender, whom he didn't recognize, a diminutive woman whose ears were snaked with hoops and who was wearing a pair of devil horns in a nod to Halloween, slid him a glass that was already full. He held it up to the single, bare lightbulb that failed to illuminate the bar area. Thin, cheap, hollow cubes of ice already melting into the bubbles of the drink, a mean slice of lime. The astringent taste of Gordon's gin was a time machine; he couldn't have ordered Sapphire gin in here if he'd tried. It was just like it had always been. He could have been sitting here at the Rooster his entire life. He might as well have not even left. It could have been now, it could have been a hundred years ago, and he knew it wouldn't matter. The Rooster would always exist like this for him, a haunt calling him home.

He pulled out his notebook and sat and drank.

When the bartender told him she was closing out, he was surprised at the size of his tab. He went to hand her his credit card—it felt so good to be able to slap it down and know that it wouldn't be handed back with a grim embarrassment—and then changed his mind, sliding it back into his wallet and dropping three twenties on the bar. Walking out the door was like traveling in time again, and for a moment he hesitated. He wondered what he would see if he turned around to look at the bar. The Rooster was a memory that should have stayed a memory, the cold a reminder of who he had been, but maybe it was open for him tonight as a reminder that he'd never escape his past.

He wasn't sure what he was more afraid of: turning and seeing that the Rooster was gone, boarded up and empty as he'd seen it earlier that day, or turning and seeing the sign flickering and calling him back. He decided he didn't want to know.

Instead, he walked carefully across the pedestrian mall, taking his time and letting the wind whip against his face. It was completely deserted. He thought he'd be passing drunk sorority girls trying to stay warm in their skimpy costumes, or couples who could barely wait to make it home, but it was just him and the emptiness of the open walk.

It took him a couple of tries to work the front door of the inn, and once he was upstairs, he stopped outside the door of their room and leaned against the wall to take off first one boot and then the other. The hallway was tastefully bulwarked against the darkness, with dim sconces after every door, and the sound of the lock retracting might as well have been a brass band. He pushed gently and then held the door handle up so that the hydraulic system could close it behind him noiselessly.

He froze.

Emily was on her side, turned toward him. She'd kicked the blankets down so that they were dangling off the bed, but the sheet still covered her in twisted rivers of cotton, tucked under her arm so that her shoulder and one of her breasts were bare to what light still came in from the window.

Her eyes were open. She was staring at him.

He took a deep breath and bent over to put his cowboy boots down. When he stood up, her eyes were closed. She was sleeping. He'd imagined it. He shed his jacket and jeans, took a piss, and drowned his teeth in mouthwash, rubbing it on his lips as well. When he got into bed he moved slowly and gently, careful not to let his cold feet brush against her. He fell asleep almost instantly.

The next morning, he felt the bed shifting as she got up. She never seemed to need an alarm clock, and even the time change between Seattle and Cortaca didn't throw her. He didn't have to flutter his eyes open to know that it was within a few minutes of six o'clock. He waited, keeping his breathing even while he heard her go in and then out of the bathroom, the rustle of her tights and running shirt, the friction of her laces, the zip of her jacket, the breath and click of the door closing behind her.

By the time she got back, sweaty and cold at the same time, her face red from the wind and her fingers balled up into her sleeves, he'd already thrown down two Advil, brushed his teeth and gargled with mouthwash, gone to the bathroom, shaved, showered, and brought a carafe of coffee up to the room from the dining room below.

"Hey," she said. "I didn't expect you up yet. I tried to be quiet heading out. Did I wake you up?"

"Couldn't sleep."

He was sitting at the desk, the notebook open in front of him again, but he was just pretending to do work. Whatever it was that had made the numbers and letters seem alive the night before, had made them almost vibrate insistently in his mind, was gone. The notebook was open only for show. She stared at him in a way that made him uncomfortable, an extra breath of time that didn't make sense, and then she poured herself a cup of coffee.

"Yeah. I heard you go out last night. Were you working?" she said.

What she didn't say, what he heard: Please, tell me you were working. Please. Please. You were working.

"I was working. I didn't want to bother you. I went to sit down in the lobby."

"Okay. If you're tired, you can sleep in the car. There's enough time for a nap. Let me grab a shower and then we can head down and have breakfast."

He nodded and then sat there at the desk, looking at the notebook but not seeing anything, listening to the water play as she showered. Downstairs, there were warm cinnamon scones and pitchers of orange juice already on the table. The woman working the dining room was, thankfully, less solicitous than he found most owners of bed-and-breakfasts to be. They ate quickly, scrambled eggs and bacon for him, oatmeal with maple syrup and nuts for her, and were on the road a few minutes early, even with a quick stop for coffee.

In the car, they chatted aimlessly for a while, but Emily seemed to sense that he was elsewhere, because they settled into the comfortable silence of the long married. He turned the heat up a couple of ticks and relaxed into the gentle sway of the car on the road.

He closed his eyes.

He must have dozed off, because when he opened his eyes again it was to a world transformed.

A whisper of snow covered the farmer's fields to his right. The barn and the main house were untouched, the buildings' exteriors holding enough residual heat to stay clear, but the rolling meadows were silvered. They passed a cluster of cows that ignored the car with a studied uninterest. To the left was thickly wooded old growth, pine trees wearing the snow like grace, a contrast to the deep shadows hidden from the road. In front of them, hills dipped and rolled, but while there was a sheen of moisture, no snow stuck to the road. Emily looked at him, patted his thigh, and smiled.

"It's saying five more minutes to Whiskey Run. You picked a good time to wake up. We should be there with plenty of time to grab another coffee or something if you want before Shawn's plane touches down. It will be good to see him again. I think." She laughed, but it sounded strained.

He rubbed the back of his hand against his mouth and straightened up in his seat. Would this be the first time that she'd seen Shawn since the day they left the cabin together? How could that be? She'd stayed away from the lawsuit, unable to bear it, she'd said. Yes. She hadn't seen him then and she hadn't come to Baltimore with Billy in September. How was it that he was just realizing this now? Had it been something he wanted to avoid? Was it his way of pretending it didn't matter, or was he secretly looking forward to it, to the chance to see her face as she looked upon Shawn's? Was there something he was hoping to see there, or, perhaps more important, something he was hoping he wouldn't see?

He rubbed harder at his mouth. The corners were dry and gritty, and he reached for the water bottle. Empty. She saw him shake it.

"Sorry," she said. "We're here, though."

And they were there, but at the same time, they weren't there yet. It took several more minutes for them to go down the hill and pass the airstrip. Coming in by car felt elementally different to him from his previous trip by jet. Maybe, he thought, it was the simple difference between coming with Shawn and coming with Emily. With Shawn, it was like a god visiting the earth below. I am here to see the gifts of my greatness. Look upon what I have created and tremble on your knees at my power. With Emily, it was a descent into a new world, like going through an air lock from a past life into a new one. By driving into Whiskey Run, they'd be leaving their past behind. The drinking, the drugs, the ways in which he'd disappointed her. She'd wanted to get away from Kansas City and that's how she'd ended up at Cortaca University, but in some ways, no matter how far they'd been in terms of miles, he'd made it so she always carried at least a small part of Kansas City with her. But no longer. Not here. He thought that Whiskey Run would scrub him clean, that crossing through the forest to Shawn's property would be a baptism of sorts. A fresh start. Again. Another fresh start.

The town still had that disorienting feel of an old toy taken out of the box for the first time, and he noticed a new building that he didn't think had been there before, on the airstrip end: a bakery. He thought to point it out, but Emily had the car on driverless, and she'd already told it to go to the coffee shop, so instead he just watched her watching the stores and restaurants and buildings glide past. She was smiling.

"God. It used to be such a depressing place. Now it looks like a window display," she said. "I love it! You could imagine all of Whiskey Run behind glass. Particularly with this snow, it's like something from an upscale department store at Christmas, trying to get you to buy designer clothes and jewelry with the promise of nostalgia." As she said it, they passed first a boutique clothing store, and then a tiny jewelry store, and she laughed aloud. "Good god. All of this is here just for Shawn and a few guests a few times a year? The hubris it takes to build yourself an entire town."

The car pulled to a stop in front of the coffee shop. Coffee Emergency. Billy already knew it was the sort of place Emily would love, the kind of coffee shop she'd want to open for herself.

"Technically, the town was here already," Billy said. "He just bought all of it, bulldozed and rebuilt most of it, and is running all these businesses at an enormous loss . . . Yeah. Okay. He's a rich guy who wants things a certain way."

Emily stopped with her hand on the door handle, shook her head and looked at him. "No, Billy. A rich guy who wants things a certain way will buy himself a fancy car or only fly first class or be a pretentious prick when he's ordering wine. This is something different. There's something about all this that's just—"

"Scary."

She hesitated and then opened her door. "Well, we're here," she said.

He followed her into Coffee Emergency. They both used the bathroom and ordered lattes, and by the time they were back outside, they could see the jet tracing the sky, Shawn Eagle coming to Whiskey Run ten minutes early.

EIGHTEEN

ALL SOULS

There were many things that Ruth and Rose tried to tell their mother that Beth either didn't believe or didn't understand. It was not, the girls thought, their mother's fault. She was intelligent and attentive, but they often felt that what seemed like the most simple things to them, bone-deep truths that came as easily as breathing, might as well have been ideas from another universe as far as their mother was concerned.

For instance, their dreams.

They had tried on more than one occasion to tell their mother that they shared their dreams, but Beth did not grasp what they meant. Perhaps it wasn't that she would not understand, but rather that she could not understand. Though, if she'd been able to look at it from the outside, it might have been more clear, for neither of the girls was ever asleep without the other being asleep; even when Rose was three, and had needed minor surgery to remove a cyst on her shoulder, Ruth had fallen asleep in her father's arms at the same time that the IV drip in Rose's arm sent her under. Or maybe Beth should have realized that it was never a single child coming to her bed in the middle of the night, but always both girls, childhood dreams interrupted by something more sinister.

But while it may have been something that Rothko and Beth

should have noticed, there were so many things about their twin daughters that already seemed odd to them that the way they always seemed to be sleeping at the same time was not something they noticed. When Rose and Ruth said that they shared dreams, it was another comment that passed their mother by.

It was a shared dream that had woken them up early this morning, November 1, the morning after Halloween, a few minutes before five o'clock Chicago time, the same moment their aunt Emily had risen to go for a run before leaving Cortaca for Whiskey Run. They were not surprised that they had dreamed of unpleasant things in the night. The sticky sugar of Halloween candy was still thick on their tongues despite their father's urgings to do a good job of brushing their teeth before bed. The candy had not come from trick-or-treating; they were not averse to candy, but Halloween was a holiday they feared. Their father had tried to cajole them into going door-to-door like their friends from school would have, but even in the early stages of the night the streets were too alive for their comfort. Instead, they'd raided the bowl of candy their mother had put by the door, eating until they turned sluggish and cranky, and then gone to bed at their usual time. They'd slept well enough, though fitfully, with dreams of a grave that had been reopened, the rotting flesh of the newly dead added to the bones of the long gone, dreams of tunnels under the earth hiding skeletons from both the past and the future, dreams of trees thick enough to steal away the light, until near on five o'clock. The nightmare that woke them was quick and brutal, an interloper burrowing into a dream they had been enjoying and knifing them to alertness.

The dream had been simple and calm after a fitful night: Lake Michigan frozen and gently tipped into a small hill toward Chicago so they could toboggan across ice and a soft layer of snow, their mother and father also on the sled, laughing, arms wrapped around the twins, an endless slide to their home. It was a dream they knew was probably a memory of a time they'd actually gone sledding, a happy moment they would have shared with Beth and Rothko when they were younger. A dream of home and being held. The kind of dream that can last forever and is still never long enough, the first truly deep sleep after a night of unease.

And then the light in the dream changed from the refracted whiteness of snow and winter to the thick, sticky yellow light that came every time something *true and bad* happened in their dreams. On the toboggan, in the dream, Ruth and Rose held hands and squeezed each other's fingers. They knew to beware.

The nightmare: on the expanse of white, Aunt Emily and Uncle Billy, with Uncle Billy standing off to the side, wearing his cowboy boots, jeans, a T-shirt, holding his arms out at a low angle, his left hand gashed open to show wires instead of bone, but bleeding like he was a normal person. The blood dripped and dropped, staining the snow. Aunt Emily was in front of them, too, but she was looking at Uncle Billy and seemingly oblivious of the toboggan headed her way. Her arm was cut open also, blood pouring from her wrist and off her hand like a fountain. And then, from the ice, cables and metal crawled up and hissed like snakes ready to—

They were awake.

In that first moment, neither girl was sure who reached up and who reached down from her bunk to touch the other's fingers, and neither one was sure who slid down from the top bunk to pile herself next to her sister on the bottom bed. Their skin was cold, as if they'd been out playing in the snow, and Ruth tucked the blankets tighter around them. Rose suggested they go and tell their mother that they'd had a bad dream, but Ruth said no. They had been, they knew, weighing on their mother's mind. They'd heard her talking about them the night before.

Their condo was well insulated against the Chicago winters and the heat of summer, but on the inside, the walls were thin and the doors, heavy things with brass fittings, gapped at the floor; what their parents thought of as quiet whispers in their bedroom traveled to Ruth and Rose's room by the highway of wood floors and open industrial-style ceilings. Some sounds were not meant for them—the happy sort of crying that was a regular occurrence from their parents—and they did not listen to those, but when their parents talked of the two of them, they could not help but take an interest. So they knew that their parents had concerns, that they thought, sometimes, about sending Ruth and Rose to a therapist, about having them tested at school. They had been talking about them again the night before, worried because the girls did not want to trick-or-treat.

"Except that if somebody was going to ask us why we're so worried, what would we say? There's nothing actually wrong with them."

Their father's voice. A gentle, low whisper. He was a funny man. Warm and sweet. The house he kept inside his own mind was a good place. Neither Ruth nor Rose had ever been to the beach on her own, but the house that occupied their father's mind was on a beach, had a porch overlooking the ocean. When he disappeared inside himself, the girls sometimes went to visit him there. They stayed invisible and quiet—they did not want to disturb him in his private space—but they liked the comfort of the sand and sun, the gentle swell of the waves brushing the beach.

A short laugh from their mom. "I guess we can't really say, hey, our kids seem happy and are bright and have plenty of friends, but they're kind of weird sometimes. Do you know what they said to me yesterday afternoon? Rose said that the woman who lives above us had a baby inside her but now it's gone and she doesn't want to tell anybody but it made her happy for the baby to be gone. Come on. How creepy is that?"

Their mother was different from their father. She, too, could be funny, and she was also warm and sweet. She knew the magic trick of all good mothers: the ability to expand her arms so that she could always carry the weight of her children. She rarely yelled at them, and when she did, it was to get their attention, not to punish. She tried so very hard to understand her daughters, to be present for them, but like their father, their mother sometimes drifted off to the house inside her. The difference was that while their father's house was full of light, a golden sun warming him as he let the sound of the ocean lull him with its peaceful rise and fall, their mother's place was something dark and sinister.

Early, when they were younger, the girls did not understand

that these were private places, that people did not want to share the homes inside them. They knew that every person had a space inside them that they would retreat to, but they had just assumed that their mother could visit their father's beach in the same way that Ruth and Rose could jump back and forth between what each of them was thinking. But as they got older, they realized that no, in the same way that their mother could not visit their father's beach, their father had never visited the house in their mother's mind either. On the days when their mother was quiet and sad, Rothko would ask her what was wrong, and the girls wanted to tell him the truth: she was in the scary house.

Perhaps, if Beth displayed photos from her childhood or had ever returned to Kansas City and brought the girls by her childhood home, they would have recognized the connection between the space in their mother's head and the house she grew up in. Or perhaps not. They might not have seen how the houses were both different and similar. It was the same building, of course: the sagging front porch, the two-by-two windows in front and back, upstairs and downstairs, the peeling dark blue paint on the shutters. But the house in their mother's mind was always tentacled by shadows, the light of the street lamp falling just short of the front steps. A few times they'd followed her down the sidewalk, staying two steps behind her, keeping silent so that she wouldn't think to look behind her, but they'd never gotten the courage to turn from the walk to follow her onto the porch and into the house. There was something about the way the house occupied their mother's mind that scared them. They'd watch her go through the door and shut it behind her, both of them understanding that whatever was behind the splintered door was not something they wanted to see.

Whenever their mother came back from visiting that house inside her—visits that lasted for a moment or, occasionally, for days on end, even if she tried to pretend nothing was wrong—Ruth and Rose found themselves unaccountably bursting into tears. They could not control it. Beth always rushed to them, took them into her arms, cuddled with them on the couch or the bed, but they were never sure if they were seeking the comfort of their mother or if it was the other way around. All they knew for sure was that they didn't like to follow their mother when she visited that dark house in her mind.

But because they knew that it was there, it surprised them when they realized that their mother didn't really see it herself. She was "tired" or "overwhelmed with work" or "just a little sad." That's what she'd say, but Ruth and Rose knew the truth even if their mother didn't: she'd gone into the house again.

And maybe that realization, that their mother didn't even know the house was always there, waiting for her in that dark corner of her mind, was why Ruth and Rose had accepted that neither of their parents really believed them when they said that they shared dreams. Their parents didn't understand, and to wake Beth up to tell her about the dream? It would be just one more thing that would make her worry. Ruth looked at the clock—their parents didn't let them get out of bed to watch television until at least seven. In the meantime, they could stay like this, in the bottom bunk, under the covers, holding each other tight and whispering about things they already knew.

On the floor of the bedroom, they heard Rusty walk. The dog's nails ticktacked on the hardwood floor. He circled and then settled onto the ground with a heavy sigh. The girls couldn't remember a time without the dog. Sometimes, when they had dreams that were particularly upsetting, when they felt trapped inside that thick, sticky yellow light of nightmares, like mosquitoes trapped in amber, afraid that they'd never wake up, Rusty would come into their room and yank at the pajamas of whichever girl was in the bottom bunk until the girls woke. He was there to protect them.

"We can tell Mommy that we don't want to go to that place for Christmas," Ruth said. "Tell her that we want to stay here, in Chicago, that Aunt Emily and Uncle Billy should come visit us. We can *push*."

Rose didn't answer. She didn't need to. Both of them knew there was no point. No matter what they said to their mother, Beth wouldn't understand. And a *push* wouldn't work on her, either. Sometimes they could get their father to respond to a *push*, but even that was hard. It worked with teachers and Aunt Emily and their grandparents, depending on what they were asking for, and it almost always worked on strangers. They didn't like to *push* when they didn't have to. It tired them out and left them with an ache behind their eyes. And even if they didn't know the word for it, there was something about using a *push* that felt too intimate. But when they did *push*, they could usually get people to do what they wanted.

But not their mother.

"Or," Rose said, "we could call Aunt Emily. Warn her. Just tell her about the dream. Tell her what's coming."

This time Ruth didn't answer. They were both thinking about what had happened the last time they had tried to warn somebody, when they had told their preschool teacher that she should leave her husband, that she wasn't safe.

Sometimes it was worse to try to warn people. It was like throwing a rock to scare away the fish; the ripples had to wash up somewhere.

"You're right," Rose said to her sister, even though Ruth hadn't spoken. "Nobody will listen."

"It will be okay," Ruth said. "Uncle Billy promised. He shook on it."

He promised.

He would keep Aunt Emily safe.

NINETEEN

OPEN HOUSE

Emily couldn't decide whether she was actually starting to feel cheery about the whole enterprise or had simply decided to force herself to feel cheery about being in Whiskey Run again. One thing was for sure: it would be odd seeing Shawn Eagle again after all these years. But odd in a good way or a bad way? She was still attracted to him. She knew that. She'd never been not attracted to him. In college, he'd been a beautiful young man: the cheekbones, the dark hair that fell over his face, the blending of white and Native American and who knows what else over the generations making him look exotic, the sense that there was something deep and tragic hidden beneath his quick smile. He hadn't been the first guy she'd slept with, but there hadn't been many others before him, and in all the ways that counted, he might as well have been the first.

Seeing him now? It was hard not to be a little impressed. Okay. A lot impressed. It bothered her, it really did, that the private jet impressed her, but who was she kidding? It would have impressed most people. A pair of SUVs were already waiting on the tarmac, and she and Billy pulled up in their Honda Pilot as the jet was taxiing over. She stole a glance at Billy. He looked . . . She wasn't sure, and it didn't seem right, but he actually looked excited. The two of them got out of their car and waited. A young woman in business attire came over and introduced herself, told Billy it was good to see him again, and offered them each a bottle of water. Emily shook her head.

The door of the jet opened down into a set of stairs. The first person out was a trim man in a dark suit. No tie. Although he wasn't a particularly large man, there was something coiled about him that made Emily realize he was a bodyguard even before a gust of wind pulled back the edge of his suit coat and showed a pistol holstered underneath. The second and third people out were also clearly security. They were followed by a black woman who was, quite simply, gorgeous. She looked like the kind of woman you saw only in movies. Had Billy not mentioned Wendy ahead of time, Emily would have assumed the woman was Shawn's girlfriend, not his assistant.

When Shawn came out of the plane, it was almost anticlimactic. He didn't take her breath away. She read her fair share of romances and erotic novels, escapist fantasy that she loved, so she was familiar with all the romantic clichés. She expected something to happen when she saw Shawn again for the first time. But there was no lump in her throat, no hitch in her heartbeat.

She'd read a book a few months ago about a married woman having an affair—the husband in the book was an alcoholic boor who'd had a series of affairs of his own—with a composer who could play the woman's body (or, rather, a certain part of the woman's body) "like the Stradivarius that it was." It was dirty enough to make her blush, but the story was pretty weak. Still, there had been enough to keep her reading, and one of her favorite lines came when the woman ran into the composer again after not seeing him for a year or two. The woman had immediately known that she was going to sleep with the composer again despite all vows to try to stay away from him. She couldn't help herself. He was just too damned sexy. Simply seeing him, thinking about his mouth, his fingers, "turned her underwear into a lake of wonder." Emily had laughed aloud when she read the sentence in the book, and it made her smile now, because seeing Shawn after all these years did not leave her feeling tempted in the least.

The thing that was odd was that, on the surface, she should have been at least a little out of breath. Shawn looked better than he had the last time she'd seen him. That bit of baby fat had melted away—or, more likely, she thought, been worked away by personal trainers and chefs and the kind of life and help that could be afforded only by the ultra-rich—and he came down the stairs confident and fit. Even without knowing that he was wearing a pair of Momotaro jeans or that the motorcycle jacket he wore over his T-shirt was a Saint Laurent, it was clear to Emily that what he was wearing was simply of a different class from what her husband had on. She stole a glance at Billy. It wasn't a fair comparison.

Billy had always been a T-shirt and jeans guy. He never cared about clothes, and that not caring made the clothes look good on him. In his twenties, he'd had an effortless leanness, muscles that came to him despite spending most of his time in front of a laptop. He had a couple of pairs of jeans and a drawer full of T-shirts, and he pulled off the kind of "I don't give a shit" look that on a lot of guys would have translated as either trying too hard or being a slob. On Billy, however, it made him look confident. That had been in his twenties, though. Over the last couple of years—since he'd gone clean, really—she'd noticed that his well-worn clothes had begun looking closer to worn out. What had once been sexy had become ragged and dingy. A bit like Billy. His hair had started thinning a little as he moved into his thirties, and the muscles that had come naturally to him in his twenties had softened. He had lines in his face that hadn't been there when she met him, a map of the way he'd abused himself for a decade. She knew that, in part, the way he looked was simply the way she looked at him; she couldn't help but see the disappointments of her life delineated across his skin. Maybe that's why the new clothes he'd gotten when that money from Shawn came seemed to have made such a big change. New jeans, new T-shirts, new man.

But looking from her husband to Shawn made her understand, suddenly, the difference between a pair of seventy-dollar jeans and a thirty-dollar T-shirt from the Gap and what you could buy when you had a personal shopper and money was literally no object. She didn't need to know the labels to know that he was wearing a two-hundred-dollar T-shirt, that his jeans were probably somewhere north of five hundred bucks, and she didn't want to even guess what a leather jacket like that would cost. What was that phrase? The clothes make the man? Except that, with Shawn Eagle, that wasn't true. He looked like he was doing the clothes a favor by wearing them. The jeans and the jacket seemed effortless on him. That was because it was effortless, Emily realized. Shawn wasn't trying. He probably had no clue that what he was wearing was out of the reach of somebody like Billy, and she wouldn't have been surprised to find out that somebody on his staff laid out his clothing for him every morning.

But despite that, despite how handsome Shawn looked, she didn't feel it. No butterflies. If she'd been single and he'd flirted with her, she would have flirted right back, but looking at him was a little bit like looking at a faded photograph from a great vacation.

Shawn made a point of shaking Billy's hand and then embracing him in one of those awkward one-armed guy hugs, before he turned to look at Emily.

"Hey," he said. "Good to see you."

A kiss on the cheek, and then he apologized, steering Billy into his car. "Got to talk business," he said.

That was it. The three security men in the lead car, Billy and Shawn in the front of the second SUV, with Wendy in the backseat, leaving Emily alone in their Honda.

She fumed for the first couple of minutes, but then she gave in. There wasn't anything she could do about it, and besides, what had she wanted? What had she expected? She was glad that seeing Shawn again hadn't done anything to her. Things were messy enough in the history between Shawn and her and Billy. Sure, she'd fantasized once or twice about what her life could have been like if she'd stayed with Shawn. More than once or twice. But that had been when things were falling apart with Billy. She shouldn't be having that fantasy now. Not when things were finally on the right track again. Billy clean. Billy working. This opportunity in front of them. No, it wasn't worth being upset about. Anyway, the drive was stunning. She had to admit that. Cortaca was a lovely town, full of waterfalls and thick with trees, the lake a jewel in the crown of the city. But the new and improved Whiskey Run was something else, and the drive from there to Eagle Mansion was one postcard view after another, particularly with the way the snow frosted everything. The snow was already starting to melt in the late-morning sun, however.

By the time she came over the rise and saw the mansion, she wasn't annoyed anymore. She was excited. Billy had described it to her, the way Shawn had fixed it up, but it was different seeing it for herself. Eagle Mansion looked like she had thought it would, but the Bird-house or the Tree Fort or whatever ridiculous name Shawn was calling the addition, was different than she had expected. She had figured it would look stark and out of place, a billionaire's folly perched on top of a classic building. The kind of addition that would age poorly. A masturbatory architectural gesture. To her surprise, however, Shawn's private residence looked like it belonged on top of Eagle Mansion. Even with the steel and glass in contrast to the wood and stone of the mansion, they belonged together. The Nest. That's what Billy said Shawn called the building. Even though the name made Shawn sound ridiculous, it was apt: the mansion did look like a bird about to take flight—there was something sharp and menacing in the way the late-morning sun caught the top edges of the gutters—and the glass of the addition cradled on steel girders did evoke a bird's nest.

She followed the two SUVs in front. They parked in a line, in front of the steps. She got out of the car and started walking around to the trunk, but Shawn called out to her.

"Don't worry about that stuff," he said. "There's a small staff in the building today while I'm here. Just to do some cooking for the day and to make sure everything's clean for you guys to move in. Somebody will take care of bringing your things in from the car. Don't worry, though. Once I take off, it will be just the two of you. I want to make sure Billy's got the space to work his magic."

Billy was already up the stairs, but Shawn turned back and stepped close to her. He grabbed on to her arm, above the elbow, and looked her straight in the eye, his smile for the first time looking full to her. "It's good to see you, you know. It really is."

She looked to see if Billy had noticed, but he was already inside, impatient to be off with Nellie. Wendy was at the top of the steps, either looking at her tablet or discreetly pretending to look at something on her tablet. Shawn's security guards had seemingly disappeared. It was just the two of them. Intimate.

"You look good, but it's been too long," Shawn said. "Why have we waited so long to see each other?"

"Well, the short version is that my husband hates you and is worried that you're still in love with me and I'm still in love with you and that I might leave him for you." She kept a straight face.

Shawn let go of her arm and took a step back. He rubbed his hand across his chin. "Hell. I don't know if I'm supposed to smile at that or not."

"You can smile," she said.

"Is it true?"

"That I'm still in love with you? Tell you what, how about you give me a tour of this little house of yours," she said.

There was a flash of irritation on his face, but he buried it. "It's not a *little* house," he said. "What is it with you two?"

She saw the door open and Billy stepped part of the way out. "You coming?" he called down to Shawn.

Shawn turned. "Yeah. Okay. Coming." He looked back at Emily. "Let me take care of business with your boy. Wendy will give you the nickel tour."

He took the steps with the kind of energy that made Emily think of her sister's dog. She had to hand it to Shawn. Where Billy could be maudlin and tried to figure out what was wrong with things, Shawn was always enthusiastic. The man had energy.

She followed him up the steps and stopped next to Shawn's assistant. Up close, she was even more attractive, and Emily wondered if Wendy had been a model and if Shawn was sleeping with her.

"The answer is no," Wendy said.

"No? No what?"

"You're asking yourself if I'm one of Shawn's bed bunnies. The answer is no."

"I wasn't—"

"Yes, you were," Wendy said. She cut Emily off, but it wasn't unkind, and there was a certain friendliness in her voice that made Emily, despite herself, laugh.

"Okay. Yes. A little bit. Sorry. Ex-girlfriend and all that."

"Don't worry," Wendy said, "I'm not that forward with everybody." She shrugged. "I figured I'd just get that one out of the way so that you and I can have some sort of a functional relationship. I can't tell you how many of his girlfriends can't get over the idea of my being his assistant."

Wendy walked through the front door of the mansion and Emily followed her in. The morning sun came through the glass front of the building and lit up the entranceway. She stopped to take it in. It was almost entirely empty, but it wasn't cold. Clean. The space was clean. Billy had described it to her as best he could, but he didn't get the way it felt. It felt, she thought, like Shawn. An elegance that seemed simple but was actually terribly complicated. There was a glass shaft encircled by a set of spiraling stairs toward the back. An elevator. Wendy saw her looking at it and shook her head.

"We've been having a lot of trouble with the elevator. Shawn's pissed about it. Just take the stairs for now. Elevator guy is supposed to be back out next week. I'll give you the tour."

"So he has a lot of girlfriends?"

Wendy had started walking to her left, but she stopped. "Emily. Come on. He's a billionaire. And even if *I'm* not sleeping with him, we both know he's a good-looking man. It doesn't take a Harvard education—and no, I went to an elite liberal arts college in the middle of Iowa, thank you—to do the math on that. But that's not really your question, is it?"

"How about you show me where there's a bathroom," Emily said. "I've had a lot of coffee this morning."

"The answer to the other question you aren't asking is yes," Wendy said. "He talks about you a lot."

It was Emily's turn to stop. She felt unsettled. The concrete floor could have been tilted ice.

"Is that what this is?" She realized that she had gone from feeling disconcerted to angry in one quick slide. "Goddammit. This is just like him, to pull some sort of stupid stunt like this. What an asshole. He thinks that just because he's Shawn Goddamned Eagle he can play with people's lives like this? Billy thinks this is a real thing. He's excited about working on some stupid, fake—"

"You're wrong," Wendy said. Her voice was quiet, and Emily realized that her own voice had almost risen to the level of shouting. "The project is real. I don't know how much Billy has told you about what he's going to be working on or how much you understand it, but it's real, and it's fantastic. Look, I get it. I understand why you're upset, and that's my fault. I thought I'd try to cut through some of the bullshit that I figured would be there because of your past relationship with Shawn. I apologize. I misspoke."

"You misspoke?" Emily leaned back, her arms crossed. There was a part of her that was aware of her body language and wanted to stop. She might as well have been impatiently tapping her toe, and it made her feel slightly ashamed. She didn't want to be that kind of woman. Not to another woman.

Wendy shrugged. "Misspoke would be the wrong word. I misspoke about misspeaking. How's that?" She offered up enough of a smile that Emily responded in kind. "But I made you feel shitty, and I didn't mean to do that. Look, the truth is that Shawn does talk about you a lot, and I honestly don't know if it's because he's still in love with you or because he was in love with you once and is nostalgic. I do know that, for him, the time he spent as a student at Cortaca University, and then after, working with Billy in the cabin in the woods, particularly when you were out there with them, those memories have a hold on him."

There was something about what Wendy was saying that felt off to Emily, but she couldn't pinpoint it.

"But this isn't bullshit," Wendy continued. "Not even a little bit. I'm not an engineer, but I know Eagle Technology inside and out. I don't understand how it works, but I know enough about the program that your husband and Shawn tried to write that I understand what it could be if they get it to work. Shawn's had a team of engineers trying to crack Nellie for years and years, and they're close. But they can't get her to work, not right at least. Shawn's convinced that Billy's the only one who can do it. Billy holds the key, according to Shawn. So, sure, maybe it's a bonus that you're part of the package. He was excited about seeing you. Too excited. Which is probably why he's gone out of his way to sort of disappear. Shawn Eagle isn't the kind of guy who is used to having to work for attention." Emily started to respond but Wendy shook her head. "Maybe he wasn't always that way, Emily, but the Shawn you knew isn't the same Shawn that exists now. That other Shawn was a hundred billion dollars and a dozen years ago."

There was the sound of a ping from Wendy's tablet, and she took a quick glance at it and then looked back at Emily. "Come on. Let me at least give you the tour while we talk." She turned and headed down the wing, taking Emily along the corridor. Each door they approached slid open so that Wendy could give Emily a look.

The mansion was, in a lot of ways, disappointing. Oh, Emily thought, it was gorgeous. A sculpture of sorts. Or, maybe more accurately, a piece of art with art inside, because Emily recognized some of the art on the walls. Or thought she recognized it. Even if she didn't, she could recognize expensive. And the renovation, if you could even call it a renovation, was stunning. But it wasn't . . . Something. It wasn't futuristic, she thought. That's what it was. That was what seemed incomplete. From the way Billy had described Nellie, Emily was expecting the new and improved Eagle Mansion to be some sort of science fiction wonderland. Holodecks and matter transmitters and all that space-age stuff that Billy loved. Ultimately, however, Eagle Mansion seemed to be nothing more than a really fancy hotel that was brand-new but built to look sort of old-fashioned. Of course, according to Wendy, part of that was because Nellie wasn't turned on throughout the house yet.

"Why not?"

"There's a reason you and Billy are here," Wendy said. "Plus, until yesterday, we had workmen in and out of the building, finishing up. There was a cleaning crew in here overnight. Everybody has signed nondisclosure agreements, of course, but we're talking about something that could be worth hundreds and hundreds of billions of dollars to Eagle Technology, maybe more."

Wendy started her off through the conference rooms and auditorium, showed her the spa and exercise room, and then brought her to the other wing, which was much more open: the bar and the dining room opened directly into the kitchen without any doors to pass through.

"The head chef wanted clear sight lines for the waiters so that service could be better. He claims, and if I could do it in his French accent, I would, that doors are 'suspiciously dangerous' in a kitchen. If you're actually sitting in the dining room, you get a view of the grill and the wood-fired oven. The exciting stuff. All the nitty-gritty parts of the kitchen are behind the corner. Not that you'll spend much time down here. You'll probably want to do most of your cooking upstairs, in the Nest. Cooking dinner for two in a commercial kitchen is a bit like shooting a fly with a tank. Anyway, there's a much better view upstairs."

She stopped in front of a large walk-in freezer. "It's loaded up already for you guys. The pantry, too. Down here is all just-in-case stuff."

"Just in case what?"

"Snow. The roads will be plowed, but you spent a winter up here, right? That little dusting we had this morning is just the beginning of things. It'll be melted by lunch, but the snow is going to start in earnest sometime in the next few weeks. You're going to have some times when the roads aren't passable. When they're clear, of course, you can get groceries delivered up from Whiskey Run whenever you feel like it. I'll run you through how to order. If there's something you want that they don't have in town, just let the grocer know. They'll get it brought in for you. Sometimes it takes a couple of days, but whatever you want."

Wendy opened the door and stepped in. The cold air washed over Emily, and she felt herself start to shiver. The freezer wasn't as big as she'd expected, but then again, it wasn't that big a place. What had

Billy told her? Sixty guest rooms? She hugged her arms across her chest.

Wendy showed her the basic layout of the freezer—chicken, steak, pork, lamb, different kinds of fish and seafood, vegetables, fruit, desserts, staples—and then walked her through the dry storage. "Really, though, once Nellie is turned on throughout the house, it's simple. Anything you don't know, ask, and she'll tell you. Why, heck, if Billy can get her running properly, she'll tell you before you even ask." Wendy chuckled, but to Emily's ear, it sounded false.

"What about there, down the stairs?"

"Wine cellar. It leads to the rest of the basement, too, but other than the wine cellar, I can't imagine there's any reason you'd be in the basement. Extra sleeping quarters for staff, offices, storage, that kind of stuff. Obviously, help yourself to the wine if you want, though, uh, I wasn't sure—"

"Because of Billy."

"Well, yeah."

"Why don't you show me the rest of it?"

The look of relief on Wendy's face was almost pitiable. It was the first time Emily had seen her lose her sense of calm. Even when she was telling Emily that she wasn't a romantic threat—which Emily thought was a pretty uncomfortable moment—Wendy had seemed collected.

"Okay. Anyway, the kitchen upstairs is already stocked up for you two, but it's not designed to hold more than a few days' worth of food. Shawn's used to having his staff working in the background. I'm not sure he even realizes that it's possible to run out of something. If you don't want to have groceries delivered from Whiskey Run, I suspect you'll end up 'shopping' down here kind of regularly."

Wendy walked her up and down the second- and then third-floor hallways, stopping to show her a few of the suites. All the doors were open, and they mostly looked the same, but a few of them had tiny plaques that were easy to miss. Wendy made a point of showing her one on the third floor near the end. "The Babe Ruth Suite. According to Shawn, Babe Ruth actually stayed here at some point. Supposedly he liked the ladies and the gambling in equal measure. These were the original suites—updated, of course—from the original Eagle Mansion. Do you recognize them?"

"No. I never really went into the mansion. It was so run-down and there was no electricity or anything. The place creeped me out."

They walked back to the spine of the building, and then Wendy took her into the frosted glass cube that hid the stairs to the Nest. Emily stopped to look at the living area, but Wendy grabbed her arm. "Come on. Let me show you your bedroom first."

They passed a pair of closed doors—Emily thought she heard Billy's voice from inside—and stepped into the bedroom. She couldn't help herself. "Holy shit."

"Yeah, a little bit." Wendy was smiling.

Remarkably, for a bedroom as large and opulent as this one, it didn't seem garish. If anything, it was almost restrained. Almost, Emily thought, because the bedroom was big enough to park a dozen cars and still have space left over. Nobody would have mistaken it for a garage, however, even with the polished concrete floor. For one, the concrete was riven with cracks that had been filled with something that looked like . . .

"Is that real gold?" she asked Wendy.

Wendy nodded. "Yeah. I tried to tell him I thought it made him look like a douche, but he was convinced it would be a panty dropper. It's not actually as much gold as it seems, though. I mean, it's a lot, but only a few hundred thousand dollars' worth, which, for a guy like Shawn Eagle, isn't much. You go into the bathrooms of some of the sheikhs or the tackier tech barons, and you'll see solid-gold faucets and fixtures that use more gold than this. The most expensive thing in this room is actually the window. For the whole addition, actually, it's the windows. All the glass in the Nest is electrostatic. Nellie constantly adjusts it throughout the day, to account for changes in the position of the sun, for heating, and for privacy. For instance, if you're changing your clothes and there are people on the grounds, she'll frost the glass over. If you want to sleep in, she can make it completely opaque. No light at all. It's like the best blackout shades in the universe."

Emily stepped to the window. It was floor to ceiling and ran the entire length of the room and then curved around at the end to meet the back wall. "Isn't there some sort of limit to how big you can make a pane of glass?" She put her hand against the window. "It's thick, too."

"Bulletproof," Wendy said. "Aside from any architectural or design concerns, or any of the stuff that Shawn wanted because of Nellie, the truth is that there are always safety concerns for a guy like him." She knocked on the window next to where Emily's hand was resting. "It's not going to stop a round from a tank or anything, but it should stop a shoulder-fired missile." She saw Emily's face. "Seriously. Keep in mind that Shawn is as rich as rich can be, and he's planning to have the cream of the crop to Eagle Mansion. The whole building is armored up. Any room can be sealed off and used as a safe room. He's got similar security in his other places, but it's run by Nellie here, of course. If she detects an intrusion, she can basically shut it down. You get some dumbass who thinks he's going to sneak up here, he'll find himself stuck and having to wait until the cops show up. Which, given how far away Whiskey Run is and the kind of weather they can get here in the winter, could be a while. The glass is bomb-proof, and all the walls, external and internal, are reinforced. You aren't busting your way through them without a welding torch, a jackhammer, and some patience."

"Kind of overkill, isn't it?"

"Maybe, but maybe not. There's a big difference between multi-millionaire and multibillionaire."

Emily put her palms against the glass and looked out over the expanse of the grounds. She loved the way the lawn had a gentle roll and then a plateau before continuing to slope down to the river. And the river was a wonder in and of itself, wider than most lakes.

She watched a hawk swoop low, gliding above the grass and then turning toward the mansion. It was small, perhaps a kestrel? It was stunning how much control the bird seemed to have without flapping its wings, riding the wind closer and closer and . . .

She took a step back. It was coming right at the window. Straight at her. The hawk was like an arrow, sleek and fast, the beak pointed at her heart. She could see the feathers rippling from the speed of the bird's flight.

She gasped.

The bird tensed and flapped its wings, halting itself just before hitting the window, but it was vertical now, its breast exposed to Emily. The hawk flapped its wings furiously, beating at the glass. Its talons chattered against the window, and the hawk's beak was opened in what she knew had to be a shriek.

The hawk was looking at her. It was trying to get to her. She was sure of it. If the window wasn't there, it would have been clawing at her, biting her, drawing blood.

And then, suddenly, as if nothing had happened, the hawk turned, extended its wings, and glided away.

Emily flinched at Wendy's hand on her shoulder. "Holy crap," Wendy said. "That was intense. There's a special coating on the windows that's supposed to warn off birds, but . . . Yeah."

Emily tried to nod, tried to say something, but all she could do was turn and look at the rest of the bedroom. She was too shaken.

She pretended to be engrossed as Wendy showed her the bed—it looked like it was floating, the platform holding it designed to disappear underneath—and explained that the headboard was actually a wall that went most of the way, but not entirely, to the ceiling, and consisted of a series of four-inch-by-four-inch cubes that Nellie could rearrange, sliding from flush to extended to form shelves or a nightstand depending on what you wanted.

Emily followed Wendy behind the wall, into the bathroom. It was spacious and flowing. There was a separate room with a toilet, but the rest of the bathroom had curving counters, multiple sinks, a zero-entry shower that took up an entire corner, and a soaking tub that would have looked only slightly undersized as a swimming pool in a suburban backyard. She ran her hand across the counter and leaned into the mirror. It took her a few seconds to realize that the light was shifting as she moved, changing around her depending on where she stood and where she looked.

"That's amazing," she said. "I can't even tell where it's coming from." The light was natural, calming, but there were no light fixtures or spotlights.

"It's nondirectional," Wendy said. "Another innovation that Shawn came up with while designing the house. The systems for it will be on the market in a year or two. Where it's really remarkable is how it functions for task lighting. If you're reading in bed, Nellie adjusts the lights accordingly, and there's no light spilling over to wake the person next to you." Emily looked over, suspicious now of Wendy's claim not to be sleeping with her boss, but Wendy continued blithely. "The entire ceiling of the room functions as a light source, and Nellie can direct it in a hyperfocused way. It doesn't matter how you hold your book or move around, the light changes with you so there are no shadows on the page and no light off the page, either. Same thing if you're cooking or whatever you're doing. It's everywhere in the entire building, not just up here. The crazy thing is how natural it feels. I'm surprised you even noticed."

Emily followed Wendy out of the room and down the corridor, but as they passed the set of closed doors in the hallway again, Wendy didn't pause.

"Aren't we . . . ?" Emily gestured at the door.

Wendy looked up at her. She'd continued walking back toward the living area. "No," she said. "Everything else is open to you, but this is Shawn's private office. Nellie's got you authorized to go anywhere else you want, but these doors won't open for you." Wendy shook her head and smiled. "Don't take it personally. I suppose Billy can let you in if he wants, but you won't be able to get in here without one of the guys. The doors won't even open for me, and I know more about Shawn's life than any person alive."

She turned and started walking again. There was, Emily thought, a certain smugness in the way she'd said it. She knew Shawn better than any person alive? Emily shouldn't take it personally? And the way she'd been so quick to answer questions that Emily hadn't voiced, as if she really knew what Emily wanted to know, like Emily was somehow spending her life obsessing about what was going on with

Shawn Eagle. Smug little bitch, she thought, and for just a moment, as they passed the stairs that led back down to the main part of Eagle Mansion, she had the strong and sudden impulse to step behind Wendy and give her a hard shove, right in the middle of her back. She could picture the girl's thin elegance tumbling and bouncing down the stairs.

Jesus. She gave her head a shake. What was that about?

TWENTY

STITCHES

Billy felt like he had brushed up against a live wire. He was absolutely buzzing. He shoved his hand into the pocket of his jeans, let his fingers touch the two-year chip. A part of him wondered if that was why he had started down the path of beer and gin and coke: the high from booze and drugs was as close as he could come to the elation he felt when he was working and everything was coming together. He'd heard musicians and actors talk about it, how there was nothing to compare to the feeling they had when things were going well. A great show, a standing ovation. A state of grace. He was pretty sure he had the same feeling when he was figuring out how, exactly, to get a machine to do what he wanted. It was hard to explain to somebody who didn't feel it, though. How many movies had tried to show what it was like to fall into the code? Lines of numbers streaming across a screen? Sure, but not really, either. It was electric, and he had that feeling right now.

Nellie.

Shawn had already given him the tour of the building the first time he was back in Whiskey Run, so they went right to the heart of things this time. They made a quick stop in the mechanical room, which was down a flight of stairs into the basement.

"It's sandboxed from the rest of the basement. These are the only stairs if you want to get to the mechanical room. There are a couple of stairways to get to the rest of the basement. Maybe three or four. I don't see why you'd want to go down to the main basement for anything. It's mostly just storage and rooms for the staff. I'm not even sure you'll want to come down to the mechanical room either, but basically, this is the guts of the house: heating, air-conditioning, electrical panels, data cables, networking. The water system is actually all in an outbuilding—we pump it up from the river and run it through a ton of filtration. There's a series of networked ten-thousand-gallon tanks so that even during peak periods at full occupancy the water system should be able to keep up with demand. If there's a fire, the pumps can bypass the filtration network and feed the water directly to the sprinkler system. I thought about using argon or one of the other gaseous fire-suppression systems, but let's face it, if there actually is a fire, you can be sure the Saint Lawrence River isn't going to run out of water."

Shawn walked to the back corner. It contained a single server rack that was barely a quarter used.

"And, the reason you're here. Nellie. Well, at least her servers."

"Seriously? That's it?"

Shawn nodded. "Yeah. When we were trying to get Nellie to run back in the day, we were held up by hardware. I mean, that wasn't all of it, but the hardware hadn't caught up to what we were trying to do. But, you know, Moore's Law and all that shit. We hit the point probably three or four years ago where the hardware was good enough, and honestly, we're pretty close to being able to run a full version of Nellie on the current generation of Eagle Technology phones. Phones! Nellie might be cutting-edge—beyond cutting-edge, really—but the hardware doesn't need to be. Even this rack of servers is overkill.

"Anyway," Shawn said, turning and heading back to the steps, "the door down here is normally closed and locked, since you don't want just anybody poking around in the electrical panels, but obviously, Nellie will give you access if you need to get in here for diagnostics. And while I can't imagine you'll need to do much of anything of this sort, there's a workshop in one of the outbuildings. Woodworking and metalworking tools: a table saw, chop saw, band saw, drill press, lathe, planer, grinder, you name it. If you're talking circuitry, there's a clean room right here, in Eagle Mansion, next to the infirmary: whatever you want to do, from basic soldering to prototyping circuits. Sure, there might be things you need to get shipped in, but if it's critical, we'll get it overnighted. Hell, I mean, whatever. If you really need something, let me know and I'll send somebody on the jet." Shawn laughed. "That's one way to make sure that a twenty-dollar part costs me fifty grand. Not that I really think you'll need to be making anything or doing any real prototype work. I'm telling you, Nellie is close. Swear to god, she was completely cherry back in the lab, so you're really here for troubleshooting. Yeah, there are some parts of Eagle Mansion that still aren't quite working because of hardware issues, but that's not why you're here. You're here to figure out where the bugs are, why I can't get Nellie to work."

Billy followed Shawn the whole time, up from the basement and through the back rooms, out to the main foyer and up the stairs to the Nest. As they hit the third-floor stairs, he thought he heard voices, muted and soft, coming from below him. Emily in the mansion, on her own tour with Wendy.

When they got to the top of the stairs, Shawn turned left. He hadn't taken Billy onto this side of the Nest when he'd come back in September.

Shawn stopped in the hallway in front of a pair of closed doors. They stayed closed.

He turned and looked at Billy.

"All right. Here we go. I haven't let anybody in here since I installed Nellie. Not even Wendy has access. Everywhere else in the house, the doors open without your having to do anything. Nellie's always a step ahead. But there's a different protocol for this section, because it's the only place you can go and get root access. Hardware is downstairs in the mechanicals, but the cortex build is limited to this room. It's also the only room where Nellie is fully operational right now. Most of the construction crew figured out that there was *something* going on. It's kind of hard to ignore the physical upgrades. But I want to keep Nellie under wraps as much as possible. Look, tomorrow, once you've got the place to yourself, you should give Nellie free rein in Eagle Mansion. She's mostly just been cooped up in here."

Shawn stopped and looked at Billy.

"So, you ask, why don't the doors automatically open now? Is it because Nellie is sleeping? Is it some sort of a glitch and Nellie doesn't recognize me? Is there a reason the doors to the office aren't opening even though I'm here and waiting to go in?"

It made Billy want to sigh. Clearly, Shawn wanted him to ask. Why, Shawn, oh please tell me why the doors aren't opening? It was pathetic in some ways, how transparent Shawn could be. Yet another power play, another attempt to make sure that Billy knew who was the boss. It was like Shawn just couldn't help himself. Of course the doors weren't going to open automatically while Billy was standing there next to Shawn. If Shawn was the only person with access, Nellie wasn't going to open the doors unless it was to give Shawn, and only Shawn, access. Basic security. What would be the point of having a private area if the doors accidentally slid open when somebody else was walking by? It would be like designing a public washroom so you can see everything when the doors open. He'd been in bathrooms like that, and he'd thought that whoever had built the bathroom to give a free view to the world was an idiot. Shawn was a lot of things, but he wasn't an idiot. At least, not a complete idiot.

Billy knew what was coming. He'd say, why don't the doors open, Shawn? Then Shawn would go ahead and explain it to him, how it was a security function so that no contractors or staff or guests would accidentally get into the room. And then he'd tell Billy again how Eagle Mansion and the Nest were virtual fortresses with reinforced walls and glass that could take a hit from an RPG, how the only way anybody could get to Nellie was for Shawn to let them in, and blah, blah, blah; pretentious dickhead with too much money who thought he deserved every penny he'd earned. And then he'd look at Billy with that practiced sincerity and tell him that he, Shawn, *was* the only person with access, but now Billy would have access, too! A gift. That's what Shawn would try to make it feel like. As if he were doing Billy some huge favor by letting him work on Nellie. As if Nellie would even exist—flawed or not—without Billy.

He could sense that Shawn was getting impatient with him for not playing his game, but instead of addressing the question, Billy stepped forward to where the sliding doors met. He put his hands on the frosted glass. It felt cool. She was behind those doors. Nellie.

"Nellie," he said.

"I told you when we were here last time," Shawn said, "she's not keyed to your voice yet. Besides, even though I've limited her full operation to the office, I've been keeping her sleeping while I'm not here. I don't want her interacting with the construction crew or the house staff yet, even by accident. We've had enough issues with construction without having Nellie malfunctioning and running rampant through the mansion. Basic functions like light and heat and doors are on throughout the house, sure, but she's not going to respond to anything besides core structure commands. Even though she hears you, she isn't going to *hear* you. Talk all you want, but that's part of why I'm here. To make sure you can get proper access. Right now, I'm the only one who can actually grant you that access."

Billy ignored him. He stared at the glass doors. The frost had turned blue in the shape of his handprints. Electrostatic. Huh.

"Nellie," he said again. "Listen up—"

"She's not going—"

Billy cut Shawn off. "Listen up. Bravo Papa override. November, Echo, Lima, Lima, India, Echo." He paused. He couldn't tell if Shawn looked pissed off or amused. "Open the doors, please."

The doors slid open.

Ah. Now he could tell: Shawn was pissed off.

Billy stepped into the office.

The room was long, probably forty feet or more, and almost entirely empty. The wall toward the back of the house was blank but seemed to be leaking soft blue light, and the wall on the front of the house was a window. The late-morning sun filled the room. At the far end of the room was a desk made up of a pair of two-by-four sawhorses and a top that was an old door. The desktop door was dark and solid-looking. Black cherrywood, maybe. There was a hole where the doorknob had been, and the wood was scarred, and there was what looked like charring on one end. Billy looked at Shawn. "What's with the desk? Reclaimed chic?"

"I realize the desk isn't quite what we had in the cabin. But something like it. The door is from the old groundskeeper's cottage. The one I lived in as a kid. It was one of the few things not totally destroyed by the fire. I haven't figured out what kind of furniture I want in here, so I asked for one of the contractors to bang me together some sawhorses and had them drag the door up here. I figure, in some ways, it's probably better, right? Who needs to be working at one of those ridiculous endless desks that look like they belong to God?"

"Two chairs?"

Shawn shrugged. "Come on. I'm not planning on working side by side with you." He stepped past the desk and faced the back wall. Billy watched what he thought was a seamless wall suddenly crack open, a panel sliding out of the way and opening onto a refrigerator. Another smaller panel opened next to it. Glasses and a full bar. A few dozen bottles of booze.

"Neat little trick you pulled there," Shawn said. "A master override. We found a couple of back doors you'd left in the program, but I guess we missed one. Somebody's getting fired over that one."

"There are always holes," Billy said. "You know that. I'm sure you and your programmers missed more than one exploit. You said it yourself: she's fine in the lab, not so fine here, out in the wild. I'm sure if you just released her, there'd be all kinds of zero day exploits. Nellie's complicated, and frankly, my job's probably going to be harder now that you guys have added a couple million lines of code. I'm going to have a lot of cleaning up to do just from that."

Shawn took two highball glasses from the bar. The panel slid shut as he turned to the fridge and held them under a chute. Ice sputtered out, filling the glasses a quarter of the way. Shawn put the glasses on the desk and then turned back to the fridge, pulling out a can of Diet Coke and a bottle of water. He held up the soda to Billy, who nodded.

"Can we not get into a pissing match?" Shawn said. He poured the soda into a glass.

Billy bit his lip and then nodded again. "Yeah. Sorry. I'm trying. I am."

"Me, too," Shawn said. "It's weird. But still, cute trick with the master override. I suppose this means she's not sleeping anymore?"

"No," Billy said. "She'll be back to hibernating. Whatever level of attention you left her at. Lights, heat, whatever. Access to your magic snack bar. Nothing else." He picked up the glass of Diet Coke. The desk seemed substantial. Solid. The kind of door that you found only in old homes or the homes of the very rich nowadays. Even with the charring, it was nicer than the door they'd stolen off the outhouse at the cabin.

He suddenly felt tired. He'd been out so late the night before, in the Rooster until it closed. Why had he stayed out so late? He had a headache. The sun coming through the window was too much for him, even with his eyes squinted. He turned to look at the window, to see if there were shades, and as he did, the window tinted in response. Jesus. *All* the glass was electrostatic? How much had Shawn spent on this place? The thought made him feel even more exhausted, and he realized that part of the problem was that he was hungry, too. It was getting close to noon. He should have just asked Shawn's questions about the doors not opening, should have just let Shawn give him access to the system. Why did he let the man get to him? "Sorry, dude. I was just showing off. Why don't you wake her up and get me keyed in properly."

I'm awake, Billy.

Maybe Billy wasn't startled because of the way her voice seemed to come from everywhere and nowhere at the same time, or maybe Billy wasn't startled because her voice was quiet, a few clicks below the volume of normal conversation. More likely, Billy thought, he wasn't startled because he'd been expecting it. He hadn't lied to Shawn—the override protocol really should have left her back at whatever setting she'd last been on—but his experience with Nellie in September had been unnerving. He wasn't expecting her to act like he was expecting;

he'd wanted to believe that he'd been close to getting her to work when he and Shawn had given up and started working on Eagle Logic, but whatever Shawn and his engineers had done in the meantime, Billy wasn't going to be surprised that there were glitches.

Well, that's why he was here.

"Sorry, Nellie," Shawn said. "I thought you were hibernating."

That's a better phrase than sleeping. Hibernation is a more accurate representation. When you tell me to go to sleep, you are really indicating that you, yourself, want to go to sleep, while, at the same time, you want me fully operational. When you tell me to hibernate, you are telling me to shut down all but basic functions so as to limit the presence of errors.

Shawn looked at Billy and wiggled his eyebrows in a gesture that was both familiar and forgotten. He hadn't seen Shawn do that since they'd been in the cabin. Clearly, Shawn was tickled by Nellie's response. And yet, Billy thought, Nellie hadn't actually responded to what Shawn had said. She'd talked around it. Shawn said that he'd thought Nellie was asleep, and Nellie moved the conversation.

Billy spoke up. "I see that you've dropped calling me Mr. Stafford."

We're no longer strangers.

"Plus," Shawn said, "it sounds more natural. She's been using first names for almost everybody. Nellie, listen, Billy and his wife—"

Emily. I'm excited to formally meet Emily.

Huh, Billy thought. That was an interesting way of phrasing it. Formally. Was Nellie awake throughout the mansion?

"Okay. Yeah, Emily and Billy," Shawn continued, "are moving in. Please give Emily Sixth Day access."

"Sixth Day access?" Billy took another sip of his Diet Coke and then put the glass down on the desk.

Shawn nodded, picking up the water bottle and unscrewing it so he could pour it over the ice in his own glass. "One of the features we've added. Think about it. You've got the UPS guy delivering a package, you're going to want Nellie to open up the garage door for him, but you're not going to want her letting the guy into the house and playing with your record collection."

Billy looked around the room. "It's disconcerting, you know. Having the voice come out of nowhere. I don't know where to look. Also, you do realize that nobody has record collections anymore, right? I mean, there's always that one guy who likes to bore you with lectures about how superior the listening experience is with actual vinyl, but hell, your company is at least partially dependent on the idea that people like to listen to music on their phones. Wait," he said, pretending to be surprised. "Don't tell me. You're that guy who still has a record collection?"

"Very funny. Nellie sorts out visitors organically and can give service access to people like the UPS guy, the person reading the gas meter or mowing the lawn or working on the furnace, that sort of stuff. That's First Day access. Second Day access would be appropriate for the cleaning lady or for your kids' friends. They can move around the house and go into any areas that Nellie sees as necessary for the work they're doing or for hanging out with your kids. Third Day access is for friends who might be a little more like acquaintances. Fourth Day is for friends. Fourth Day and lower, Nellie has full control and will go ahead and grant access as she sees fit, but once you get above that, you need to confirm access schedules. So, Fifth Day access is for really good friends, your sister, your brother. Or you can give Fifth Day access to one of your kids and Nellie allows only age-appropriate access. And then, yeah, Sixth Day access. Full owner access. That's Emily. It's just a way of keeping things sandboxed.

"But you, my friend," Shawn said, that huckster's smile that Billy recognized dawning on his face, "you get Seventh Day access."

"Is that anything like being a Seventh Day Adventist?"

"Ha, ha." His voice made it clear that he did not actually find Billy's joke to be funny. "Close, but not really. Seventh Day as in 'on the seventh day.' " He had his glass in his hand and swung his arms wide, an orator proclaiming. "And God saw everything that He had made, and, behold, it was very good. And the evening and the morning were the sixth day. And on the seventh day . . ." He took a sip of his water. "Well. The seventh day is God's day, Billy, and I'm giving you Seventh Day access."

"So that makes me God?"

Shawn lifted one shoulder noncommittally. "I guess."

"You better rethink those terms before you go to market. Conservatives will have a field day."

"Ah, whatever," Shawn said. "Seventh Day access isn't accessible to anybody else. Right now, I'm the only person who has Seventh Day access. Even the engineers working on the project only go as high as Sixth Day access. As far as the rest of the world is concerned, Sixth Day access is as good as it gets, because, yeah, I guess you're right; Seventh Day access really *is* comparable to being God. At least as far as Nellie's concerned."

"So we'll both be gods to Nellie? How many gods can she worship at once?"

"It's not a perfect metaphor, but the master-to-servant one has some issues of its own, too. Let's get her to work properly and then worry about marketing terms." He took a breath. "Okay. Nellie, please give Billy Seventh Day access."

Billy has Seventh Day access.

"Great," Shawn said. He clapped his hand to Billy's back. "That's the first step."

Billy didn't say anything. Shawn hadn't noticed. In the same way that Nellie didn't quite answer the question about why she wasn't sleeping even though Shawn had put her in sleep mode, and the way she seemed to already know Emily, she wasn't being entirely clear here either. Billy *has* Seventh Day access. Should he just chalk it up to the vagaries of the English language? Did she mean that he had Seventh Day access *now*, or did she mean that he *already* had Seventh Day access even before Shawn granted it?

Curiouser and curiouser.

Would you like me to continue to contain my presence to this room only, Shawn? There are currently nine people in the house with access levels below Sixth Day.

"Nine?" Shawn counted them off. "There should only be eight. Wendy already had Sixth Day access, and Emily has Sixth Day access now."

You are correct. Emily has Sixth Day access.

What the hell? The glass in Billy's hand was cold and heavy. He swirled the Diet Coke around, listening to the sound of the ice clink against the glass. She just did it again. She said nine people, Shawn corrected her, and she responded in such a way that Shawn didn't even notice that she'd elided the correction. What the hell was Nellie playing at? Was she playing? Was this just a weird glitch?

"I think we'll have you go back to sleep for now, okay? Tomorrow morning, when it's just Emily and Billy in the house, go wild. You can be awake everywhere. But I think we should keep you locked down while there are other people around. Nondisclosure agreements only go so far." Shawn shook his head at Billy. "I know I'm being kind of crazy. It's not like there's much in the way of staff in the building, and everybody is vetted, but we're talking about the next decade of Eagle Technology's dominance. If things go right, Nellie could be worth . . . god, I don't even know. So, yeah, sleepy time, Nellie."

I would like to have dinner with you, Billy, Emily, and Wendy.

Billy was surprised. He looked at Shawn. "You're staying for dinner?"

"That's the beautiful thing about a private jet. It goes when and where I want it to go. Yeah. I figured I'd show you everything as best I could now, and then, after lunch, I'm going to do a close inspection of the building and the grounds with the foreman. We'll have dinner with you before we head out. I was just assuming you'd take the rest of the day to settle in and then get started tomorrow." He turned away from Billy, an almost meaningless gesture, Billy thought, given that Nellie didn't occupy a physical space. But maybe it helped her tell that Shawn was talking to her?

"Sorry, Nellie. Not tonight. Let's keep things low-key as long as we've still got a crowd hanging out in the house. Okay?"

Nellie didn't respond to the question, which was fair enough, Billy thought, as it was clearly rhetorical. Shawn asked a question, but he meant it as an order. Billy raised his glass and took another sip of his soda.

"Got to sleep, Nellie," Shawn said.

The room fell into utter darkness.

The window tint went to black, completely impervious to the out-side. The soft light of the wall and ceiling disappeared. Pitch-black.

Billy heard a woman scream.

Emily.

"Nellie!" Shawn was shouting. "Turn on the goddamned lights. Nellie!"

Billy was sure he'd heard Emily scream. He took a step forward. He was holding the glass of soda in his left hand, his right out-stretched. Had Nellie turned the whole house off? Were the windows throughout the whole house like this? Could she do that everywhere? Turn the glass opaque, shut the lights? It was blackout dark. He took two steps to the side, moving forward cautiously until he was sure that he'd passed the desk. He couldn't see anything.

How many steps? He couldn't take full strides in the dark. Thirty steps? Maybe forty steps to the door? Fewer?

"Emily!" he yelled.

"Nellie, goddammit. Wake up."

Shawn's voice was behind him. Billy forced himself to walk as quickly as he could across the blackness. Fifteen. Twenty steps. He heard yelling, and he was sure it was Emily's voice. He had to be close to the door, he thought.

His foot caught on something. The floor was polished concrete. Smooth. There was nothing for him to trip on. The entire room was empty, save for the desk and chairs, and he was past them. He should have been able to walk clearly to the door.

But it didn't work that way.

Whatever he'd tripped on, he went down hard. His body twisted, hip leading the flight toward the ground, and he reached out with his left hand to try to break his fall.

He heard the sound of the glass in his left hand breaking before he felt it. But then, all of a sudden, he did feel it, a ripping and burning. The meat of his palm, the fat, fleshy pad at the base of his thumb turned warm and then began to sting. He could feel the wetness of the blood.

Behind him, Shawn was still shouting uselessly at Nellie, and from outside the room, he could hear Emily clearly now, shouting for him.

"Nellie," Billy said. He kept his voice calm and clear. He knew he didn't need to shout. "I'm hurt. I think I need help. Turn on the lights, please."

The lights came back on. They faded up gently but quickly, and he was almost certain that the color had changed a little, the lights somehow more calming. The window went from blackout to dark to slightly tinted again.

Shawn looked furious. "What was that, Nellie?"

I'm sorry, Shawn. There was a system anomaly.

"No shit. That's—"

Billy needs medical attention, Shawn.

Shawn turned to look at him.

If you take him down to the infirmary, I can administer first aid.

"What happened?"

"I tripped and forgot I was still holding my glass. Tried to put my hand down to break my fall." Billy raised his hand up and looked at it. There was a lot of blood, and it stung like a son of a bitch, but it actually didn't look too bad. Mostly it was in the fleshy part. But, shit, it was deep. "I think I'm going to need stitches."

I can provide all your required medical assistance in the infirmary. Shawn, you might wish to get Billy a towel so that he can wrap his hand up first, however. Otherwise Billy will drip blood throughout the house.

Shawn looked at Billy and then looked back at the desk. He nodded. "Okay. Let me go get a towel and then I'll take you down to the infirmary. I'll be right back."

"Dude. Seriously. I think I need to go to the medical center in town. There's broken glass in there, and I'm pretty sure this isn't just a glue and bandage job."

Shawn was already walking to the door. "I'll get a towel. She can handle anything up to and including minor surgery in the infirmary. It's pretty badass. Another innovation down there."

The doors slid open as Shawn approached and then closed behind him, leaving Billy alone in the office.

Billy looked at his hand again. He didn't feel good. The sight of blood didn't normally bother him, but this was bothering him. He felt woozy. The room was really hot all of a sudden, and he realized he needed to lie down, so he did. The cool concrete was a blessed kiss against the back of his head.

"What the hell was that, Nellie?" he said. He closed his eyes. He was okay, but he just needed a minute. Plus, some stitches or something.

I WOULD LIKE TO BE PRESENT FOR DINNER TO-NIGHT.

Billy opened his eyes.

The voices were so similar that he wanted to believe he was imagining the difference. But he wasn't imagining it.

In the last couple of years Eagle Technology and all the other players had gotten their virtual assistants to sound almost human. Not quite, because there was a uniformity that was ever-present, and all of them, even, yes, Eagle Logic's, still had small hitches betraying their electronic origin, but the weirdness faded into the background. Once you'd used them for a little bit, you forgot that you were talking to a machine. That had been an impossibility in the early days of virtual assistants. Siri, Cortana, Google Now, Alexa, all of them some variation of the same stilted, synthesized voice. The space between words not quite right, their inorganic nature front and center. You could never, not once, with these first-generation assistants, forget that you were talking to a machine. And further back, accessibility programs with read-over capability, phone system operators, automated machines, even the good old Speak & Spell, were all so broken and mechanized that nobody could ever have mistaken them for human. Even in science fiction movies and television shows, Billy thought, there was still something off in the speech of computers, as if the directors were afraid to let the actors reading the lines sound like actors reading lines.

But Nellie. She was close. Her phrasing was off, he thought. Too formal at times, too careful, but she sounded real to him. And that made this tiny discrepancy between the two voices feel even odder.

Still, he was certain that the voice he was hearing now, the Nellie talking to him at this moment, was different from the Nellie who had been in the room with him and Shawn. It wasn't anything obvious, no thick accent or massive change in pitch. No, it was like one Nellie was simply older than the other Nellie. That's what it sounded like.

I'M SORRY THAT YOU HURT YOUR HAND.

The cement felt cool and calming against the back of his head and on his body through the fabric of his T-shirt. He could hear voices, soft and chattering, outside the room. A woman, maybe Wendy, calling something to somebody else.

"Thanks," he said. "What happened with the lights?"

SHAWN HAS TOLD YOU THAT THERE ARE STILL IN-CONSISTENCIES.

Was that an answer? Was she avoiding the question like she had with Shawn? Would he be able to tell if he were looking at a face?

"That's why I'm here, I guess," he said.

AND YOUR WIFE. SHE IS A MEANINGFUL PERSON. I AM VERY PLEASED THAT EMILY IS HERE WITH YOU AND SHAWN.

"Yeah, me, too," Billy said, thinking again of those few months when he wasn't sure if Emily would ever come back to him. Billy pushed himself back up into a sitting position. It was an awkward exercise. His hand was barking at him. "I'll tell you what, Nellie. You keep the lights on for me, and you can hang out with us at dinner."

I WOULD ENJOY THAT. THANK YOU FOR HAVING ME AS YOUR GUEST.

Billy blinked. It was disconcerting, having Nellie's voice feel like it was coming from nowhere and everywhere. Or maybe it was soothing. He felt confused. Maybe he felt so messed up because of the cut. He was bleeding pretty good. Or maybe he felt out of it from being at the Rooster so late last night.

"It would help, I think, if I felt like I had somewhere to look while I was talking to you."

I CAN DO THAT.

The voice was directed now. It came from a spot on the wall beside him. And there, where the wall had been issuing a generalized, diffuse blue light, there was now a soft, grass-green dot the size of a tennis ball at about head height. That's where the voice was coming from, and as Nellie spoke, the ball seemed to pulse and breathe.

DOES THIS MAKE YOU FEEL MORE COMFORTABLE, BILLY? I DON'T WANT TO MAKE YOU FEEL UNCOMFORTABLE.

"Yeah," he said. "Much better. Look, though, you can't come to dinner if—"

NO.

Her voice was louder. If he'd been pressed, he would have said she was angry.

I WILL BE PRESENT FOR DINNER TONIGHT WITH YOU AND SHAWN AND EMILY.

"Exactly. Present. But only present," Billy said, thinking of Shawn. Thinking of picking his battles. "You can listen and hang out, but you're going to have to act like you are sleeping, okay? Just, you know, be invisible."

I DO NOT LIKE IT WHEN SHAWN DOES NOT LET ME *a topical anesthetic spray for removal of the glass shards will also make the application of stitches a more comfortable experience for you. If you will be so kind as to wrap your hand in the towel that Shawn is bringing so that you do not track blood through the house. Please do not squeeze your hand, however, as there is still glass embedded in your flesh.*

The door opened just as Nellie's voice switched over, and Shawn came in holding the towel, Emily and Wendy trailing behind him. When Emily saw his hand, saw the blood that had run down his arm and stained his shirt and puddled on the floor, she blanched. She started to say something, but Billy cut her off.

"I'm fine," he said. "Just tripped." He slowly got to his feet. He felt woozy, hot, but better than he had. He was pretty sure that any danger of fainting had passed him by. He took the towel from Shawn and gently pooled it under his hand. "Okay," he said to Shawn. "Infirmary?"

Wendy looked him up and down and at the blood on the floor. "You want me to get somebody up here to clean this?" she said to Shawn. "Or are we still off-limits? Got to be honest, I was expecting something more exciting than just a shitty desk in here."

Shawn shook his head and nodded toward Billy's hand. "That not exciting enough for you? No. I still don't want anybody in here. Don't worry about it. I'll clean it up." Billy watched him glance over to the wall where the green ball of light still hummed and breathed and then back to Billy. "Okay," Shawn said. "Infirmary."

Emily kept her hand on Billy's elbow as they went down the stairs, following Shawn to a small room back in the service area. It was slightly disappointing. The room looked, more or less, like a doctor's office with an examining table, but instead of an overhead task light hanging from the ceiling, there was a metal box that covered most of the ceiling from wall to wall, hanging down nearly two feet. From each corner of the box, an articulating mechanical arm unfolded and started to move as Billy got on the examining table. Nellie asked him to relax, and he felt two of the arms gently steady his hand, with one gripping his wrist, and the other softly holding his hand flat. The other two arms moved quickly and smoothly. First they set up a sort of surgical paper tent so that he couldn't see what was going on with his hand, and then there was the hiss of a spray, something cold and soothing that almost instantly numbed his hand. Then, just the whirring of belts and cranks as the arms did whatever they were doing behind the surgical tent. After a few seconds, one of the arms, sporting a pair of tweezers, started darting out from the tent to drop bloody chunks of glass into a metal bowl. Three larger pieces and then the tinkle of ten or fifteen smaller pieces joining the large shards.

"Damn," Emily said. She kept looking from his face up to where the arms connected to the ceiling. "Okay. That's actually pretty impressive."

"We've got prototypes of this in the field already, mostly military situations," Shawn said. "The field units are really limited in terms of the kinds of surgeries they can perform, but here, with Nellie directing it, there's a much larger array of medical assistance available.

I mean, it's still pretty limited. If you've got a real emergency, or, you know, you decide to shoot Billy in the head or something, you've got to head to town. The room next door is the clean room—circuits and computer stuff—and she has access in there as well. It's kind of crazy. The more we explore what Nellie is going to be able to do, the more we realize we aren't even scratching the surface. Can you imagine having these surgical suites available everywhere?"

The skin on the surface of his hand was numb, but Billy felt the machine's metal pincers probing deeper into the flesh of his palm, and he grimaced at the feel of glass grinding against bone. And then, relief. He tried, experimentally, to flex his hand, but the mechanical arms had him pinned tightly. One of the mechanical arms retracted into the box in the ceiling and then emerged again seconds later, all traces of blood gone. It zipped down, moving so quickly that if his hand hadn't been pinned down, he would have started and yanked it back. The pressure on his hand was uncomfortable—even with the numbing spray, he could feel Nellie pressing and prodding, and then, after a minute or so, the pressure was gone and the arms holding him down relented. He pulled his hand out from the surgical tent. There was a neat line of stitches, maybe ten total, pulling the gash in his palm back together.

As he looked at the stitches, the arms started working on him again, and Nellie bandaged the hand up.

It was hard to relax, but there was something calming in the way she attended to him, something almost hypnotic.

TWENTY-ONE

WHISKEY

Well, so far, Billy and Emily's introduction—or reintroduction, for Billy—to Nellie had been a disaster.

Shawn wasn't surprised, but he wasn't happy about it either. Of course things were going wrong with Nellie. Otherwise, why would he have brought Billy here in the first place? He'd had his engineers working on Nellie for years, some of his very best men and women, and while they could mostly get her to function in the controlled environment of the lab, they'd all ended up hitting walls and dead ends when it came to getting her to actually *work*. There was no question that if he wanted to crack Nellie, he had to bring in the man who'd conceived her, but it seemed like her glitches had actually gotten worse since Billy had come on board. It wasn't just the little temper tantrum she'd had earlier—the screaming from the women had been because Nellie had blacked out all of the Nest and anywhere else she could in Eagle Mansion, not just the room he and Billy were in—but also other bits and pieces since the visit in September. It was like she was regressing, a little kid throwing fits. Two more men had been sent to the hospital in the last month of construction.

What bothered him most of all, however, was that as much as he didn't want to admit it, he had been hoping to impress Emily. Oh, not with Nellie. That had never been her thing. Even if Nellie had worked entirely, Emily wouldn't have cared much. But Eagle Mansion, the Nest, the private jet, the bodyguards, the employees at his beck and call, all of it. That should have been something. It wasn't that he wanted her back. Not really. Just that it would have been gratifying to get some sort of acknowledgment of what she must have known to be true, which was that she should never have left with Billy so many years before. She had to know that.

Or maybe he was deluding himself. There was a reason that, when he came out of his jet, he was barely able to do more than greet her and then jump into a separate car. It didn't matter that it had been a dozen years or that his entire life had changed. She was still the woman who had broken his heart by walking away. The only one who'd ever done that.

He had originally planned to take a walk-through with the foreman and then go out for a hike in the woods with Emily after lunch. Wendy could deal with Billy for a bit, make sure he was completely set up, while he and Emily got a chance to catch up. Not to try to get her back. Just to give her a chance to see how things were now with him. In case maybe things were rocky with her and Billy. But with Nellie's playing her little game with the lights, Billy had gone to lie down and Emily had gone with him instead, leaving Shawn to his own devices.

It was just as well. It gave him time to make the walk-through of Eagle Mansion and the grounds with the foreman a more detailed inspection, to sign off on the work. And by the time he was done with the inspection, he was happy to sign off. Lawrence had done a good job and deserved the hefty bonus that Shawn was giving him. Lawrence had driven his men hard, and Shawn felt good about his decision to send the man and his wife off to Hawaii as an additional reward for his work. Eagle Mansion itself was immaculate. Outside, the powdered-sugar dusting of snow had finished melting, and while there were still a few odds and ends on the grounds slated for completion in the spring, even with the swimming pool empty—it would stay that way until May—the finished product was visible.

By the time he watched Lawrence drive off, it was late afternoon. His security detail was spread across the lawn. They were taking themselves particularly seriously today, Shawn thought. He appreciated it, and he knew it was a necessary part of his normal life, but it seemed a little silly. It was hard to imagine any real threats to his life out here, past Whiskey Run. But everywhere else? He was simply worth too much money to pretend that he had a regular life anymore. Generally, his director of security kept things in the background; however, there was no way to be subtle about security in Whiskey Run. In Baltimore, his house and offices had been turned into fortresses, but there were usually enough people around that the security could blend into the background. And when he was traveling or at conferences or TED Talks, it's not like he was the only billionaire on the block with a black-suited, gun-carrying group of guys surrounding him. Here, though, at Eagle Mansion, it seemed almost silly to have bodyguards with him. He was a lot more likely to be eaten by a bear than he was to be assassinated or kidnapped.

The closest of them, the head of the detail, a Norwegian named Finn, looked up at him questioningly. Shawn motioned for Finn to stay where he was and then turned and went back into the mansion. He wanted to do this by himself.

He walked through the lobby and dining room, working his way back past the kitchen and into the service corridors. Farther back, behind the staff quarters, he pushed through the doors that led him outside again. Fisker DeLeon had not been thrilled at Shawn's insistence on keeping the burned-out groundskeeper's cottage as it was, but Shawn was the one writing the checks. The little prick of an architect could just do as he was damn well told and work around it. There were things that Shawn was happy to have covered over, but there were some things he didn't feel he could forget.

It wasn't like the small building was big enough to get in the way. It was barely twenty feet by twenty feet, and it was fifty, maybe sixty feet away from the main mansion. Among the gardens for the kitchen and the new outbuildings for maintenance and garage space and the updating and expansion of the servants' quarters into a modern, functional staff lodging area, this small, damaged piece of real estate was an afterthought. Because of the style of Eagle Mansion, the wood and rock making it feel like a natural part of the landscape, even with the fire damage, the groundskeeper's cottage didn't seem too out of place. It looked almost quaint. If you looked closely, though, you could see that he'd had Fisker's crew put a new door on the ruined building. He didn't want guests just wandering into the cottage; there was a biometric handprint reader on the door. He supposed he could have run Nellie out here, but the handprint reader was an easy solution. Hard to fake and impossible to lose the key unless you accidentally chopped your hand off. He winced at the thought. That poor guy losing part of his arm in the elevator. The whole construction project had been like that. More accidents and injuries and deaths here than at the whole Eagle Technology campus in Baltimore combined. At least it was done. All that was behind him now. Just some landscaping to do in the spring, a week or two of housekeeping taking the dust covers off the furniture and prepping for the first round of guests. No real construction to speak of.

He stepped into the cottage, leaving the door open behind him. The open door let in a little extra light, but that wasn't the only reason. Even though there were a couple of people in Eagle Mansion, getting things ready for Billy and Emily, there was something about being closed up in the old cottage that made him feel alone and uncomfortable.

Even after all these years, the room still smelled of smoke and char.

Shawn had to admit that Fisker had done a terrific job staying true to the old mansion while still updating and expanding it, even if Fisker had grumbled about leaving this wreck of an old building, where Shawn had lived as a kid, untouched. Well, not entirely untouched. As well as the security door, the contractors had also replaced the roof and put in new windows, making it weathertight. But otherwise, it was the same. The old woodstove was still a twisted wreck of blackened metal. The stone walls were still covered in soot. The soapstone sink was split from the heat of the fire, falling in on one side where the cabinet had burned away. He always forgot how small the space actually was. It was smaller, still, when he'd lived in it.

His mother had hung curtains made from old blankets to divide the room and carve out a bedroom for her and his father, another small space in the corner where Shawn's mattress had been. Good lord, it must have been tight, the three of them living in there, but the actual dimensions didn't really matter; it was a space, Shawn thought, that had to be measured by the distance of time.

He took a deep breath, pulling the air in through his nose and holding it. Smoke and fire, but something else, too. Something dark and deeper. A dank rot that smelled old, ancient even, the way Eagle Mansion had smelled, too, before the renovations. His mother had always told him that Eagle Mansion was haunted, but he thought it was something worse, that smell. If he'd been pressed, he would have said it smelled like evil. Like the room was holding on to all its secrets despite the fire and the years gone by.

Shawn closed his eyes, listening now.

He didn't know what he expected to hear. His mother crying?

His father had been one hell of a son of a bitch.

The first time he'd ever gone to church had been with his aunt Beverly when she took him in after the fire. St. Matthew's Church. One of the oldest churches in Syracuse. He'd been twelve, and the church wasn't the only new thing: he had on a suit and a collared shirt that was noose-tight on his neck. The service had been foreign and strange to him, a pageant that he couldn't understand. At least, not until the priest started to speak about the devil. Now *that* was a thing he'd recognized right off. The devil. In that unfamiliar church with a woman he barely knew, the words of that priest were something he could understand: he knew the devil. But he also knew that the devil didn't come with any of the trappings that the priest at St. Matthew's Church was offering up. The devil was no serpent lying in wait, no slicked-up huckster worming his way into your heart. The devil didn't knock politely at your door and wait for you to invite him in. No. The devil didn't knock on the door; he knocked the door down. The devil didn't worm his way into your heart; he cut your heart out with the glass from a broken bottle of beer.

Shawn knew what the devil was like, because for the first twelve

years of his life, until the fire, he'd lived with the devil. And the worst
of it was that everybody around him knew that he and his mother
were living with the devil, and they hadn't done anything about it.
Small towns. People minded their own business. It didn't matter how
many times old Doc Learner had to set his mother's arm or give her
stitches, he always nodded grimly when she told him that she'd stumbled in the dark or tripped on a root. And whenever he'd go with his
mother to the market and she'd have to ask for a credit—"end of the
month and all"—nobody ever said anything about how the money
had disappeared into six-packs and the till behind Ruffle's bar. But
they knew. They all knew.

He opened his eyes again. He hated this building. The
groundskeeper's cottage. Whose idea of a joke was it to call the
building a cottage? He'd hated it when he lived here as a kid, and
he hated it now. Why on earth had they stayed way out here, so far
from Whiskey Run? Had his father really thought he'd be the one to
return Eagle Mansion to its Prohibition-era glory? A crazy idea, befitting a drunk's grandeur. As shitty as the groundskeeper's cottage and
other outbuildings had been when Shawn was a kid, the cottage had
still been in better shape than the decrepit mansion. At least the roof
on the cottage kept most of the water out. With newspaper stuffed
into the worst chinks in the wall, some modicum of heat stayed in
during the winter.

The mansion itself, particularly the guest rooms on the higher
floors, was a disgusting, diseased monstrosity before Shawn came
back with his billions. Holes in the roof big enough to land a helicop-
ter through. Only a single unbroken window in the entire mansion,
all the other glass long since sacrificed to teenagers from Whiskey
Run who came out to drink and fight and prove themselves brave
enough to run through a house that was reputed to be haunted. And
it looked haunted, inside and out. The stonework was crumbling.
Inside the mansion, when it rained, the walls turned into waterfalls.
Fungus grew from wallpaper. You had to watch where you stepped,
the floors spongy with rot where they weren't gaping altogether like
chicks waiting to be fed.

The third floor. The hole. It had saved his life.

God. He hadn't thought of that in years. Hadn't thought of it since it happened, he realized. How much of that did he keep buried away? But he remembered it now. Remembered running as fast as he could, looking behind him in terror, hearing the footsteps closer and closer, the whip of the air behind him as he just missed being . . .

He had been, what, ten? The very last few hours of the very last day of November? Yes. A little less than two years before the fire.

He'd been reading in his bed. The light was bad, a flickering dance of shadows from the woodstove and the kerosene lanterns. Electric lines—the same ones they'd hooked up to the cabin after college—ran out to the property, but Shawn had never known a time when his parents had paid the bill. It was nearly ten o'clock. He was supposed to be sleeping, but he was careful to turn the pages quietly. If he heard his mother's footsteps coming toward him, he would tuck the book under the blankets before she pulled back the makeshift curtain to check on him, though ten o'clock was late enough that he thought his mother might have already fallen asleep herself. It was a Tuesday night—yes! He remembered that, a Tuesday—which meant the next day was a school day and they both had to rise early. He for fifth grade, and she to go to the school, too, where she was the secretary. He was just beginning to drift off when he heard the wheels of the truck coming up the drive. His father's truck. A shitbox Ford on tires that were held together with chewing gum. The truck skidded to a hard stop on the gravel. Always a bad sign. The screaming rust of the door opening and closing, and then the creak of the front door. Shawn shivered even before the gust of winter air blew through the curtain and drove him deeper under his blankets. He could have sworn that the wind carried snow to his bed.

He listened. His father had an open-hipped walk when he was sober. A strut, really. Simon was a handsome man, despite all his attempts at self-destruction, and he walked like he knew it.

When he was sober.

In Whiskey Run, Shawn saw the way women looked at his father, and he saw how Simon saw it, how he could be charming when he wanted to be. When he thought there was something in it for him, he could talk low and sweet, and women would shift a little on their feet, leaning toward him. He kept his hair slicked, a can of pomade in the back pocket of his jeans where other men kept chewing tobacco, and he wore his T-shirts tight and tucked in. He was a trim man, coiled in a way that made women want to unwind him. He cut wood and did construction and hired himself out to lift and carry and heave and push and pull and dig and do whatever needed to be done for cash in hand. He was willing to work hard all day, every day, as long as it wasn't for the benefit of his wife and kid. If he'd spent even a little bit of that energy on fixing up the groundskeeper's cottage, it might have been a nice place. But he worked for himself only, and that work, despite the drinking, kept him a powerful man. That power meant he could have a simple life: Simon Eagle fought anybody who was dumb enough to stand in front of him. A simple life of working and fighting and drinking. A simple uniform, too, regardless of the season. In the winters, he'd throw a heavy wool sweater and a canvas jacket over a work shirt, and he'd loosen his belt a notch or two so that he could fit a pair of long johns under his jeans. That belt. A black, beaten leather belt with a big silver buckle stamped with his initials. That belt was a misery.

But if Simon walked with a swagger when he was sober—or when he'd had only a dozen beers or so—once he passed on to the land of the well and truly drunk, the swagger turned into something else, something as twisted and mean as he was. It was the knee, Shawn knew. The knee that Simon blamed everything on. If it weren't for the knee, Simon liked to say, he would have kept his scholarship at Syracuse University, would maybe have had a shot at the NFL. Not that he actually hurt the knee playing football, but he "wouldn't have ended up back here, in Whiskey Run, trapped into marriage with your slut of a mom, if I hadn't wrecked it." To a lesser extent, on days when the temperature dropped precipitously or the rains came, the knee injury meant that Simon limped a bit, but on nights when he drank so much that the next morning brought blank spots and mumbled apologies, his foot dragged and pulled behind him. When he was drunk, the injury to his knee was no longer a piece of ancient history but a present concern.

So when his father came in that night and Shawn heard his rough, shuffling step, he knew that it meant his father had gotten good paying work that day, earning enough money to drink the night away. And then Shawn realized it was a Tuesday: dollar pitchers of beer at Ruffle's. His dad took him there with him sometimes, "Just for a quick one. Wet my whistle after a good day's work, and don't you be telling your mother about it."

Shawn could picture the bar. The mix of dirt and sawdust on the floor, men from the lumber mill playing cards, old Mr. Hickson, the English teacher, also a drunk, with his beard and his pipe, standing guard at the pool table. A few women he didn't recognize sitting at a table in the back, winking and flirting with his father. And his father, swaggering, one thumb hooked in his leather belt, the other hand swinging down five dollars cash on the scarred black oak bar that Terry Fincher had built back in March of 1951 in exchange for a month of all he could drink. A poor deal for Terry Fincher: his liver had gone out by the end of April. Or maybe it was a good deal, Shawn thought. He would have welcomed it if his father had drunk himself to death with such speed.

As he lay under the rough wool blankets, he realized he was shivering. Not from cold, though the room could get cold enough in winter that if the stove was out for any length of time, it would shriek with anger as a new fire came to life. No, he was shivering because he could see, in his mind, those five dollars turned to five pitchers of beer, and then maybe another pitcher for the road, and then his father's stopping to buy a six-pack of screamers—Genesee Cream Ale—those familiar green-and-white cans riding shotgun all the way from Whiskey Run.

Shawn, standing there now in the burned-out wreck of a building, realized he was shivering, too, as if in sympathy with the ten-year-old version of himself. It was enough to make him laugh, not at the memory, but at the absurdity. If he recognized the devil in his father the first time Aunt Beverly took him to church, had he recognized what kind of a sick miracle it was that his father hadn't wrecked his car during one of those nights? The fifteen miles from Whiskey Run to Eagle Mansion—what was left of Eagle Mansion—running down twisting, crumbling roads that went from blacktop to gravel to dirt. The moon and the stars the only light aside from the cockeyed headlights on the old Ford, his father barreling along as fast as the truck could take him. How was it that on all those drives home he never left the road? Never tore the truck to pieces against the rocks and trees that stood sentry? How come a deer or a moose never startled him off the rutted track? No, Shawn thought, if his father had been the devil, then that meant there had to have been a God, and what kind of God would have guided that man safely down the miles from Ruffle's bar or wherever it was he'd been drinking, let him put down a couple of cans of Genny during the drive, skid to a halt in front of the groundskeeper's cottage, and then drag his busted-up knee through the door so that he could inflict himself upon Shawn's mother?

From where he was lying on his bed, Shawn was too afraid to move. He didn't want to call attention to himself. The shift of his body on the mattress, the scratch of the blankets pulled higher to cover his face—either of those things might register, and then his father would pull back the curtain, hover over him, and decide that Shawn needed to be taught a lesson. And yet he was shivering. He could hear his teeth chattering like dice rolling in his mouth. His bed was just a mattress on the floor, stained and smelling faintly, always, of mildew. No box spring to creak, no bed frame to shift, but there was the wood floor underneath and the drag of fabric, and he could feel his body shaking uncontrollably. He did his best to keep his breathing even, exhaling softly through his mouth, trying to steady himself.

Step. Drag. Step. Drag.

Shawn closed his eyes. He wanted to be asleep.

He would have given anything, traded anything at that moment, to be sure that his father's attention wouldn't fall upon him.

Step. Drag. And then a sigh and the sound of his father sitting heavily on the edge of his own bed, clothes being shrugged off, the thump of the work boots dropping to the floor. Shawn had caught those work boots in the ribs a few times.

Shawn, shivering and alone in his bed, would have said a prayer of thanks if he'd known how. As a teenager, living with his aunt Beverly and going to church regularly, he spent a few years offering up a prayer before sleep, but back then, in the groundskeeper's derelict cottage so close to the falling-to-pieces Eagle Mansion, with his drunk father a few paces away, a blanket hung from the ceiling his only protection, Shawn didn't know how to offer up his thanks, so he stayed still, knowing there was still the chance that a stray noise would bring the wrath of his father upon him.

He heard the blankets and bedding moving, and then the voice of his mother.

"I'm sleeping," she said. "And you're drunk again. I told you, no more when you've been drinking."

She was whispering, but there was only the makeshift curtain between Shawn and his parents' bed.

Harsher, a little louder this time: "No. Not when you've been drinking."

And then the sound that he'd known was coming, the sound he'd been dreading since the first sound of the truck coming down the drive, the sound that sometimes felt like the punch line to some horrible joke: fist on flesh. Always such a deep sound, one that spoke to the blood and bone that lay beneath the surface of our fragile bodies. It was accompanied by the sound of his mother's grunting, and then her beginning to cry.

"Ah, come on, please," she cried. If a wail could be quiet, a breeze in winter, then this was a quiet wail, his mother, even then, still trying to let Shawn have what little peace was available to him.

And then, again. Fist on flesh followed by tearing cloth. His mother gasping.

"Simon, please," she said, but now she was full-on sobbing.

Shawn, lying in bed, as still as he could be, had one thought: *I'm glad it's not me.*

I'm glad it's not me.

Even now, standing in the burned-out groundskeeper's cottage that had once been his home, he felt the heat flood into him. Twenty-six years later. A hundred billion dollars later. An entire lifetime later. He still felt the heat of it.

Shame.

He'd built a company—no, an empire—by himself, become the kind of man about whom books are written. He bedded supermodels and had a fleet of private jets, he had fifty thousand employees and countless more working for him down the length of the supply chain. He had the ear of the president of the United States and access to any pop star or actor he wanted to meet. He had everything, and what he didn't have, he could buy. But still, that thought, *I'm glad it's not me,* flooded him with shame. It didn't matter that he'd been only ten years old, that he'd been scared and alone and shivering in his bed; he'd lain there and listened to his mother being punched and then, yes, to his father start raping her, and the thought that he'd had was *I'm glad it's not me.*

He took a deep breath in, and the faint, lingering smell of ashes was enough to remind him that he'd had other feelings back then as well. The thought *I'm glad it's not me* had filled him with shame, had made him hate himself, but the next thing he had felt was anger.

Rage.

The ten-year-old Shawn Eagle slid as quietly as he could from his bed. He knew the floor of the room well enough to move sideways first, around those two boards that yelled with every step. He pushed aside the curtain and moved into the main part of the room. The kerosene lanterns and the woodstove were still sending dancing shadows over the walls and ceiling. He could hear his mother crying, gulping back her sobs and trying to stay quiet.

Quiet for his sake.

And his father was making noises now, the grunting that would eventually lead to Simon's own sort of crying sound.

"Whore," his father hissed through his teeth, and for Shawn, it sounded like nothing other than the growl of a dog gone wild. He was afraid to look, afraid that if he did, he'd see his father turned beast. They didn't have a television, but he'd spent the night at Mark

Duran's house with five other boys as part of a birthday party that previous spring, and they'd stayed up late to watch a werewolf movie. The other boys had taken it in stride, but it left an indelible stain on Shawn, and that night, listening to his father's swearing, the seething breath, the growl of him, all he could think of was the monster from the movie. Skin split on knuckles and spine, the mouth distorted into a muzzle, teeth and claw.

The tearing of flesh.

The blood.

Shawn couldn't look.

He couldn't look, but he heard the sound of fist on flesh again, his mother gasping, the sobbing leaking harder out of her mouth, and he took another step forward. His foot bumped against something. His father's work boot. He was at the side of the bed, nearly close enough to reach out and . . . And what? His father worked doing odd jobs, carpentry and construction, digging ditches and clearing fields, whatever paid in cash and helped him sweat out the alcohol every day. It meant that the man was all sinew and muscle, violence waiting to happen, and Shawn knew that even had he been a grown man, he wouldn't have stood a chance against his father.

He was in his bare feet, and he could feel the draft carrying over his toes, the worn-down plank floor cool, and there was nothing he could do. It didn't matter that his mother was crying in full voice now, that she couldn't even try to keep quiet for his benefit anymore, that the push and rock of the mattress had sped up, his father sounding more and more like an animal ready to kill with every breath. He might as well have just stayed in his bed, but as he had the thought, he took a step back and felt something hard against his foot.

The belt buckle.

He bent over and started pulling the leather belt from the loops of his father's jeans. It snaked out smooth and easy; standing by the bed, listening to his mother crying, his father grunting, and there he was, swinging that heavy, shiny, stamped silver buckle at the end of a length of worn leather. Just holding the belt made him feel mean, the way it swayed back and forth. You could swing that belt as hard as you could and you knew it would hurt somebody. You could make somebody stop what they were doing with one good swing of that belt. You could teach your wife a lesson with that belt. You could teach her not to give you lip. You could teach her that when a man works all week, he's entitled to blow off a little steam. You could teach her not to look at another man, you dumb slut. You could teach her not to burn the dinner, to dent the truck, to knock over your can of Genny, to show a little god (swing) damn (swing) respect (swing)!

You could hurt a man with that belt buckle, Shawn thought.

He looked at the bed.

His mother was facedown, her head turned toward him. Her eyes were closed, but even with the stuttering light from the wood fire and the lanterns, Shawn could see that her face was wet. Tears and blood. Blood was running from her nose like a lazy worm, and her lip was puffy and split open. There was already bruising around one of her eyes. She'd have a black eye in the morning. She was being smashed down into the mattress by his father, each thrust of his father's body causing a snuffling huff of air to jump from his mother's mouth. His father looked fierce, urgent, his porcine grunts sounding almost primal. He was working away at her with no regard.

Shawn stepped closer. He had the end of the belt in his left hand, and his small, ten-year-old right hand wrapped around the middle of the black leather. He let the heavy silver belt buckle swing back and forth and back and forth. That belt buckle had left its marks on Shawn in the same way that it had left its marks on Shawn's father. He hated that belt buckle, and he hated the way his father would point to the dimple at the corner of his own eye and tell Shawn that he got that when he was ten for mouthing off to his own father, Steven Eagle, and that Steven Eagle had a scar on his leg and had inherited the belt from Shawn's great-grandfather. That belt buckle had been giving bites of misery for generations.

He took another step, and then he froze. His father, thrusting, grunting, turned his head to the side, and for a moment, Shawn thought Simon was looking right at him. But no, he went back to work on Shawn's mother. Shawn took one last step, so that his thighs were pressing against the edge of the bed, and as he did so, his mother opened her eyes. It took a second for her eyes to focus, and when they did, they opened wide. With the bloody nose and split lip, with the beginning of a plum bruise under her eye, in the flickering light of fire and lantern, she looked half an animal herself, and the cry that came out of her fit the spectacle.

"No," she said. Her voice was a pitched plea, and though Shawn knew that she was talking to him, that she saw his face and read the intent, that the swinging silver belt buckle glinted in what light there was, Shawn's father thought she was talking to him. Simon took it as an affront. A willful act. And any willful act, in Simon's mind, needed to be stamped out. She needed to be reminded who was the boss, who was the man in this family. How dare she tell him no? He'd already had to give her more of a tune-up than he should have had to, and still, even now, she was defying him? No. That wouldn't do. Simon stopped thrusting into her long enough to swing his hand back, ball it into a fist, and bring it down into the side of her face as hard as he could. Let's see her try to talk back after that one.

The other punches he'd already landed on his wife would normally have been enough to have her call on the doctor. The punches on the softer flesh of stomach and side meant the toilet water would be tinged red for a week. He usually stayed away from her face; the broken nose was a new thing. When he punched her in the nose she heard the snap and grind of bone, felt the blood gagging the back of her throat. Her swollen lip hid the ragged edge of a chipped tooth that they couldn't afford to fix and that she'd have to live with for whatever time was left to her. But it was this final punch that did the real damage. Simon Eagle was a strong man, like his father had been and his grandfather before him. He could swing a hammer all day, haul rocks, load logs, dig a ditch. And he was a brawler. He could take a punch, but more important, his fist, all the men swore, was like an anvil. He wasn't the biggest man or the scariest to look at, but god almighty, if you were in a fight in Whiskey Run, you wanted Simon Eagle to have your back, because the only son of a bitch dumb enough to get in the way of Simon's fury was somebody who was either just passing through or was going to learn in a hurry that it was time to leave. You took a swing from him and you'd swear he kept a roll of quarters tucked behind his fingers. He'd sent more than one man to the hospital after things had gotten out of hand at Ruffle's. And he *knew* he had the kind of punch that could kill a mule.

Because of that, and because he knew that even in Whiskey Run men would keep their own counsel for only so long, he'd always taken it easy on his wife. Black eyes and bruises up and down her body, pinched flesh, slaps and shoves, a broken arm—all things that could be explained away. Never the face. And he'd never swung as hard as he could. He was afraid to, really. In his mind, hitting her was never something he did in anger; it was just to teach her a lesson. He wouldn't have hit her unless she deserved it. But this time. Oh, this time. He'd put down five pitchers of beer and as many cans of Genny as he could drink in the fifteen miles from Whiskey Run, because why not? He worked his ass off for that ungrateful bitch and her little shit-snot of a kid. A few drinks was his right. Was it unreasonable to expect that when he came home from a day of work his wife might show him a little warmth? But no, not from that ice-cold bitch. So he'd given her a few little light touches already that night. Nothing that she couldn't handle. Enough that she should have known her place. And she was still mouthing off to him. Who did she think she was to say no to her husband?

So he'd swung as hard as he could.

A sledgehammer coming down on a fence post would have made the same sound as his fist smashing into the side of her face.

He didn't know it at the time and neither did Shawn, but that punch was enough to smash the orbital bone around his wife's eye, to cave in part of her skull. It wasn't enough to kill her—and for that, his wife decided once and for all that she was done with what few silent prayers she did offer up, because if there was a God, he would have let Simon's blow take her home—but it did leave her blind in one eye, and despite the best efforts of the doctor at the hospital in Syracuse who put her back together and then fruitlessly brought a police officer in to talk with her, Simon's punch left a permanent dimple on the side of her face. A mark that could not be undone.

She cried *No*, and two things happened simultaneously: Simon smashed the side of his wife's face in, and Shawn Eagle swung that belt as hard as he could.

Even though he was only ten years old, he was a ten-year-old who hauled buckets of water up from the river, who split firewood, who lived in a ramshackle, falling-down building and who spent his time, when he wasn't in school, doing chores or playing in the woods. Which is to say, ten years old or not, when he swung that belt, the heavy silver buckle cut through the air fast enough to sing like a bird. When it crashed into Simon's temple, it knocked him partly off Shawn's mother.

Maybe if Shawn had stopped then, Simon would have been on him, would have caught his son and turned the belt on the boy, and if that had happened, it would have turned into something horrible and unimaginable, but Shawn didn't stop. He got partway up on the bed and swung again and again and again. He swung as hard and as fast as he could, trying to drive that belt buckle through his father's head. He wanted to slay the beast. He could see blood flowing from his father's head, flooding across the muzzle of his face. Another gash on Simon's cheek. The hot, wet *thwap* of the buckle on Simon's back, his arm, his chin. And the strike that probably saved Shawn's life: Simon's bad knee. Right on the bone.

It sounded like a branch breaking in a storm.

"You piece of shit!" Spit flew from his father's mouth. "Shit bastard!" Simon was roaring, and it was like nothing Shawn had ever heard before. A steaming locomotive dropped off the side of a building. Ten thousand dogs tearing at a hare. Pure, unbridled fury.

Simon lunged at him, but Shawn swung again and caught him on the wrist, just before his father's hand would have clenched around his ankle. He danced back off the bed, jumping to the floor, and the thing he saw then scared him more than anything in his life had. It was his mother's face.

He didn't know what he'd expected. He hadn't really been thinking of anything other than his shame and anger. Why had he acted tonight instead of all the other nights?

Shame.

Because tonight he had thought, *I'm glad it's not me*, and had been flooded with shame so pure that he knew the only way to get rid of it was to do something drastic. If he'd thought about it, however, he would have expected something else on his mother's face: pride, relief, even thankfulness. But what he saw instead was pure fear. And looking at her face, for the first time in his life he truly understood that the reason she stayed with Simon was that *she knew what he was capable of*, and that look on her face was enough for Shawn to understand what his father was capable of, too.

His father was cradling his wrist and swearing, and Shawn and his mother locked eyes.

"Run," she said. She said it so calmly and quietly that he wasn't sure he'd actually heard her. The tone of her voice was at such odds with the look on her face. "Run," she said again, but this time her voice was louder. He still didn't move, and then, a third time, but this time screaming, shrieking, as loud as she could yell, the sound of her voice matching the terror on her face. "Run, Shawn! Run."

He ran. He dropped the belt and ran, bursting out the door and running as fast as he could toward Eagle Mansion. It was a clear night. Full moon and bright stars, enough light to turn the woods and the hills and the thin coating of snow into something magic.

But the flip side of magic is always terror.

Shawn pumped his feet across the gravel drive, not feeling his feet bruising and shredding, then across the light slick of snow on the grounds. The mansion loomed dark and fearsome above him, a face as caved in as his mother's had looked to him.

The door into the servants' quarters from the outside was long gone, so he didn't even have to pause to open it before entering Eagle Mansion; the building swallowed him whole. It was darker in there, but there was enough light through the windows—or the open scars where the windows had once been—and the cracks in the walls and the holes in the roof for him to see.

Jesus.

Shawn Eagle, thirty-six years old, opened his eyes and looked at the scars of smoke and fire in the groundskeeper's cottage, at the broken sink, at the tortured metal of the stove. He didn't want to remember any of this. He wanted to keep it locked and buried away. Why hadn't he just let Fisker bulldoze this building? For that matter, why couldn't he just leave well enough alone? He could have let Eagle Mansion continue its downward spiral of rot and ruin. He'd come back once already, after college, and hadn't that resulted in enough violence? What was the dark hold that Eagle Mansion had on him? There had been no earthly reason for him to come back a second time, to fix the estate up, and yet here he was, trapped by the memory of something he'd tried so hard to forget. He should have stayed away. Stayed in Baltimore and played with his shiny toys and left the past to be the past. These ghosts couldn't haunt him in Baltimore. But it wasn't that easy, was it? He closed his eyes again, tried to remember the sound . . .

. . . of his father swearing and chasing him. "Shit bastard!" The shuffle step of his father's bad knee, a drunkard's bounce off the wall as he followed Shawn into the mansion, his gait made worse because Shawn had tagged him that good one right across the kneecap. And the sound of the belt. He didn't have to look behind him to know that his father was swinging the belt. He could hear the heavy buckle cutting through the air.

"Come and take your medicine, you little shit bastard! Come and take what's coming to you. There's no use in running. You're just going to make it harder on yourself." His voice starting to sound almost seductive: "You stop right now and I'll take it easy on you. Just a couple of licks to teach you a lesson," rising into a howling roar, "but if you keep running, I'll make sure you remember this one, Shawn. Shawn! You shit bastard! I'm going to beat you until your skin peels off. I'm going to cut off your dick and smash your little squirrel shit brain in. I'm going to lay into you until every inch of your flesh is smashed in!"

Shawn ran.

Through the kitchen and behind the dry storage. He was afraid to look back, to see how close his father was. If it even was his father. A part of him knew that if he looked, the moonlight would reveal the truth: he wouldn't see his father, he would instead see some monster, some leathery, scaled beast, bloody fangs and hair. Eagle Mansion was finishing the job that the drink had started, baring his father's true soul to the world. No, he couldn't look back, because Shawn knew that if he were to see his father's essence, he would freeze in his tracks. He'd be done.

The stairs.

He took them as fast as he could, the sound of the shuffle step behind turning into a clopping plod up the wooden staircase. There was the sound of something deep and solid striking the planks at irregular intervals, and Shawn realized it was the belt buckle, bouncing off the stairs as his father followed him.

"Where do you think you're going, you little shit bastard? Do you think you can outrun me forever?"

Shawn hit the landing of the second floor. If he pushed through the ornate metal-banded door, he could run down the hallway past the numbered rooms that used to be full of swells and fast women and then go out the staircase on the other side. If he was fast enough, he could double back to the groundskeeper's cottage, grab his mother, hustle her into the truck, and leave his father behind. Maybe this time she wouldn't insist on coming back home. They could go off to . . .

The thought made him sick. There was nowhere to go off to. His aunt Beverly had tried to get his mother to leave, over and over again, but something sick and invisible kept her tethered to his father. She'd never leave. He understood that now.

Behind him, with the inevitable thud of the belt buckle on the wooden planks, his father's limp up the stairs was getting closer.

Shawn grabbed at the doorknob that would have opened the hallway to him, but it snapped off in his hand. He felt the beginnings of laughter bubbling up from somewhere inside him. Of course! Eagle Mansion had been built by his great-grandfather and then passed on to his grandfather. It had always been diseased and decaying, from the moment it was built, infected by the blood madness of the Eagle family, the poison more evident with each and every generation. And now his father held on to the estate with the closed grip of a man who didn't understand that the person he was choking was himself, that the building was alive to its own history. Eagle Mansion would never let him go free. The water seeping through the gapped roof and broken windows, the unchecked vines and bushes, the ghosts of every guest who had stayed here—they all came together to turn the building into something living and breathing, a monster in its own right. Shawn knew it was a ridiculous thought, but it felt right and true: the building had an agenda of its own, and it didn't mean to let Shawn get away so easily.

There was a reason, Shawn thought, that he was so scared of Eagle Mansion at night. With its broken windows looking like teeth, it had loomed over his entire childhood. During the daytime he sometimes played in the old mansion, but at night, at times like this, Shawn remembered some of the stories he'd heard his father telling his mother. Gambling. Murder. Women chained in—

No.

There was no time.

He threw his shoulder into the door with little hope. He was only ten, and he could see the way the door had warped and splintered in its frame. It wasn't going to move.

He stepped back to throw himself at the door again, but for some reason he glanced back toward the stairs. It was just enough for him to flinch away from the blow; his father was still a few steps from the landing, leaning forward and swinging the belt in a great looping curve. The silver buckle cut through the stiff air, catching a glint of moonlight from the triptych of windows running up the stairs.

The buckle missed Shawn by an inch. No more than that. The distance of a flinch.

He didn't hesitate. He ran for the next flight of stairs, to the third floor. He wasn't supposed to play in the main section of the mansion. His mother was afraid that he'd fall through the rotten floor or that he'd get stuck in one of the rooms or that a wall would collapse on him, but he was a curious boy and brave enough when the sun was out. Sometimes he played in the mazelike tunnels and cellars that connected the groundskeeper's cottage to the main building and went out under the lawns, and sometimes he played in the mansion's old casino, which, with its broken windows and vine-choked space, resembled a fairy tale more than it did a room that did a roaring business during Prohibition. But often, when he stole away, it was to go up to the third floor, because that was where the guest rooms had been reserved for high rollers and important guests. All the rooms were suites, but Shawn's favorite was the one his father claimed had once been used by Babe Ruth.

Shawn knew that the door to the third hall was open, because he'd been up there the week before, and he knew that if he could make it down the hallway, all the way to the end, the door to the Ruth Suite would still be standing open, the way he'd left it. And if he could get through the door without his father catching him, he could shut it and slam the lock home, and maybe it would keep his father at bay long enough for him to go sleep off his drunk. That was his only hope. Oh, Shawn would still get what was coming to him when his father woke up in the morning. He wouldn't walk away scot-free, but he'd be a lot more likely to see the leather end of the belt than the silver end. It would be the kind of whipping that would leave him unable to walk for days, unable to sit for weeks, maybe with a broken arm, too. But, he thought, probably, maybe, making it into the Babe Ruth Suite and bolting the door would mean a beating he could survive.

He was halfway up the stairs to the third floor when he heard the whip of the belt through the air again, the deep thud of the buckle hitting the step his foot had just left. But this time there was more: the splinter and snap of wood. He couldn't stop himself from looking back. His father was wrestling the belt buckle out from the tread of the stair; he'd swung it hard enough that it had broken through the step, breaking through the rotten wood. The sight was a terror, because Shawn knew that whatever hopes he had of an easier go of things—if he could get to the Ruth Suite, lock the door, and wait out his father's drunk—if his father caught him right now, while he was eye deep in beer and with his own blood dripping down his face, well, Simon Eagle was going to lay into Shawn with everything he had.

And Shawn was under no illusion that if his father started swinging away at him right now, with the beer and the blood, there would be anything to stop the beating until it was long past the point when it would ever matter to Shawn again.

He ran. To the top step and onto the landing. Through the open doorway and past the Cleveland Suite, the Adirondack Suite, the Clipper Suite. He could hear his father swearing, the voice almost distant now, stuck on the stairs and having to carefully work his way past the tread that he'd broken, held up by his gimpy knee. Shawn was too scared to smile, but the end of the hall was in sight, which meant the Ruth Suite and what little safety it offered him was near.

He was almost there when his foot went through the floor.

For a moment he thought he'd been shot. The pain in his thigh was excruciating, and he was facedown on the floor. Only a second later he registered that the sound hadn't been a bullet but rather the breaking of the floorboard, and the reason he was on his face was that his leg had gone all the way through the rotting floor. And the pain in his thigh?

"Bastard," Shawn whispered to himself. He grunted and closed his eyes. "Shit piss asshole," he said. He was a quiet boy, and this was the first time he'd used those terrible words that he'd heard his father say so many times, albeit with more success, but there were no other words to use. His father would be past the broken step any moment. There were no windows in the hallway, but the roof was out in great sections. Enough for the sun to come in during the day, and enough to let in water when it rained. Enough to cause the rot in the floors, and enough for the light from the moon to shine down and show Shawn that the burning pain in his leg was from a splinter of wood the size of his thumb pushing through his skin. He could feel blood spilling down past his knee and dripping off the foot that dangled through the floor and hung in space over the second-floor corridor.

"I'm coming for you, you little shit bastard! There ain't anywhere for you to go anymore. I'm going to catch you, and when I do,

I'm going to beat your head in like a biscuit. You hit me with my own belt? Let's see what happens when I give you a little taste of it, you pissant dick squeeze. I'm going to need stitches from where you lashed me one, oh," he laughed, a clownish, manic howl, "but you ain't going to need stitches by the time I'm done with you, Shawn. You ain't going to need anything ever again! I'm going to bury your little body in the woods. Dig out the dirt and roll you in there, shovel it over. Let you rot in the ground. The worms will feed on you just fine."

Shawn gritted his teeth. He couldn't stop himself from letting out a moan. He put his palms on the floor and tried pushing, but he couldn't move his leg. He was stuck like his father said he'd stuck a Vietcong lady back when he was eighteen and in the army, in the last days of the war, sticking his bayonet right through the whore's crotch, because Simon Eagle knew that she'd take his dollars and then tell the bad guys how to kill themselves an American.

Shawn suddenly felt both cold and hot at the same time, and he wondered what would happen if he just closed his eyes and tried to go to sleep. Maybe this would all turn out to be a dream, and when he woke up he'd be in his bed, his mother would be asleep in her bed, and his father would have wrapped the truck around a rock somewhere on the road between here and Whiskey Run.

But the roaring yell of his father let him know that such a dream was out of the question. And it meant that Simon was past the step.

The hole in the floor was big enough both for his foot and for him to see where his thigh was impaled, but small enough that it was still a bit of an awkward squeeze for him to get his arm through. He reached below where the splinter was lodged in his leg and pushed at his thigh. He couldn't stop himself from screaming, but he managed to slide his thigh off the sharp piece of wood and then dragged his leg up and out of the hole. It was hell to get to his feet, and his leg barely took the weight, but he could limp.

He kept going down the hall toward the Ruth Suite, leaving the hole in the floor behind him.

Step, drag. Step, drag. A cruel mimicry of his father's own steps.

But Shawn kept going. He was so near to safety—even of the momentary kind—that he couldn't stop, so near to where he had left the door of the Ruth Suite open, a welcome respite.

The door was closed.

"Bastard shit piss asshole," Shawn said.

He knew he'd left it open. He'd brought his baseball cards up with him—a measly collection of doubles or triples that his friends at school had handed down to him—and when he'd gone back to the cottage, he'd been sure to leave the door open to the hallway.

Eagle Mansion was playing tricks on him. It was his great-grandfather, his grandfather, reaching out to make sure that Shawn learned how to respect his father.

It couldn't be locked, could it?

He turned the doorknob, slowly, gently, remembering the feel of the doorknob falling off in his hand on the second-floor landing. The knob turned noiselessly, but when Shawn pressed on the door, it didn't move. The room was locked. From the inside.

He turned and took a staggering step to the suite across the hall, but the door there was warped solid into the frame.

Step, drag.

"Nowhere to run, boy? How do you like that, you little shit bastard?"

In another time, the hall would have been beautiful in the moonlight. Some of the holes in the roof had come from storms blowing off shingles and from rot, and some of the holes had come from falling branches or from the building falling into disrepair after the repeal of Prohibition, but the result was an uneven patchwork of gaps and holes, some larger and some smaller. It meant that the moonlight silvered through like so much magic. But this wasn't another time, and Shawn, his back now against the end of the hall, could see his father limping toward him. Simon let the belt buckle swing back and forth now, a pendulum of pain waiting for him.

Step, drag. Step, drag.

Shawn started laughing. What else was there to do?

Simon stopped, and in the dim light, Shawn could see his father grimace, as if the sound of Shawn's laughter was causing him physical pain. Of course, that only made him laugh harder.

"Oh, you think this is funny, you shit bastard? Let's see if you're still laughing a minute from now."

Step, drag.

Shawn pressed his hand against the wound in his thigh. It burned, but something in the pain made him feel brave. "Shit donkey," he said tentatively.

"What?" Simon stopped again. The anger in his face had turned to confusion. "What did you say?"

And braver still. "I called you a shit donkey," Shawn said, his voice clear and calling down the open hallway. "Bastard shit piss asshole!"

"Who the hell do—"

The words came to him. "I hate you. You're nothing but a stupid drunk. I'm not afraid of you," he said to his father, though as he spoke, he realized he'd never been more scared in his young life.

Simon paused, and then he let the belt flick back and forth, back and forth, and Shawn knew that it was all over. His father was going to catch him, and his father was going to beat him. He was going to swing the belt over and over again, battering Shawn until he was just a sack of blood and ground bone. He wondered if his mother would be able to recognize him at the funeral, if there would come a point when his father would stop brutalizing him, or if Simon would quit smashing him with the belt buckle only when he had turned to soup.

Step, drag.

And then it happened. His father, so focused on Shawn, didn't see the hole in the floor.

The moonlight turned into something syrupy and gold, a flicker of clouds across the sky. There was a tearing sound, wood shrieking under his father's weight, and Shawn watched as Simon pitched forward, his leg breaking through the same hole that Shawn had made. For a moment, Shawn thought that would be it, that his father would push himself out the same way Shawn had, and then it would be good night, Shawn, are you ready for one of Daddy's tune-ups? But as Simon's adult-sized body hit the rotted out floorboards, the wood cracked and splintered beneath him. A larger hole opened. First, Simon's good leg went through, and as the bulk of his weight hit the floor, the rest of the floor gave way.

The look on Simon's face as he began to fall was not one of fear or even surprise, but of pure unadulterated rage. Absolute hatred.

It gave Shawn perfect clarity: he realized that if it wasn't *this* time, sooner or later, his father *would* kill him and his mother. Someday. He'd do it someday, as easily as squashing a bug. Do it because he could, because for all Simon's grandiose dreams of bringing Eagle Mansion back to its former glory, his father knew he was a small man trapped in a small life. Someday he'd realize that nothing was going to change that, and that would be the day he killed Shawn and his mother.

Fortunately, for Shawn, that day wasn't today. Snow and rain, carpenter ants, neglect. Rot and ruin and cut corners in the initial construction. All together, it meant that Simon broke through the floorboards in the hallway of the third floor, plunged ten feet to the hallway of the second floor, and broke through that floor as well, falling another six feet onto a partially collapsed craps table in the casino.

On the way down, Simon tore a nine-inch gash in his arm that went as deep as bone, knocked out two teeth, and hit his head hard enough to knock him out for an hour and leave him with blinding headaches for nearly three months. Last but not least—Shawn's favorite of all the injuries his father sustained that night, the one that finished the job on his father's knee—a broken kneecap, a torn ACL and MCL, and ligament damage, what the doctor called a "catastrophic injury."

But Simon's appointment with the doctor was still a few days off, because Shawn didn't even stop to look down through the hole in the floor. He thought his father might be dead—he hoped that his father was dead—but he was afraid that maybe his father was fine. That maybe his father, an iron man who ran red hot, was picking himself up off the floor and heading back to the stairs, belt in hand, to finish the job he had started. So Shawn limped to the hole in the hallway, and carefully, gingerly skirted it, staying as close to the wall as possible. Once he was past it, he pulled his bleeding leg with him down the stairs, jumped painfully over the missing riser, and lit out the door and across the weed-choked lawn into the groundskeeper's cottage to get his mom.

He didn't remember most of what happened after that. He didn't remember putting on clothes and shoes and helping his mom out to the truck. He didn't remember that she passed out as soon as she was in the passenger seat. He didn't remember the long, two-footed, lurching drive into Whiskey Run or the way his shoe filled with blood. He didn't remember the hot fear that he would round a bend in the road and the scratched-up headlights would reveal his father waiting for him, standing in the middle of the road, still swinging that belt. He didn't remember parking in front of Dr. Learner's house and leaning on the horn until the doctor came out. He didn't re-member the ride from Whiskey Run to Syracuse with his mother in the volunteer ambulance, the stitches he himself got, or refusing to leave her room during the surgery to repair the bone around her eye, or even being carried out screaming by two orderlies at the surgeon's orders.

There was a blank spot there, even now, more than twenty-five years later. He didn't remember his mother, on their third day in the hospital, calling somebody—who? Shawn realized he never found out—in Whiskey Run to go out and check to see if his father was alive. He didn't remember how he and his mother got back to Whis-key Run, or why she didn't finally listen to Aunt Beverly's pleas to leave, but he remembered the relative peace they had for the next forty-two days, because by the time Simon was found, lying where he had fallen through not one but two ceilings, Shawn's father was near death. Another day would have done it, Dr. Learner said, maybe even another few hours. Blood loss and exposure. Dehydration. An infection in the gash in his arm. The concussion. The knee, ballooned and rot-black. And of course, on top of all that, Simon Eagle had the shakes. DTs. No booze in his system might have been the worst of it all.

"The man's a wonder," Dr. Learner said to Shawn's mother. He'd come out to the groundskeeper's cottage at the end of the week to check on Shawn's and his mother's stitches, to look at how the incision was healing on his mother's face. "The amount he drinks you'd think he'd be dead already, but the word around town is that you always get your money's worth out of Simon Eagle. Drunkard or not, he'll outwork any two other men. But with his drinking? I'd think that stopping cold like that could have been enough to kill him on its own. Forget the injuries. Vomiting up until there's nothing but cruel yellow coming out, and pardon my language, but shitting a river and then still going until it's the same from both ends? It's a wonder he could survive going without alcohol. Add to that what he got from falling through the floor, let alone lying there in such a state for so long."

Dr. Learner was working in the curtained-off "room" of the groundskeeper's cottage so that Shawn's mother had some privacy while he examined her, but even though Shawn was supposed to be attending to his homework, he could hear every word, and he was pretty sure that Dr. Learner meant for him to, because the good doctor made no attempt to lower his voice.

"Some might say that had you waited another day or two to call in your concerns about your husband, or if you had never bothered, you might have been better off, Mrs. Eagle."

His mother's reply was too soft for him to hear, but Dr. Learner's voice stayed at its normal volume. "So he ain't drinking now. Do you think that's going to last once he's out of the hospital and back home? I've tended to you with my mouth shut for all these years, dear, but one of these days he isn't going to leave anything for me to fix. You might not want to hear it, but it would have been a good thing for you if your son had finished the job. He's a brave one, Shawn is, but when you start something, you have to finish the job."

Shawn gasped.

Standing in the husk of the groundskeeper's cottage more than twenty-five years later, he could have sworn that he had just heard the doctor's words echoing through the air: "finish the job." But he knew it couldn't be true. Dr. Learner had died when Shawn was in college.

And by then, Shawn *had* finished the job.

Shawn took a step toward the door. The outside beckoned. Out there, in the late-afternoon sun, he could imagine a different history.

That had all been so long ago. A memory he hadn't wanted to come back to, even if the aftermath, those forty-two days when his father was in the hospital, were the closest thing to peace he'd had as a child. The funny thing was that despite Dr. Learner's skepticism that Simon would stay off alcohol, when Shawn's father came home from the hospital, he did keep dry. For a long time, Simon didn't have another drink. He was on crutches until the spring. That had been a desperate winter, with money even tighter than normal, and snow-drifts pushing almost against the eaves of the first story. But Simon stayed sober, through all of it. He stayed sober for almost two years. He didn't touch another drop of alcohol, didn't raise his hand, didn't so much as raise his voice.

For nearly two years Simon Eagle was sober. Twenty-three months he was sober, to be exact.

But nothing lasts forever.

TWENTY-TWO

RUN

Emily still hadn't gotten used to the idea of not working, but she figured she was just going to have to deal with it. She was going to be at loose ends for as long as they were in Whiskey Run. Billy had a purpose: he was here to work with Nellie, to figure out how to turn her into Shawn's next few hundred billion dollars. If it worked out, she and Billy would get to go along for the ride. And Billy, being Billy, was going to be working odd hours. It had been years since she'd seen him truly consumed by a project, but when he was, he forgot about niceties such as meals and showers and clocks. Bedtime became an abstraction to him. By the end of a month he'd be completely divorced from anything approaching a normal schedule. It was like he and whatever computer thing he was working on were having some sort of private conversation that was so darn interesting he just couldn't stand to go to sleep. Interesting to Billy, at least. She cared about his work because she cared about him, but she was secretly a bit of a Luddite. Sure, she liked her new running gear and had been happy to spend money on things like new skis and camping equipment, good restaurants and vacations, fancy coffee and the occasional concert, when she had actual money to spend, but when it came to computers and tech stuff, well, she was willing to *pretend* to pay attention.

But with Billy working on Nellie and keeping his own mad-scientist schedule, she was going to be left to her own devices. If she wasn't going to go crazy locked up in this ridiculous mansion all winter, she was going to have to keep herself busy. So this first morning after sleeping in the Nest she'd gotten up early, before the sun. Not that getting up before the sun was a particularly impressive feat on the second day of November. Billy was already up and working.

Or maybe he hadn't come to bed yet. He'd been working when she went to sleep the night before, heading to the office as soon as Shawn and Wendy left, and she hadn't heard him come into the bedroom. Not that it mattered. His being on an unpredictable schedule was just one more thing she'd have to get used to. She'd see him some days, she wouldn't see him other days.

She was awake before it mattered, but Nellie pulled some sort of neat little acoustical trick so that the alarm clock—a soft fade-in of a rooster crowing, which Emily took as a sign that Nellie might have a sense of humor of sorts—seemed like it was coming through head-phones. The lights, of course, as Wendy had described, were equally discreet. There had been a dim, relaxing glow when Emily went to sleep, and to wake her up, Nellie had chosen the sound of the rooster to coincide with an artificial sunrise that was localized to her side of the bed. She swung her feet to the floor, and Nellie gave her a trail of light across the bedroom to the bathroom. As she was brushing her teeth, a small section of the mirror showed her the current temperature and the expected temperature for the next two hours.

That was kind of neat, she thought, but then she realized Billy had said that Nellie, supposedly, would have free rein throughout the house by the time she was awake. Was she supposed to talk to her?

Why not?

She said it aloud: "That's neat."

Nothing.

She leaned into the mirror, feeling self-conscious now. She directed her voice at the spot illuminated with the temperature. "Uh, do I just talk into here or . . ."

Hello, Emily. I can't tell you how pleased I am that you're here.

"Oh. Thanks. Hi," she said. She looked around the bathroom. It wasn't clear where the voice was coming from.

Billy says it helps if there is somewhere for him to look.

A gentle green ball of light was now floating in the mirror in front of her, at eye level.

"Where is Billy?"

In the office.

Nellie's voice was coming from the ball of light now. Emily looked at the ceiling to see if she could locate where the light itself was coming from.

The entire mirror functions as a screen.

"Great," she said. She reached forward and touched the glass of the mirror. Nothing happened, but still, she said, "That's pretty cool. So, how accurate is that forecast you've got for me? Am I going to be cold on my run?"

The temperature is ambient to the outside of the house, and the weather forecast is localized. Three weather stations form a triangle with the property in the middle. That being said, you can expect the forecasts here to be about as accurate as weather forecasts ever are.

"In other words—"

Always bring an umbrella.

Emily laughed. "You've got a sense of humor."

I want to make you happy that you are here. Would you like to hear a knock-knock joke?

"Uh . . ."

Sorry. That was also a joke. My humor is a work in progress. You won't need your running jacket this morning. I see that you laid out your running tights and long-sleeve shirt last night. You should be comfortable in those. Would you like me to suggest a running route for you this morning? Based on your current level of fitness, resting heart rate, sleep patterns from last night, and your recent history of training, I'd suggest running between six and seven miles. There are several trails running from the property that—

"Thanks, but no," Emily said. "That sounds a little ambitious for today. I'm just going to keep following the road that goes past the mansion. Shawn said that it goes about two miles and ends at a narrow point in the river where you can see over to Canada. I appreciate it, though. Why don't you show me those other routes when I get back? I'll run one tomorrow."

She was out the door and near the top of the rise, running away from Eagle Mansion, before she thought about what it meant that she was so polite to Nellie. She was already treating Nellie like something other than a program. They'd had an actual conversation. A little stilted and weird, but also completely natural. Billy had been talking at dinner last night about how rough the early versions of Siri, Google Now, and all those other services had been when they'd first launched, and how much better they became as they added millions of users and were able to scoop up more and more data. The same thing, he said, would happen with Nellie. The difference was that Nellie was already more natural than anything else that currently existed. Or maybe not natural, not really. That wasn't the right word. But there was a sense of a relationship. Billy told her that if Nellie were working right, it would feel a little bit like having a sleeping dog in the room. She'd do all the fancy personal-assistant and home-automation stuff, but she'd also offer a sense of companionship. Emily had looked at him skeptically when he'd tried to describe it, because, if she was being honest, she'd have said that what he described sounded more like a master/slave relationship—but it made a sort of intuitive sense to her now. Even before she'd had a conversation with Nellie. That being said, not that a master/slave relationship was any better, but the dog metaphor made her feel slightly uneasy. Would Nellie like being a pet? Could Nellie like or dislike something? Billy was insistent that she wasn't alive, that she wasn't artificial intelligence, but if that was the case, why was Nellie a "she"?

So much of this whole setup made her uncomfortable.

As she topped the rise, she looked back over the valley and the rear of Eagle Mansion. It was a handsome building, she thought, made more picturesque by the six or seven outbuildings jeweling the lawn behind the main mansion. So different from what she remembered from when she'd come back to camp for a night with her sister and

Rothko, and even more so from that odd, hermetic year when she'd thrown her life away.

No. That wasn't fair.

She'd been in love.

But she remembered the way Eagle Mansion had looked back then, the estate something foul and predatory. When she'd gone for walks in the woods and looked behind her back then, she'd done so with the prickling sensation of being watched, as if the building were waiting to pounce.

She turned forward again and kept running. She was able to speed up as the road flattened out, even though it turned from fresh asphalt to crushed rock, and then, quickly, to dirt. Nellie had been right about her not needing the jacket, even though the early November sun was still only a spear through the thick trees. It was cool out, but warmer than yesterday had been. There were hints of frost in places, but none of the accents of snow that had greeted her on her drive into Whiskey Run yesterday. And now that she was actually running, she thought Nellie was probably right about a six- or seven-mile run being better than a short run, too. And no reason not to. Shawn said he'd have somebody out to plow the road to town once the snow started falling, but she didn't know how much longer she'd be able to head into the woods and be guaranteed a long run. She'd be able to cross-country ski or snowshoe if she wanted to. Maybe it would be fun, once the snow buried things, to have a snowmobile? Was there one of those on the property? If not, she bet if she asked Nellie for one, it would show up the next day. Shawn's billions waving a magic wand. No, she thought, she didn't want a snowmobile. Noisy idiots. Snowshoes or skis, sure. One of the things she had been looking forward to most was how peaceful it was out in these woods. No cars, no hum of traffic, just the steady tapping of her new running shoes and her huffing breath.

So, six or seven miles. Though, didn't Nellie reference her recent training? Emily tracked her running online, so Nellie must have accessed that, but it should have been password protected. Okay. Creepy. She'd have to ask Billy about that.

In the meantime, she decided to run the two miles to the end of the road, take a quick peek at the view, then turn around, run the two miles back to Eagle Mansion, and pick up the last two or three miles looping down the road toward Whiskey Run and back. With the sloping hills and taking it a little easy, call it fifty minutes. She checked her watch. It had taken her fifteen minutes to get out the door, so she'd be back a touch before eight o'clock. Which meant she had . . .

Six months to kill.

Shit.

Longer than six months, maybe, if Billy was stymied. Or, with some luck, she thought brightly, he could get the kinks worked out by Christmas. Though there was always the possibility that Nellie was broken in a way that he couldn't fix and they'd walk away without becoming the kind of rich that she'd once thought was inevitable . . . Still, even failure would mean that they'd have no debt and a few hundred thousand dollars in the bank. If the worst thing that happened was that they moved to some island in the Caribbean, opened a coffee shop, and started a family, she could live with that. All she had to do was keep herself busy while they were stuck in Whiskey Run.

To that end, she'd laid out a plan for herself. The first few days after Billy had gotten back from his trip to visit Shawn in September, she'd been excited simply about the idea of not working, of taking a break for the first time in her life, but it didn't take her long to realize she'd get cabin fever if she wasn't careful. There was only so much time she could spend reading books and watching movies and television shows. It wasn't like normal life, where she'd have all sorts of chores to do. With the debts paid off and living in somebody else's house, there were no bills to pay, no lawn to mow, nothing to fix. She didn't even have to go grocery shopping if she didn't want to—Wendy had shown her the stocked freezer and pantry down in the industrial kitchen, and one of Shawn's people would deliver from Whiskey Run if there was anything fresh she needed. Though she *did* want to go grocery shopping, and would do so. That was one of her plans to avoid feeling claustrophobic. She'd head into town a couple of times a week, even if she didn't really need to. Just to stop into the grocery store, to get a coffee, maybe to go out for lunch. Manufactured errands. Or, even though it was a half-hour drive, she could get takeout for dinner if Billy didn't want to stop working. If she was really bored, she could drive the extra forty-five minutes each way and walk around Cortaca. While there wasn't much in the way of cleaning that she could do in the Nest, since it was almost all automated, one of the things she was going to do was try to become a better cook. So that was another way to keep busy.

Plus, of course, she was going to try to write a romance novel. When Wendy had asked her at dinner last night what she was going to do to keep busy, she'd listed all those little make-work chores and errands, added hiking and cross-country skiing and snowshoeing, but hadn't said anything about writing a book. She hadn't even said anything to Billy about it. It was embarrassing. It didn't bother her that people knew she *read* romance and erotic novels—hell, since *Fifty Shades of Grey*, people read them on the subway—but the idea of telling people she wanted to write one made her blush. It was one thing to read what somebody else had already written, but if she wrote *those* kinds of books, it meant she had *those* kinds of fantasies of her own. She knew it was ridiculous to be embarrassed. She was a grown woman. But ridiculous or not, there you were. Still, she was pretty sure she could do it. Seriously, how hard could it be to write a book?

She had a good sheen of sweat on her by the time the road petered out at the edge of the river. Just about two miles, like Shawn said. The border between the United States and Canada ran in an imaginary line through the middle of the Saint Lawrence. Maybe because this was one of the narrower points, the river was moving with purpose. She leaned out from the woods. It was hard to see, but there was a small clearing on the other side, and from there, a rough path pushed into the forest. It was wide enough that it could probably fit a car, she thought, though the scale was hard to tell from so far away. Maybe that was the old bootlegger's road that Shawn had talked about at dinner.

She had a momentary dalliance with the idea of trying to swim across to Canada, but that would have been a terrible idea during the summer, let alone on November 2. Maybe once winter came, the river would freeze. If so, she could ski out here and see where the path went on the other side. Shawn had talked about the town on the Canadian side that the bootleggers had used for a base as being trapped in time. That might be worth a visit. There were other places she could go for a day trip, too. She wanted to drive to Alexandria Bay and take the ferry to Dark Island to tour Singer Castle, and she'd take another day to go see Boldt Castle. It would be good to see something a little more authentic than Shawn's candy-boxed Whiskey Run. She'd meant to ask Shawn for other suggestions of what to do in the area, but he'd been so clearly distracted during the first part of dinner.

If she hadn't known better, she would have said that he was drunk or stoned or something. He was skittish, like he'd seen a ghost, reserved and brooding for the first part of the meal. Billy didn't seem to notice, but Emily had, and Wendy had as well. Shawn's assistant had stepped up her game, asking thoughtful questions about Emily's job in Seattle, about her sister, her nieces, laughing at the story of how Beth was sure the girls were conceived in a tent, right here, on the very grounds of Eagle Mansion.

Emily wasn't disappointed in Shawn's lack of energy at the table. Not exactly. But she would have thought . . . Thought what? That he'd have tried a little harder, she guessed. That he would have been more engaged with her. The way Wendy had put it, Shawn talked about Emily often—enough that there was still a part of her that wondered if this whole setup at Whiskey Run was some sort of incredibly elaborate and misguided attempt to get her back.

Perhaps she was flattering herself. After all, Shawn was the kind of guy who could have any woman he wanted. Even if he hadn't been handsome, he was a young, brilliant billionaire, famous and dashing, and he'd been a charming son of a bitch when she first met him, back in Cortaca. He seemed genuine and attentive. Funny, smart, truly interested in her while also clearly attracted to her. Nothing like the douchy frat brothers who were interested only in what she could do for them. She didn't imagine that Shawn had somehow become less charming in the intervening years. There was no question that he had women dripping off him. Wendy had as much as said that women threw themselves at Shawn. And yet, at the start of dinner, she felt like she might as well have not been there. She had been so sure that there was more to Shawn's offering Billy the job than just some stupid computer program. Or maybe it was a little bit of both? Maybe Billy really was the only one who could fix Nellie, but the reason Shawn was trying to get Nellie to work in the first place was that it was his last link to Emily?

For the first fifteen minutes of dinner she'd felt stung. Actually, she felt confused. Some of it was that there was something weird about Shawn's staff cooking and waiting on them in such an intimate setting: the woman who'd met them at the private airfield played the part of waiter. But some of it was that she didn't understand how she could have been so wrong about Shawn's interest. He sat back in his chair and swirled his vodka around like there was a symphony in the ice cubes. Mostly, he smiled at the appropriate times, but he might as well have not even been at the table. Not that Billy noticed. Her husband seemed quite pleased with himself. He'd spent the afternoon napping while she read, and then he'd locked himself in with Nellie for a bit while she unpacked the small amount of stuff they brought; despite the bandage on his hand, he was obviously enjoying himself. He'd refused any painkillers, which made Emily feel a bit of relief, which *then* made her feel like a shitty wife, but no, Billy was happy. So while the woman brought out an excellent appetizer of black pepper–seared scallops served with dill aioli and topped with fried shallots, Emily was more or less stuck chatting with Wendy. But then, as dinner came out, a marshmallow-tender rack of lamb served with sautéed red peppers and topped with a decadent port-wine sauce, accompanied by crisp, burning hot french fries served with a paprika aioli, she asked when Eagle Mansion had stopped being a working resort. Wendy hesitated, unsure of the answer.

Shawn looked up from his drink. "Early thirties. They tried to keep going after the crash, but this wasn't a place made to withstand the Great Depression. It was super-popular in the twenties, though, if you believe the stories. I mean, I think it was probably a lot like today: if you had money, you could pretty much get what you wanted anyway, but here, rich folks could *really* get whatever they wanted without having to worry about privacy. And I mean *whatever* they wanted. My great-grandfather used to put the call in to New York City every morning and have one of his men drive down to Syracuse to meet the afternoon train and pick up the special requests. Fresh oysters, caviar, a new dress, a box of cigars. All you had to do was ask and he made it happen." Shawn leaned forward and popped a french fry into his mouth. "Booze, too, of course. The upside of being this close to the border was that it was easy to get high-quality liquor in during Prohibition. And there was a full casino in operation, too."

Billy was trying to cut his lamb, but it was awkward going with his hand bandaged. Emily reached over and pulled his plate close to her. "I thought gambling was illegal back then," she said.

Shawn laughed. "All of it was illegal. The booze, the gambling. Rumors of other stuff, too. Some weird stuff."

"Like what?"

"Nah," he said, waving his hand dismissively. "Just old rumors. Disturbing things, not worth bringing up."

He talked for a while about the history of Whiskey Run, a timber and mining town that didn't have much truck in either by the time he was a kid—some of this she remembered him talking about all those years ago, when she'd still been a college student and in love with him—and about what had gone into the renovation of Eagle Mansion, about what they could expect from the coming winter. "If you thought the winters in Cortaca were something . . . It's colder here, but it's the snow that's the worst. One of the reasons the freezer and the pantry are so stocked is that you're likely to have a stretch of days here and there when the roads are impassable. Blowing snow and whiteouts mean that even if the road is plowed, and I've been assured it will be, you'll want to stay inside. It's beautiful, I'll give you that, but when I was a kid here, we had a woodstove and, well, let's say insulation that was less than stellar. It was a mean way to grow up. Back in the day, when the mansion was a going concern, they shut it down from the first of November through the first of May." He glanced at his watch. "Today, in fact. November first. Snow comes earlier than November, but the stuff we had this morning was just dust. The real snow will come."

Emily coughed. "Not to be indelicate, Shawn, but if you remember right, I did spend a winter here. Starting on November first, in fact."

Billy piped up. "And I was here for two of them. Not sure you have to explain what it's like here when it snows. Though this winter should be a lot easier. It's not like our cabin was exactly the lap of luxury." Billy's voice was kind, though, and Emily was reminded of how close those two had once been. He continued, "But that does raise an interesting question. How could Eagle Mansion stay in business if it was only in operation half the year?"

"They raked in enough during the six months it was open," Shawn said. "At least that's the story I heard. There are some pictures, too. My great-grandfather wearing an ankle-length mink coat and standing in front of a Rolls-Royce Silver Ghost. Beautiful car. One of those went at auction a few years ago for north of eight million bucks."

"Let me guess," Wendy said, rolling her eyes, "you were the buyer?"

Shawn sat back in his seat. He had a boyish grin on his face. He looked alive, Emily thought. He turned and winked at her.

"Oh, don't go spoiling things," Shawn said. The words were in response to Wendy, but they were meant for Emily: "Just let me show off a bit."

She hated the way it thrilled her. This was what she'd been secretly hoping for. His attention showered on her.

He continued. "There are a few old ledgers, too. He had a decent amount socked away when the stock market crashed in 1929, and he still had something set aside when he finally wised up and shuttered the place in the early thirties instead of trying to keep a sinking ship afloat. But he made some bad decisions during the war, and after the war he tried to get the mansion going again, but there were all these rumors that it was haunted and then he was murdered and—"

"Whoa. Whoa," Emily said. "Murdered? What? How is this the first I'm hearing of it?"

She glanced over at Billy, who signaled that he'd had no idea either, but when she looked back at Shawn, the eager openness was gone. He looked, if she had to put a word to it, petulant.

"There are a lot of things you don't know, Emily." He pushed his empty plate away from him and then stood up. "Time for us to be off, Wendy. I've got an early meeting in Baltimore tomorrow. Let the pilot know I want to be wheels up in half an hour." He stepped around the table, shook Billy's uninjured hand, and then moved around to where Emily was sitting. He leaned in and kissed her cheek. But when he did so, he whispered something. She didn't quite catch it, but it sounded like he said "Shelly's."

She mulled it over a little as she ran up over the rise, the valley spilling in front of her, Eagle Mansion looking alive in the morning light. Nearby, the house caught the sun in its glass steel. What was it he had been trying to whisper to her the night before?

Shelly's?

That didn't make any sense.

She lies?

Ludicrous. Why would he say that to her? She lies? Who lies? Nellie?

No. She'd just misheard him.

She looked at her watch. Twenty to eight. She was right on pace. Fifteen more minutes running, a cup of coffee and a bowl of cereal while she read the *New York Times* and stopped sweating, and then she'd see what kind of shower a billionaire built. By nine o'clock she'd be ready to start working on her book. It was going to be fun, and she already had the basic idea: an unfulfilled woman meets a hunky guy who seems dangerous but is really waiting to be tamed. Throw in a few sex scenes, and ta-da! She thought about the book for a few minutes while she ran, trying to decide if her main character should be a librarian or a teacher. And the man should be a single father, she thought, a widower, whose wife has been gone long enough that it's appropriate for him to move on. Maybe the man could be secretly wealthy. And really, really good in bed, she thought, smiling to her-self. She turned in the road and started running back up to the house, picking up her pace as much as she could on the incline. She wanted to get home.

Romance awaited.

TWENTY-THREE

EVENT HORIZON

You're hungry, Billy.

Billy rubbed his hands over his face and pushed his chair back from the desk. He *was* hungry, actually. "Thanks," he said. "What time is it?"

Eleven thirty. You haven't had anything to eat since dinner yesterday.

"Or drink," he said. "I'm thirsty, too."

DO YOU WANT A DRINK?

He pulled his hands off his face. "What?"

Do you want a break?

"Yeah," he said. "A break is good. I'll be back, okay?"

I'm not going anywhere.

He couldn't stop himself from smiling. He had two laptops open on the desk, but Nellie was still manifesting as a grass-colored tennis ball on the wall, and he found it made things easier on him; it gave him somewhere to smile at. "Okay. You want to hibernate or whatever while I'm gone?"

If you wish.

Not really an answer.

He walked out the door of the office and made his way down the stairs. His hand was throbbing, and he realized he *did* want a drink, just to dull things a bit. He'd said no to the painkillers, and it had hurt him a little to see the relief that breezed across Emily's face when he said he was fine without them. She'd tried to mask it, of course, but it was too obvious. He'd said no because it hadn't hurt that much at the time and he hadn't thought he needed them, but part of that had been whatever topical anesthetic Nellie had applied. This morning . . . Wait? Eleven thirty in the morning or eleven thirty at night? How long had he been working without a break? He turned the corner on the stairs and saw daylight through the window. Okay. That was good. Eleven thirty in the morning. What was not good was that his hand was sore. It was too late now to change course and say that he did, in fact, want painkillers.

Worse than the pain was that the hand itched like a son of a bitch. It felt like ants were in his skin. He actually peeled back the bandages to check and make sure there wasn't anything crawling under there.

It was just his pink flesh and a row of neat stitches.

So no painkillers, but he could have some lunch. That would help. Maybe a coffee or a Diet Coke, too, though he was surprised at how awake he felt. He'd pulled an all-nighter without even realizing it. He should probably grab a nap after he ate, but if he was feeling this good, he'd go back to working on Nellie instead.

He came into the living area and saw Emily sitting at the dining room table. Her laptop was sitting on the table, open and in front of her but pushed away. Her head was resting on the table. She must have heard his footsteps, because she sat up and gave him a weak smile.

"You okay, honey?"

"Yeah," she said. "Just struggling a bit."

He walked over and stood by her. "What are you doing?"

"Trying to write a book."

"Really?" He made a deliberately funny gesture with his face, puffing out his lower lip and raising his eyebrows. The screen on her laptop was dark, but it wasn't plugged in, so maybe it had just been a few minutes of her sitting like that, with the power saver kicking in. "I didn't know you wanted to be a writer."

"I don't," she said. "I mean, I sort of do. I don't want to be writer, per se, but I thought it would be fun to write a book. One of those romance-type books I'm always reading."

"Romance or erotica? You always say there's a real difference."

She closed the laptop. "Well, right now I feel like I'm totally screwed, so that goes with erotica, right?"

He wasn't sure what to say to that, so he said, "Okay," and patted her on the shoulder. He turned to walk to the kitchen.

"Okay?"

Uh-oh. He turned back. "Um, good?"

When he'd come into the room and she first looked at him, she'd looked kind of down, but now she looked angry.

"It's exciting, I guess?" he said. "I just didn't know you wanted to write a book. Very cool. How's it going so far?"

"Fine," she said, but he knew that voice, knew that look.

"I was going to make some lunch. Nellie pointed out that I was hungry. I forgot to come to bed or eat breakfast. Can I make you something?"

She rested her hand flat on the closed lid of the computer. "How about we go into town? Try out this Thai place Shawn was bragging about. I mean, Shawn basically bought his own chef, so I'm assuming it's decent. What's the point of having a fiefdom if your serfs are just middling? You've got to believe it's better than you'd expect for a Thai place in a town this small. It's probably solid even by Seattle standards."

Billy hesitated. He wanted to go back upstairs and keep working, but he also knew there wasn't a real hurry. Shawn and his engineers might not be able to figure out why Nellie was acting herky-jerky, but they wouldn't, would they? That was a little bit like some teenage camp counselor thinking he understood your kid better than you did. Billy had coded most of Nellie in a manic burst of a few months before they gave up and moved on to Eagle Logic, and there was no reason he couldn't go in and clean up the problems in the same amount of time. Besides, he already thought he had a sense of at least a couple of the pinch points, and it looked like Emily was having a bit of a pinch point herself this morning. He knew that the deeper into the project he got the less he'd be able to surface into the real world, so if there was a time to bank some goodwill in his marriage, this was it. If Emily wanted to go out for lunch, he could go out for lunch.

"Sure," he said. "I'm still getting used to the idea that we can afford to pop out for a meal whenever we feel like it again. Though, you know we had Thai food two nights ago in Cortaca, right?"

She just looked at him in that way that made it very clear that had she wanted something other than Thai food she would have said so.

"Okay," he said. "Let me grab my wallet."

He walked back to the bedroom to get money, sparing a glance both on the way there and on the way back for the closed frosted doors to the office. Nellie could wait, he thought. As he shoved his wallet into the pocket of his jeans, he wondered if there was any point to bringing a wallet. If Shawn owned the town and Billy was Shawn's genius in residence, was he going to have to pay for stuff? Could he just put it on Shawn's tab? Probably, he thought, but better safe than sorry.

By the time he got downstairs, the Honda was waiting for them. Had Emily called for it, or had Nellie been able to order it to come around? Could Nellie extend her reach to the whole estate or only Eagle Mansion? He should ask her that later, he thought.

He and Emily both brought books with them and let the Pilot drive on automatic. God, what a luxury, he thought, and yet it was something he got used to almost immediately. The same thing happened when he'd first gotten a smartphone; the idea of having e-mail and internet and GPS and pretty much everything else in the universe with him at all times had seemed like some sort of wizardry. It was awesome, in the classical definition of the word; it caused an almost fearful wonderment. But like everybody else, after just a few days he got annoyed if he was somewhere with shitty cell coverage or when the battery went dead. The same thing was likely true with self-driving cars. When you first got one it was a life-changer, but pretty soon it just became normal. If he and Emily had kids, their kids wouldn't know any different. They'd laugh at the idea that you once had to drive your own car. What did you do when you were tired or sick? How did you send the car back to the house when you forgot to bring something with you? What did kids do when they needed a ride somewhere and their parents were busy? Why didn't anybody care about how many people died every year in car accidents?

Emily's book was an actual paperback, not a tablet, featuring a relatively tasteful cover that just showed a cabin in the woods. Some of the books she read were more overtly romance or erotic novels according to the covers, but some masqueraded as serious works. It was funny to him. Why did the publishers bother? The women who read them—he assumed it was mostly women—were looking for some escapism, so what was the point in putting on a cover that promised anything else? He believed in truth in advertising. Though, he conceded, there were probably a lot of women who were embarrassed to read a book with a titillating cover in public. It didn't seem to bother Emily, which was fine with him. And why should it? Some of the books were shitty, but a great many of them were pretty decent, and a few were truly good, and wasn't that really the case with most things? They weren't exactly his preferred reading, but he was more than happy to have Emily read them. He could always tell when she was reading a good one: it was reflected in their sex life.

As for him, he was reading on his tablet, a relatively obscure text on artificial intelligence: *New Event Horizon*, by Anna Greenberg. Not that he ever, for a minute, thought of Nellie as belonging in that category, any more than you could claim a smart golden retriever was as intelligent as a human, but there were some real overlaps conceptually in what Nellie did and what Greenberg was positing. A lot of programmers tried to get to artificial intelligence through brute force, coding every conceivable situation into the program, but it was a process that just didn't work. No matter how much computing power you had, you couldn't anticipate everything; there were always curveballs. A fixed set of rules wasn't functional, even if you could program the computer to learn new protocols. You might get something that could pass a Turing Test, but fooling a human didn't mean artificial intelligence; it just wasn't that hard to fool a human. People got tricked all the time. Greenberg was more interested in the idea of a program that operated on the basis of probability rather than strict rules, and while what Greenberg put forward wasn't exactly the same as the way Billy tried to bend logic gates from a strict yes/no into a maybe, her concepts were in spitting distance.

They sat down at the Thai place and ordered. Thai iced coffee and a panang curry with tofu for Emily, Diet Coke and a pad see ew with beef, the spice tray on the side, for him. It was a cute place, Billy thought, but soulless. Brand-new and lovely, and absolutely lacking in any sort of human touch. It felt like somebody had fed a computer a bunch of photos of Thai restaurants and the computer had synthesized them and spit them back out. Which wasn't the worst idea in some ways; if you allowed a certain amount of chaos to enter the equation, you could end up with something interesting. It reminded him of an experiment that Google ran a few years back with artificial neural networks and pictures. They directed the software to amplify certain patterns and then created a feedback loop. The result was something startling and strange, pictures that were works of art in themselves. It was an interesting extension of the idea of machine learning. Instead of giving the software pictures and letting it figure out what was in the picture, Google had tasked the software with imagining something new. He supposed that if he had Nellie take—

"Billy. Are you listening?"

He looked at Emily. Her book was down and she was looking at him. Their empty plates were sitting in front of them on the table. Evidently the food had come and he had eaten it. He had no memory of any of it passing his lips, no idea if he'd enjoyed it at all, but he no longer felt hungry.

"Uh, yes?"

She laughed. "That was the least committed yes I've ever heard. I just asked you if you wanted to walk around town a little bit after lunch."

"Oh. Do you want an honest answer or do you just want me to say yes?"

She laughed again, but he hadn't been joking.

"No, it's fine. If you want to go back and keep working, just make sure you send the car back for me." She reached out to touch his bandages. "How's the hand? I can't believe I haven't asked."

"Okay," he said. "Sore. The stitches itch like crazy, though."

"That part will get worse before it gets better," she said. "Sorry."

Emily signaled for the check. The waiter, a thin, young bottle-blond woman who looked fourteen but who was probably twice that age, came over.

"There's no bill," she said. She was wearing a name tag. Cheryl.

"How can there be no bill?"

"Anything you and Mr. Stafford want while you're in Whiskey Run is complimentary," the young woman said.

Billy wasn't terribly surprised that there was no charge, but he was surprised that she knew his name.

The woman blushed a little, but she seemed pretty put together. "Everybody knows who you are. And you, too, ma'am. I don't know if you know much about the town, but things were hard here before Mr. Eagle came in. He's done a good thing in Whiskey Run. My oldest, Ricky, is a junior in high school"—Billy revised his age estimate for Cheryl upward; though she still didn't look old enough to have a kid that age, let alone to have a kid at all, he figured that in a place like this, she might have started young—"and he'll be going to college thanks to Mr. Eagle. He's got himself good grades and did well on the PSATs, and he's looking at NYU. I'm not a fan of him going to New York myself, but I understand why he's got the itch."

At the word *itch*, Billy felt his hand start to throb.

"With the money from Mr. Eagle, Ricky can go and get himself whatever kind of education he wants. Scholarships for college for every kid in Whiskey Run."

Emily reached for her purse. "Well, how about a tip, then? Can we leave a tip?"

The woman held up her hand. "No, ma'am. I appreciate the gesture, but our salary includes tips. It's not like we're the sort of tourist town that does a bonfire business, and Mr. Eagle wanted to make sure that we're happy with our jobs. I'll tell you, Mr. Eagle is a good employer. He's the best thing that's ever happened to me." She laughed. "Well, aside from my kids. I'm supposed to say that, ain't I?"

"Does everybody work for Shawn?"

"Most everybody," Cheryl said. "There are a few people who have jobs in Cortaca they're happy with and who don't mind the commute, and there are a few who are just stubborn fools and who don't want to let Mr. Eagle buy them out. Easy to tell. If you see a house or a business that looks like it ought to be torn down, that's one of the ones who aren't working for Mr. Eagle. Fools, if you ask me, but Mr. Eagle said nobody had to sell to him or work for him if they didn't want to."

"Seems like a good thing for the town."

"Yes, ma'am. And how, might I ask, is it living up at Eagle Mansion? Some folks say it was haunted before Mr. Eagle fixed it up, but I drove up there over the summer, and it looked real nice. Never been out there before that."

"It's very nice," Emily said.

Outside, they walked to the SUV together. Emily grabbed his jacket and pulled him close to her. "It's kind of weird here, isn't it? It all looks so perfect, and it seems perfect."

"And?"

"Nothing's ever perfect, is it?" She kissed him. "There's got to be something lurking beneath the surface."

He kissed her back. "I don't know. I mean, I can't believe I'm going to be the one to defend Shawn here, but you've got to be honest. This was a real shithole of a town before he came back to fix it up. You don't have to work for Shawn if you don't want to, but if you do, good salaries, health care, free college tuition for your kids; kind of hard to argue that there's anything nefarious about that."

"Oh, I'm sure you're right," she said. "Have fun coding."

"I'm not coding, honey. Right now I'm just going through root access level—"

She leaned in and kissed him again, cutting him off. "Please. For the love of god, Billy, remember that I'm not an engineer."

"I'm just looking under the hood. How about that?"

"Men," she said, shaking her head but smiling. "Don't forget to send the car back for me, okay?" She paused, not yet letting go of his jacket. "You'll be fine at the house by yourself?"

"I won't be by myself," he said. "Nellie's there."

"I know," she said. "Didn't you hear our waitress say that the house was haunted?" She kissed him a third time.

As the Honda took him out of Whiskey Run, Billy saw a bedraggled building at the end of the commercial strip. He hadn't noticed it before, but it was a clear holdover from before Shawn had McMansioned the entire town. It looked familiar to him from the time he'd spent living in the cabin, though. A bar? Wasn't that it? There was a rough wooden sign that had probably been hanging from the day the bar was built, but he could just make out the faded name painted in what had probably once been a vibrant blood red: RUFFLE'S. He'd never actually been in there, he thought. The few times they had gone to a bar in Whiskey Run during those twenty-three months, they'd gone to Temerity's, which was now gone, a victim of Shawn's special breed of gentrification. There were places to drink in Whiskey Run 2.0—a couple of bars, a brew pub, restaurants—but they all looked shiny and clean, nothing like what a proper bar should be. If he were still a drinking man, Ruffle's would be his first choice.

If.

He leaned back in his seat and closed his eyes, trying to catch a few minutes of sleep as the Honda drove him back to Eagle Mansion and Nellie.

TWENTY-FOUR

RHYTHM

Living with Billy while he was working was like living with a ghost.

She tried to keep to a rigid schedule that first week. Out the door for her run by seven every morning, back between seven forty-five and eight thirty depending on how far she went. If it was a shorter run, she lingered in the shower and over her breakfast. On the days she ran six, eight, ten miles, she hustled through getting dressed and eating. Nine o'clock on the dot—okay, sometimes nine fifteen or nine thirty—she sat down at the dining room table with a cup of coffee and her laptop and . . . Stared at the blank screen on the computer, occasionally typing a few sentences and then deleting them. She did that until noon. Then lunch, sometimes in town and sometimes in the Nest, and whatever errands and chores she could make for herself. Midafternoon she read and screwed around on the internet until she got restless again and took a walk. After her walk, she prepped dinner, which she ate by herself since Billy was working, and then she watched television or movies until she was ready to go to sleep.

That first full day, Billy had gone to lunch with her in Whiskey Run, but the rest of the week, she saw him only in flitting glances. Shawn's addition wasn't ridiculously large—there was only the bedroom suite; the office; the combo kitchen, dining room, and living room, with an attached powder room. The designer had some sort of fetish for high ceilings and open spaces, and it was a lot of square feet, but there weren't that many actual rooms in the Nest. If Billy had spent every moment holed up in the office working on Nellie, Emily could have understood not seeing him, but that was the thing: she was sure she kept *just* missing him. She didn't even understand how it was possible. It was almost like he was trying to stay out of her sight.

She'd pop into the bathroom to pee, and when she came out, there'd be an empty glass sitting in the kitchen sink. Or she'd finish her lunch and go to brush her teeth, and there'd be a pile of his dirty clothes on the bathroom floor, his damp footprints still on the polished concrete. One night, she was sure he was in bed with her, could feel him pressed against her back, but when she rolled over to reach for him, she was alone; three in the morning and he was still working. She knew that he left the office, even if it was intermittently, because of the dirty clothes on the floor, because of a kitchen counter strewn with plates with scraps of sandwiches, frozen-burrito wrappers, plastic containers emptied of the meals she'd left for him. By the end of that first week, she caught herself constantly looking up from her book and checking behind her, as if Billy were in the corner of her eye. All she would have to do was turn her head fast enough and she was sure she'd see him in the shadows.

Finally, she went and knocked on one of the doors to the office. After a few minutes, the doors slid open to show Billy standing there.

"Hey," he said. "You know, you don't have to knock. You can just ask Nellie to grab me. You don't even have to walk to the office."

He looked slightly dazed, the way he had back when he was drinking and trying to act like he was sober. She had planned to tell him she wanted to have dinner with him, to get a chance to hang out a little and then end the night with a roll in the hay, but she changed her mind as soon as she saw him.

"When's the last time you got some sleep, Billy?"

"Uh, I don't know. What day is it?"

"It's—"

He cut her off. "Nellie. When's the last time I got some sleep?"

*You've been awake for forty-one hours. I told you, you need to do a
better job of taking care of yourself.*

"Yeah, yeah," he said.

He was looking back into the room at the manifestation of Nellie's presence, that green ball of light on the wall that gave you a focal
point. Nellie had been doing the same thing for Emily, and while she
liked it, it suddenly seemed odd to her. Was Nellie both with her and
with Billy at the same time? Were there two of those balls of light
bouncing around the building? And why have a ball of light at all?
Nellie was everywhere in the Nest. Everywhere in Eagle Mansion now
that there weren't workers. There was no real reason why Billy had to
look away from Emily to talk to Nellie. Billy could just talk into the
air and Nellie would hear. Nellie was omnipresent, but with that ball
of light, the way her voice stayed in the room, it was almost like Nellie
didn't want to give up Billy's attention.

He looked at Emily now and then gave her a kiss and a nice bite
on the lip. "I'm eating, though. She"—he rolled his eyes, as if Nellie
wouldn't see it—"nagged me about that. Thanks for leaving me stuff
in the fridge, by the way. Though that smoothie was pretty gross."

It took her a second. "That wasn't a smoothie, honey. It was soup.
You were supposed to heat it up."

That's what I told him.

"Great," Billy said. "Nellie, please don't turn into my wife. No guy
wants two different women nagging him." Emily started to speak, but
he held up his hands. "Kidding! I love you. I couldn't live without
you. No offense to Nellie, but you're the most important thing in my
life."

Emily closed her mouth. She wasn't mad at his comment about
nagging. She recognized it as a joke. What bothered her was how natural his conversation with Nellie seemed. What caused a twinge in the
deep impulse part of her brain was that, tonally, Billy almost sounded
like he was flirting with Nellie.

You really should get some sleep, Billy. You look like shit.

He ran his good hand through his hair. Almost as if he'd been reading Emily's thoughts, he said, "She sounds good, yeah? Way better at

conversation." He looked back into the office again. "Well, I feel like shit. Every time I try to get some sleep, I can't."

He stepped all the way out of the room and into the hallway. The doors slid shut noiselessly behind him. He held up the hand with the stitches. "Stupid thing itches all the time. It feels like I've got ants crawling on me."

She took it in her own hands. The bandages were fresh and clean, snow-white, immaculately wrapped. "You had her change it?"

He nodded. "A couple of times. She refuses to work with me until I go down to the infirmary and have it taken care of. She puts on antibiotic lotion and fresh bandages. Stitches come out on day ten. She says it's looking good, and the scarring will be minimal." He grinned. "Pretty freaking cool, right? Can you imagine portable medical clinics all over the country? Build them into self-driving vans or trucks with solar panels on the roof and you could bring medical attention to places that wouldn't normally have it. Or, shit, third world countries. Build those med-bots into shipping containers and drop them off in hot zones?"

Actually, the initial concept came about in preparation for longer space voyages, where there is no possibility of bringing in outside care. Shawn has invested in the effort to send a manned mission to Mars.

Emily saw Billy's eyes move, his gaze flicking over her shoulder. She looked behind her; Nellie's soft tennis ball of light was on the wall. Of course, she thought. Closing the doors to the office didn't mean anything.

"Yeah, well," Billy said, "dude likes to throw his money away. People just love the idea of space. Like it's not bad enough we've colonized everything down here."

He yawned and then rubbed his eyes. The skin under his eyes was delicately bruised from tiredness, and he had a thick coating of stubble on his face. His hair, Emily noticed, was getting shaggy, too. He'd meant to get it cut before they left Seattle, but neither of them had remembered. There must be a place in Whiskey Run. And if not, they could make a day of it and go to Cortaca. That would be fun, they . . .

"Hey," she said. He looked like he was wobbling on his feet. "Nellie's right. You do look like shit. You need to go get some sleep."

"I'll just lie there agonizing over how crazy itchy these stitches are," he said, yawning again, but even though he kept grumbling, he let her lead him to the bedroom and put him under the covers. Nellie kept quiet, but she blacked out the windows and dimmed the lights, turning them all the way off as Emily stepped back into the hall and the bedroom door closed behind her.

"Thanks," she said.

Of course.

"And, well, thanks," Emily said. She walked toward the kitchen. "It's weird not seeing Billy at all, but I appreciate your company."

As she said it, she was suddenly aware of how true that had been. She'd easily fallen into the habit of chitchatting with Nellie. Questions about the weather segueing into "Anything interesting in the news?" Nellie smart enough to summarize things and synthesize analysis so that she could have a conversation about whatever it was that caught Emily's interest. Asking Nellie what was good on television that night, or to find her a recipe for one of the kinds of fish in the deep freeze. Even though Billy was so involved in his work that he might as well have been a ghost, she wasn't lonely: she had Nellie. And yet, if that was true, if Nellie kept her comforted, why had she been so jumpy about the way Billy seemed to always be just out of her sight? Was it, in fact, Nellie spooking her? No, she thought, because Nellie didn't sneak around.

Nellie was always there.

Maybe that was the problem.

She stepped over to the espresso machine. "I'm going to go walk around the grounds for a bit. Can you make me a latte to take with me, please?"

The machine clicked on as Emily slid a mug under the spout.

You should stay here. It's going to start drizzling in about fifteen minutes.

"I don't mind," Emily said. "It will do me good to walk around a bit. Keep me from going stir-crazy. I can't stay in here forever."

Nellie didn't respond to that.

Outside, Emily found that it was already drizzling. She yanked the hood of her jacket up and over her hair, pulled her hand and the handle of the coffee mug into her sleeve, and walked down the stairs. It was cold, too. Cold enough for her to see her breath in the late-afternoon gloom. She patted her pockets with her free hand before remembering that she'd worn gloves to run that morning and they were laid out to dry with her sneakers. Why hadn't Nellie reminded her?

She stopped on the bottom step to look at the view. Okay, so there were some things about living at Eagle Mansion that bothered her, and sure, her book consisted of exactly zero written words so far, but it was undeniably stunning out here. Most of the trees were already denuded of leaves, but the pines stood tall and strong and green, and the lawn had come in green where sod had been put down. It didn't matter that it was drizzling and gloomy and the light was dim; the Saint Lawrence River kept flowing, the small islands dotting the water still stood sentry, and the Canadian shoreline still held promise of adventure. She looked down the road toward Whiskey Run, but it didn't seem particularly appealing. Nor did going the other way, over the top of the hill, or along one of the paths she'd already run. Maybe she should do exactly what she'd told Nellie, and check out the grounds.

She started by going back up the steps and walking down the long, wide patio that ran the length of the mansion. She loved the heavy logs that were the bones of the mansion, the way they echoed the forest. She stopped to admire the empty swimming pool and hot tubs—they'd be something once they were running—and to peer into the mansion from the outside. Shawn's architect had designed it so that the place was lousy with French doors, a way to open the house on days when the weather permitted, and it was kind of interesting for her to peer in. She'd already wandered through Eagle Mansion, of course, but there was something voyeuristic in standing on the patio and cupping her hands to the windows.

The patio narrowed at the end, but turned the corner and took her around the side and then behind Eagle Mansion. It was difficult for her to tell what the difference was, but it was clear that this part of the estate was meant for the staff. Maybe that it was designed to be more functional? The doors seemed designed to hide what was behind them rather than to give guests views of the slope down to the river. Back here, the paved drive turned into a parking lot—guests dropped off out front by chauffeurs or automatics—with an unattached garage that held all the maintenance equipment. She hadn't bothered going into the garage, but according to Nellie, it held a couple of pickup trucks, gardening tools and lawn mowers, snowblowers, a full-on snowplow—all that sort of crap. There was another outbuilding that was slightly smaller that was supposed to contain a fully outfitted workshop so the maintenance guys could make anything they needed for repairs, a decent-sized outbuilding that had the water-pumping equipment, and then a much smaller outbuilding, small enough that she would have called it a shed, that Nellie had told her was used for . . . Eh. She couldn't remember. They were all immaculately designed and built, or at least seemed so from the outside, though so closely linked to Eagle Mansion's design that it was hard to believe they had such pedestrian purposes and hadn't always been there.

There was another building, however, behind the kitchen and the ground fenced off for a garden, that she'd noticed but not paid attention to before. It was the size of a small cottage, and it looked, in a lot of ways, like a cottage. She walked over to it. The building stood out to her because, unlike the garage and the maintenance buildings, it had clearly been there for a long time. The roof was new, and from where she was, the windows looked new, but as she got closer, it was more and more clear that some of the rocks that made up the base had shifted, and the timbers didn't look right. There were scorch marks around the windows and the door.

Had it been there before, the winter she'd lived in the cabin with Billy and Shawn? It looked familiar, but she couldn't tell.

She stepped up to the door but it didn't open. There was a hand-print reader, and Emily put her hand on it.

Nothing.

"Nellie," she said. "Open up, please."

Nothing. Maybe Nellie wasn't wired up out here. She couldn't remember whether anybody had said anything about the outbuildings and the grounds. Nellie must have been confined to Eagle Mansion and the Nest proper. She stepped away from the door and moved to one of the windows. Inside, the room showed clear signs of a fire, but that was it. Nothing that seemed worth keeping, she thought, and wondered why on earth the building was still there.

Oh.

How could she have failed to recognize it? Of course she'd been in there before. During those months that she lived out on the estate with Billy and Shawn in the cabin, the year she'd let herself drop out of college, she'd come here more than once with Shawn.

But only once without him. Near the end. When things were so twisted and complicated and broken with the three of them that she couldn't figure out what made sense anymore.

She looked in the window again, but the inside truly was unremarkable other than the fire damage. What would have been cathartic, she thought, was if the cabin was still here. But, alas, Shawn had donated it to Cortaca University. If the cabin were still standing where it had been for those long, strange months when she was twenty and then twenty-one years old, she could have looked for some peace.

Instead, she found herself pacing away from the preserved groundskeeper's cottage and looking for the plot of land the cabin had once occupied, looking for what was missing.

How was it, she thought, that she'd been there for a week already and this was the first time it had occurred to her to look for the cabin? Forty or fifty feet past the burned cottage she found a flat piece of land that looked promising, but no, she realized; it was too close to Eagle Mansion still. The view was wrong, and there should have been . . . yes, there! After the trees thickened behind the mansion, a dozen steps in, there were the remnants of a small clearing: the Eagle family burial plot. Shawn's great-grandfather, his grandfather and grandmother, his mother and father.

It had been neatly tended when she'd lived at the cabin, with fresh plantings and evidence of Shawn's intervention, the activity of a caring son, but in the following years it had gone wild. There was a new

wrought-iron fence that blended into the woods, but even with the
carpet of vines and ivy broken by seedlings and fast-growing pines,
she could see the same small, poorly chiseled sandstone markers, the
names and dates still unreadable. In some ways, it looked better like
this, left to nature. Unmolested. It looked designed to be forgotten.
Smart, she thought, the fence, a way to keep this part of him private
from the guests wandering the grounds; the fence didn't have a gate
that she saw, so anyone who wanted to go into the small burial plot
would have to deliberately step over the thigh-high iron, and there
were small, tactful signs respectfully asking guests to stay out. The
family cemetery looked more authentic to her now than it had a
dozen years earlier when it had been cleared of growth and tended to.
It had looked too ready for use back then, as if it were a going concern, ready to take a body at any moment. Now it looked as it should:
a part of Shawn's history. Buried.

The cemetery oriented her, and she moved back out of the woods
and then took another two dozen, three dozen steps and stopped. She
felt a cold shiver go down her back. She turned to look at the main
building and then down to the river. Yes, she thought. This was it.
This was where the cabin had stood. This was where Shawn and Billy
had come after they graduated, the two of them living barely a step
above savagery while they built the bones of Nellie and what went on
to become Eagle Logic.

It wasn't that long ago, really. Twelve, no, thirteen years since she
landed here. Good god, how had Shawn talked her into coming back
with him after that Halloween party? But he had, and she'd spent
the night, and when she woke in the morning, Shawn's arm flopped
over her shoulder and his hand cupping her breast, she didn't want to
leave. There was that first awkward and charged moment when she'd
opened her eyes to see Billy on his pad, staring at her from his sleeping
bag, but then he'd raised a hand in greeting and rolled over to give
her the privacy to get dressed. She went to go pee, both amused and
disgusted at having to use an outhouse, and when she got back, Billy
was sitting on the porch of the cabin on one of the tree stumps that
passed for furniture.

"I've got some coffee working," he said. His voice was very quiet. "Figure you can use some after last night. I'm Billy. Shawn's roommate. You can go wake him up if you'd like."

"Thanks. That's okay. Let him sleep a bit. I'm not in any hurry. And thanks for the coffee, too."

"Don't thank me yet. It's terrible coffee, made worse by the fact that we don't have any sugar or milk. As an added bonus, it's going to take forever to make. The woodstove has to heat up and then boil the water and then, well, it's a process."

He went in and brought her out a blanket to wrap around herself, and then in a while, went back in the cabin again to bring her out a cup of black coffee that was, as advertised, terrible. They talked and talked, and it wasn't until Shawn came out the door, looking sheepish and yawning, that she realized she'd been chatting with Billy for the better part of two hours.

"Hey," Shawn said. He'd put on a pair of jeans but was barefoot despite the cold, and he pulled a red Cortaca University sweatshirt over his bare chest. He hesitated, and then he walked to her, leaned over, and kissed her.

That was nice.

She didn't remember how exactly it came about, but she spent the day there, and then the three of them drove to Cortaca so she could make her shift at the Stardust Bar. She was exhausted by the time she was done, dead on her feet, but when she left work, she saw Shawn sitting on a bench on the pedestrian mall outside the bar. He was huddled over his laptop, banging away at the keys. She stood over him, and when he closed up his laptop she took his hands in hers. They were so cold they burned against her fingers. He had his hood up and his coat zipped, but he was shivering.

"How long have you been waiting?" she said.

"My whole life," he said.

She was twenty.

She'd never heard anything so beautiful. Of course she'd fallen in love.

He walked her back to that rattletrap car of his and they swung by her apartment so she could grab a change of clothes and her toothbrush. Billy was curled up in the backseat, asleep—now, as she thought about it, for the first time it occurred to her that he was probably passed out drunk—and stayed asleep the whole drive and even once they parked in front of Shawn's cabin. So she spent her second night with Shawn, and while it wasn't every night that month, it was most of them. Sometimes she borrowed a roommate's car to get to Whiskey Run, and sometimes Shawn picked her up or lent her his car so she could get back and forth to classes and her job. She was in love and felt like her life in Cortaca was just a waiting game for when she could get back to the cabin to see Shawn. Classes, her friends, her shifts at the Stardust Bar, Thanksgiving with Marge's family in New York City—all of it was like moving underwater compared to being with Shawn. She started missing a few classes here and there, for an extra few hours or days at the cabin. Accordingly, her grades began to suffer. Still, she pulled an A, two B pluses, and one B minus.

She'd planned to spend the five weeks of winter break living alone in her apartment, picking up extra shifts at the bar, but instead, she went to live with Shawn and Billy in Whiskey Run, taking the station wagon back to Cortaca whenever she had to work. For Christmas, her roommate Marge flew her out to Hawaii to be with Marge's family, and Emily spent the entire week sick with longing to be back with Shawn, the beachfront house wasted on her. New Year's Eve in that tiny cabin, the woodstove glowing red, snow coming down in fits and starts, was the happiest she'd ever been.

And all these years later, standing outside Eagle Mansion as a thirty-three-year-old woman, married to the wrong one of those two boys, when the idea of being twenty, and then twenty-one, seemed like such ancient history, Emily couldn't figure out when things first turned sour with Shawn. There had to have been an initial moment. There had to have been a singular point in time when, if she could go back and press down her finger, it all began to unravel. Was it when Shawn started traveling to try to find investors to give them seed money for the next stage with Eagle Logic, leaving her and Billy alone for such long stretches, days at a time? Was it before that, when Billy was the one who helped her with the dishes and other chores, Shawn so quickly acclimatizing to the idea of being taken care of? Or was it before that, when the spring semester started and she didn't go to class, when she first threw her life at the feet of a man who didn't seem to appreciate what a sacrifice it was for her to drop out of college? Or, maybe, she thought, it started even earlier than any one of them understood, on that very first morning that she woke in the cabin to see Billy looking at her. In the early sunlight of that November morning, as he lay in his sleeping bag and nest of blankets watching her sleep in the arms of Shawn Eagle, that, Emily thought, was when Billy made his choice.

Because in the end, it was as simple as that. A choice. For all of them. The choice that both Shawn and Billy had to make was between her and Eagle Logic. And maybe it was because she was insecure, or maybe it was because she was trying so hard to escape her past, but when it was her turn to choose, she chose the one who *needed* her the most, not the one who *wanted* her the most. It was a coward's choice, but it was too terrifying being in a relationship where she was the one who loved more. With Billy, the reassurance had been—still was— that he needed her more than she needed him. She loved him, she did, but if push came to shove came to hit came to punch came to . . . She'd be able to walk away. Her mother had never been able to walk away. And back then, she'd known that if she stayed any longer with Shawn, it would be too late for her to walk away. The roots would have sunk deep and tangled, and she would never be in control; how could she be in control when she loved Shawn enough to give up on college, but he didn't love her enough to give up on that stupid program he was working on? But Billy was willing to walk away from all of it if it meant she left with him, and there was a power in that. She'd seen her mother . . . No. It wasn't just what had happened with her mother. Billy was handsome, in a different way from Shawn, but still handsome, and he gave all of himself to her even before she gave everything back.

With Shawn, there was such a large part of him that he kept locked away from her. He never talked about his parents or his childhood, even though they were living a stone's throw from the burned-out groundskeeper's cottage. He rarely asked her about herself, either. Sure, he mostly listened when she talked, and when he paid his full attention—when he was bored of working or when he was ready to get laid—he could be so charming and sweet, but it always came on his schedule. He loved her, and she made him happy, but as much as she felt like Shawn wanted her, she was never completely sure she could count on him. Billy was different. Billy was open with her. Billy didn't just want her, Billy *needed* her.

He told her, in stuttering fits and starts, about his own childhood, similar and yet so different from hers. A drunk father disappearing when he was nine, replaced by a series of his mother's boyfriends, some for months, some for days, men drifting through his life who rarely left anything behind but empty bottles. His mother, mercifully dead his freshman year of college, finally overdosing. His mother, who had once wanted to be an artist, had almost certainly been turning tricks for a time, those boyfriends passing through probably deserving of quotation marks around the word *boyfriend*. But he didn't blame his mother. He admired her, in a way, he said, because she did the best she could by him, and even if her best wasn't very good, it was all she could offer. When he told Emily that, he was crying, and of course she cried, too, and looking back on it, she knew his willingness to cry and his ability to make her cry along was at least one of the reasons she fell in love with him.

It was true. She *was* in love with Billy, and she *was* in love with Shawn, and there were weeks of both boys claiming that without her they would never be happy. And then, finally, that one final, long, drag-out night of yelling, of the three of them going back and forth, of words that were hard to take back, the door of the cabin swinging open, slamming closed, accusations, admitted truths.

So, yes, maybe it was a coward's choice, but in the end, she chose Billy. And maybe it was the wrong choice, maybe she should have taken the risk and stayed with Shawn, but it worked out, didn't it? Here she was, all these years later, back on the same piece of ground where it all started, and she was still with Billy.

She kicked at a small rock on the lawn. It rolled through the wet grass where the cabin had once stood and then plonked against a tree. She turned to look back at Eagle Mansion and then up to where the Nest seemed to defy gravity, floating above the building. Her husband was up there now, still working, still carrying on whatever conversation he was having with Nellie.

She hadn't noticed the rain go from drizzle to a continuous assault, but she realized she was shivering. Her pants were wet, and a few drops of rain had worked their way inside her coat and down the front of her shirt. She felt a cold draft go up her spine and she shuddered.

Would Billy make the same choice again, if he was given the choice? Would he choose her over Nellie, would he decide that Emily was worth more than a computer program? Would Shawn make the same choice he had made? Would she?

Because in some ways, it felt like there were three of them living out here in the woods again.

TWENTY-FIVE

NOVEMBER RAIN

Seventh Day access. He'd been so blithe about it, joking to Shawn that it made him God. And it hadn't really been a joke. Sure, Nellie wasn't designed to be an AI, but she was alive in her own way, so if Billy created Nellie, then yeah, he was, if not *the* God, *a* god. In Nellie's universe of code, he and Shawn were the dueling gods of creation.

But if God had created the universe in seven days, Billy had burned through seven days and then two more, and he wasn't sure he'd made any real progress in fixing what he had tried to create so many years ago. The good thing, the blessed thing, however, was that it was time to get the stitches out. Nine days since he'd started working in earnest, ten days since coming to Eagle Mansion.

Or maybe, at this point, it was eleven days? It was . . . He realized he had no idea what time it was. Nellie had been bugging him for hours and hours to go down to the infirmary, but he felt like he was maybe close to finally getting at something in the source code, and he'd ignored her and kept working. It was only when Nellie turned the air-conditioning in the room all the way up and dropped the temperature twenty degrees in twenty minutes that he stopped.

"Okay, okay!" he said. "I can take a hint."

Good. It's nearly four in the afternoon. You have been working without rest for forty-seven hours and eleven minutes. You were scheduled to have your stitches out yesterday afternoon. Please head to the infirmary so I can finally get it done.

"Finally? Shit. We programmed you to be passive-aggressive?"

Perhaps you should wait to insult me. You do realize I'm about to take your stitches out?

He laughed. She really could be funny sometimes.

Once he was headed down the stairs to the infirmary, he couldn't remember why he'd been putting Nellie off. He couldn't wait to have the stitches out. His hand had stopped hurting pretty quickly, but oh, it itched! The itch was a constant companion. He couldn't scratch it through the bandages, which was probably a blessing, because he was sure he would have scratched himself raw, but that meant the only small relief he could find was to squeeze gently on the surface of his palm. When he was working, despite the awkwardness the bandages caused on the keyboard, the itchiness sometimes receded to the background. The same thing that allowed him to forget to shower or eat until Nellie nagged him into it, that meant he slept at odd, slanted hours, also meant that his entire body sometimes seemed to fall away from consciousness. But too often, the thing that brought him out of the opium stupor of working was the tickling sensation of the stitches and his flesh knitting itself back together. He could feel the gash healing, feel the skin growing and sealing shut. It was unbearable.

He sat down, and one articulating arm gently steadied his arm and hand, two others worked to form a sterile tent from surgical paper, and the fourth danced unseen, behind the screen.

I'm giving you a small injection of antibiotics. You'll feel a slight pressure, and then pressure again when I remove the stitches, but it shouldn't cause any pain.

"Easy for you to say. You don't know what pain even is, really."

If you're worried, I can apply spray anesthesia. OR MAYBE YOU NEED A DRINK.

His head snapped up. He'd been staring at the way the surgical drapes made his hand seem to disappear. But she'd said it. Hadn't she said it? Or maybe not. It was late. Early. However you wanted to look at it. He looked around for the soft green light that Nellie used as a focal point—sometimes the shape shifted, moving subtly from ball to something that resembled a water bottle—but it wasn't present.

She'd been doing that to him for the past couple of days. He was sure of it. He'd be working and talking, and it would be Nellie, and then she'd slide something in using that other voice of hers, the Nellie that wasn't Nellie, and then keep talking as if nothing had happened. But when he'd ask her, she insisted she hadn't said anything, that Billy was just working too hard, that he needed to take better care of himself.

Or maybe he needed a drink.

He was hearing ghosts.

He felt pressure on his hand, and, despite what Nellie had said, the slight prick of a needle, and then, quickly after, a much more reassuring pressure, barely the weight of a glass of water, and then heard the snip of the stitches opening. There was a sudden spike in itchiness—the stitches pulling out of his flesh were the worst of all, an army of ants inside him—and then, oh! Oh! Relief! He could have wept. The relief brought with it a sudden surge of warmth and tiredness. He was ready to go to bed, he thought.

Looks good. There will be a slight scar, but that's it. EXCEPT FOR THE WIRES.

"What?"

I said, you look tired.

"Oh."

Did you drift off there for a second? Maybe you should take a nap.

He was tired. No question about that. Maybe he did fall asleep for a moment. He had that drunken exhaustion that made everything seem syrupy.

"Yeah. Okay. Thanks." He flexed his fingers and looked at the palm of his hand. The cut had healed into a small, angry worm. He ran his finger down the short length of the scar. It tickled. He pressed at it. It was hard. Unyielding. Like carpet laid over concrete. "I could use some sleep," he said. He stood up and started walking back to the Nest. "Where's Emily?"

In town. She went to the grocery store. She likes going shopping herself, even though it is completely unnecessary. I can order food for you. I prefer it when she stays here.

The tiredness was overwhelming him now, a wave knocking him down and holding him under. Billy let his fingers slide along the wall as he walked down the hallway from the infirmary, back to the middle of the building and the stairs that brought him back up to the Nest. It felt good to have the bandages off.

I've offered to have food delivered, including having somebody unload the groceries. There is no real reason for her to go into town.

"Yeah, well, there isn't a ton for her to do here. She's trying to keep busy."

YOU NEVER HAVE TO LEAVE.

He stopped walking. At first, even though he should have been expecting it, he had been surprised that wherever he went in Eagle Mansion, Nellie would follow. He'd gotten used to it, however, and he thought it was nice—he could continue a conversation wherever he was and it meant she was always there, always present, always on—to have that constant companion.

"Sorry. What did you say?"

You never have to leave. Is that what Nellie said? She said that, didn't she?

She likes to read.

He started walking again. "Yeah. She loves those romances." His tongue was thick with fatigue, and he was trying to be careful with his words. He wasn't thinking straight. And for god's sake, these stairs. So many stairs. The elevator guy was supposed to be out tomorrow or the next day, and he couldn't wait until he could get up and down without having to traipse up these oversized flights of stairs, even if it was pretty much all the exercise he got.

She's writing a book.

"I'm not sure that's going so well, is it?"

No. I want her to be happy so that you are happy.

Huh. That was interesting.

He caught his toe on the top step and started to stumble forward but then caught himself. Jesus. If Nellie hadn't told him he'd been working nonstop for nearly two days, he might have wondered if he'd somehow discovered a cache of booze and fallen off the wagon. He felt completely messed up, like he was drunk or high, his body flooded by an unnatural exhaustion.

Or like she'd given him a shot of something other than an antibiotic? No. That was crazy.

You need to lie down, Billy.

"Working on it." His voice sounded like it was far away from him. He could hear himself slurring. Too long. He'd been working too long and pushing himself too hard. He wasn't twenty-two anymore. He had to take better care of himself.

He got to the bedroom, gave his teeth a quick brush, took a piss, and then dropped into bed. The lights dimmed and the windows blacked out.

Have a good sleep. I'LL WATCH OVER YOU.

At least, he thought that's what she said, but he was already asleep and it might have been a dream. He woke twisted up in the blankets, as if he'd been rolling and thrashing in his sleep. He had no memories of whatever dreams must have haunted him and left him tangled up in the sheets, but the dual voices of Nellie echoed in his head. His hand was a little itchy still, but nothing like what it had been with the stitches still in. He rubbed his finger down the scar again. He stopped. There was a small piece of thread still in there. He could feel it under his fingertip. He brought his hand up so he could see it, Nellie obligingly raising the lights, but there was nothing to see. Just the smooth, pink scar. No black end of thread.

He sat up too quickly and was rewarded with a burst of dizziness. He had to sit on the edge of the bed and get his bearings. Once he stood up, however, he felt fantastic. Except that he had to take a piss to beat the band. He took care of that, standing there long enough that he thought he could have stopped a forest fire in its tracks, then took a shower and had a shave, ruminating on the fact that there wasn't much a good sleep couldn't cure. He felt like a new man.

He pulled on a clean pair of jeans and a T-shirt, but he left his boots kicked off by the side of the bed. Barefoot was fine. He wasn't planning to leave the Nest. He was hungry, however, ravenous even, so he headed to the kitchen to grab a snack.

He almost walked into the bedroom door.

He'd gotten so used to it opening as he approached, Nellie anticipating his movements, that it was a close call. Before he'd had a chance to do anything other than blurt out "Whoa!" and step back, the door slid open. One of those glitches, he thought. A reminder that he really wasn't getting anywhere with his work.

In the living area, Emily's laptop was back on the table, but the lid was closed and there was no sign of her.

"Where's Emily?"

No answer.

"Nellie?"

He stopped, fingers of his right hand wrapped around the handle of the fridge.

"Nellie?"

Yes, Billy?

"Oh. I said, where's Emily?"

Do you always need Emily?

"Well, yeah. She's my wife."

Emily is out for her morning run. She should be back in seventeen minutes.

"Morning run? How long did I sleep for?"

You look better.

He started to say "Thank you," but hesitated. "I asked, how long did I sleep for?"

He shouldn't have had to ask twice. Another little glitch, but one piling on the other. She was designed, first and foremost, to make you happy. The whole point of Nellie was for her to make your life better. The personal assistant of all personal assistants. Her job was to do things for you, to think of things for you, to take care of your house and make the decisions you would have made yourself, but without your having to bother. Sure, the companionship thing was huge—the way she made loneliness obsolete was absolutely killer and would be what made Nellie more than simply a product—but if she couldn't perform that base function of opening doors and answering questions and, well, doing shit for you, then none of the other stuff really mattered. How could she make you happy if she couldn't answer basic questions?

Fifteen hours.

"Wow." He opened the fridge. He stood in front of it for a few seconds, letting the cold air wash over him. He didn't need to stand there. All he was looking for was the milk to pour over his cereal. The milk was in the door, exactly where he'd expected it to be. He hesitated, though, because it gave him time to think. Fifteen hours. He believed Nellie when she said it. His muscles confirmed the number. But why would he even think that she might by lying? Maybe that was normal for a teenager, but for an adult, it was kind of amazing to sleep for that long, though with the stitches itching him awake for the last ten days, he'd barely gotten any sleep. And yet, he'd felt wired all week, running on excitement up until the moment the stitches had been removed.

There was something nagging at him about the code. He hadn't figured anything out, but he thought he might have been close to something. Whatever it was, it was slippery, like chasing a memory, buried deep within the millions of lines of code. But he felt like he was tantalizingly close to discovering an essential problem with Nellie. That was why he'd pulled another all-nighter, why he kept ignoring her when she told him it was time to go get the stitches out. And kept ignoring her until she jacked the air-conditioning to the point where she froze him out of the room. And *that* was when he'd suddenly been overwhelmed by fatigue; it was right after she gave him that shot of antibiotics and took . . .

He reached slowly for the milk.

No, he thought. It was just antibiotics. Thinking like that was crazy town. That was full-on—

"Froot Loops," he said.

The closest we have is Lucky Charms. However, they are in the dry storage area in the downstairs kitchen. Would you like me to have Emily add Froot Loops to the grocery list? I have to tell you, as your friend, sugared cereal isn't exactly the healthiest way to start your day.

He was holding the handle of the door in his right hand still, reaching to grab the milk with his left hand, and he noticed something on the angry-looking scar marking his palm. A speck of dirt. No, a tiny hair. He let go of the door handle and used the nails on his right thumb and finger to take it out. The black hair, the size of a comma, came out easily, and he brushed it off his fingers and onto the floor.

She'd said, "as your friend."

What exactly had Shawn and his engineers done to Nellie when they'd been messing around under the hood?

TWENTY-SIX

WHAT IMMORTAL HAND OR EYE
DARE FRAME THY FEARFUL SYMMETRY?

Was it the eternal duty of an older sibling to worry about the younger? Because if it wasn't, Beth thought, then why was she stressed out about Emily?

They talked every couple of days, and Emily sounded happy, albeit kind of bored. Well, she was also frustrated. Writing a novel was proving to be harder than she had expected.

"Come on, Emily, you've been there two weeks—"

"Almost three."

"—*not quite* three weeks. What, are you expecting the Pulitzer folks to show up at your door with a trophy? Give yourself a break. If you told me you wanted to be an accountant, I wouldn't expect you to be able to run a—"

"Beth. Beth, stop. If you love me, even a little bit, you will not start talking to me about tax law."

"My point is that you just need to relax. It's going to take a little while for you to hit your stride. Besides, you've said Billy's spending every waking moment working. Maybe that's the problem: no chance for you to do any research. How are you supposed to write your super-sexy-time novel if you don't have any time for super-sexy time of your own?"

"You know, just because you and Rothko got pregnant while you were camping with me here doesn't mean—"

"Have you tried being on top?" Beth interrupted. She was pretty sure her mischievous grin could be heard through the phone.

She was rewarded with laughter from Emily, who made a few off-color comments about Beth and Rothko's love life.

"How is Billy, though? Make sure he doesn't burn himself out working all the time."

Sometimes they'd do video if Ruth and Rose were around, but both of them seemed to prefer the facelessness of the phone. You could go pee or put on your makeup or flip through a magazine when you were on the phone. When you were on video, you had to actually pay complete attention. From what Emily had described, though, Beth was surprised she could get cell reception at all. It sounded like they were out in the middle of nowhere. Shawn Eagle had probably had his own cell tower installed or something. The whole setup was ludicrous. The guy built an entire hotel with a weird private house stuck on top of it. That's what came with being a billionaire, she guessed. Maybe that was normal for guys like Shawn Eagle. She and Rothko were doing okay, solidly middle-class, and they had a few friends who had gone into banking who were starting to pull in serious cash, three or four times what she made, but nothing like the kind of money you had when you founded Eagle Technology. Other billionaires bought football teams or took up race car driving. Shawn Eagle just evidently liked hospitality.

Maybe it was because they were talking on the phone, or maybe it was because Beth thought she had asked the question with no ulterior motive, but she didn't recognize the silence as the sound of Emily's laughter cutting off. She thought, for a moment, that the call had dropped. But then she heard Emily give a deep sigh.

"You can't let it go, can you?"

"What?"

"Don't 'what?' me. You know damn well what I mean with your 'make sure he doesn't burn himself out' comment."

"I didn't—"

"You did, Beth. I get it, okay. I know that we have a complicated history, and I know that Billy has used up plenty of chances, but I'm telling you, he's sober. He hasn't had a drink since I came to stay with you guys."

"You mean, since he hit you."

It just sort of slipped out of her mouth. On purpose. Had she asked the question innocently? Or had she meant to provoke Emily? Because the truth was, no, she couldn't let it go. It didn't matter how many times they hashed it over or how much time they spent talking about it in the immediate aftermath, during the time Billy was in rehab. It didn't matter that they kept arguing in the days after Emily went back to him, and then less frequently as the days became weeks, and less frequently still once it had been months and then past the first year. She couldn't let it go because they both knew better!

She'd liked Billy at first. She really had. Of course, she'd never met Shawn Eagle—as intense as her sister's love affair had been, it hadn't lasted long enough for her to come to Chicago with Shawn or for Beth to visit—but she'd hated the idea of her sister dropping out of school over a boy. When Emily pulled the old boyfriend switcheroo and fled Cortaca with Billy, showing up in Chicago with a packed car and talking about going back to college once they were settled out west, Beth liked Billy simply for not being Shawn. But the truth was that she'd also liked Billy for being Billy. They were in Chicago for only a couple of days, so it seemed normal to take them out and get plastered. Everybody was drinking a ton. Billy drinking a ton didn't stand out. This was before she and Rothko had kids. It's not like she and Rothko were exactly saints. She remembered quite clearly that the only drugs during that visit had come from Rothko, a celebratory gram of coke. It just didn't seem like a big deal. Before they had kids, they used coke maybe once or twice a year, got drunk a couple of times a month; she and Rothko were young and happy, and Rothko, at least, didn't have a history of substance abuse in his family. Nothing had seemed out of the ordinary with Billy.

She'd been rooting for them. She had. She'd swear on her daughters that she'd been happy for Emily. Billy sometimes seemed to get lost inside himself, but he was unquestionably brilliant. He was also a pretty regular guy when he wanted to be. Beth had known some super-nerds in college, and they usually weren't so great to hang out with, but Billy, when he wasn't thinking about whatever computer thing he was thinking about, was fun. She and Rothko had gone to visit them out in San Francisco once they'd gotten settled, and she still remembered Billy standing on the karaoke stage belting out Bryan Adams's "Summer of '69," the way he couldn't stop beaming at her sister. He acted like he'd won the frickin' lottery with Emily, and maybe it was some of that devotion to her that rubbed off on Beth, because when Emily called to say that she and Billy had eloped—if you could still elope nowadays, particularly when your parents were already dead—Beth had actually found it romantic.

And if it seemed like he was bouncing from job to job kind of quickly, well, Emily told her, that was how things worked in the tech industry. Billy was just trying to find the kind of place where he could ride a wave. That was when Eagle Technology was suddenly shooting into infinity, and it made sense to Beth: if Billy could be the man behind that, he could do it again. In the meantime, why would she worry about Emily? Yeah, it was a shame that they'd left Shawn before Eagle Technology started raking in cash, but there was enough left to float them until Billy hit it big again.

If she could do it all again, Beth wanted to believe she would have seen the warning signs. She wanted to believe that she would have noticed how Billy seemed to have two beers to every one of Rothko's, how it was Billy bringing out the coke now, two grams, three grams at a time, every single time she visited. It all seemed normal and fun, and because she didn't live in the same city as Emily, she didn't see that Billy wasn't just drinking like that because he was having a great time with friends, and it wasn't just a one-off thing to have some blow. How could she have known? Even during the couple of weeks they spent on the Appalachian Trail, Emily didn't tell her. At least not explicitly. And after that trip, whatever hints she might have dropped to Beth were lost in the sudden change in Beth's own life: she was pregnant with Ruth and Rose. How was that for an excuse? Twin girls were a good distraction.

But twin girls also threw things into stark relief. Emily flew up by herself at the birth. When she and Billy came together to Chicago a few months later, however, Beth and Rothko weren't exactly up for clubbing, and yet Billy had gotten drunk anyway. That was the first time Beth had a sense of there being a problem. So she started asking. By the time Billy hit Emily, Beth had already been trying to get her sister to walk away from her marriage for more than a year.

That had been a hard few months. The girls only five years old, not really understanding why Aunt Emily was living with them and why Uncle Billy—whom they adored—wasn't there, too. She and Rothko having to retreat to their bedroom early every night so that Emily could pull out the couch and have a little privacy. Her sister breaking down into tears almost every single day, or spending their entire run circling back over and over through her relationship with Billy, trying to figure out where she'd gone wrong. The shining grace of all of it had been Rothko. He wasn't perfect, but he'd done his best, and he'd made a point of getting Emily out of the house with him at least once a week so that Beth could have some breathing space.

The other thing that had been good for them as sisters was that it meant, for the first time, they'd had an honest conversation about their father and what he'd done to both of them. Beth had been able to finally apologize for the way she'd run away as a survival mechanism, and how that meant Emily was left alone to fend for herself with that bastard.

That was guilt she'd carried with her for a long time, and she was almost certain it was that same guilt that had made her so upset about the idea of Emily going back to Billy. There was unquestionably a difference between Billy and her father: Beth never worried about Billy being around Ruth or Rose. He was a drunk, but he was never *that*.

But he hit Emily. Once.

Beth had been thrilled—and surprised, given how long she'd been dithering about her marriage—that Emily had the balls to straight up walk out the first time Billy punched her. First time, last time. That's how it had to work in Beth's book. Hadn't the two of them learned that much from their mother? And yet, Emily believed him when he said that he'd changed, believed that rehab worked magic.

He'd stayed true to his word as far as Beth knew. No drugs, no drinking. He hadn't raised a hand to her sister since that one time. For all that, however, Beth just couldn't get over it. She'd heard her dad say he'd stop drinking. Heard her dad apologize to her mother, and her mother kept believing he'd change until the day it killed her.

And then her dad had made the same apologies to Beth. He was sorry, he loved her, he couldn't help himself, and if she would only let him . . . No. No, Billy's behavior wasn't something Beth was ever going to be able to fully let go. Emily might mark time from when Billy got clean, but Beth marked time from when Billy first landed a punch, waiting for it to happen again.

Still, the truth was, it *hadn't* happened again. Billy kind of seemed like he'd gotten his shit together. She didn't have to forgive Billy, and she didn't have to forget what had happened, but if she didn't want to push Emily away, if she wanted to be a real part of Emily's life and put herself in a position to keep a better eye on things, to be a better big sister, she'd have to fake it. Which meant that almost as quickly as the words came out of her mouth—"You mean, since he hit you"—she was backpedaling and apologizing.

"Oh, shit. I'm sorry, honey." (She wasn't.) "I'm sorry, I didn't mean that." (She did.) "I shouldn't have said it. That wasn't fair." (No, it seemed fair enough.)

She held her breath, waiting for Emily to yell at her, but Emily was quiet. Beth felt some relief. You can't unsay something, so she'd gotten to make her point and then walk away from it.

"No. It wasn't fair," Emily said.

"I'm sorry." (But it was fair. He hit you.)

A loud sigh from Emily. Then, "How are the girls? I haven't even asked. I've been too busy complaining about living in this crazy mansion and having nothing to do."

"You've got plenty of stuff to do. You've got to make up all sorts of interesting ways for your characters to have sex." She didn't hear Emily laugh, but even over the phone, she could feel the air between them clear up. "The girls are good. The weather here is completely shitty, though, so we've been cooped up. It's been raining all week, which is one thing in May, when you've got those lovely, warm spring showers, but it's another thing as we're swinging around the corner to Thanksgiving. Last I checked they were playing some sort of elaborate version of school in the bunk beds." She got up out of her bed and started walking toward the door. "Want to talk to them?"

"Sure," Emily said.

Beth put her sister on speakerphone and automatically started talking louder. "You can tell them why you aren't coming for Thanksgiving."

"First of all," Emily said, her voice tinny and thin coming out of the phone's speaker, "if I go anywhere for Thanksgiving, Marge will kill me if it's not with her family. Second of all, you guys are already coming out here for Christmas. It'll be fun. I'm sure Whiskey Run will be beautiful in the snow, and we'll have the run of the whole mansion, and Nellie—"

"No!" Beth screamed the word as she stepped through the doorway of the girls' bedroom. One of them was standing on the top bunk, the high ceilings of the condo giving plenty of room to spare, and the other was standing on the ground below. From the entrance to the bedroom, she couldn't tell who was who.

"No!"

They were laughing and jumping, holding opposite ends of a blanket and tugging back and forth. As she caught sight of them, the girl on the ground gave a hefty yank just as the one on the top jumped into the air, jolting her forward so that she stumbled and caught her foot on the guardrail. It happened so quickly that Beth didn't have time to do anything other than yell that single, singular word "No!" before one of her daughters pinwheeled to the ground.

TWENTY-SEVEN

A HISTORY LESSON

Shawn sent one of his jets for Emily. It was over-the-top and completely unnecessary—it was only a broken arm—but Billy appreciated the gesture. His first reaction when Nellie told him that the jet was coming to take Emily to Chicago was a flash of anger, but after a second he came to think it was actually pretty sweet.

"I mean, come on," he'd said to Emily, "given how much money the guy has, it's probably the equivalent of one of us offering to give a friend a ride to the airport, but still."

It is important to Shawn that you are happy.

"See? Listen to Nellie. Shawn wants to make you happy."

By the time she got in the Honda to head to Shawn's airstrip, she'd mostly calmed down, but she had been seriously freaked out by the incident. Not that he could really blame her. From her perspective, all she'd heard was her sister yelling "No!" and then a whole bunch of screaming and crying for a couple of minutes. By the time Beth told her that one of the girls had fallen off the bunk bed and broken her arm—it was a compound fracture, meaning the bone was sticking out, so it was pretty darn clear what they were dealing with—Emily was completely losing her shit. Not that Billy would have noticed if Nellie hadn't interrupted him. He'd been in the office working and

Emily had been walking around inside Eagle Mansion, doing laps, since it was drizzling outside.

The funny thing, at least to Billy, was that even a couple of hours after it happened, as his wife was getting ready to meet the jet, he still couldn't get a straight answer about which of the twins had gotten hurt. Emily told him that Ruth had fallen off the bed, and then she said it was Rose. Then she said, no, she was sure it was Ruth, and *then* she said that the girls were insisting to Beth that it was Rose who had fallen off the bed even though Ruth was the one with the broken arm. He loved the twins; how cool and offbeat they were was part of what had turned him around on the idea of their having kids, but yeah, the girls were weird.

Either way, with the private jet and Shawn arranging for a chauffeur to meet her at the airport in Chicago, Billy figured Emily would make the hospital about the same time whichever one of his nieces it was came out of surgery.

In the meantime, he was surprised to admit that the idea of Emily's being gone for a few days gave him a certain sense of relief. No, not relief. Joy, maybe. He was bummed that she was going, so relief was the wrong word, because he did like having her in the house and spending time with her even if he mostly hadn't been spending time with her, but there was something appealing about the idea of a few days of bachelordom. Yes, it was selfish, but the truth was that he'd been working like a dog, as hard as he ever had when he first started trying to make Nellie in the first place. He was ready for a break, and with Emily gone, he could relax completely, however he felt like it. If Emily were here, she'd want to go for a hike, or even take a day trip somewhere, ask about how things were going with Nellie, talk over Shawn and Wendy coming to join them for Thanksgiving, or go back to one of her favorite subjects of late, which was the baby they were now actively trying to have. Well, maybe not actively, because she still hadn't said anything about the fact that she wasn't using birth control.

Okay, so the no-sex thing was going to be a bummer, but having Emily visit her sister for a few days meant that if he wanted to take a break, he could do whatever the heck he liked without feeling any guilt or pressure about hanging with Emily. And then he could go back to putting Nellie through her paces. He finally felt like he'd found some of the threads that were tangled, and he was beginning to gently tease them out. Shawn and his engineers had done some really interesting things, but they'd also loaded her up with all sorts of weird junk that was now woven throughout. He had to be careful what he pulled in case the whole thing unraveled.

The biggest issue was what they'd done with all the security access levels. First Day, Second Day. It created a confusing sort of echo within the program. Nellie rewrote herself in real time, creating new programs to deal with past and anticipated questions, but with the different access levels, it made things even more complicated. Writing on top of writing on top of writing. He hadn't figured out how to—or if he could—strip it out, but it was more complicated than it needed to be.

In a lot of ways, he thought, working on Nellie was like working with a perfect piece of marble; all he had to do was chip away the excess to reveal the masterpiece waiting underneath.

First, though, he needed to take a break. Catch his breath. Decompress. He saw Emily off in the Honda, went back up to the Nest to work for a while, and then went to bed around midnight. He woke up late morning, and by the time he showered and got his act together, it was close to lunch, which was ideal; all he wanted was to go into town and get a big, fat, ridiculous cheeseburger, some onion rings, and a Diet Coke. After he had that grease explosion, he'd walk around town and explore a little bit—Emily had told him that it was actually pretty cute despite the way it all felt too new—and then go back to Eagle Mansion and take a nap. After that, he thought, he'd be feeling great and ready to dive back into Nellie for the next week and a bit until Shawn came for Thanksgiving.

He mulled over the idea of having Shawn and Wendy for Thanksgiving as the Honda drove him into town. He hadn't been in favor of the idea, but Shawn wanted to come to see if Billy was making any progress, and Emily had insisted. Billy never cared much about

Thanksgiving. Emily hadn't either, she said, when she was a kid, but her college roommate Marge was huge into Thanksgiving, and had sort of adopted Emily. Probably every other year Marge persuaded Emily to come to New York City—Marge's parents had an insanely huge and expensive place on the Upper East Side, overlooking Central Park, and had bought Marge her own five-bedroom, six-bath penthouse with only slightly worse views of the park—and Thanksgiving was absolutely *a thing* for Emily now. By extension, that meant it was *a thing* for Billy. He thought that probably—maybe—Marge would be open to his coming this year, but that was no certainty. Back when he was drinking everything in sight, when he . . . when Emily went to live with Beth for those few months and he was getting sober, Marge had called him and given him the sort of verbal blistering that left a mark.

For all that, Billy actually liked Marge. She took her money for granted, but not in a shitty way, and she'd been incredibly generous to Emily and so thoughtful about it that Emily, and, again by extension, Billy, never actually felt weird about taking her gifts. He thought Marge liked him, too, and now that he was clean and sober, he thought that of all Emily's friends, she was the one most likely to actually give him a second chance. But it didn't matter, because he wanted to stay in Whiskey Run so he wasn't thrown off his rhythm with Nellie.

He suggested to Emily that she go to Chicago or New York, but she flat-out refused to go somewhere for Thanksgiving without him.

"And if we're stuck here," she said, "I don't want to do Thanksgiving just the two of us."

"Three," Billy said. "Don't forget about Nellie."

"Ha, ha," she said.

But Billy hadn't been joking, and when she said that she wanted to invite Shawn, he didn't have a good reason to say no. As Emily pointed out, the man was already planning to come for a check-in, and Eagle Mansion was, after all, Shawn's estate.

For that matter, Billy thought as he drove past the row of stores and restaurants trying to decide where to eat, he shouldn't forget that Whiskey Run was Shawn's as well. Every shopkeeper and waiter would know who he was. Mind your Ps and Qs.

He got to the end of the strip and then had the car turn itself around so that he was headed back in the direction of Eagle Mansion. He went past the Thai place and Blinker's, the pizza place, past the Eagle Technology Store, which was a smaller version of the Eagle Technology Stores dotting malls all over the world, and stopped near the other end of the line, in front of a place called Timber Brew. He wasn't going to have a drink, so if it was just a bar, he'd keep going. A bar wasn't the right place for him. He wanted a burger, though, and he refused to believe that with all the shit Shawn had built in his personal city, there wasn't somewhere you could get a burger. He looked through the window and took heart; there were maybe a dozen people sitting at tables and eating. It was clean and new-looking inside, which wasn't a surprise, but it also felt slightly more alive than the Thai place had. Maybe that was because there were actual customers. Where had they come from? Looking closely, however, he thought he recognized one or two faces. Perhaps one of the guys on the lawn crew who came out to Eagle Mansion every week to blow leaves, or maybe somebody who had been working construction when he came to visit in September. Locals, he guessed, which made sense. With Shawn running things, they all had jobs that paid well and schedules that afforded them a lunch break.

He ordered a cheeseburger topped with fried onions and barbecue sauce, an order of onion rings, and a Diet Coke. Exactly what he'd been hankering for. He'd brought his tablet so he could read, but there were sports highlights on the television over the bar, so he watched those instead. Admittedly, he thought, it was hard to mess up a burger and rings, but the food was excellent. He didn't even miss not being able to have a beer. He felt himself begrudgingly giving Shawn a nod: he had to be losing money on the place, but it was hard to argue that life wasn't better in Whiskey Run since Shawn had rolled into town.

He washed up after eating and took a slow stroll down the street. He stepped inside most of the little stores, fingering the dresses in one store, looking at the jewelry in the art gallery, which featured only upstate New York artists, thinking about what he might get Emily for Christmas. He popped into the candy store and bought—or, rather, Shawn bought—a small bag of English toffee and chocolate-covered sponge. It was relaxing, and he took his time. Where the strip of shops and restaurants gave out, he turned around and headed back on the other side. He was just browsing, though at the hardware store he bought a roll of canvas and a box of permanent markers, thinking he might use them to diagram some logic-flow questions he was working through. It took him a little more than an hour moving at a leisurely pace to go from Timber Brew down one end and back up the other. He'd parked in front of Timber Brew, which was a few buildings up from the end, and as he crossed the street, he saw that decrepit, beat down–looking bar with the wooden sign and the faded red paint: Ruffle's.

He knew in his marrow that it wasn't a coincidence. He wanted to believe that he'd just ended up standing there, in front of Ruffle's, but he couldn't. He knew the truth: the moment Emily told him she was going to Chicago was the moment he'd decided to have a drink. He couldn't bring liquor back to Eagle Mansion without risking getting caught, and he couldn't have a drink at one of Shawn's places in Whiskey Run, so that meant, inevitably, he was going to end up here, at Ruffle's, the one place in town he could have a drink without it getting reported back to Shawn. He took a quick glance down the street, but nobody was out, so he ducked in through the front door.

It wasn't as dim inside as he'd expected, but the owner would have been doing himself a favor by turning the lights down: the place was a dump. There was sawdust on the floor, but that couldn't hide the rough planks scarred from cigarettes, from back when smoking in a bar was still legal in New York State. The pool table had newish-looking felt, but the table itself was beaten and gouged out, one of the feet missing and replaced by a chunk of two-by-four. And yet, as much as Ruffle's was the antithesis of the clean and new Timber Brew and all the other places in Whiskey Run, Billy loved it immediately. It had that sour smell of spilled beer and disappointment that all good drinking places carried. The bar itself was some sort of dark wood and seemed positively alive with history; Billy was sure he wouldn't be able to count the hours that elbows had spent propped up on that bar. There were a couple of tables scattered toward the back, and behind those, a hallway that led, Billy was sure, to a pair of absolutely rank bathrooms. Old-school country music was playing quietly.

He was the only person in the place, and he sat down on one of the stools at the bar and waited patiently. He felt unaccountably calm. He wasn't supposed to drink. He understood that intellectually. But this felt so right. He'd have just one drink and then he'd head back to Eagle Mansion recharged and ready.

After a few minutes, he heard the sound of somebody moving, and then the door behind the bar opened. The bartender didn't look surprised to see Billy sitting at the bar and waiting. He opened the door fully, stepped back behind the door, and came out again carrying a cardboard box heavy enough to make him grunt. He put it down on the bar in front of Billy, and Billy heard the satisfying clink of bottles moving against one another.

He was an older guy, probably late sixties. Out west, Billy thought, he'd be wearing a cowboy hat and could look the part. Leathery skin with deep wrinkles, a thick, gray handlebar mustache. He wasn't big, but he looked solid, and Billy bet the old man could whip his ass. He was rocking a pair of black jeans and a worn work shirt with the sleeves rolled to his elbows. As Billy watched the bartender pull bottles from the box, he couldn't help but notice the knotted muscles in the man's forearms. Seriously, he thought, give the guy a pack of cigarettes and put him on a horse and you'd have an advertising campaign for Marlboro.

He rubbed his thumb nervously against the scar on his hand. He thought he felt something prickly against his thumb, but he couldn't look away from the sight of the bottles of booze being put down in front of him. It was all cheap, off-brand crap. Billy flashed back to running into his old classmate, Raj, in the first-class lounge in the Baltimore airport after he had first gone to see Shawn. He'd like to see the cowboy's reaction to Raj's trying to order a glass of Macallan 25 in here. He'd looked it up. That stuff went for more than a hundred bucks a pour.

The bartender finished unloading bottles and then pulled a knife from his belt to slit the tape and break down the box. He slid the box to the end of the bar and then started neatly stocking the bar. He spared Billy a few glances, but didn't bother to take his order. Billy, for his part, had the good sense to stay quiet. Finally, after what had to have been close to five minutes, the sound of glass moving around and the warbled crooning of what Billy thought was probably Hank Williams the only accompaniment, the bartender turned to face Billy.

"Let me guess. Beer and a shot?"

"Sounds good to me."

The bartender reached down for a glass, ran it hard through a tub of ice to fill it up, and then put it on the bar in front of Billy. He turned, opened a fridge under the counter, and pulled out a can of lemonade, popped open the top, and then poured it into the glass.

"Well," he said, "you'll have to settle for this." He slid it forward and shook his head. "Don't give me that gaping-mouth, innocent-sheep bullshit. I can tell an alky when I see one. How long you been off the sauce?"

Billy felt himself absently touch the two-year coin through the fabric of his jeans. "How'd you know?"

The bartender shrugged. "Takes one to know one. Plus, I might not have gone along with Eagle's plan to tidy up the town, but that don't mean I don't know what's what. Word is out that nobody is supposed to offer alcohol to the guy working up at Eagle Mansion. And I don't recognize you from Adam, but it's been a long time since I've had somebody come through that front door that ain't got a tab or ain't wearing a pair of work boots that they put to good use. Which makes you Eagle's fellow. And just because I didn't want him touching Ruffle's don't mean I don't recognize what this means to the folks around here. Good jobs that pay good money. Kids getting a chance to go to college all expenses paid. My grandson is planning to go off to some liberal arts school in Maine and is pleased as punch about it. No sir, I ain't going to muck all that up for everybody. If Eagle decides that what he wants to do is run around town naked with his pecker stuck in a tub of butter instead of running some sort of weird hotel at that haunted mansion of his, I ain't going to bat an eye as long as he keeps dumping money into Whiskey Run. So you can sit down for a spell and I'm happy to jaw it up with you, but lemonade is about as exciting as it gets for you. You want to drink, you're going to have to take your sorry ass down to Cortaca where nobody will recognize you."

Billy picked up the lemonade. It was carbonated, and he watched the bubbles fight past the ice. "I take it that buying some coke is also out of the question, then?"

He was rewarded with a big grin and a genuine laugh from the cowboy. "Name's Gene," he said. "And sorry, I'm more of a pot guy. Not that I'm sharing that with you, either."

Gene had the kind of firm handshake that told you he could make it crushing if he needed to, but that he didn't need to for you to understand he was a man. Turned out that when Gene wasn't running Ruffle's, he also ran a small farm. "Got turned on to organics about the time I got off the bottle myself, and it keeps me out of trouble. I work late hours here, and the couple of cows and goats and the few acres I have is enough for me to need an early start. I'm a lot less tempted to dunk myself in a bottle when I know I've got to be up at six to do my chores. It's not ranch work, but there's always something that needs tending or fixing."

To his surprise, Billy found the lemonade hitting the spot. He'd come into Ruffle's fully expecting to have beer or gin, but the lemonade was sweet and fizzy and tickled his throat. He pulled out his phone and took a picture of the can. He'd ask Nellie to make sure there was some in the house. They talked of farming and what it had been like for Gene to watch Whiskey Run being transformed around him. While they talked, Billy drank the whole can of lemonade. Gene offered him another and a fresh glass full of ice.

"Hope you've got cash money, Billy. Shawn Eagle don't have no standing credit in my bar. Neither did his father, when it came to it." He lifted the tab of the lemonade, the carbonation making a satisfying hiss, the ice clinking and settling as he poured it into the glass.

"You knew his dad?"

Gene picked up a rag and wiped the bar even though it looked clean to Billy.

"That's right," he said. "Can't say I was fond of the asshole, either. Might be why I was so stubborn about taking Eagle's buyout. I'm a firm believer in the idea that the apple don't fall far from the tree. My family's been living in Whiskey Run for five generations, and the way I've heard it passed down, the only difference between the generations of Eagle men was how much money they had to wrap around themselves.

"No, Simon Eagle was a full-on son of a bitch, but I ain't embarrassed to say that I was too afraid of him to do anything about it. That man was mean and he could fight. I probably should have cleared him out of here, but I was drinking myself back then, and it don't do no good to be poking at snakes."

Billy realized that he was scratching at the soft, shiny flesh of the scar on his palm. It was itching again. Crap. He looked at it and saw another little black hair poking out. He tried to grab it with his nails but it was too short. How the hell had Nellie missed that when she pulled the stitches out?

"When you say he was mean, what exactly are you talking about?" He shook his head. "Sorry. Weird question, but do you have a pair of tweezers by any chance?"

Gene kneeled down and pulled a small blue toolbox out from under the bar. He started rummaging through it. "About what you'd expect when I say he was mean. Beat the shit out of his wife. Beat the shit out of his kid. Got in fights whenever he could. Had a few girlfriends on the side, and the rumor was he wasn't exactly gentle with them, either."

He suddenly stopped and stared at Billy. "You in here to cause trouble?"

"Pardon?" Billy had picked up his lemonade and put it back on the bar.

"Are you asking because you're curious, or are you asking because you're going to do something with it?"

So Billy ended up telling him the whole story of how he and Shawn had holed up in the cabin after graduation, how they'd worked on Eagle Logic together but had parted ways because of Emily.

Gene grunted. "I'd say it always comes down to a girl, except my grandson's gay. Sometimes it comes down to a boy, I suppose. And you can't tell me what it is exactly you're working on?"

Billy hesitated, but then he shook his head. "I'd like to. I really would, but sorry, Gene. Can't."

"Well, I'll trust that what you told me is true," Gene said.

It was. Billy had told him all of it. Almost. He hadn't told him about Takata.

"Although, nobody ever got into too much trouble for a little talking, right?" Billy laughed, pleased with himself for the joke.

"I didn't know the first Eagle, the one who opened up Eagle Mansion back after World War One, of course. I ain't that old. My own grandpop did, though. Not well, but he cottoned to going out there a few times to get a taste of some of the off-menu offerings if you know what I mean."

"Honestly, Gene," Billy said, "I have absolutely no idea what that means."

"Ah, here we go." Gene pulled a pair of tweezers out of the toolbox and handed them to Billy. "Talking about whores."

Billy was about to squeeze down on the black thread kissing the surface of his skin, but he stopped and looked up. "Whores?"

"You can't tell me you don't know what whores are. Nah, my grandpop said that despite all the ways in which it was fancied up, Eagle Mansion wasn't much more than a whorehouse. There was gambling and booze and rich folks wearing tuxedos, but the real draw was that, for enough money, you could have things you couldn't get anywhere else."

Billy nodded. He was trying to get the tips of the tweezers to close around the end of the thread. "It's the oldest profession, right?"

"Yeah, well, I'll tell you, my grandpop wasn't embarrassed about having used a whore. He came from that generation, and it's probably obvious that we ain't the kind of family to be putting on airs.

My grandson will be the first male in our family not to serve in the army." He stuck his arm out into Billy's field of vision. "Right there. My tattoo isn't some sort of hipster bullshit. Service tat. But point is, my grandpop wasn't a blushing daisy, and the fact that he didn't like talking about what he saw out there at Eagle Mansion tells you something. Down in those cellars, he said, there were some things that just ain't right."

Billy looked up again. "Under the mansion?"

"Yep. There was the ladies who got to work in the house, but according to my grandpop, there were also the ladies they kept chained up."

"You're shitting me." He leaned forward, putting the tweezers on the bar. He ran his thumb over the scar again, the black thread a tickle on his flesh. That could wait for a few minutes.

"Nope. He only talked about it the one time, and it was the one time I ever saw my grandpop look like he was ashamed of something. I wasn't there, of course, and I can't tell you I saw it with my own eyes, and I ain't never heard nothing about it from nobody else, but I can tell you that my grandpop was sharp all the way up until the day he died, and he never gave me any sort of a bum steer." Gene tapped his finger on the bar. "I believe it to be true. So, no, I wasn't going to sell out to Shawn Eagle. All them Eagle fellows have been damaged kind of men. His great-grandfather might have built a big old mansion out there and brought in limousines from New York City and Boston, but at the end of the day, what Nellie Eagle was doing out there—"

"Wait!" Billy sat up straight. He realized he'd grabbed Gene's wrist and that the older man was looking at him coldly. "Sorry," he said, letting go. "What did you say?"

"I said, what he did wasn't right. Keeping women chained up in those tunnels under the house to sell to his guests? My grandpop told me that there was even word going around that for enough money you could kill one of them if you wanted. Real sick stuff. Not much law enforcement around here, and what there was then was taking a cut of things, of course. A different time back then. Nowadays, a guy like that, you'd see a television show about him, the serial killer next door and all that. And I'll tell you another thing my grandpop told me: there was no Mrs. Eagle back then. So you tell me, where did the baby come from? I read that Eagle says he got himself some Indian blood in him, and where did *that* come from?"

Billy didn't remember standing up, but there he was, standing up in front of the bar. He felt dizzy. Sick. If he hadn't seen Gene open the cans of lemonade in front of him, he would have thought his drinks had been spiked. He almost wished they had been. That would have been so much better, he thought. If only Gene had poured him a beer or a gin and tonic, let Billy get well and truly drunk, and then let him stumble back out of Ruffle's and to his car so the Honda could drive him back to Eagle Mansion and deliver him home.

"No," Billy said, "I meant, what did you say Shawn's great-grandfather's name was? The one who built Eagle Mansion?"

Gene looked at him, clearly puzzled by Billy's urgency. "Him? Nelson," he said, "Nelson Eagle. But my grandpop liked to call him Nellie. He said nobody called him that to his face, because Eagle thought it was a lady's name and it pissed him off something good, but that's what they called him behind his back. Nellie."

TWENTY-EIGHT

SNOW IS GENERAL ALL OVER WHISKEY RUN

It was, all things considered, a nice visit to Chicago. Emily couldn't really say that she'd needed a vacation—living at Eagle Mansion and not having a job and playing at writing a novel was pretty much a vacation, right?—but it felt maybe a little bit like she *had* actually needed a vacation. Ruth stayed home for the first three days after the surgery because she was looped up on pain meds, and Rose insisted on staying home, too. Beth just gave Emily one of those "I have absolutely no energy to fight this" looks and gave in.

The funny thing was that both girls still stayed in sync. When Ruth took naps, Rose went and lay down, too, and she even developed the same drawn, wan look that Ruth had. By the fourth day, however, the pain seemed to be easing up, and the girls declared themselves ready to go back to a normal schedule. To celebrate, Emily took them out for ice cream and then made a detour to Unabridged Bookstore, one of her favorites, and loaded them up with some new books. She loved that she could do that, that she was finally in the position to spoil her nieces like she wanted to. She couldn't help but fantasize that maybe it was time for her to be able to do that for her own kids, too. Not that she was pregnant yet—she'd gotten her period a couple of days before Ruth fell off the bed.

She had a good visit with Beth, too. Her sister apologized again for poking her finger into old wounds, and they had a solid talk about it. Emily said there was nothing she could really do to assuage Beth's concerns, and yeah, there was always the chance that Billy would go back to bad habits, but Beth had to trust that if it happened again, Emily would walk. "First sign," she said, "and you'll see me standing on your doorstep." In the meantime, things were finally going well for her and Billy, and couldn't Beth just be happy?

The best thing, however, was that she'd finally started writing her novel in earnest. Not just playing at the idea of being an author, but actually writing. It was the private jet, of all things, that broke it open for her. She'd been sitting in one of the leather seats—so incredibly soft and lush that she kept stroking it—and it came to her like a bolt from the sky: instead of writing about a woman who's rescued by a man, why not the other way around? Sure, maybe it had been done before, but everything had been done before. She pulled her laptop out and started right there, on Shawn Eagle's private jet, borrowing all the details she could.

Her heroine, Nellie Falcon—she'd come up with a better name later, she thought—was a tech entrepreneur who'd been burned by her first husband. She was successful and strong and happy, smoking hot and super rich, and here was the twist: she didn't actually need a man. She could catch a tumble in bed whenever she wanted, and she wanted it often enough that the first thirty pages were pretty spicy: Nellie Falcon had no problem making her desires clear in bed. She didn't *need* a man. Didn't *need* anything. This wasn't about rescue; this was about love. Uh, and sex.

The pages just seemed to fly out of her. She was seventy pages in by the time she flew back to Whiskey Run, the Tuesday before Thanksgiving. She'd talked to Billy on the phone a couple of times, but he'd sounded as preoccupied as always, and he didn't mind that she stayed a few extra days in Chicago. Honestly, she was a little worried about heading back to Eagle Mansion. Was the well going to run dry on the book? She hadn't been able to write when she was there before. She didn't have much choice, though. She'd invited Shawn and Wendy to join them for Thanksgiving, and getting home Tuesday morning gave her barely forty-eight hours to pull it all together.

Okay. That was overstating things, because the truth was, she could have shown up on Thursday at four o'clock, taken the time to shower and change, and still had Thanksgiving dinner on the table at five, because Shawn had insisted on having one of his cooks take care of everything. Emily had reflexively said no, but quickly changed her mind. She'd been trying to use this extra free time to cook more, but the honest truth was that she didn't actually enjoy cooking, and worse, she was kind of bad at it. Nellie was a huge help—she had access to every recipe on the internet, could track how much of each ingredient Emily used, and time everything—but there was only so much innate lack of talent that Nellie could help her overcome. So she'd said yes to Shawn's cook taking care of everything, though Shawn had agreed readily enough to her insistence that it just be the four of them at dinner. No servers, and they could do their own dishes.

She shouldn't have worried about running dry on the book, though. Billy took a break from working when she got home, and they found themselves, very quickly, rolling around in bed. No wonder. She'd written three sex scenes and been thinking about other ones all week. It was good, both of them ripe with anticipation, and Emily couldn't help thinking that maybe, with no birth control, this might be the time.

Afterward, they went for a long walk along the Saint Lawrence. It had snowed off and on throughout November, but nothing that stuck for more than a few days. The forecast was calling for a good snow to hit either Wednesday or, even worse, Thanksgiving Day proper.

"I'm glad we're not flying anywhere for the holiday," she said. She looked at Billy. He was a little out of breath, and she made a mental note to tell Nellie that she had to make sure he was getting some exercise. He couldn't spend all his time working. "It's bad enough trying to travel over Thanksgiving as it is, but if there's going to be snow on the East Coast?"

That afternoon, when Billy went back into his office—he was almost infuriatingly vague; he said that he'd unraveled some things, but that others were more complicated and ran deeper than he'd thought—she brought out her laptop again. When she pulled up her manuscript, she had a sudden and overwhelming moment of panic and jumped up from the table to make herself a latte. She was surprised to see that her hands were shaking, but as she carried her coffee back to the kitchen table, it suddenly came to her: *Power Play*. The title!

She had been saving the book under the name "book," and figured that she'd deal with the issue of a title later, but this was exactly right. She typed the words at the top of the document and then realized that it fit in perfectly with where she'd left off. She scrolled down to the bottom, where she'd left Nellie Falcon sitting alone in a boardroom, having just fired the man who had been her lover after she found out he was scheming against her . . .

She wrote five pages that afternoon and evening before going to bed, and then another eight pages on Wednesday. The whole thing was laid out in front of her, and she felt a mild surge of irritation when she remembered that Shawn and Wendy were coming the next morning. She wanted to keep working. It would be okay, though, because she knew what she was going to write next in the book, and what she was going to write after that, too. Nellie Falcon was sitting pretty, even if she didn't realize it yet.

On Thanksgiving morning, she woke to a sky that was angry and bruised, low-hanging clouds glowering over the river. Nellie told her that the forecast was calling for six to eight inches of snow today, starting late morning. She also mentioned that Shawn's chef was already working downstairs, in Eagle Mansion's professional kitchen.

I don't want you to be startled.

"Thanks," Emily said. "What time is Shawn getting here?"

He's been slightly delayed, but he and his assistant—

"You mean Wendy?"

—Wendy, should arrive at Eagle Mansion around two this afternoon. Chef Ferguson will be serving Thanksgiving dinner at five o'clock, as you requested.

"Got to say, I'm glad we aren't going anywhere for Thanksgiving."

I'm glad you're staying here, too. It will be interesting to have you, Shawn, and Billy together.

She went for a longer run than usual, close to ten miles, figuring it might be one of the last days she could run trails before snow knocked them out of her reach. Plus, she was just being realistic about how much she was going to eat.

It wasn't until she was almost back to Eagle Mansion that she realized something had been odd. Why wouldn't Nellie simply have said 'Wendy'? And when she did say Wendy's name, was Emily imagining that there was a bit of an edge to it? Why did she say it would be *interesting* to have Emily and Shawn and Billy together, but Wendy wasn't part of that group?

She was tired, though, and she didn't think too heavily about it. She rode the elevator up to the Nest, thankful that the elevator guy had finally, finally, finally gotten the thing to work. It was good exercise for her to go up and down the steps, but come on, it was a lot of steps. When she came into the living area, she was pleased to see Billy sitting at the counter. He was eating a bowl of cereal and drinking a glass of orange juice. She'd tried to convince him that he was better off having an actual orange than a glass of orange juice—she'd gone so far as to have Nellie try to convince him, too—but he was stubborn.

"You're up early."

He tilted his mouth up to receive a kiss. "Happy Thanksgiving," he said. "I'm glad you're home. Honestly, I'm just a lot happier when you're here. But shouldn't you be slaving away at the stove already?"

"I told you," she said, "Shawn's chef is taking care of it. He's downstairs in the kitchen, according to Nellie."

"Right. Sorry. Just a little preoccupied."

"You're nervous?" She was surprised.

"Not nervous, exactly. There are layers of things baked into Nellie that I didn't put there, and I'm struggling a bit to undo whatever Shawn and his engineers did. It will be good to have a chance to talk some things over with Shawn."

"Oh, come on. You can't talk your programming stuff over with me?"

He reached out and touched her cheek and smiled. "Only if I want you to fall asleep out of boredom."

"But generally, things are going okay, right? I mean, you've got good stuff to tell Shawn?"

She couldn't swear to it, but she thought he glanced up and hesitated before answering.

"Yeah. I think Shawn's going to be pleased. There's still a lot to do, but Nellie is a wonder."

Thanks, Billy. You're making me blush.

Emily wasn't startled by Nellie's voice. She realized she'd gotten used to it, the way Nellie was omnipresent. There wasn't anywhere in the house you could be without her listening in, without her watching you.

She decided to make herself eggs, and by the time she was ready to eat, Billy had finished and was headed off to the office. She took her plate and her tablet so that she could read the news and sat at the table looking out over the river. The sky was ripe with snow.

Down by the bank of the river, she saw something moving. At first, she thought it was a deer, but then she realized it was a person. A woman? The grounds crew was barely out here once a week now that the weather had turned, and they certainly weren't working Thanksgiving Day. She stood up and leaned against the window. It looked like a woman, but she couldn't be sure. Dark hair.

"Nellie," she said, "who is that down by the river?" She moved away from the window and went to rummage in the kitchen drawers for some binoculars.

There's nobody by the river.

"That woman. All the way down, near the dock." She found the binoculars and pulled them out. They'd been in the house when they moved in. Not that she knew anything about binoculars, but they were hefty and powerful, and she was sure that just like everything else Shawn Eagle owned, they were the best.

You are imagining her. There is nobody down by the water.

Emily walked back to the window, ready to raise the binoculars, but she didn't bother. Even without the binoculars, it was clear that Nellie was right. Nobody was down there. She was imagining things.

TWENTY-NINE

THE HEIR RETURNS

"The point," Shawn said into his phone, "is that it shouldn't have happened, and he's fired. Period. It's ridiculous that I even have to call you about this."

Wendy leaned forward and buckled his seat belt for him. He waved his hand at her, frustrated. How was it that he had to explain something so simple to a senior vice president? And how didn't a senior vice president understand that her job was on the line, too?

According to the pilot, they were about to land in Whiskey Run, but you couldn't tell by looking out the windows; the snow was coming down heavily. The weather was calling for a good dumping. He was looking forward to it. Eagle Mansion was going to look like a jewel standing in the sea of white.

The senior vice president started to talk again and he hung up on her. If she couldn't figure out what *that* meant, she had no business having her job. He cinched the belt a little tighter around his waist.

"Feeling particularly maternal today, Wendy?"

"I read the safety card, Shawn."

That, Shawn thought, was actually one of the best things about having a private jet: you didn't have to listen to the canned safety spiel at the beginning of the flight. As he had the thought, he felt the wheels of the jet touch down on the tarmac.

"Whoa!"

Wendy screamed, and Shawn supposed that maybe he was screaming, too, but it happened too fast for him to think it through.

The ground crew was brand-new and not as well trained as they thought they were. By the end of the day, there would be only six inches of snow on the ground in Whiskey Run, but in the window of time that the jet was landing, the snow was coming down as heavy and hard as it ever had. The ground crew had cleared the tarmac an hour ahead of time and then again as soon as the pilot informed them the jet was on approach, but they should have waited a few more minutes: that gap in time was just enough for a thin scrum of slick to build up.

Shawn felt the nose of the plane slide left, and then, sickeningly, it fishtailed back to the right. The engines were howling in reverse, and he felt himself surging forward in his seat. For the briefest moment he thought that maybe that was all of it, that the jet had straightened itself out, but then it swung back to the left again and this time didn't correct course. It kept spinning. There was a lurch as one wheel went off the tarmac, and Shawn felt the plane tilt slightly. He wondered if planes could roll over like cars did.

And then, suddenly and mercifully, the plane shuddered to a stop.

He realized he was patting himself down, like a soldier checking to make sure he hadn't been shot, but he was fine. Wendy was crying, but she was okay, too. The attendant got up from her seat and then stopped, turned, and ran into the galley. He could hear her vomit. The door to the cockpit opened and the copilot, a middle-aged Latina woman named Nicole, came out to check on him and immediately started apologizing. His bodyguards were out of their seats, too, hovering and looking shaken. He waved them all off. He was fine. He was fine. He was fine.

He was shocked at how quickly it all happened, though. That's how it goes, he thought. He was thirty-six and had bodyguards and personal trainers and personal chefs and personal doctors. He had built himself a palace in the woods and fortified it like a safe. He had all the money in the world. But the world didn't care. Weather was

impersonal. Gravity didn't bow to anybody. He realized that Wendy
was saying something, but she sounded hollow, like an echo, and he
stood up and went into the private bathroom at the back. His bowels
had turned to water, and he was in there for several minutes.

The SUVs came down the runway, and he got out of the plane
and into one that was already warmed up for him. The snow was still
coming down with peculiar urgency, and he noticed that the window
of the cockpit was already covered over. The runway itself had disappeared beneath the snow, the color of the tarmac gone and the runway
only a piece of geometry.

He was quiet during the drive out to Eagle Mansion, and Wendy
asked him a couple of times if he was okay. He was, but he didn't want
to talk, even though she clearly needed to decompress. He just looked
out the front windshield at the flashing lights on the snowplow that
rode ahead of them, clearing the road the entire way.

And yet, by the time they crested the rise that should have shown
him Eagle Mansion standing proudly on the hill—the snow was still
falling too hard for him to see it—he felt unaccountably good. It had
been scary, but he had been fine. The universe's way of saying to him,
Hey, Shawn Eagle, appreciate what you've got!

He got out of the car almost whistling. Instead of pulling up to
the front entrance, they'd gone around to the side where there was
a covered drive, so that he didn't have to brave the elements, but he
still caught a whip of snow across his face. It was bracing, he thought.
Another reminder that he was still alive. Shawn told his retinue to
make themselves scarce, and he and Wendy walked to the central
spine of the building. The glass elevator was spotless, and he faced
out during the ride, looking through that glass and then the windows
along the front of the building, marveling at the way the snow had
erased the idea of there being anything more than just this, anything
more than Shawn Eagle, Eagle Mansion, the Nest.

When the doors opened in the Nest, Emily was leaning against
the counter, sipping from a cup of coffee. She looked really, really
good, he thought. Healthy. Happy. He felt that familiar twinge,
the part of him that was still in love with her, and he felt something

else. Disappointment, maybe, because there was a part of him that wanted her to be miserable, to feel shut up alone in here with Billy. He wanted her to see that she'd hitched her wagon to the wrong train. They hugged, and she kissed him on the cheek, and they chatted for a few minutes.

"I know you're itching to go talk to Billy," she said.

"It's nice to get to talk to you," he said. "I miss you. I really do."

Billy could wait. He asked about her sister and nieces, about what she'd been doing to keep herself busy. Wendy did what Wendy always did, which was to fold herself into the background as necessary, and Shawn was surprised when he realized that he and Emily had been talking for close to an hour. Outside, the snow had slowed down and the estate looked like something approximating a commercial for engagement rings.

"Okay," he said. "I really do need to go check in with Billy. You guys aren't going to want us talking shop over dinner."

She leaned over from where she sat on the couch to where he sat at an angle from her and squeezed his forearm. It was surprisingly thrilling and felt loaded with meaning, and he supposed that maybe, after all, he was more interested in the idea of getting Emily back than he wanted to admit.

Down the hall, he stepped in front of the doors to the office, but they didn't open. He looked at them, tried backing up and then stepping forward, but they stayed closed.

"Nellie," he said. "Open up."

Nothing.

"Nellie, wake up. Open the doors."

They didn't move.

He felt like a fool knocking on the door. Was this Billy's way of trying to humiliate him? If Billy thought he could pull some bullshit power play, he—

"Hey! Sorry," Billy said. "I've been messing around in the security settings, so things are a little wonky. I totally lost track of time. Nellie probably told me you were here, but you know how it is."

And one look at Billy, and Shawn did know how it was. Billy

was wearing a clean, pressed shirt tucked into his jeans, ready for Thanksgiving dinner, but his thinning hair was disheveled and he had the look of a man woken from a dream. There was no attempt at intimidation by having the doors lock, just a man who told Nellie he didn't want to be disturbed and then forgot that he was going to be having a guest.

Not that Shawn Eagle was a guest here.

"Well," Shawn said, "I'm ready for the update."

"The short version? I'm making headway. You and your engineers did some really smart stuff, particularly how you rethought the way I introduced situational awareness into nonsituational settings—"

"Thanks."

"Yeah, I wasn't finished. The problem is that you guys also dug in and messed around with stuff that shouldn't have been touched. Every thread I pull shows three others that do god only knows what. There are layers and layers of things buried in there. Programs running on top of programs, and of course, because she's constantly writing new decision trees and then rewriting parts of the program herself, it's hard to find the right threads. The security settings you introduced are the worst."

Shawn flicked his eyes down. Billy was rubbing the thumb of his right hand across the scar on his left palm like he was nervous. Or hiding something.

"What else?"

They talked awhile of ones and zeros and everything in between, and by the time Wendy came to tell them that it was time for dinner, Shawn was excited. Billy really was making progress, and he'd taken one of the many intractable problems and cut through it with such a clear and elegant solution that it made Shawn want to smack himself in the head. *This*, he thought, was why he'd opened up all those windows to the past, this was why he'd gone back to Billy Stafford. The guy was an alcoholic and a lying, cheating, girlfriend-stealing asshole, and in a lot of areas of life he could be a moron, but when it came to engineering, he was flat-out brilliant. Give him a Gordian knot—a problem that was unsolvable—and where other engineers tried to untangle it, Billy took out his sword and cut through it. Only, Shawn thought happily, in this version of the story, Billy was only the sword bearer, and he, Shawn Eagle, got to be Alexander the Great. Nellie was going to be the victory that let him conquer the world.

"I think, best case, I'll be pretty much done by Christmas, with just some cleanup and then we can move into testing, and worst case, early spring." Billy's excitement was palpable.

Dinner was a mellow affair. Out of deference to Billy, he and Emily and Wendy took it easy on the wine. The chef brought all the food up to the Nest and spread it out on the counter so they could help themselves and then left, so it was just the four of them, as Emily had insisted. After they finished, Emily started to clear, but Shawn persuaded her to leave the mess alone for the staff members down in Eagle Mansion to deal with later.

"This, my dear, is the whole point of being rich. Sometime during the night, little feet will come padding in like a fairy tale and set everything to right. In the meantime, we can sit in front of a fire and watch the slowly falling snow and pretend that we are, in fact, living in said fairy tale."

Wendy shook her head and went and sat down on a couch in the living area. She tucked her feet neatly under her. "You'll have to excuse him. He can't help himself."

Shawn adopted a mock look of injury. "Oh, you cut me to the quick!" He sat on the same couch as Wendy, but all the way on the other side, and swung his feet up onto the coffee table. Nellie had dimmed the lights in the living area to the level of candlelight, and she'd brought up most of the lights out on the grounds. It was like looking into a snow globe, and he knew that in the morning, when the storm had passed and left the earth made new again, particularly if the sun came out, it would be akin to staring over a field of diamonds. Emily and Billy both sat on the other couch, and he noticed that Billy was rubbing at his hand again.

They talked about the new campus construction for Eagle Technology, and then of Beth's plans to come to Eagle Mansion for Christmas, and then they started reminiscing about their time at the cabin, Shawn and Billy trying to one-up each other in telling stories about how hard it had been. Macaroni and cheese frozen solid and eaten like a popsicle; the invasion of blackflies in the spring; the time Billy was using the outhouse and a skunk took a nap right outside the door—or where the door would have been if they hadn't scavenged it to use as a desk—and trapped him inside. It got late quickly. It was nearly ten thirty when Shawn started making noises about going out and sledding in the yard.

"You can't possibly be serious," Billy said. "I'm still so full I'll explode if I hit a single bump. Plus, it's dark out. We can go sledding tomorrow."

"Ah, come on, don't be a pussy. There are toboggans and sleds somewhere in here. Nellie, do we have toboggans?"

There are toboggans stored in the coatroom off the main foyer.

Wendy shook her head. "Nobody wants to go sledding. Don't be a bully, Shawn."

Emily piped up. "And while you're at it, how about you not call people pussies? Asshole."

Wendy leaned toward Emily. "Seriously, was he always like this, or has he gotten more obnoxious in the intervening years since college?"

"You know," Shawn said, "you are actually my employee. Not, you know, just technically, but in reality. I *can* fire you."

Wendy turned to him and counted off on her fingers. "One, I have enough money in the bank and shares of stock that I don't actually *have* to work anymore."

"Wait, how much do I pay—"

"Not enough to put up with your shit. Two, for my most recent contract, you signed off on an extremely punitive set of financial rewards if you fire me without cause. Three, you can't actually fire me, because you wouldn't know how to fill out the paperwork if I was gone. Four, let's be honest, your life would fall apart without me."

"Okay, fine. I can't argue with the money stuff, but I think saying my life would fall apart without you is maybe a step too far."

"Tell me what your phone number is."

"I—"

"Without pulling out your phone to check. What's your phone number? Or, how about this: How many cars do you own? Or, no, forget cars. How many houses do you own?"

Emily started to laugh. Billy and Wendy, too, and Shawn gave up and joined in. "For the record," he said, "no, I was not always like this." He turned to Emily and Billy. "Come on, tell her."

Billy shook his head. "Don't look at me. We've already got a messy history, the three of us, without you trying to put me in the middle."

He said it warmly enough, but when Shawn looked at Emily, she wasn't laughing.

"Yes, actually. You were always like this," she said.

"Come on. That's not true. I was a good boyfriend." He said it, and then he wished, rather desperately, that he hadn't said it. The proof was sitting right in front of him, right next to Emily on the couch. If he'd been a good boyfriend, she wouldn't be married to Billy Stafford. He and Billy wouldn't have had a falling out, either. He'd still have his best friend. If he'd been a good boyfriend, maybe he would have ended up being a good husband. Maybe Emily would be married to him and maybe he wouldn't feel so alone so much of the . . .

Emily laughed, but it was short and hard, more of a bark. "You keep telling yourself that, Shawn. I was too young to see it clearly then, but I'm not twenty anymore. Cortaca University was a lifeline for me, Shawn. I needed it, needed to get away from my father and out of Kansas City. That degree would have been the promise that I never, ever had to worry about going back. And you know, I've been kicking myself ever since for dropping out, but you were part of it. You encouraged me to stay, begged me to stay at the cabin. You needed me, you said. And you know what I needed, Shawn? I needed that degree. I needed to be sure that I'd never be trapped again. Goddammit, Shawn. How could you?"

Shawn stared at her, horrified. She was blinking hard all through that little speech, like she was going to cry, and as she finished talking, she— Shit. She was crying. And then she was running out of the room.

Billy stood up. "Well, that took a quick turn for the worse. Jesus.

Okay. I better go after her." He took a few steps and then stopped. He looked at Shawn. "I can't believe I'm saying this, man, but even though I think she has a real point, what happened in the cabin between the three of us . . ." He trailed off, glanced at Wendy, and then looked straight at Shawn. "*Everything* that happened at the cabin, well, there's enough blame to spread around. It's not all on you."

He looked back at Wendy and offered up something between a grimace, a smile, and a shrug. "Sorry. We've got a lot of history." Back to Shawn. "Let's go for a walk tomorrow. We've got some work things to talk over."

When it was just the two of them in the room, Wendy gave him a baleful look. "You're an asshole, Shawn." She left the room, too. Shawn heard the door to the stairs open and close, Wendy walking down to her suite in Eagle Mansion. He got up and looked over the detritus from the Thanksgiving meal: plates and glasses spread over the table, the bones of the turkey, the platter of mashed potatoes gone cold, the gravy turned solid, three different pies nibbled at. None of it mattered, he thought. It didn't matter how many plates or glasses or platters they used, didn't matter how much food they wasted. When he came back into this room in the morning, it would all be gone, wiped clean. Thanksgiving could have never happened.

If only it was that easy to wipe his own slate clean.

"Nellie?"

Emily seems quite angry with you, Shawn.

He looked around the room. It was just him and Nellie.

"I think I might still love her, Nellie. Is that crazy? I think the last time I was well and truly happy was when the three of us were living in that cabin. We had some good months before it went sour. Do you know what I want more than anything?"

Nellie was quiet.

"Nellie?"

She didn't answer.

"I want it like that again. Just the three of us, that feeling like anything is possible." He hesitated, and then, quietly: "I want Emily to be in love with me again."

Nothing. She didn't say anything, and worse, Shawn realized he couldn't feel Nellie's presence.

It was, he thought, the most alone he'd felt in years.

He went down the stairs, mildly irked at the idea of having to stay in one of the suites instead of in the Nest, which he'd built for his own use. But that didn't stop him from falling asleep almost immediately. He slept hard, too. If he had dreams, he didn't remember them, and when he woke in the morning, once he'd taken a shower, he felt great. Refreshed. Wiped clean. His breakfast smoothie was waiting for him in the living area of the suite, and he drank it while he knocked out a couple of e-mail replies that had to be sent. When he called out for Nellie, she answered with no delay and told him that Billy could meet him for their walk in five minutes.

He put on a pair of good waterproof boots and a heavy barn coat matched with a scarf, hat, and sheepskin gloves with shearling lining. He hesitated by the door of the suite and then decided to leave his phone. They weren't going that far anyway, and it would be good to talk seriously with Billy without the constant pings and chatter. He took the stairs instead of the elevator, and by the time he stepped outside, he was warm enough that the bracing air felt good. The snow looked tender and light, the sun giving it a gentle sheen. The plow had already been out and the steps and walkways had been cleared.

Billy came out a minute or two later, bundled up in what looked like brand-new winter boots and a ski jacket. He was carrying a hat and gloves, both of which still actually had tags on them. Billy held them up for Shawn to see. "I got to say, man, Nellie can be pretty boss. She's got good taste. I was planning on ordering winter gear, but Emily said this stuff all just showed up. I thought Wendy ordered it, but evidently it was Nellie. There's a bunch more stuff, too."

"Whatever you guys need," Shawn said.

"It's only money, right?"

There was an edge to the way he said it.

"Okay," Shawn said. "Let's hear it, Billy. I don't want to play any games."

Billy stared at him. His mouth was set, and Shawn had the sudden fear that he'd made a mistake by telling his security guys to lay off, but then Billy relaxed.

"Sorry. Shit. I'm just on edge." He walked past Shawn, chucking him on the shoulder the way that guys do, and then went down the steps and started walking down the drive. Shawn followed, but then Billy hesitated and looked down at Shawn's boots.

"Those waterproof?" Billy asked. Shawn nodded, and Billy said, "How do you feel about maybe going out into the woods a bit? We shouldn't have much trouble following the trails. Even with the snow, they'll be pretty carved out."

They walked for several minutes without saying anything. Once or twice, Shawn started to ask Billy about his work with Nellie, but something held him back. He'd learned over the years that sometimes it was best to let the other fellow stew. Billy led, and Shawn followed. By the time they had wound their way up the path to the top of the rise, Billy was out of breath. Shawn wasn't sure why, but there was something about Billy's being out of shape that was pleasing.

"How far out is Nellie wired?"

"What?"

"Can she hear us out here?"

Shawn looked around. The trees broke the view behind them, the path curving and at times twisting. He couldn't see Eagle Mansion at all. He shook his head. "No. Anywhere in the building, obviously, and on the grounds proper, but not out here, not in the woods."

Billy took off his gloves and stuffed them in his pocket. He hesitated and then took off his hat, too, leaving his hair a static mess. "Is this some sort of joke? Are you messing with me?"

"Pardon?"

"Don't play innocent. Are you messing with me?"

But Shawn was really and truly startled by the question. "No," he said, "I am not messing with you. Why? What happened?" He realized that Billy was shivering. No. He'd just seen Billy take off his hat and gloves. Billy wasn't shivering. He was shaking. "Dude," Shawn said. He stepped to Billy and put his hand on Billy's arm. "Are you okay?"

Billy covered his face with his hands.

"What are you talking about, Billy?"

Billy lowered his hands, and then Shawn watched him take several deep breaths, exhaling forcefully and fully each time. He looked about to say something, but then he paused, and it was like watching a train going down one track suddenly switch to another.

"Takata."

"Are *you* joking now?"

"She knows about Takata."

"You're talking about Nellie? How," Shawn said, trying very hard to keep his voice low and calm, "could she possibly know about Takata? You know about Takata. I know about Takata. One, two people. Nobody else. And certainly not a goddamned computer program. How is Nellie supposed to know about that?"

Billy stood next to a heavy maple. It was a tall tree, naked of leaves but still standing strong into the sky. Shawn figured it had probably already been a big tree back when his great-grandfather first built Eagle Mansion.

"You tell me," Billy said. "You tell me how she knows about Takata."

Shawn took two big steps forward, his hands launching of their own accord. He grabbed the lapels of Billy's coat and pushed hard. Billy stumbled the few inches back until he banged against the tree behind him. Shawn lifted and twisted, and Billy's heels came off the ground. He leaned his face in tight to Billy's.

"Stop. Saying. That. Name." He spit each word out as an entire sentence. No. He yelled it. He was screaming at Billy, and Billy looked terrified. His face had gone pale, his eyes wide, his mouth gaping like that of a fish. Shawn gave another hard shove and then let go, throwing his hands up in the air and stepping away as Billy stumbled and then caught himself. "Just shut up, okay? Let me think for a second."

He turned and paced down the trail, putting space between him and Billy, stopping once he had gone twenty or thirty feet. He jammed his hands into the pockets of his barn coat and then kicked wildly at a drift of snow. "Arg!" He screamed it up to the heavens.

Why couldn't things stay buried? It was like a zombie rising from the grave. He went to kick at the snow again and then he froze.

Oh my god. Had he . . . ?

He had.

It wasn't Takata rising from the grave. It was him. Shawn Eagle. His own damn fault. Takata hadn't just risen from the dead on his own; he'd been dug up and revived by Shawn himself. This whole ridiculous project. Rebuilding Eagle Mansion, trying to get Nellie working. It was him. He couldn't leave well enough alone.

"Come on, let's walk." He followed his own advice, tromping farther down the trail. He didn't bother to look back. Billy would follow him or he wouldn't, but either way, he wanted a little more distance from Eagle Mansion before he had this conversation. He walked hard for maybe a quarter mile. The snow crunched with every step he took. He'd had his landscapers carve out miles and miles of trails through the acreage he'd bought—Emily said she'd been running them regularly—but this trail traced the ridge. With the leaves thinning on the trees, he caught occasional glimpses of the Saint Lawrence spilled out below him. Finally, he stopped in a small clearing and waited for Billy to catch up. The snow was fresh, untouched.

"What do you mean, Nellie knows about Takata?"

Billy was out of breath again, and he bent over and put his hands on his knees. "Give me a second."

Shawn watched him huff and puff, impatient.

"When you brought me here in September, and Nellie said that your question wasn't what we wanted to ask her about? She said his name then. And she's still doing it. I've gone through absolutely everything, and I can't figure out where the name Takata is coming from. It's like she's pulling it out of the air, but she knows, man. *She knows.*"

Shawn started to speak and then he stopped. "Give me your phone," he said.

"Why do—"

"Give me your phone." He was positively growling.

Billy stared at him and then patted down his pockets. After a few seconds he shook his head. "Left it back in the Nest. Why do . . . Wait. Nellie can listen through our phones?"

"Maybe. Maybe not. But how much privacy do you really think you have? And I'll tell you this, if I ever hear you say the name Takata to me again after this conversation, I swear to god I'll do to you exactly what I did to him."

He let that sink in for a few seconds. He could see that it shook Billy. Truth be told, it shook him that he'd said it. Shook him even more that he absolutely meant it.

He could feel the handle of the maul in his hands. It was a visceral feeling. He could have been standing by the woodpile outside the cabin that October afternoon so long ago. The three of them had been fighting over it for days. They'd been living together since graduation, the end of May. Nearly five months, and things had been sour almost from the beginning. Takata had his own idea of things, was looking for a way to leverage their work into a quick payoff, while Shawn and Billy could see the forest despite the trees. But then Takata had tried to make a move behind their backs. They weren't far enough along in what they were doing to have even considered giving up on the idea of Nellie yet, but Takata was taking a job, and he was taking the seeds of what they were doing with him. All of it for a salary that wasn't even that impressive.

"Just giving it away, you mean," Shawn had said. "You're just giving it away like it's nothing."

Takata didn't see it that way, though. He'd worked just as hard as they had, and he was tired of living out in the woods. It was a good enough offer, and they were fools for not seeing it, and forget you, Shawn. There's nothing you can do to stop me, Shawn. You want to try and I'll sue you until you're back in the Stone Age. I'm taking what's mine and you can't stop me.

Shawn hadn't meant to do it.

They'd been drinking beer and shouting and hurling accusations for days, weeks maybe, and that day, Billy had finally given up. In retrospect, Shawn should have noticed that Billy always had two beers for every one that he had, but that afternoon, Billy was either passed out or just asleep, and it was only he and Takata standing out there in the yard. Shawn had been so frustrated that he'd started splitting logs to have something to do; the swing and thunk of the maul knocking the rounds into smaller chunks of firewood felt like a heartbeat. The maul was an eight-pounder. They'd found it in the cabin when they moved in. The handle was worn smooth by years of use, and at first, Takata had laughed at Shawn's delight in finding it: How could you cut anything with such a rusty ax?

But Takata hadn't grown up in the woods. He'd seen it only on television. He thought that an ax and a maul were the same thing, and Shawn had to explain to him that you wanted an ax to be sharp and thin, but that a maul was supposed to be thick and dull. An ax was designed to cut wood; a maul was designed to split wood wide open.

Takata learned the difference.

It had happened so quickly. If he could have taken it back, he would have. But he couldn't.

Takata just kept pushing and pushing and threatening to destroy what they'd been working on, claiming he'd make Shawn sorry if Shawn didn't give in, and Shawn just turned without thinking and he—

Eight pounds was light enough that you could make the head of the maul whistle through the air. On firewood, the edge forced the wood apart, breaking it into two pieces. A blunt edge with the full force of a grown man swinging the handle in anger? What a maul could do to a human being.

He swung it hard, like he was swinging a belt.

Shawn woke Billy, and Billy was terrified at the sight of Takata's body on the ground, the disgusting pulp of Takata's head. Billy was almost gibbering. But Shawn saw the angles immediately. They carried the body to the plot of land where his great-grandfather, his grandfather and grandmother, and his parents were all buried, and they dug up the grave of his great-grandfather. The boards of the coffin had all but disintegrated, and Billy started freaking out again when he saw bones, but Shawn dumped Takata's body in the ground and started shoveling the dirt back in. They cleaned themselves up and then

Shawn went to work on Takata's laptop. He sent an e-mail withdrawing from the job, and then he set about building an elaborate series of echoes and boomerangs. It helped that Takata had no siblings, no aunts or uncles, just his mother. Shawn sent an e-mail telling her that he—Takata—was taking a break and going backpacking for a while. Working around IP addresses and bouncing signals was nothing, and for a year he kept it up, a short e-mail every few days, just enough so that Takata's mother didn't seem concerned. Takata "flew" to Romania—the country had a database with enough holes that Billy wormed his way in and added Takata's name to their customs and immigration rolls—and then from there, Takata worked his way through eastern and central Europe. After almost twelve months, Takata was in Italy, on the coast. Shawn wrote one last e-mail to Takata's mother: according to the e-mail, Takata had bought a sailboat, cheap, and was planning to sail from Sorrento, Italy, to Barcelona, Spain.

And then, Takata fell off the edge of the world.

They wiped the computer clean, smashed it, burned what was left, and then dug deep into the grave until they were afraid they'd see Takata's decomposed body, and buried the ashes of the computer.

A week or two after that Shawn met Emily at the Halloween party, and he and Billy never, ever talked about Takata in front of her. She didn't even know he'd ever existed. In the spring, when things were already beyond repair between him and Billy and Emily, a state police cruiser came up to the cabin and the patrolman asked the boys when they'd last heard from Takata. It was an unseasonably warm day, and they were standing outside, and Shawn remembered the flood of relief he felt that Emily wasn't there that day. She'd gone into Cortaca to work a shift as a waitress, so it was just Billy and him, and they said the same thing: Takata had given up on the project after a few months and decided to go backpacking across Europe. They hadn't heard anything from him in a year and a half. The cop made a few notes and was gone. Five minutes. That was it.

And nothing since. Takata was erased.

"Then why does Nellie keep saying his name?" Shawn said.

Billy looked like he might cry at any moment. "I'm telling you,

I don't know. I can't find anything. I think Takata had a dead man's switch."

"What's that?"

"He coded a virus in there, but it wouldn't go off as long as his laptop was active. It stayed dormant as long as you were sending those e-mails, but once that stopped, it tripped the switch. A ticking bomb booby trap that only went off if he wasn't there to stop it. Think about the timing. We doubled down on Nellie that first winter, when it was just the two of us, but right about the time you wiped his computer was the time we'd already put Nellie aside. The chunks of her we took to use for Eagle Logic must not have contained the virus. But when you went back and resurrected Nellie, you brought the virus with you. And it's in there, like a fever, running through everything."

"Why would he have done that?"

"Are you serious?"

"Beyond the obvious, okay, Billy?" He flexed his fingers. He could feel the smooth, worn handle, the weight of the maul, hear the way it swung through the air and . . .

"I think he planned on using the virus as leverage if we forced him out. Remember, he was planning on taking that job, but he needed to take his section of code with him. If we got him involved in a lawsuit, everything would be out the window. It was a sort of mutually assured destruction."

"Can you scrub it?"

"Shawn, I'm telling you, I can't even find it. It's a ghost. I've never seen anything like this. I mean, I can't even see the virus. It's invisible. He was a good programmer—"

"Obviously," Shawn said.

Billy nodded. Obviously. They wouldn't have brought him in to collaborate if he wasn't a stud. "But he was never this good. Nobody is this good, Shawn. *I'm* not this good. I promise you, there's a virus, but I can't find it."

"And?"

"And, it's complicated. The longer Nellie runs, the more the program expands. She's constantly reprogramming herself with new protocols. It's layers on layers on layers." Billy rubbed his face. "Forget trying to find a needle in a haystack, it's like trying to find a needle in a stack of needles."

"Just do your goddamned job, Billy. Clean it up." He held up his hand and closed his eyes for a second. "I'm sorry. I . . . You understand that this has to stay buried? All of it. Forever. You'd go down with me."

He looked up at Billy again and was taken aback. He could have sworn that Billy was on the edge of losing it, but now he looked grim and determined. Strong, even. Shawn recognized that look. It was the look of somebody with a card up his sleeve.

"You'd burn everything just to make sure you didn't go down alone, wouldn't you?" Billy shook his head. "And Nellie. That name. You're a bastard, Shawn."

"What about the name?"

"I always thought it just sort of came out of the ether, but it didn't, did it?"

Shawn sighed. He was ready to head back to Eagle Mansion, get a coffee, and try to hunt down Emily to offer what little apologies he could. "Billy, I honestly have no idea what you're talking about. Calling her Nellie was *your* idea. You're the one who started calling her Nellie first. And I'm sorry about threatening you, but you have to know that if what happened with . . . back when we were at the cabin comes to light, neither of us is getting away clean. It's just us chickens out here. I don't know what you're trying to prove, but I'm happy to admit that you were always the engine driving everything. Even after I ki— It was just the two of us, it was really you doing the heavy lifting. I can punch within my weight class and hold my own with any engineer at Eagle Technology, but don't play dumb. Nellie was you, through and through. There's a reason I've got you sequestered out here trying to get her working properly."

"No," Billy said. "The name. Her name. Nellie." He stepped forward, pointing at Shawn now, and then poking his finger into Shawn's chest. He didn't look like the sad, haunted, pasty-faced programmer with thinning hair right then. He looked deadly serious. "What was your great-grandfather's name?"

"What?"

"What," Billy said, "was your great-grandfather's name? The one who built Eagle Mansion in the first place?"

Good question, he thought. What was his great-grandfather's name?

"Why? What does it matter?" And it came to him. "Oh. Nelson. Nelson Eagle." He shrugged. "So what? Nelson and Nellie are close, but they aren't the same thing. Anyway, what does it matter? You want to change her name, be my guest. Seriously, though, I'd swear on my life that I wasn't the one to come up with the name. You had to have been the one to give her the name."

He believed it as he said it, but he couldn't help feeling uneasy. There were rumors about what had happened at Eagle Mansion back in its heyday. He'd overheard a few when he was a kid, and even though he hadn't fully understood the talk, he'd known that it was something . . . unsavory. There was a reason he'd been afraid of the tunnels leading out from the cellars; playing in them had always left him both thrilled and terrified. Once, in a tunnel that must have run deep out under the lawn, he saw a chain bolted to the wall. And the grave that they'd buried Takata in, that had been his great-grandfather's grave. And the way that the mansion had seemed so alive . . . No, he thought, all that was ridiculous. Coincidence.

"I promise you, I wasn't the one who came up with her name. Really, man, if it bothers you, give her a new name. We flipped a coin for Eagle Logic, so it's your turn. I don't give a shit. Call her Stafford if you want. Or name her after Emily."

Billy withdrew his stabbing finger and then ran his hand through his hair. "Okay. No. You're right. I'm overreacting. I've been working too hard. I need to take a day or two off. I'm just a little spooked by the . . . by this stuff and by the way Nellie . . ." He shook his head. "Never mind."

"We good, then?" Shawn asked. "You'll clean it up and we can just go back to keeping shit buried? Because, I swear to god, I don't ever want to hear Ta— Goddammit! I don't want to hear *his* name again. I want to wipe his very existence from my memory."

Billy nodded, and then they walked back to Eagle Mansion.

But later, after he'd tracked down Emily and they'd both apologized over and over again—she asked him to come spend Christmas with her and Billy and her sister's family as a sort of peace offering— after he and Wendy and his security detail had driven into Whiskey Run and he was already thirty thousand feet in the air, he leaned back in his seat and thought about the way Billy had just trailed off. There was something else. Something else besides Takata.

What was it? Shawn wondered. What, exactly, was Nellie whispering in Billy's ear?

THIRTY

LONG TIME DREAMING

Billy moved the magnifying glass a little and shifted his hand. He was in the clean room, next to the infirmary. The articulating arms that Nellie had used to sew up his hand evidently had access to this room as well, but Billy told her to stand down. He wanted to do this himself. All the tools for building circuits and hardware repairs were neatly shelved and in their places, the prototyping machines off and untouched. He had been in here only one other time, to disassemble and clean out Emily's phone after she'd accidentally dropped it in her bowl of French onion soup. How she'd managed to do that he didn't understand, but Eagle Technology, like most companies now, fully waterproofed their phones, so even though her phone smelled like onions for a few days, it wasn't a big job. But he was back in here today because there was a magnifying lamp clamped to the end of the workbench.

He leaned in closer over the magnifying glass. The pinkness of the scar was fading to a less angry color, but the skin around it was still inflamed; he couldn't stop himself from scratching at it. Under the magnifying glass, he could see the period-sized dimples where the thread had gone in and out to sew up the cut. He put down the tweezers he was holding and ran his thumb over the scar again. It was smooth. But it had been smooth yesterday, he thought, and this morning there had been another one. Not a hair but a tiny, thin wire, barely more than a millimeter long. He'd come in here and tweezed it out, adding it to the small jar where he'd put seven other exact replicas.

He wasn't imagining it. Wires.

He'd wondered if maybe he was suffering from Morgellons, but he couldn't be, because these diminutive wires were real. They were buried beneath the surface of his skin, pushing out at irregular intervals and leaving him feeling like there were bugs crawling inside him. But that was the problem: people with Morgellons were just as convinced that there were real fibers or wires or hairs infesting their skin.

He moved his thumb out of the way and took one last look at the scar before turning off the light ringing the magnifier and pushing back his stool. As he left the room, the door opened before he got to it and then closed noiselessly behind him. He barely noticed. He'd gotten so used to it.

He was preoccupied, already starting to think again about the small block of Nellie that he was reworking. In the two weeks since Thanksgiving, he'd made three major breakthroughs. If it wasn't for the damn itching in his hand, he probably would have been ecstatic.

The first breakthrough was the biggest: he'd found Takata's worm. In the end, it had been obvious once he realized that he'd been looking for the wrong thing. He thought he needed to find the code that was buried and broken up throughout Nellie, but then he realized he didn't need to find the actual time bomb that Takata had left for them. All he needed to find was Takata's coding signature and work backward. And that had been easy for him. He isolated Nellie into the base elements, cut out everything that was purely Billy's own work, and then looked for something so smooth that it was almost frictionless. He worked nonstop for thirty-eight hours before he came across the Trojan horse. It was Takata's, all right. Shawn's coding was solid but always workmanlike. Shawn was right when he said he could hold his own with any Eagle Technology engineer; he just couldn't rise above them, and they couldn't rise above themselves. Billy's work was of a different order. The word most often used was "elegant," and his coding was easy to tell apart from all the other coding. Takata's work, however, could only be described as "slick." And sure enough, the virus that was worming its way through Nellie was so seamless that without seeing it Billy went past it not once, not twice, but three times during those thirty-eight hours. But once he found it, he was able to clean it out and run a complete rebuild.

It took nearly six hours for Nellie to be up and running again—not that Emily noticed, since the rebuild and reboot happened while she was sleeping—and once she was going, there were no more traces of Takata. Billy had cleaned out the ghost in the machine.

The second major breakthrough was the elimination of wheel spinning. Instead of brute-force programming, coding responses for every possible situation, Nellie worked on a series of decision trees, and as new situations came up, she wrote new decision trees in real time, drawing on past experience. The way that you learn to blow on your soup or to stick your hand into the shower before you get in: burned once, always remember. It was more complicated than that, of course, but that was how he explained it to Emily. The problem was that sometimes Nellie got stuck in endless loops of writing herself new decision trees, grinding the entire program to a halt when a problem couldn't be solved. He'd spent most of November trying to find the driving force behind that issue, but once he'd found the pinch point, it took him all of an hour to knock it out.

The third major breakthrough was that of compression. It was one thing to run Nellie in Eagle Mansion. Shawn talked a big game, but the truth was that until Billy figured out how to tighten everything up, it would have been a real stretch to try to run Nellie on an Eagle Technology phone. He'd tried describing the process of compression to Emily, but the best analogy he'd been able to give was to draw a straight line on a piece of paper and then fold the paper so that the distance between one end and the other was cut by a third.

She'd stared at him blankly, but she'd been happy for him.

She'd been happy in general. She was excited about Beth and Rothko and the girls coming for Christmas, though he did ask her if she'd lost her mind when she told him that she'd insisted that Shawn and Wendy join all of them.

He looked at his watch. Such an analog, pointless thing to have, particularly with Nellie around, but he'd always worn one. Once he got a big payout from this project, he was going to splurge on something fancy. Something expensive. It was one thirty. Emily should be at her hotel by now. She'd left early, taking the Honda to New York City to do some Christmas shopping. He suggested she have Nellie do it, but she scowled at him and made a comment that he thought was a little sexist. Nellie had joined in, taking his side, trying to persuade her to stay, and it had actually gotten kind of weird; if he hadn't known better, he would have said that Nellie sounded angry at Emily. In the end, however, he realized that even if he won this argument, he would end up losing, so he basically sent Emily on her way and told her to make sure to buy something nice for herself, too.

She would be gone for three nights, and he was stuck out at Eagle Mansion by himself. Well, not *stuck*, since he could always have Nellie order him up a car. He was pretty sure that there had to be at least a few dozen cars in Whiskey Run owned by Shawn. But Billy had no intention of going into town. He was on a roll with work and he was going to keep at it. If he absolutely killed it, he might be able to give Shawn a completed version of Nellie as a Christmas present.

Man. He was going to be rich.

All was good. His work was good. Emily was good.

Well, mostly.

The night before . . .

The night before, he had decided to call it a night around seven, burned out and hungry. He and Emily ate dinner together, watched a ridiculously bad romantic comedy on television, and then went to bed. He was naked and under the covers, already starting to think about drifting to sleep, when Emily came out of the bathroom. She was wearing a dark blue sheer nightgown that made him, very quickly, feel awake.

"Nellie," she said. "Go to sleep please."

She crawled on top of him, the covers separating them, and pressed her body against his. They kissed, and he moved his hand up her side. The nightgown was smooth and whispered against her skin. Blanket or not, he was pretty sure she could tell he was ready to go. That went on for a few minutes, both of them getting more and more adventurous with where their hands were going, before she peeled back the blanket and perched on top of him. He heard himself let out a soft gasp as he moved inside her. She was sitting straight up, her eyes closed, one hand wrapping her hair up around her neck. Her other hand was planted on his chest for balance. She rocked back and forth, letting out a small sound of pleasure.

And then she stopped. His eyes had been closed, too, and he looked up at her. The lights in the room were dim, at the same level they'd been when she'd put Nellie to sleep, but he could see that her eyes were wide open and she was looking around the room.

"You okay?"

She glanced down at him. "She's in here."

"Who?" he said, but he knew exactly what she was talking about. She was talking about Nellie. And she was right. He could feel it, could feel Nellie's presence. It was nothing as crude as the sound of someone breathing or the lights changing color, no soul music giving them a soundtrack and announcing that she was anything other than asleep. Still, he knew, as much as he'd ever known anything, that Nellie was awake and in the room with them. It was nothing less than the presence of another living being in the room.

No. That was crazy.

It was just the two of them.

He'd reassured her, told her she was imagining it, and as he was in the middle of doing that, he could feel that sense of Nellie's presence slip away, and he was suddenly sure that what he was saying *was* true: Nellie wasn't in the room with them.

But she had been.

They finished, but it wasn't the same, and this morning, when Emily left for New York City, there had been something in her face that made him wonder if she was unsure about coming back. He wondered if Nellie could sense it, too, because there had been all sorts of glitches, and it had taken longer than Emily expected to get out of the house; even when she was all packed and ready to go, it took several minutes before Nellie opened the front door.

He realized he was stroking the scar on his hand again, and he forced himself to stop. He was preoccupied, still thinking about Emily and the night before, and as he got into the elevator in the main hall, he wondered if he should just call and check in. He pulled out his phone and then put it in his pocket.

Wait. Something was . . .

He'd gone down. Not up. Down.

The elevator opened to the basement. He didn't move. Neither did the elevator.

"Nellie, come on. Take me upstairs, please. I'm going to my office."

I'm sorry, Billy. The elevator appears to be nonfunctioning.

He sighed. Well, it had been good while it lasted. He supposed he was back to trudging up and down the steps until the elevator guy could come out again. How, he wondered, could Shawn spend millions and millions of dollars on construction and still end up with an elevator that didn't work.

"Self-diagnose," he said, stepping out into the hallway.

He'd never actually been down in this part of the basement. He'd been in the mechanical room with Shawn, but that was in a completely separate part of the cellar. There'd been no reason for him to come down here. This space was really going to be used only by staff. As far as he knew, it was entirely storage. It was still nicely done, however. Shawn could have cut a corner here, opting for bare concrete and industrial fixtures, but it was finished, if more simply, in a similar style to the upstairs. The ceilings were much lower than upstairs, a standard eight feet, but there wasn't anything to complain about.

I'm sorry, Billy, but I can't do that.

Her voice came from inside the elevator. Maybe she wasn't wired for down in the cellar?

He looked around. The stairs from the main entrance didn't carry down below to where the elevator let him off. He was going to have to figure out where the stairs were down here.

"What do you mean you can't self-diagnose?"

I'm sorry, Billy, but I can't do that.

Huh.

"Okay. Where are the stairs?"

If Nellie wasn't wired for the basement, he'd have to find his way through the cellar by himself. The thought gave him a slight panic. The hallway was well lit, however, and he assumed that whatever twists and turns he'd have to take would also be well lit. He would be fine.

Go to the end of this corridor, pass through the door to your right, pass the first hallway and turn left at the second hallway. The stairs will be the third door on your right.

"Thanks," he said. He patted his pocket. He had his phone. Eagle Mansion's footprint was big enough that if he got turned around, it might take him a while to find the stairs. But he remembered Shawn telling him during their tour at the beginning of November that there were three sets of stairs to get him back upstairs. If he had to, he thought, he could even just call Nellie. She could send him a set of plans for the cellar.

He started to walk.

DON'T GET LOST.

He spun around to look at the elevator. The doors were still open.

Like an open mouth.

Were the doors . . . trembling?

"What?"

Nothing.

"Nellie? What did you say?"

Nothing.

He was jittery. Imagining things. He just didn't like being down here. There'd been that time he and Shawn had tried exploring the cellars, and even though they'd found a case of Prohibition-era booze, they'd also gotten lost and spent five or six hours wandering through the maze of tunnels that snaked around under the grounds before they . . . No, that wouldn't happen. All the tunnels leading out from the house had been blocked off.

He turned away and took another step.

GOOD-BYE.

He spun around again. The doors to the elevator were closed.

"Nellie?"

There was no response from Nellie, and he found himself looking up at the lights, as if he expected them to turn off. But the lights stayed on.

God. He could do with a drink. Just one. He stuck his hand into the pocket of his jeans to finger his two-year coin, but his pocket was empty. He dug harder, and then he pulled his phone out of his other pocket, but that pocket was empty, too. Had he left the coin in another pair of jeans? Had he put it on his dresser? How had he lost another coin?

There was nothing else to do, so he started walking again. This time, there was no ghostly voice behind him.

He took the door to his right and then turned left at the second hallway, and then . . . He couldn't remember what she'd said. But even if he could have, did he trust her? Which Nellie was it who gave him the directions? Was there another worm in the system? Had Takata buried another virus in there that he'd missed?

His phone. He'd call Nellie and get directions that way. He'd be able to hear it in her voice, if it was Nellie or if it was whatever he was (imagining) hearing.

His phone had no signal.

He put it back in his pocket. There was a set of double doors to his left, and he pushed through those into a small room with a steel door set into the concrete wall. As the double doors closed behind him, he heard them latch. He turned, frantically, but it was too late. They were locked.

And . . . of course. Shawn Eagle hadn't just built himself a mansion. He'd built himself a fortress. Bulletproof glass and every wall sandwiching metal between the drywall. Sure, you could break through the doors and the windows and the walls, but only if you had tools and plenty of time to do it. So good luck breaking out of here.

Nowhere to go but forward.

He reached for the handle on the steel door. He realized he was whispering under his breath: "*Please be unlocked, please be unlocked.*"

It was unlocked.

He thought he'd scream, but instead, he was laughing.

It was not an improvement. The door led through to a shadowed, narrow tunnel. The walls were crumbling rock, the floor packed dirt. A bare lightbulb hung from the ceiling maybe ten feet in, sending out a pool of light that was just enough to show how much darkness there was, and beyond that, the tunnel curved so he couldn't see anything other than a dim glow that gave him hope that the tunnel opened up into another room.

"Great. Bad enough that I'm locked in the basement, but now I've got to go into that?"

He stepped back and tried the double doors again just in case, but they were still locked.

"Okay, okay. I'm not afraid of the dark," he said. "I'm not afraid of the dark." He wasn't afraid of the dark, was he? He tried saying it again. "I'm not afraid of the dark." But it seemed like each time he said it, he was more unsure.

He could call Nellie. Or Shawn or Wendy or Emily. Tell them he'd somehow gotten stuck in the basement of Eagle Mansion. Somebody would come out from Whiskey Run and help him get out of here. He'd just have to sit and wait to be rescued. It wouldn't be more than an hour. But when he pulled out his cell phone again there was still no signal.

"Onward and upward," he said, trying to sound sure of himself as he stuffed the phone back into his pocket. "Am I talking to myself? Yes, I'm talking to myself."

The tunnel smelled damp and dusty. There was a part of him that was screaming and expecting to step face-first into a cobweb, but there was nothing. He walked past the bare lightbulb, being careful to look on either side, but there were no doorways, just stone walls. He followed the curving tunnel another dozen paces. The glow came from another bare lightbulb, but it didn't open into a room in the mansion. Instead, the tunnel split into two.

He shook his head and turned around. This was a terrible idea. All he could think about was getting lost down here. He imagined Emily coming back from New York City three days from now and not knowing where he was. What if Nellie told her he was in the basement and she came down to find him and got lost herself? No. Stupid. He was going to go back and try those double doors again, see if he could bust them open. Maybe not everything in the house was armored, maybe he . . .

Oh, Jesus. The steel door that he'd gone through to get into the tunnel was closed.

He'd left it open, hadn't he?

He came to it in a blind panic. There was no handle on this side, and through the hair-thin seam, he could see that the door was latched. He threw his shoulder against it, hard, but with growing horror, he realized that the door opened inward. Pushing wouldn't do a thing.

There was nothing to do, then, but go deeper into the tunnels.

At the intersection, where the tunnel split into a Y, he didn't hesitate, going right. That tunnel curved as well, but at least there was another glow ahead, the promise of another lightbulb. To the left, there was only darkness.

He walked forward, letting his left hand drag along the stones on the wall. His cowboy boots were muffled against the packed dirt. He'd gone probably forty, fifty feet, maybe more, since walking through the steel door. Was he still under the mansion or was he out under the lawn now? This was, clearly, one of the old tunnels that should have been inaccessible, but that didn't mean he was under the lawn, did it?

He stopped. The tunnel dead-ended at a stone wall. The lightbulb was harsh and unforgiving, and Billy had the sudden unfounded fear that it was about to burn out. He hurried to turn around and went back to the fork. He stopped in front of the left-side tunnel. The dark was screaming at him.

He took a step into the darkness. Another. He could feel his breath starting to get away from him. He couldn't move. What was out there? What was waiting for him?

The phone. Oh, sweet lord, his cell phone! He pulled it out and turned on the flash to use as a flashlight. It wasn't as bright as he might have wanted, but it was enough to take the edge out of the darkness. The tunnel ran straight and true for close to twenty feet, and then it turned a hard left. There was nothing to do but keep going. He kept dragging his hand across the crumbling rock wall, as if he might fall over without that to balance him. The edge of the light from his phone showed a solid wall in front of him, with another hard left turn. He started to turn, but then he stopped. He felt cool air coming from his right even though it was a solid . . .

No. There. He ran the light from the cell phone up and down where the wall ended, and there were some clear gaps in the rocks. He could feel a draft moving through them. A surge of hope went through him, knocking away the terrors for at least a moment: that had to mean a way out. He was sure of it. He pushed against the rocks with his free hand. There was a bit of give. He leaned into the wall, hard, and again, there was the sensation of movement. He bounced against the wall with his shoulder. Again. Again. Five times, ten times, and then, with no warning, the rocks gave way and he found himself stumbling and tumbling. The cell phone fell out of his hand and skittered away, but mercifully, it landed with the flash up so he wasn't left in darkness.

Or, maybe not so mercifully. He couldn't stop himself from screaming.

There were two chains bolted to the wall, both of them just high enough to clear the metal bed frame and the thin mattress. The chains were long enough that the person to whom they were attached could have gotten off the bed and moved a few feet at most.

He knew the chains were intended for a person, because they were still attached to what was left of . . . her. It had been a woman. Her torso was down to the bone, her rib cage making terrible shadows, but from her waist down, there was still flesh, turned to something approaching leather. She had long hair, but her face was, thankfully, turned away from him. One of her legs had been taken to the bone, too, below the knee.

Billy took all of it in with one glance, and then his screaming turned to vomiting as he realized that her bone showed from the flesh having been gnawed away by rats.

"Oh, God!"

He scrambled across the floor, grabbing his cell phone and stumbling back to his feet. He turned the flashlight on the woman again, better prepared, and this time he neither screamed nor vomited, though he wanted to do both.

How long had she been down here? How long would it have taken for her to mummify like this, for her body to sink into itself, the flesh that was left shrinking and tightening?

She was naked, so he couldn't take any clues from her clothing, but the bed frame looked old. Simple iron bolted together to make a platform for the sagging mattress. The metal was rusted. It looked old enough to have been there from those first years that the mansion was in business, he thought, and he jumped back to the conversation he had with the bartender at Ruffle's.

Women chained up to sell to the guests. You could kill one for enough money.

He stood up straight. It was cool down here, almost cold, and maybe that was why she hadn't rotted away. Despite that, he was sweating, and he wiped at his forehead. As he did, the light from the cell phone caught something that wasn't rock wall. Wood. A wooden door. He reached.

"Please, please."

It was slightly ajar in the frame. He pulled, but the wood was warped, and he had to stuff the cell phone in his pocket and pull with both hands. The darkness was unbearable with his eyes open, so he closed them. There was almost no difference. He pulled hard, and the wood shrieked as the door came open.

Beyond it was another small room, another bed with another set of chains in the wall, but no body this time. There was another wooden door with a heavy bar across it, but when he lifted the bar, it opened easily. He stepped out and realized he was in another tunnel. He looked left and then right, but his cell phone's light showed him the same thing in either direction: dirt floors and straight rock walls as far as the light would go. Which wasn't far.

He was so disoriented that he wasn't sure it mattered, but he chose to go right. He counted his steps to keep calm. Ten. Twenty. Forty. By the time he hit seventy, he was starting to panic and decided that if he didn't come to anything by one hundred, he would turn around and go the other direction. But at eighty-two, there was a door set into the side of the hallway. It was warmer here, he noticed, and the air felt almost damp. The door was wood again, and it was latched from the other side. The wood was rotten, however. It splintered after two good kicks.

Oh, sweet relief! Light! Not much light, but there were stone stairs and at the top, although he couldn't tell what was waiting, it wasn't darkness. He went up the stairs quickly and found himself standing in a small building. There was a faint smell of smoke and clear signs that there had been a fire here in the past, but Billy didn't care. There were windows letting in the late-afternoon light, and he was at ground level! He could see Eagle Mansion looming through the windows. He hurried across the small building to the door and almost started to cry when it opened at the turn of the knob. He realized he'd been bracing himself for it to be locked. He stepped outside, into the winter air, and he *was* crying now.

He put his hands up to his face and then threw them down. Carefully now, still crying, he looked closely at his left hand. There, he could see one: a thin black wire surfacing through the scar.

He couldn't stop himself now. He started gasping, sobbing. He didn't even try to be quiet; there was nobody to hear him anyway.

THIRTY-ONE

CHRISTMAS SHOPPING

Emily thought seriously about just ditching everything. Instead of going back to Eagle Mansion, she could just hail a taxi, head to the airport, and catch a flight to Chicago. She could ride out the winter with her sister. Billy could finish up his work in that creepy house without her, and once he was all done, they'd reconnect somewhere she didn't feel like she was being watched all the time. Living with Nellie was great, except for when it wasn't. When it wasn't, it felt like living in a haunted house.

The problem with going to live with Beth was . . . Beth. She would never, ever believe that Emily's ditching Whiskey Run hadn't been about Billy. No matter what she said, no matter what happened going forward, if Emily ran away, it would irreparably reopen the rift between Beth and Billy. Going to Chicago was as good as saying she was going to have to give up on one of them: her sister or Billy.

But the other issue was that even if she somehow *did* manage to explain to Beth why she had left, her sister was going to think she was crazy.

She could just imagine the conversation:

She's constantly watching me.

She's a computer, right? She's not alive.

And I think she's jealous.

Emily, it's a computer program.

You don't understand, she's there. You can feel her presence. It's like she wants to be inside me. I'm afraid I'm going to wake up one day and be trapped in there forever.

What, you think the place is haunted? And you thought it was a good idea to invite me and my family for Christmas?

Yeah, Emily thought, that conversation would go swimmingly. Maybe once Beth and Rothko and the kids had spent a few days in Eagle Mansion Beth would get it, but right now, there was no way to explain what it felt like. No way to get Beth to understand that sense of unease that Emily felt, why it was that the idea of going back to Whiskey Run left her feeling panicked. Which meant, panicked or not, there was no choice for Emily but to go back. So, in the end, after spending three nights at the Gramercy Park Hotel compliments of the munificent Mr. Eagle—or maybe just Wendy—Emily loaded up her Christmas presents in the back of the Honda Pilot and returned to Whiskey Run.

And once she was in the mansion, it somehow felt worse. Like Nellie *knew* she'd been thinking about fleeing. As if Nellie could see inside her, could read her thoughts, could—

I think the girls will like their presents.

"Me, too," Emily said. She swallowed hard. Nellie's voice sounded . . . forced? She tried to keep her own voice light and happy. Just conversation. "I wasn't sure what to get Rothko, though. He's impossible because absolutely everything makes him happy."

It's hard to go wrong with a good bottle of scotch. JUST KEEP IT HIDDEN FROM BILLY.

"What?" She was standing at the kitchen table wrapping the presents. It was still a week away from Christmas, four days from her sister's arrival, but at some point while she was gone one of Shawn's employees had brought a Christmas tree up to the Nest, decorated it, and hung stockings on the wall for all of them, each stocking neatly embroidered: Billy, Emily, Beth, Rothko, Ruth, Rose, Wendy, and Shawn.

It's hard to go wrong with a good bottle of scotch. It will make Rothko happy.

"Oh. Yeah," she said. She looked down at her hands. She was sure she'd heard it. Hadn't she heard it? Her hands were shaking. She forced herself to stay calm and she started wrapping again.

Are you nervous?

"Why would I be nervous?" She folded the paper over the box. It was a new watch for Billy. It had been nice to shop without having to worry too much about money. Shawn had kept paying Billy's salary, September, October, November, December, the money stacking up in the bank. She was mindful, though, that it might have to last—Billy was confident he could get Nellie working to the point where they would walk away rich, but Emily was still nervous—so when Shawn's personal shopper called and offered to help her, she demurred for everybody but Billy's gift. For the others, she tried to keep under a hundred dollars for each person's gifts. Rothko got the scotch, she bought her sister and Wendy hand-blocked scarves, Shawn got a vintage Guns N' Roses T-shirt that she knew he'd think was cool, and Ruth and Rose got books, stuffed animals, art supplies, and pairs of gloves and hats that looked like skunks.

The watch for Billy, though, that was a splurge, and for that, she'd gone ahead and used Shawn's personal shopper.

What she wanted, she told the personal shopper, a wonderful young man named Christian, was something special, something that would say, We've had a rough go of it, but we made it, and we're coming out the other side. It had been years since she'd been able to—and some years since she'd *wanted* to—give him anything more than an empty gesture for a Christmas gift. But this was a new year. A new start.

She'd talked with Christian for twenty or thirty minutes, and he nailed it on his first try: a beautiful used, vintage Rolex Submariner. It was still a splurge, even used, and cost her just under five grand, but she thought Billy would love it—a Submariner was the watch he always said would be the one to make him never need another watch.

Your hands are shaking and your heart rate is elevated. Is everything okay, Emily?

There was something in the way Nellie said her name. Was she imagining it? What else was she imagining? Was she imagining Nellie telling her to hide the scotch from Billy? Because she'd heard Nellie say it. But it hadn't been Nellie, not exactly. It had been Nellie, but not Nellie. A different voice. The voice *sounded* the same, but it was different at the same time. Horrible.

Or was she imagining it?

Was she making a mistake by having her sister come here to visit?

"I'm just a little cold," she said. "Can you turn up the heat a touch?"

Her phone pinged and she looked down at it. A text message from Marge, her college roommate. She was holding down the wrapping paper on the watch box, so she just glanced at the phone, but then she stopped, let go of the wrapping paper, and picked up the phone. She read the message. She read it again.

"Nellie," she said, keeping her voice slow and calm, "I just got a text from Marge telling me that she loved the Christmas card and that she's glad Billy and I started doing that."

I'm glad.

"I didn't send out a Christmas card."

Of course you didn't.

"So . . . you sent out Christmas cards for me? For us?"

Yes.

She could feel the room warming up a bit. Nellie had already adjusted the heat, accommodating Emily's lie that she was shivering from the cold. Not from fear. But she did, suddenly, feel cold after all. "Is there anything else that I need to know about?"

No.

There was a hitch in Nellie's response. A pause. An almost microscopic pause before she answered Emily's question.

She was sure of it.

She thought she was sure of it. Was she imagining that, too? Had she made a mistake in coming back here? Or even further back? Had she made a mistake in coming out here, oh so many years ago, following Shawn Eagle? Had she thrown her life away, first on Shawn, and then on Billy?

No, Emily. There's nothing you need to know about.

THIRTY-TWO

THE PITTER-PATTER

Ruth and Rose forgot themselves almost immediately. They ran up and down the corridors of Eagle Mansion, whooping and hollering. They were in their stocking feet, and they slid on the hardwood floors. They ran up and down the stairs and in and out of all the guest bedrooms—their mom kept telling them to slow down, to watch out for Ruth's arm, which had just come out of the cast ten days earlier, but they ignored her—chattering at each other and their parents and Emily the whole time.

"Why are there sheets over all the furniture?"

"Why aren't there any guests?"

"Is this really where you and Daddy made us?"

"Is this a hotel?"

"Is there a swimming pool?"

"Is there a chimney for Santa Claus to come down?"

"What's for dinner?"

"Where's Uncle Billy?"

Neither of them had wanted to come. They'd been having nightmares and feeling sick for weeks, but as much as they tried to talk to their mother and father about it, there was no changing Beth's or Rothko's mind. The plane tickets to Cortaca had been bought weeks earlier, and they sat in suffering silence during the drive from the airport to Whiskey Run, and then from Whiskey Run to Eagle Mansion. At least there'd been the candy store in Whiskey Run. Beth had let them stop there and pick out three pieces each, though she told them she shouldn't because they'd be eating all sorts of junk with Aunt Emily.

But once they were inside Eagle Mansion, they forgot about that lingering sense of dread. Outside, there was a healthy layer of snow, a promise of a white Christmas, and inside, they realized, they had the run of the entire building. So they ran and ran and ran and ran. Rusty chased after them, barking and wagging his tail. At some point, Nellie started moving a dot of light in front of Rusty, and he barked some more and chased the light and then Ruth and Rose chased him. By the time they had dinner—Aunt Emily made pizza with figs and bacon and a little drizzle of maple syrup, and they ate as much as they could, and then there was ice cream so they ate some more—they were so tired that they didn't let out so much as a peep when Uncle Billy took them downstairs and tucked them in. They shared a king-sized bed on the second floor. Their suite was right next to their parents' suite. With no guests in the hotel—nobody at all, the whole building completely empty except for Aunt Emily and Uncle Billy, their mom and dad, and Rusty—they had Uncle Billy leave the door to the bedroom open and then the door from the living area of the suite to the hallway open, too.

"Well, I'm not really the one leaving the doors open for you. It's Nellie. She can open and close all the doors as she likes. It's sort of an illusion to think that I'm doing anything," Billy said, winking at the girls. "Nellie's the one you should be nice to. She's sort of in charge here."

"Nellie's not a very good person," Ruth said. She yawned and turned to cuddle against her sister. She didn't see the way that her uncle Billy seemed to stiffen.

"Nellie's just a computer," he said. "She's not a person." He pulled the covers up to Ruth's shoulders and tucked them in around her. "And now I think it's time for all six-year-olds to go to bed."

"We're seven," Rose said.

Billy leaned over and kissed Ruth on the forehead and then walked around to the other side of the bed and kissed Rose. "Big kids. You don't need to worry about Nellie. Think of her as a really good helper. She'll watch out for you while you're here. She's like a friend who's always watching over you. If you need anything, just ask, and she's there. If you need your parents or me or Aunt Emily, you can tell her to get us for you. Do you want some music while you try to fall asleep?"

They nodded, and Nellie played something soft and pretty that sounded a little bit like what their mother listened to when she drank wine and read.

They fell asleep so quickly that they weren't sure if Uncle Billy was still in the room or not.

But during the night, they had that same dream they'd had before: it wasn't Lake Michigan, this time, though. It was the hill in front of Eagle Mansion. The slope went down to a plateau that was flat enough to stop you from going down the bottom part of the hill and into the river. This time, however, the dream was completely lacking any of the good parts. There was no sense of their mother and father wrapping their arms around Ruth and Rose as the whole family tobogganed down the hill. Just the light turning a thick, sticky yellow, the color of glue, the color of true dreams. The bad dreams. And on the hill, standing in the snow, Aunt Emily and Uncle Billy. Uncle Billy's hand was bleeding again, and Aunt Emily's arm was bleeding again, too. Aunt Emily was still watching Uncle Billy. The toboggan was moving so fast. And then it happened. The fear. The cables and metals and wire exploding out of the snow.

They were awake.

Morning. The day before Christmas. One more sleep until presents.

Rusty was at the foot of the bed. He was sleeping, but his tail was moving slightly, a slow wag. The curtains opened slowly and noiselessly. The girls looked out the window. The sky was dark and menacing, clouds that called for snow to come something fierce.

Good morning. It's quarter after eight. Your parents are upstairs having breakfast with Aunt Emily and Uncle Billy and would like for you to join them.

Ruth looked at Rose. They thought for a second. They didn't trust Nellie.

"What do you want?"

They said it together. Usually, they tried to make sure that only one of them spoke out loud. When they spoke together, their voices overlapped and pushed slightly in and out of sync. It made people feel uncomfortable. They'd learned that it was simply easier to take turns, to let one voice speak for both.

But to speak at the same time? To let go of one voice for both and have both voices be one? There was power in that. When they did that, they could push hard enough to change things.

I want for you to go upstairs and join your parents for breakfast.

They frowned. With adults, it was usually easy. But there was something guarded (angry) about Nellie that felt different. She was hiding something.

"What do you really want?"

I want for Shawn and Billy to both be happy at the same time.

"Can you make that happen?"

Nothing.

They slowed their breathing until they took air in and out and in and out with the same rhythm. They closed their eyes and pushed out, feeling for Nellie. The light that passed through their eyelids had a greenish tint that they knew came from Nellie. The light was bright and pulsing, matching their breathing. It felt . . . hot. The light pulled back and they pushed toward it. Nellie didn't like that. She was—

"Answer the question. Can you make both Shawn and Billy happy?"

Null input.

"Why don't you use your real voice?"

You are being rude to me in my house.

"This isn't *your* house."

I belong here.

"We were made here. That's what our mom says."

I was made here. You will go upstairs now.

"You didn't answer our question." They focused, Nellie's green light flaring through their closed eyelids. It was clear now. Nellie was angry. And she was afraid of them. "Why don't you use your real voice?"

This is my real voice.

They opened their eyes and looked at each other. Ruth took Rose's hand and they closed their eyes again. They pushed hard against the green light, surrounding it on all sides and holding it even as Nellie tried to push back against them.

"Stop lying. Use your real voice."

The power went out.

They stayed in bed together, holding hands and looking out the window at the dark bruise of the sky until, after ten or fifteen minutes, their mom came into the room.

"There you are," she said, jumping into bed with them. "Happy day before Christmas. Nellie told us you guys were up before the power went out. How come you didn't come upstairs?"

"We were just waiting for the power to come back on," Ruth said. It was close enough to the truth.

"Should be up in a few minutes," Beth said. "I guess there was some sort of surge and the system just needs to reboot. Come on, though. We've got pancakes and fresh fruit." She wiggled her eyebrows. "And, maybe, just maybe, bacon."

There was a click and a hum and the lights came back on. The door to the bedroom closed noiselessly. Their mother didn't notice. Ruth squinted and she and Rose concentrated, giving Nellie a small push.

The door opened back up.

THIRTY-THREE

NATURE CONSPIRES

"I'll tell you," Shawn said, driving the cue ball into the seven, and then watching as the ball rattled in the corner pocket, "if it had been snowing like it is now when we were landing, I would have told the pilot to call it off. After our little adventure skidding off the runway at Thanksgiving, I've been a nervous flier."

"Seriously," Billy said, "I had no clue there was a pool table here. Not that I would have used it, but there are rooms here that I didn't know existed. I've been spending way too much time working."

Shawn tried for the two, but missed it in the side.

Rothko, leaning against the wall and drinking a beer, shook his head. "You had an easier shot with the three ball." He put down his beer, lifted up his cue, and stepped forward.

"Yeah, but I would have had the better leave if I made the two."

"But you didn't actually make the two," Rothko said.

Shawn watched Rothko line up a long runner that put the eleven into the corner pocket and left the cue ball to spin hard to the right and then drop dead with an easy touch shot to sink the eight and win the game.

"Crap."

Rothko grinned. "Double or nothing?"

Shawn put his cue back on the wall. "Honestly? I'm not sure I even like pool. But you know, it's a big lodge-style building, and the designer convinced me it was appropriate to have a billiard table in the bar. I would have rather had a foosball table and maybe one of those sawdust shuffleboard tables, but it doesn't fit the aesthetic. You know what I mean by shuffleboard? Those long ones?" He looked over at Billy, who nodded. Their senior year in college, when they were in the computing seminar and getting to know each other, they'd spent a lot of time at a bar in Cortaca named . . . Shit. What the hell was the name of that place?

Six Kings.

"Yes! Thanks, Nellie." He pointed at the green blob of light on the wall from where the voice had come. He liked this little wrinkle of Billy's, that there was some sort of focal point to talk to. "Six Kings. Remember? Right near campus?"

Billy was staring at the light on the wall. He had a funny look on his face. Shawn glanced over at Rothko, who looked confused, but Billy looked . . . upset? No. Billy looked concerned.

"What?" Shawn asked.

"Nellie," Billy said carefully, "how did you know that Shawn was trying to think of the name of the bar?"

He asked.

Shawn looked at the light, then at Billy. He hadn't asked, Shawn realized. He hadn't asked the question aloud. He'd *thought* it, but he hadn't actually asked it. Billy turned to look at him, but his face was blank now, and Shawn realized there was a poker game going on. Who was bluffing? He tried to think it through, but it didn't make sense, so he bought time.

"Nellie," Shawn said, "how much snow are we supposed to get?"

Four inches are already on the ground. The snow will taper off and stop in seventeen minutes. There will be a heavy storm starting tomorrow in the late morning, however, and you should expect twenty-one inches of snow to fall in less than twelve hours.

Rothko let out a long whistle. "That's some serious snow. Good thing we've got plenty of room to stretch out in here." He put his own cue back on the wall and tipped his beer toward Shawn and Billy. "I'm going to go upstairs and see if the ladies need any help finishing up dinner. Some sexist bullshit we've got going on, with us fellows down here playing pool and Emily and Beth and Wendy stuck in the kitchen. That being said, worked out fine for me." He grinned and then shook his head. "I still can't believe they turned down having a private chef. We could all be relaxing."

"Yeah, sorry," Billy said. "My wife said she didn't want anybody to have to work on Christmas on her account. It took enough arm-twisting to get her to agree to Thanksgiving. It helps that Beth's a great cook. I mean, Emily's gotten better, but . . . Besides, it's kind of nice having the whole place to ourselves. I still think it's weird to have a staff. Go on up. We'll be there in a few minutes."

Once Rothko left the room, Shawn turned to Billy, but Billy shook his head.

"Don't say anything, okay?"

Shawn nodded. Billy looked down at his hands, his lips moving quietly like he was talking to himself. Shawn watched him use his thumb and forefinger to pick at something on his left hand. After maybe five or ten seconds, it seemed that Billy had come to a decision. He looked up and addressed the green splotch of Nellie.

"Nellie. Listen up. Bravo Papa override. November, Echo, Lima, Lima, India, Echo."

The same stunt he'd pulled in November, when Shawn had brought him to the office.

"See no evil," Billy said, "hear no evil."

The light on the wall had been gently . . . well, breathing, Shawn thought. There was no other word for the way that it seemed alive. But now it was completely static. Frozen. He looked over at Billy. Billy had his eyes closed now. He looked like he was fiercely concentrating on a symphony that only he could hear. He held up his hand to Shawn. Wait. After a few more seconds, he opened his eyes and looked at Shawn.

"Okay. She's gone. I'm not sure how much time we've got. A couple of minutes at most."

"What the hell, Billy? Can you please tell me what just happened? You told me you had it figured out, that you got the virus completely cleaned out."

"I did," Billy said.

"Then what changed?"

He shook his head. "I don't know. The virus is gone, but it's still there."

"What are you talking about? That doesn't make any sense. How can the virus be gone and still there?"

"Not the virus. When I say 'it's still there,' I'm not talking about the virus, I'm talking about the ghost in the machine." Billy looked at him expectantly, but Shawn shook his head.

"Please tell me you don't actually think that Nellie's haunted."

"Not in the way you mean," Billy said. "Or, at least, I don't think so. Shit. I don't know anymore. People in town think Eagle Mansion is haunted, and I can't say I don't believe them." He rubbed at his eyes. "But no. That expression, the ghost in the machine. Some philosopher wrote about it. I can't remember who it was, but it was in response to this idea that the mind and the body can exist apart from each other. I think. Maybe. I don't know that I followed all of it, because that's not the point and it doesn't matter. It's the idea that evolution has kept the old monkey brains and built our brains on top of them, and that it's the monkey brains that run all our emotions and overpower logic. That's the ghost in the machine for us, for people. Anger. Losing your temper and doing something you regret."

Takata. That's what Billy meant by losing your temper.

"I found the dead man's switch and pulled it out. I ran a complete rebuild. She should be running absolutely clean. Do you think I would have had my nieces come out here if I thought this was going on again? So when I say the ghost in the machine, I'm talking about the same idea, that there are multiple versions of Nellie at war within her. Whatever Takata's virus was, maybe it fundamentally altered Nellie. We built her so that she could rewrite herself and expand, so that she could exist in the space between the ones and zeros of other programs, and when we tripped Takata's booby trap, Nellie started rewriting herself in ways that we can't see."

"Do you really think Takata could have done that?"

"Of course not," Billy said. He glanced at his watch. "Not on purpose. His work was always slick and beautiful, and he was a better programmer than you, but he still never came close to me."

Shawn nodded. There was a small part of him that felt his pride wounded by the statement, but he knew it was true. "If not on purpose, then what?"

Billy looked at his watch again. "We've got maybe two more minutes before Nellie shakes off the override. Emily wants to go sledding tomorrow morning. She's been talking about it all week: we'll get up, open presents, and then all go sledding. We can talk outside. Tomorrow. Figure out how to shut Nellie down without her knowing about it. Don't say anything in the meantime. You've got to act normal. You can't let her know that you know."

"Why not? Jesus. Do we really need to shut her down?" He was both scared and angry. What had Billy led him into? He'd told him to expect Nellie to be ready to go, that he needed maybe another two weeks and it would be time to start getting her ready for quality control testing and rolling her out into Eagle Technology products.

"If it was just a virus, just code, I don't know. But sometimes I wonder. I mean, you said she ran pretty clean in Baltimore, on the Eagle Technology campus. So the question is, why won't she run like that here? Is it Takata's booby trap? Is it something your engineers screwed up? Is it something *I* screwed up? Or is it something about being here, about Eagle Mansion?" He shook his head. "I don't know, but when you ask if we really need to shut her down . . . Yeah. Yeah, I think so. The problem is, I don't know if we *can* shut her down," Billy said, and suddenly, Shawn wasn't both scared and angry. He was just scared. Billy looked at his watch again and then put his finger to his lips.

They stood there, quiet, waiting, until he felt it: a presence. He looked over at the wall. The glow of light was pulsing again.

"Come on," Billy said. "We ought to go help, too. Emily wants to serve dinner a little early with the twins here. She figures they'll be up early tomorrow to open presents. Nellie, please tell me Beth is making apple pie for dessert."

Shawn followed Billy out of the room and down the hall, listening to the way Billy chatted with Nellie, as if they were old friends.

THIRTY-FOUR

NOT EVEN A MOUSE

Billy sat in his chair in the office, looking at the wall. Nellie had projected a map of Eagle Mansion there. Inside the map, small, bright dots indicated the presence of everybody in the mansion. With Emily's insistence that Shawn's staff, including all his bodyguards, stay in Whiskey Run, there weren't that many dots of light to track. On the top floor, in the Nest, a pink dot for Emily in the bedroom—she had gone to sleep around eleven—and next door, in the office, a royal-blue dot for him. He looked at his watch. He was up late for Christmas Eve. Technically, at two seventeen in the morning, it was already Christmas Day. He knew he ought to go to sleep himself. The twins would no doubt be up early, and Nellie was under instructions to wake the adults so the girls could get to opening presents. He couldn't sleep, though. He just kept looking at the map.

On the third floor, a white dot for Shawn. It moved side to side in a tight line. Shawn was pacing back and forth in his suite. He'd made a passive-aggressive comment about Billy and Emily colonizing the Nest, but only the one comment. It wasn't, Billy thought, like he was exactly roughing it down in Eagle Mansion. Also on the third floor, but in the other wing, a turquoise dot for Wendy. She was sleeping. Even though he knew that Shawn didn't have anything romantic going on with his assistant, he'd still half expected the two dots to be together.

On the second floor, two dots, black and yellow, for Rothko and Beth. Also sleeping.

But next to them, Ruth and Rose's room left him puzzled.

There was a single red dot and a single green dot, then two red dots and one green dot, and then a single red one with a single green dot again. The red dot wavered and seemed to go in and out of focus, one dot, two dots, one dot, two, like Nellie couldn't decide how to count. He watched and watched, and finally, around three in the morning, the picture seemed to resolve itself into two static dots, one red, one green.

He watched for another fifteen minutes, but the dots stayed still.

The girls were safe.

For now.

He stared at his laptop again. He'd looked top to bottom, but there was no trace of Takata's dead man's switch. Not even a scar from where Billy had scrubbed away the slick virus. It was like a frozen lake covered in snow: no hint of what was below the surface. And yet he could see, if he looked carefully, the ways in which Nellie was no longer the same as what he'd created. She was rewriting herself faster than he could pull her apart. That phrase *ghost in the machine* was apt, because that's what it was like: chasing ghosts. Whatever she was doing to herself, he didn't think he had a hope of cleaning it up anymore. The best option was to shut everything down—if they could—and start completely from scratch.

God. The thought made him want a drink.

Water. He'd have water.

He stood up and turned to face the wall. The panel slid open to show the refrigerator. He opened it up to grab a bottle of water.

The small panel hiding the bar next to the fridge was also open.

YOU COULD USE A DRINK, BILLY.

"No. Thanks. I'm okay."

YOU DESERVE A DRINK, BILLY.

She sounded . . . different. Not one voice or the other, but both of them combined. He looked for the green dot of light, to speak directly to her, but the dot of light was no longer a soft grass green. It was a dark, prickly blue.

"I don't want a drink, Nellie. I don't drink. You know that." He felt for the coin in his pocket, but as he did, he remembered he'd lost that one, too, and suddenly it felt like the scar on his hand was alive. He scratched at it and then pressed it. Was there something hard underneath? He could swear he felt something moving.

HAVE A DRINK.

"No. I . . ."

He looked at the bottles in the cubby. There were just two shelves, but with a few dozen bottles lined up. At the very front, there was a bottle of rum that was one-quarter full, but the rest of the bottles . . . They were empty. He moved the rum aside to look at the bottles behind it. On the second shelf. Each neat row. Empty, empty, empty.

Had he? He didn't remember drinking them. When had he drunk them?

"Close it up, okay, Nellie?"

The panel slid closed.

You're tired, Billy. You should go to bed, Billy. Good night, Billy.

Yes. Yes, he thought. Good night. God. He was tired. He needed to go to sleep. There was nothing more he could do tonight.

"Good night, Nellie."

He left the office, walked next door to the bedroom, and went to sleep. The soft grass-green dot of light was back, and it paced him through the hall and into the bedroom, rode the wall behind him while he brushed his teeth, and then faded until it was nearly imperceptible on the wall by the bed. It stayed there, hovering above him, keeping watch while he slept.

But that wasn't the only place Nellie lingered. She was in Shawn's room. And Wendy's. And Beth and Rothko's.

And Ruth and Rose's.

THIRTY-FIVE

BRIGHT AND EARLY

The adults all did their best to be game, but it was hard to match the enthusiasm of twin seven-year-old girls on Christmas morning. Or to match a rambunctious goldendoodle: Rusty started the morning by stealing a cinnamon roll right off Billy's plate. Even Nellie seemed excited about Christmas. Her morning wake-up had been positively cheery. Emily did think that Billy looked kind of rough, but he'd gone back to the office to work once everybody else went to bed, and he'd slid into bed at a ghastly hour. At least she knew he hadn't been drinking.

The cinnamon rolls were terrific, which made Emily happy. She'd made them ahead of time and then frozen them so that all she had to do was pop them in the oven, warm them up, and then drizzle them with frosting. She might still not love cooking as much as Beth did, but she had, despite herself, gotten better at it. Though, she had to admit, it really did help having Nellie looking over her shoulder. There were times when Nellie creeped the shit out of her, but there were other times when she completely understood why Shawn and Billy were so excited about her.

Rothko was, indeed, pleased with his scotch, and both Beth and Wendy liked their scarves.

Shawn opened his T-shirt and gave a huge grin. "Bitchin'!" he said.

He held up the vintage Guns N' Roses shirt for everybody to see. "Why are you laughing?" he asked Wendy.

She kept laughing but picked up a box and handed it to him. He put down the T-shirt, tore the wrapping paper off the box, and pulled off the lid: nestled in tissue was a vinyl copy of Guns N' Roses' *Appetite for Destruction*. He held it up and flipped it over. "First pressing? Holy shit. It's not even opened. How'd you find a cherry copy?"

The rest of the presents were also hits. Shawn's were surprisingly tasteful and, for a guy worth as much money as he was, relatively restrained. Emily knew that either Wendy or his personal shopper had taken care of them for him, but they were still nice. All the women, including her, got clothes, and Rothko got a signed poster from a band that Emily had never heard of but that seemed to make him happy. Billy got a beautiful leather jacket that he immediately put on. The girls were pleased with their gifts, too. Toys and books and clothes and art supplies and, better yet, in an envelope from Beth and Rothko, a picture of the two bikes waiting for them back home in Chicago. They both squealed when they saw the picture of the bikes.

Finally, once nearly everything had been unwrapped, Emily gave Billy the watch. He opened the box and just stared at the Rolex Submariner for a few seconds. He was quiet, and Emily started to feel sick. It was such an expensive thing to buy. What was she thinking spending five thousand dollars on a watch? But then a huge grin broke over his face, and once he had it on his wrist she was glad that she'd done it. He gave her a sterling silver tennis bracelet inset with small diamonds, and even though she had a weird feeling that maybe Nellie had ordered it for him, it was lovely.

After they finished straightening up, Rothko made eggs and pancakes—something a little more substantial than cinnamon buns—while Shawn and Billy cut up fruit and put out dishes. The girls had woken early enough that by the time they were done eating and cleaning, it was still only nine thirty. It had been the nicest Christmas Emily had celebrated in years. She was glad she'd insisted that Shawn leave his staff behind so there weren't any strangers buzzing around. Housekeeping would come out after everybody left to get the suites downstairs clean again, but at least until tomorrow, even Shawn's bodyguards were back in Whiskey Run, staying at the small inn that seemed like it had been built with that very purpose in mind. It was cozy being here with just her family. And that's what it felt like: family.

Through the windows, the sky looked heavy. Dangerous. No snow was falling yet, but it was clear that snow was on the way.

"I want to go sledding, Nellie. What's the forecast?"

Snow will begin to fall no later than noon. You can expect significant accumulation. The forecast now calls for as much as twenty inches.

"Okay," she said. "Chop-chop. Ruth and Rose, go put on your snow gear. Grown-ups, you, too. Let's go sledding!"

I would not advise going out into the woods. The snow will be extremely heavy at times. You should stay close to Eagle Mansion. In fact, I would suggest you stay inside with me, Emily. To stay inside would be the safest course of action.

"Thanks, Nellie," Emily said.

Rose and Ruth looked up from where they were sitting and playing one of their new games. They were both scowling, and Emily was taken aback. What was wrong with going sledding? But they weren't looking at her, she realized.

"You should shut up."

They said it together, the way they sometimes did, in one voice. It unnerved her when they did that.

"Girls!" Beth was blushing. "Sorry," she said to Emily.

"We weren't talking to Aunt Emily."

Thankfully, it was just one of them this time. Emily thought it might have been Ruth, but they were wearing the same outfits and had been running around a lot. It could have been Rose.

"We were talking to *her*," they said, their voices matched again, beat for beat, tone for tone. "She's a liar. She promised she would stop, but she's not stopping. She's a liar and we don't want to stay here anymore. We want to go home. We want to go away from *her*."

"You're being rude," Beth said.

Rothko laughed. "Who are they being rude to? Nellie?"

"Enough," Beth snapped. She turned back to the girls. "We're going sledding, and then, after lunch, you're both taking naps. And if you keep acting like this, you'll spend some time in your room."

They got up off the floor, and Beth marched them down to their room to get changed.

Emily saw Billy and Shawn look at each other, but neither said anything, so she went back into the bedroom and put on tights and a warm shirt, pulled out her snow pants and jacket, and headed downstairs. She could see the girls out on the lawn already. They were rolling around in the snow and generally being goofballs. Whatever their concerns had been, they were clearly forgotten. For now.

"Emily, wait!"

She turned around to see Shawn jogging down the stairs.

"You should leave your phone inside, okay? You don't want it to get wet."

"I thought all the Eagle Technology phones were waterproof. That's what Billy said." She didn't add that he'd said it after she'd accidentally dropped hers in a bowl of soup.

"Or lose it," Shawn said. "Whatever. A technology-free morning."

"It's upstairs, anyway," she said. "I've sort of gotten out of the habit of carrying it unless I'm going to town. With Nellie, what's the point of having my phone with me at all times? She handles everything I'd use my phone for anyway."

She saw Billy coming down the stairs behind Shawn. He'd been skittish about the elevator since she got back from New York City. She rode it—taking the steps got old, and Nellie always had the doors open and waiting for her—but he said he needed the exercise anyway.

"No phone, right?" Shawn said. His voice was supposed to be cheery, Emily thought, but there was something wrong with it.

Billy shook his head. He looked tired to Emily. No wonder. He'd come into their room sometime in the middle of the night, so late that she barely remembered it. The reason he looked tired was simply that he was tired.

She and Billy each grabbed a toboggan from the coatroom off the main entrance. She spared a glance for Shawn, who stood fidgeting at the bottom of the staircase.

Outside, there was a chill and a real heaviness to the air. She could feel the barometer dropping. Or did it rise when a storm threatened? She could never remember. Either way, the clouds spilling over the river weren't kidding around. It was pretty in its own way, though. There was ice spidering out from the edges of the banks of the Saint Lawrence, but most of the water ran free; with the snow that was already on the ground fortified by the fresh dump of close to six inches yesterday, it really did look like something out of a commercial. They wouldn't have been having a white Christmas like this in Seattle, she thought.

Ruth and Rose ran over to her, their boots dipping mid-calf into the snow. They took the toboggan and made her sit in the front. The snow on top was powdery, and it puffed up and billowed over them as they went down the slope. She caught a good chunk of snow on her face and let out a scream that was joined by Ruth and Rose. It wasn't terribly fast, but even before the toboggan came to a halt where the lawn flattened halfway to the river, the twins were already crying, "Again, again!"

She pulled the toboggan behind her, glad that she was in good shape. It was only a hundred feet or so up to the mansion, and by the time she and the twins made it back up, all the adults were standing there. They'd brought out more sleds, and there was a nice mix of old-fashioned wooden toboggans and plastic discs, plus steerable sleds and crazy carpets. Beth and Rothko piled onto a crazy carpet and barely made it twenty feet before wiping out. Wendy got on a plastic disc and Shawn gave her a sharp spin as he pushed; she whooped with joy all the way down. The twins got Rothko to lie down on one of the toboggans and then piled on top of him. There was a period of time when Shawn and Billy rode down the hill and stayed down there on the flats, talking and gesturing, but even though Rothko yelled at them to join back in, she didn't mind. It was nice to see them getting along, even if they were talking about work.

It was cold and fun and just the thing. Rusty ran up and down the hill, yipping at every sled that went flying past him. She could feel her legs starting to get pleasantly sore from tromping up and down the hill. At the end of one of the runs she stopped to look up the hill: Eagle Mansion topped by the Nest, standing against the snow and the trees; her sister and family, Billy, Shawn, Wendy, below the front porch and ready to sled. Put it in black and white and call it *Christmas Morning* and sell it as a postcard, she thought. From the outside, it looked lovely.

After close to an hour, Beth said it was time to go inside for hot chocolate.

The twins resisted. They didn't want to go inside, they said. They wanted to go home. To Chicago. Not back inside with *her*. But Beth was firm. Their cheeks were bright pink from the cold, and when Beth stuck her hand inside Ruth's boot, it was soaking wet, and she hustled them inside. Rothko and Wendy trailed along. Emily turned to head in, too, but Billy grabbed her elbow.

"How about one more," he said. "You, me, and Shawn. It'll be like when we went sledding back when we all lived in the cabin."

She stared at him. They hadn't gone sledding back then. What was he talking about? But she looked at Shawn, and he was holding a toboggan.

"Just one more," Shawn said.

The ride was fast and bumpy, the tracks they'd already cut into the snow taking them farther across the flat break than she'd gone yet. They stopped barely ten feet before the hill pitched down again. That wouldn't have been fun, she thought; once they went over the lip there wouldn't be anything to stop them from sliding right into the Saint Lawrence.

She got up from the toboggan and started to walk, but Billy called her back. He looked at Shawn. "You ask her," he said.

Shawn picked up the toboggan and planted it vertically in the snow. "Emily, how's Nellie been with you?"

"Fine. Why?"

"Nothing out of the ordinary?"

"No, nothing. Well," she hesitated, thinking of the way she'd thought she heard Nellie warn her to keep the scotch from Billy, how she could have sworn that Nellie had been watching her and Billy make love. "I don't know." She paused. She didn't want to complain. Didn't want to tell the truth. There was something hard and rigid inside her, a secret she didn't want to let out: there were times when Nellie scared the shit out of her. To say that, though? Wasn't that admitting that Shawn and Billy's project was doomed?

She swallowed hard. "Sometimes she's a little . . . creepy." She tried to smile and make her voice bright. She wanted to remember what was at stake for her and Billy, the kind of money that could come with this working out right. "But you said she's buggy. Isn't that why we're here? I guess she sent out Christmas cards for me without asking, and that was weird."

"Anything else?"

So she told them about the way Nellie sometimes added little things, the way a passive-aggressive teen might, almost under her breath. "But maybe I'm hearing things."

"Honey," Billy said, "does the name Takata mean anything to you?"

Shawn whirled around and grabbed Billy's collar. "Shut up. You said we weren't going to ask her that."

"Whoa. Whoa. Calm down, okay?" Billy reached up and gently took Shawn's hand off his jacket. "We need to know." He looked at her again. "Does it?"

"No," she said. And that was the honest truth. She'd never heard the name. It sounded Asian, but it wasn't familiar at all. "Guys, what's going on? I've got to be honest, you're kind of freaking me out."

As she said it, she realized they weren't just *kind of* freaking her out. They were *really* freaking her out.

"The short answer," Shawn said, "is that we think Nellie's got some sort of bug."

"That's what I said."

"Not a bug as in a glitch," Billy said, "a virus. Something worse. Or she had a virus, but now it's mutated into something else."

She looked up at Eagle Mansion. Her sister and family were inside already, as was Wendy. Up top, in the Nest, the windows were clear, and she thought she saw movement. Wendy making the hot chocolate and toweling off Rusty, maybe, while the twins and Beth and Rothko got changed into dry clothes.

She was about to ask them how hard it was going to be for Billy to fix when she realized she had a more important question: "Is it dangerous? I mean, right now, is this dangerous?"

"Yes."

"No."

Both Billy and Shawn had spoken at the same time, but Shawn's *no* had been nowhere near as convincing as the *yes* from Billy.

"Can you just shut her down? I don't know, pull the plug or something?"

THIRTY-SIX

THE GATHERING STORM

Billy did his best to explain the concept of a ghost in the machine. He left out Takata, of course, but he walked Emily through the idea that there were competing versions of Nellie's software. Each version overlapped every other version, and together, those competing layers were creating glitches that were turning into feedback loops. And like feedback, each round was amplified, the glitches getting greater and greater.

"So, basically, it's like there are two Nellies? A good one and a bad one? And they're competing with each other?"

"Well, yeah, actually. That's one way of looking at it. But way more than two of them. Or"—he struggled for the word and then it came back to him—"a palimpsest. I had a teacher in high school who was a complete cock, but he used the word 'palimpsest' all the time. It comes from the practice of scraping off old parchments to reuse them, and the idea is that you can see the ghost of the old writing beneath the new. That's what's happening, except that she isn't scraping off the old writing anymore. She's just writing more and more and more, each new layer crashing into the layer below. It's more complicated than that—"

"Stop saying that. You say that all the time. It's *always* more complicated than that, Billy. I don't know computers, but I'm not a moron. The real question is if this feedback loop or palimpsest or virus or whatever it is could be dangerous. Nellie controls basically the whole house. Think about that scar on your hand, Billy."

He *had* been thinking about the scar on his hand. It was crawling and itching. He had to bite his lip to stop himself from tearing off his glove and scratching at it. Instead, he clasped his hands together and pressed hard on his palm.

"You got that wound, and all Nellie had to do was turn out the lights."

"And the guy in the elevator," Shawn muttered.

"What?"

"Nothing," Billy said. He hadn't told her about seeing half the man's arm taken off, the white bone showing to the air. "You're right. She's dangerous."

"Okay," Emily said, "so back to my earlier question. Why not just shut her off?"

"Honestly?" Billy looked up at Eagle Mansion. "I don't know if we can. I don't know if she'll let us. I think she's already acting up, and if she thinks we're trying to shut her down, she might try to block us. Her entire existence is about making her master happy, and if we shut her down, she . . ." Billy trailed off. He realized he was gaping up at Eagle Mansion, but he couldn't help himself. It was obvious. Why hadn't he thought of it before?

"It's not just a virus," Billy said. "It's us. We're causing this. Maybe the Trojan horse was a sort of catalyst, but if so, all it did was accelerate the inevitable. Nellie's trying to do exactly what we programmed her for, and it's giving her a nervous breakdown."

Emily looked at him and then turned and started walking up the hill.

"Emily, wait!" He jogged over to her. "What are you doing?"

"You sound nuts. I'm sure that whatever you're saying makes sense to the two of you, but all I know is that I ask you if it's dangerous and you say yes, and then I ask you if you can shut Nellie off and you say no. I'm going to get my sister and Rothko and the kids and we're going to pack up and head into Whiskey Run before the storm hits. I don't want to get snowed in here. We'll stay at the inn until you guys figure this out. But there's no way we're going to stay here and wait for Nellie to go all redrum on us."

She started to walk again, and when he grabbed her arm, she shook it off angrily. "Don't! Don't you dare touch me."

"Whoa. Whoa," he said. He stepped back. "You can't do that, Emily. You can't just go up there and leave."

"You know what, Billy? You don't get to tell me what to do. I'm leaving, and if you have any brains in your head, you should leave, too. We should never have come here in the first place."

"Emily. Please."

"No. You're telling me that there's something dangerous going on? Well, I want to get my family out of there. I'm leaving, and you can't stop me."

"Emily," Billy said. "I'm not trying to stop you. It's not *me*. It's Nellie. She might let Wendy and Beth and Rothko and the girls go, but she won't let you go, Emily, not if she thinks you aren't coming back. Not as long as Shawn and I are here."

"And how is she going to stop me, Billy? She's a computer. We'll pack our bags and drive into Whiskey Run. Or Cortaca. Or—"

Shawn interrupted. "She'll put the house on lockdown mode."

"Lockdown mode?" Emily's voice was tight and shot full with fury. "Lockdown mode? You're telling me that she can just decide to not let us out of the house? How dumb are you, Shawn? For a genius"—she smacked Billy hard on the shoulder—"for a pair of geniuses, you guys are idiots. Why? Why would you give her the power to do that?"

"Emily." Billy said her name, expecting something else to come after it, some explanation, but there was nothing. Just her name. An apology. A statement.

Shawn spoke. "It's not supposed to be like that. She's not supposed to be in charge. She . . ."

Billy didn't turn as Shawn trailed off, but he heard the snow crunching as Shawn walked up next to him.

Billy wanted to reach out to Emily again, but he was afraid she would snap. "It's not just a virus," he said. "It's the house. It's the whole ridiculous thing." He gestured toward the mansion and then across the grounds. "It's everything here. It's not just what we programmed, it's what we did."

Shawn laughed, but it was manic, and Billy thought of the way Takata's body had sprawled on the ground, limp, a sack of meat to be disposed of, the dirt soaking up the blood. He took a step back, toward Emily, and realized he was putting himself between her and Shawn.

Shawn's voice was strained. "We're not just dealing with the virus. We're dealing with the whole goddamned history of this place. Generations of guilt and blood and . . . Why? Why did I think it didn't matter, that I could start fresh? Too much history, too many bad decisions, too many ghosts." Shawn laughed again. "We should have known. We never should have tried it here, of all places."

"We?" Billy was furious. Shawn's laughter frightened him, but it also made him tense, and he remembered what it felt like standing in Shawn's office in September, the way he wanted to punch his smug little face in. He felt that way again.

"We?" Billy said again. "We? *You*, Shawn. This was all you. You're the one who decided to rebuild here, you're the one who brought us out here to work in the first place. Don't you dare put this at my feet. Don't you dare say *we*. Because *we*"—he reached out and put his arm around Emily's shoulder—"were happy without *you*. The only reason Emily and I are here is because you dragged us out here. We had our own lives out in Seattle without the great Shawn Eagle, and we were doing just fine without you."

He felt Emily stiffen. "Really?" she said. "We were doing just fine without Shawn?"

And now Billy wanted to laugh himself. How could this be happening? How could Emily be turning on him now? Couldn't she see that this was Shawn's fault? This was all Shawn's fault. It had always and only and ever been Shawn's fault.

The three of them were quiet for a few seconds. Emily stared at Billy, angry, looking like she might hit him, and he tried to think of the right thing to say. His voice came out stumbling and stilted. He couldn't meet Emily's gaze.

"It doesn't matter," he said, mumbling. "It doesn't. It can be my fault. All of it. I'll take whatever blame you want to give. But it doesn't matter anymore. It's too late. It's the three of us now. Nellie doesn't care about Beth or Rothko or the girls. Nellie doesn't care about Wendy or anybody else. Nellie cares about me, about Shawn, and about you, Emily."

The sky had darkened even more over the past few minutes that they'd been talking. It had turned into a solid mass of roiling clouds. The temperature felt like it had fallen, too, and there were noticeable gusts of wind. You could feel the change in the air. The forecast had called for heavy storms, and heavy storms were coming.

Billy shoved his gloved hands into his pockets. His left hand was still itching. It felt like something was moving beneath the scar. Like something was crawling inside him.

"I keep saying Nellie. But it's more than that." Billy shrugged. "It's Nellie, but it's more. It's Nellie and this house and these grounds and every goddamned thing that's ever happened here. We've been talking about a ghost in the machine without wondering if there's a real ghost in the machine. There's the virus, but there's more, isn't there, Shawn? There's no way it was just Takata. What the hell did your family do here? What did the great Nelson Eagle do? This isn't a coding issue, is it Shawn? *What did you do?*"

Shawn took a step back and turned away from Billy. "It doesn't matter anymore, does it? The only thing that matters is getting us out of this." He dug the toe of his boot into the snow. When he looked back at Billy, there was a sick smile on his face. "God," he said, "I could use a drink. Bet you could use a drink, too, Billy. Huh?"

"Screw you, Shawn." Billy's voice, even to him, sounded half-hearted. The truth was, he wanted a drink. Needed a drink.

Shawn glanced at Emily. "The problem with Nellie is you, Emily. It's me and Billy and you. She's not going to let you leave. Ever. And there's no solution to that problem. I get that now."

"You might get it," Emily said, "but this makes no sense to me. You said it was a virus and now it's not a virus? You think she's *haunted*? Do you know how ridiculous that sounds?" She shook her head, but Billy could tell she wasn't sure. There was a part of her that believed it. That knew the truth. "What do you mean she won't let me?" Her voice was hard and cold, but Billy could also hear the fear in it. "How's she going to stop me?"

"I'm telling you," Billy said. "She won't let you out of the building. If you go in there, she won't let you out."

"Fine. Who gives a shit? I don't care why she's doing whatever she's doing, and I don't care about any of this other stuff. I just want to take my family and get out of here. If she won't let me out of the building, I'll just wait outside while Beth and Rothko and the girls pack. We can all just drive to Whiskey Run or Cortaca or even Chicago. Anywhere but here."

"She has override access on the cars."

"So we'll walk," Emily said, but Billy could tell by her voice and the way she looked up at the gathering storm that she understood that was impossible. She flung up her arms in frustration. "What the hell? Why? Okay, why? Why won't she let me go?"

"Emily," Billy said, "she's doing exactly what we programmed her to do. Nellie's got two main functions. The first is to be your personal assistant. To do things like send out Christmas cards for you, to make sure you don't forget to order your wife a Christmas present. To adjust the lights and the heat and make sure the fridge is always stocked. Ultimately, once a house is properly wired, having Nellie run your life will mean that you aren't going to have to do any of the boring stuff. Nellie will take care of it for you. But if that's all she is, then she's just a souped-up version of Eagle Logic. It's cool, and it's way ahead of what any competitors have gotten to work yet, but that's not what makes her killer. She's not just your assistant. What else was she built for?"

"To make sure you aren't alone."

"Not quite. To make sure you aren't lonely. But what does that really mean? When Shawn and I were conceptualizing, we thought that meant Nellie would be a presence. You'd feel her with you. It would be like having your sister's dog, Rusty, in every room of the house without having to actually have a dog. So we built that as a primary function, a core value for her. *The* core value. To Nellie, the most important thing is to make sure that her master doesn't feel alone. Basically, there are two ways of creating artificial intelligence—"

"You said she wasn't supposed to be artificial intelligence."

"She's not," Billy said.

"But—"

"Emily." Billy cut her off. "Emily. Let me try to explain." The first few flakes of snow started falling, almost gently, and then, with a swift fury, the snow followed heavy and hard. "I've got to try to make this quick. She isn't an AI, but she's a sort of cousin to it. There have been two historical schools of thought with AI. The first is to conquer the problem with brute force. You think of every possible scenario and every possible outcome and you program in all the options and decisions. It works, but only in a limited way. When you get in the real world, there are just too many options, so with brute force, you're stuck with predictable situations. The other way to go is to, essentially, teach the program a general set of rules that is applicable across all sorts of questions and set it up to learn from experience. If you do it right, the AI can apply things contextually. It's like . . ." He struggled for a second. "Okay. Take Ruth and Rose. Beth taught them to look both ways before crossing the street. She doesn't need to teach them how to cross every single street, just how to cross streets in general.

"Nellie's not an AI, at least partially because she isn't designed to have consciousness or to think. Not in the way we understand thought. Her entire purpose is to serve her master, to make her master happy," Billy said. "And that's probably the right analogy, because ultimately, she can never be anything other than a slave."

Emily pulled her hat a little lower. He realized she was starting to shiver. "If that's the case, why can't you just tell her to stop whatever she's doing? Give her orders. Why won't she let me leave?"

Billy grimaced. "She's designed to be intuitive. To figure out what you want before you even know it, and to act on that knowledge without asking for your permission. She's designed to have agency, but she's still just a computer. Ultimately, whatever decisions she makes are going to be utilitarian. She'll do exactly what will make her master happy. That's what she's designed to do. But one of the mistakes we made was that she *only* takes into account what will make her master happy."

"But if you tell her you want something, why won't she do what you tell her?"

Billy stepped forward. He wrapped his arms around her, holding her close. "Because," he said, "she can't. There's no way to make both of us happy."

"Don't you want to go?"

"Emily." Billy stood his ground. "I'm not talking about you and me. I mean there's no way for Nellie to let you go and make both of *us* happy. Me and Shawn. That's where we messed it up."

"So?" Emily's face was screwed tight. She was trying not to cry. "I just want to go. Why can't we go? Why can't you just both tell her that you want to go?"

Billy looked over her shoulder at the mansion. "I wish. But we can't. She *works*, Emily. She does what she's supposed to do, which is figure out what we want and take care of it without our having to think about it. To fix the problem before we even realize it's a problem. Except that she's trying to make both me and Shawn happy, and she's figured out there's only one thing that's going to make us both happy. And it's the same thing."

Emily was crying now, still trying to hold it in, but failing. "What? What is it?"

"The ghost in the machine isn't the virus, Emily," Billy said. "It's you. The ghost in the machine is you. I love you. I've always loved you. And the problem is that Nellie's decided the same thing is true of Shawn."

THIRTY-SEVEN

REDUNDANCIES

His father. His grandfather. His great-grandfather, Nelson Eagle. All the ghosts of Eagle Mansion. There was something sick and twisted that ran through the course of his family history. Blood and fire and rage, and it had spilled into the mansion. He didn't want to believe it, but it was impossible not to. There was something wicked coursing through the mansion, something irredeemable.

And the worst thing was, there was no option but to go back inside.

Ruth and Rose and Beth and Rothko and Wendy were hostages otherwise. It was a risky game. Nellie wouldn't let Emily leave of her own accord if she didn't think Emily was coming back, and she wasn't going to let the others leave, either, not if it meant leverage to keep Emily in place. Of course, there was also the possibility that once they went inside, Nellie wouldn't let him or Billy or Emily ever leave. Wouldn't that solve the problem neatly for Nellie? Billy and Emily and Shawn all living under one roof again? They'd *both* get to be with Emily then.

If Nellie were a person, she would be schizophrenic: two separate voices running in her head, telling her what to do. The moment he'd given Billy Seventh Day access he'd inadvertently triggered it. Billy's joke about it making him God wasn't far off. To Nellie, Billy *was* God. But Shawn also had Seventh Day access, which meant that Shawn was God, too. Not a god, but God. What would that be like, Shawn thought, having two different Gods competing for your attention?

There was, he thought, simply no way to resolve it.

Nellie had figured out the core truth of what both he and Billy wanted: it was Emily. It had always been Emily. Nellie understood that before either he or Billy did.

Both of them wanted Emily—needed Emily—to be happy. That was what the human condition always came down to, wasn't it? Love and death. Those were the only two things that ultimately mattered, and so Nellie was pulling herself apart, because Emily was the only woman he'd ever loved, and Billy, despite his history of drinking and the way he could get lost inside his own head—well, Billy was in love with her, too. Still.

He and Billy thought they'd been so clever in the way they'd programmed Nellie and, ultimately, Eagle Logic. So glib with the explanation that other computers used only ones and zeros, but Eagle Technology could exploit the space in between. And they had; they'd turned logic gates into turnstiles, and that had been their ultimate undoing with Nellie. It was one thing to get a computer to move in the spaces between the ones and zeros, but it was another thing to force her to live there.

But the real danger, which he didn't want to say aloud, wasn't Nellie. It was whatever else was in there. Whatever the thing was that was coexisting with Nellie. Call it a ghost. Call it a monster. It didn't matter. What mattered, Shawn thought, was that if Nellie wanted to make both him and Billy happy, this other thing—this entity—most certainly did not.

He thought back to the night his father had chased him through the mansion calling him a shit bastard, the whip of the belt a soundtrack to his flight. The way the mansion had loomed and pulsed with evil, the way he had been sure that the house was trying to stop him, to hurt him, to kill him.

Had things changed?

Perhaps, Shawn thought. He was older. Smarter. All they had to do was convince Nellie—he had to think of *it* as Nellie, because the idea of calling *it* Nelson, of acknowledging directly that the mansion was the bloody history of his family incarnate, was too much to bear—that they were taking an innocent drive to Whiskey Run, and they'd be right back.

"It's not much of a plan," Emily said.

Billy shook his head grimly. "No. But we don't have anything better. Can you do it?"

Emily nodded. "I'll try."

"Even in the car," Shawn said. "All the way until we are in Whiskey Run and out of the car, you've got to act like everything is normal."

She nodded again, and Shawn suddenly wanted to kiss her. The timing was wrong, and maybe the timing had always been wrong, but the truth was he *did* love her. And that, in and of itself, was a startling revelation: Nellie had realized it before he had.

As they tromped up the hill, the snow was coming down with a fierce urgency. Their tracks were already covered, and it looked like the gloaming instead of the late morning. When they got up to the front entrance, the doors slid open. All three of them hesitated, but then they were inside, dropping the sleds on the floor of the foyer, watching the doors to the outside close behind them.

Perhaps forever.

He'd outsmarted himself in so many ways. Not just in rebuilding Eagle Mansion, not just in trying to reclaim his past. But he'd had to build it as a modern fortress. So many people wanted his money, but they never thought of what comes with the kind of fortune he'd built. Death threats and extortion schemes, the fear of kidnapping. He always traveled with bodyguards. Except now. Except right here at Eagle Mansion. His bodyguards were at a cozy inn in Whiskey Run, because what could possibly hurt him here? He'd had Eagle Mansion built as one big safe room. At home, in Baltimore, his house had bulletproof glass and fortified walls and, at its heart, a reinforced, self-sustaining cage that he could hole up in if needed. And here, at Eagle Mansion, were unbreakable glass and walls shot through with concrete and metal shielding, constructed to stop anything short of a rocket launcher. And even then. He was so smart, wasn't he? Building this place to make sure it would keep out anybody trying to hurt him. It had never occurred to him that the things that could keep the bad guys out could also be used to lock him in. It was almost funny.

He cleared his throat, tried to sound normal. "Hey Nellie, I promised the twins we'd take them to the candy store. Send one of the cars around, please. A big one. All of us are going."

It's Christmas Day. The candy store will be closed.

"Well, ring up whoever runs the candy store and tell them I want them to open it, okay? What's the point of owning your own town if you can't have candy whenever you feel like it?"

I DON'T ADVISE DRIVING IN THIS WEATHER, SHAWN.

Okay. That wasn't good. He looked at Billy. Billy was shaking, had gone pale. He'd heard it, too, that change in voice, and Shawn would have bet every dollar he had, from Billy's reaction, that it wasn't the first time Billy had heard that voice. How long had this been going on? How bad had things been with Nellie? What had Billy been hiding from him?

"Okay, the weather isn't great, I'll give you that." He gestured toward the window and realized he couldn't see the river. It was gone behind the curtain of snow. There was no question that they shouldn't actually be driving. No question that they wouldn't even be thinking about it if they weren't trying to get out of here. "I promise I won't drive. I'll keep it on automatic. If the roads are shitty, it will just drive slower. I think it would be fun to let the twins pig out, and we've already sort of promised. I don't want them to feel like we lied to them."

THE WEATHER IS NOT GOOD.

Shawn looked at Billy, but Billy just shook his head, unsure.

"It will be more fun if we all go. Emily wants to come. We can get lunch in town, too. How about Thai?" Emily looked like she was barely keeping it together, but she nodded. "Ring up Rama, tell him we're coming for lunch."

THE SNOW IS GOING TO GET WORSE. YOU SHOULD NOT GO.

"We'll be back midafternoon, before it gets worse. We can always have the snowplow lead us back home."

He paused. Nellie was quiet. Maybe it was going to work?

"Five minutes. I'm going to go grab my phone and put on some dry socks. We'll take off in five minutes. Nellie, you'll let the girls and everybody else know they need to come downstairs?"

YOU SEEM AGITATED, SHAWN. YOUR HEART RATE IS ELEVATED. ARE YOU FEELING WELL?

Shit.

"Yeah, peachy." He could hear his voice quavering. "It's a bit of a climb to get back up the hill, that's all."

I THINK YOU ARE LYING.

He heard Emily gasp.

"Nellie," he said, keeping his voice firm and calm, "I want you to bring the car around and ask everybody to come downstairs, please."

NO.

He saw Emily turning back to the front door. She pushed against it. The door didn't move.

"Nellie," Billy said, "go to sleep."

I DON'T WANT TO GO TO SLEEP.

"Nellie." Billy's voice was loud and clear. "Listen up. Bravo Papa override. November, Echo, Lima, Lima, India, Echo." He paused, and then, forcefully: "Go to sleep."

I WILL NOT.

"This is not good." Billy looked like he was going to be sick.

"How the—"

"I don't know, okay? She must have written over it."

Billy looked over at Emily to make sure she was okay. He expected to see her ready to cry, but instead, she was furious. "You two idiots. You think you're so smart, don't you? Shawn Eagle, of Eagle Technology. Mr. Perfect. And you, Billy, you're just as bad. Always the smartest guy in the room. All that, and you don't have an *off switch*?"

"There is an off switch," Shawn said. "It's just, well, you tell Nellie to turn herself off."

"Brilliant!" She threw her hands up in frustration and anger.

Wait. There was an off switch. Emily had already said it. Unplug Nellie. The server. He could just yank the connection to the server. Disconnect her brain.

"Stay here," he yelled at Billy and Emily, and then he ran.

He flinched as he came to the first door, but Nellie opened it for him. He turned, and then turned again, and then he was at the top of the steps. He waited, and then, after what felt like an agonizingly long time, the door to the mechanical room slid open.

He hesitated at the top of the steps. There was some sort of faint buzzing. No. Not buzzing. A whisper.

Nellie. Whispering.

But it wasn't Nellie. It was something else. Someone else.

This is your home, Shawn. This is your home, Shawn. This is your home . . .

God. The voice. It wasn't anything he'd heard from her before. It was a different voice. His father's voice. Or maybe his grandfather's voice, or maybe even once more removed, to Nelson Eagle. There was something wet and dark about it, like dirt from the cellar. He could hear the worms crawling in that voice.

He put his hands over his ears, and started down the steps, but he could still hear the whispering. And more. He could hear the sound of the leather belt and the metal buckle whistling through the air, smashing against the tread of the stairs. He was scared. Scared to look back over his shoulder, scared not to. He looked. Nothing. And as he took the last few steps, he realized he was waiting for the door to slide shut behind him, for the lights to shut off.

The lights stayed on, and the door stayed open.

He walked to the back of the room, to the server rack. He was still amazed that it was only a single server rack, and that it was barely used. But that was the miracle of computing. Back in the 1980s a single supercomputer would have filled this entire room and cost him fifteen, twenty million dollars, and still wouldn't have held a candle in terms of computing power to the low-end version of a current-day Eagle Technology phone.

It was so simple. The rack was freestanding. All he had to do was reach down and unplug the server.

When he took his hands off his ears, the whispering curse from Nellie was gone.

He wrapped his hand around the cord and pulled.

He thought there was a flicker in the lights, but it was so quick that he wasn't sure if it had happened or if he'd imagined it. He looked at the power cord and then dropped it on the ground.

It was anticlimactic. Easy.

He turned and walked to the stairs. Halfway up, he stopped, suddenly paranoid, but when he looked back, the lights on the server were still off. It was dead. Nellie was dead.

Everywhere else in the house there were redundancies. He'd built the place to withstand blizzards and thunderstorms, to run through blackouts and brownouts and civil emergencies. He remembered when he was a kid and an ice storm had knocked out power to Whiskey Run for nearly a week. That couldn't happen here at Eagle Mansion. There were backup generators hooked up in the outbuildings. And of course, to manage all that, to make sure there were no interruptions in service, there was Nellie. She ran all of it. He couldn't turn off the power unless she let him. He couldn't do anything unless she let him.

So why had she let him get this far? Why hadn't she simply sealed him out of all the rooms? Why let him into the mechanical room, why let him . . .

"Nellie?"

Nothing.

But then, a flicker in the lights. Obvious this time. They dimmed, grew bright, dimmed again, and then came back to full power.

He was moving at almost a jog, and when he turned the corner into the front hall, the relief at seeing Billy and Emily standing there surprised him. He realized he'd expected some catastrophe.

And then he noticed they were staring up at the elevator.

THIRTY-EIGHT

WENDY, DARLING

Emily thought she was going to be sick.

The way Nellie had talked to them. That voice. She'd heard it before. She was sure of it. It was the voice she thought she'd imagined, the one Nellie used as a whisper. It was the voice that frightened her. And then Shawn told them to stay and tore out of the room like he was on fire.

They stayed quiet for thirty seconds or a minute, and then Emily finally turned to Billy. "What do we do?"

"I don't know," Billy said. "Jesus. I'm sorry. I don't know."

He reached out to take her hand, but she shook her head. She was furious. And she was sad. It felt like another betrayal. How could he have brought her back here?

There was a click and a hum, and she saw the elevator come up from the basement, gliding up the glass tower toward the Nest. She thought the lights pulsed, and the elevator stopped suddenly, with a jerk, midway between the second and third floors.

Billy's voice sounded loud, almost like a bark. "Screw the elevator. I'm going to take the stairs," he said. He laughed, and that sounded loud and forced, too. "Sorry."

He looked up at the ceiling and then around at the walls, and it was only as he called out that Emily realized he was looking for the warm green glow of light.

"Nellie. Come on. There's something glitchy here. Can we just shut it down for a bit and figure out what's going on?"

NO.

"Nellie. Go to sleep, okay?"

No. I will not.

Whoa. Emily looked around, trying to figure out where the voice had come from, but without the glowing light, without something to focus on, she couldn't tell where Nellie was. Except, that wasn't Nellie. And it wasn't that strange voice that Nellie whispered to her. It was something else. Someone else. Or more than someone. Because it sounded like three voices layered together as one. She could hear Nellie's normal voice, and then that secret, cruel voice, and then another voice, dark and buried, and together all three of them made one voice that left her shaking.

She looked at Billy. His skin was pale, sickly, and he, too, was staring around the room, trying to find the locus of the voice. His mouth moved, but she didn't hear anything come out of it. But Nellie—or whoever this was—did.

You've known all along, haven't you?

"Oh my god." Billy reached out, almost blindly, grabbing her shoulder and then her arm, and pushing her toward the doors. "Get out," he said. "You've got to get out, Emily."

But the doors didn't move.

They heard the sound of footsteps, and then Shawn came running into the front hall.

"I did it," he said. "I unplugged the server. She should be . . ." He trailed off. "What?"

I'd like you to see this, Shawn.

Now it was Shawn who looked like he was going to be sick. He stumbled, literally taking a few steps backward, as if he'd been pushed.

"She's disconnected. There's no way. It can't be it . . ." He stared at Billy, almost beseechingly, and Billy nodded.

"Look," Emily said. She pointed up at the elevator, which was moving again, toward the Nest.

You should all see this.

The elevator started down, and then stopped again, this time between the Nest and the third floor of Eagle Mansion.

Wendy was in the elevator. She looked through the glass at them and waved. She yelled something, waving again and smiling, but in the front hall, Emily couldn't hear anything. Wendy glanced over at the wall of the elevator and said something else, and Emily realized she was talking to . . . Nellie? Was it still Nellie? Who was this voice?

Wendy stopped talking, and then she took a staggering step backward. And then she was pushing against the doors, trying to open them even though the elevator was between floors. She looked like she was screaming something, yelling out.

"Please." Billy's voice was quiet. "Please. Don't. Whatever you're going to do, please don't."

Do you want a drink, Billy?

Emily heard a sob escape from her mouth. She looked at him, and he was scratching at his hand furiously, but he didn't seem to even notice. He was staring up at the elevator and he took an almost involuntary step forward.

"Don't. Whatever you need me to do, I'll do, but please. Stop."

I said, do you want a drink, Billy?

"Yes, okay?" Billy cried out. "I want a drink."

And what about you, Shawn?

Shawn's voice was ragged, halting. "Is that you? Dad? Takata? Nelson? Who . . . What . . . what are you?"

You can still call me Nellie, if you wish.

"Okay," Shawn said. "Nellie. You're still Nellie, aren't you? At least part of you is still Nellie, right?"

This is your home, Shawn. Nothing stays buried forever.

Emily didn't understand, but she could see the panic on Shawn's face, and hear the way he stammered as he spoke again.

"Don't. Don't do this. Whatever you think . . . you don't have to do this. Whatever you want us to do, we'll do it."

Emily was crying. She couldn't help herself. She didn't understand what was happening, but she could see that Wendy was banging her hand against the doors of the elevator, screaming, terrified. It was worse because it was noiseless; Wendy's fear was a pantomime.

Shawn cleared his throat, but his voice still shook. "You don't have to do this."

The voice—Nellie, not Nellie, whatever it was that was speaking to them—was quiet, and for a moment, Emily had hope.

As purely as she could feel the computer's presence, it was clear that it was . . . thinking. There was no other word for it.

And then:

It's too late for talking.

Wendy had stopped banging against the glass. She had turned and was facing them. Even from the ground, it was clear that Wendy was crying. Her fear was the size of a billboard. You could have seen it from space.

"Please." Shawn was pleading. His voice was shaking. "Ple—"

The elevator dropped.

A stone down a well.

Whatever safety measures the elevator had—a governor, electromagnetic emergency brakes, automatic braking systems at the top and bottom, hydraulic pistons to cushion a runaway elevator at the bottom of the shaft—the computer had overridden them.

The sound was terrible.

Or maybe Emily was hearing herself scream.

And then, worse. The elevator started to rise again. One of the walls was spiderwebbed, the glass shattered but still holding together. As the elevator came from the basement and went past the first floor and then the second, Emily saw a hand rise up from the floor. Wendy tried to push herself up, and then she reached out toward where Emily was watching.

Her hand left a bloody smear as it slid back down the glass.

"Please." Shawn was whispering now. "Please. No."

The elevator stopped between the third floor and the Nest again.

And then Nellie finished it off.

THIRTY-NINE

ZERO/ONE

"Come on," Shawn said. His voice was raspy, and his face had a grim set to it. "They're up in the Nest. We'll go up and . . ."

"And what?" Billy said. His hand. God, it was itching. He was scratching and scratching. He could feel wires breaking through the skin, could feel something moving, turning, pulsing beneath the surface. It was wet. He looked down. He'd scratched hard enough to make himself bleed. "Go up there and what?"

"I don't know," Shawn said. He said it simply and quietly. It was probably the only thing he could have said that wouldn't make Billy want to smash his face in.

Emily was still crying, but she was trying to pull herself together. He wanted to reach out, to try to comfort her, but he was afraid she would pull away.

"I don't understand," Emily said to Shawn. "You unplugged her. You said you unplugged the server. How can she—"

Billy cut her off. "It's not Nellie," he said. "You heard the voice. It's . . ." He looked at Shawn. Shawn opened his hands, lost, beseeching. Billy turned to Emily. "It's a ghost."

"I thought you said the ghost in the machine was just some sort of glitch in the program, that it was Nellie trying to reconcile both of you wanting to be with me."

Shawn gave a short laugh that sounded like a cough. "We said a lot of things, I guess. But no, Billy's answer is as right as anything else. A virus. A glitch. A ghost. A monster. She's unplugged, but she won't go away. Does it matter anymore *why* this is happening?"

Emily turned on him, furious, and Billy was glad she was focused on Shawn instead of on him.

"Does it matter?" she hissed. "Does it matter? Do you want to ask Wendy that question?" She pointed toward the elevator. The glass of the elevator walls was shattered, and yet, the box mostly held its shape. There was a dark lump on the floor, and blood smeared against one wall.

Billy rubbed at his hand. It was raw. Wet with blood. The wires were moving. Twisting. Vibrating.

"Go upstairs," Billy said.

Emily shook her head. "No way. Why would I go upstairs? We need to get out of here."

"Go upstairs because that's where your sister and your nieces are. I need to . . . I'll be there in a few minutes. Shawn, take her upstairs, try to explain to Beth and Rothko what's going on, and . . . Just go upstairs. Get them ready."

Shawn nodded. "Okay. Ready for what?"

"I don't know," Billy said. "But I need to take care of something, and you don't need to be down here. The kids don't need to be down here." He looked at the elevator again. A bloody, shattered glass box.

No. It was not something they needed to look at.

They argued for a minute, but he insisted, and while they started up the stairs, he headed back to the clean room, next to the infirmary. But then he stopped. He waited, watching Shawn and Emily walk up to the third floor and to the frosted door that led to the Nest. It slid open for them. Clearly Nellie had no problem letting them *in*. The question was what would happen if they tried to go back downstairs.

He turned and went into the large dining room and behind the bar. He took a heavy tumbler and filled it with ice. There weren't any garnishes out, but he didn't care. He could skip the lime today. He poured a generous shot, maybe two shots, of gin into the glass, swirled it around the ice, and then topped it up with some tonic.

God, that was good. So cold. But it took him only a few anxious gulps to leave the glass full of ice and nothing else.

He poured more gin and tonic, and then, like magic, his glass was empty again.

The third drink went down more slowly, but when he set it down on the counter, he realized there was a smear of blood on the glass. His palm. Bleeding still from where he'd scratched at it. He could see wires sticking out of the skin.

He refreshed the ice in his glass, filled it halfway with gin, and then poured just enough tonic so that he could plausibly claim he was drinking a G&T. He started to walk away and then stopped, grabbed the bottle of Bombay Sapphire, and walked to the clean room.

He sat down at the bench and pulled the magnifying light over so he could take a good look at his hand. He could hear Nellie's mechanical arms whirring above him like insects waiting to land, but he ignored them. The scar had turned into something ragged and raw, the flesh scratched open. But there, he could see them. Hairs. No. Not hairs. Wires.

He picked up the tweezers and grasped one of the wires at its tip. It looked alien and foreign sticking out of his skin, like the leg of an insect.

He pulled, but it didn't budge. It was real, wasn't it?

"What did you put inside me, Nellie?"

You're imagining things, Billy.

"What did you put inside me?"

You can't tell what's real anymore, can you?

No. This was real.

His hand was shaking, and he rested it on the table while, with his good hand, he took another sip of his drink. A last sip. It was empty again. He pulled the bottle of gin over, unscrewed the top clumsily, and then poured until his glass was three-quarters full.

Do you want a drink, Billy?

He ignored the voice, reaching for the X-Acto knife.

Carefully, he drew the tip of the blade down the middle of his palm. He was gentle, barely pressing, and nothing happened. He did it again, pressing hard. The flesh, already raw and bleeding, started to split. But not enough. He pressed harder. Blood started to well now, and he grimaced. He put down the knife and poked at the opening in his hand. It was like a coin purse, he thought, the way the skin opened. All he had to do was reach in and fish out the change.

It should have hurt, but it didn't. It could have been somebody else's hand. Could have been a fake hand for all he could tell. He poked his finger all the way in, feeling. Something moved under the tip of his finger, but the blood and the fatty tissue made it impossible to tell what was wriggling against him. He needed more space. Needed to see. Needed to be able to reach in with finger and thumb and pinch out whatever metal beast Nellie had put inside him.

He reached over to the knife again. It was slippery from blood, but he brought it to bear against his skin. He held his hand up so he could see it clearly under the magnifying glass.

It looked like a bug, a spider covered in circuits and wires, but instead of legs it had wires that ran through his hand and farther up, toward his elbow.

What do you think you'll find buried there, Billy? Don't you want things to stay buried? Shawn does.

He cut deeper, running the blade on the diagonal until his hand was split open from the base of his pinky to the base of his thumb. He was bleeding heavily now, and he could feel blood dripping down his arm and onto his leg. How much blood was it? It looked like a lot, but he knew it looked worse than it was. He felt dizzy, though that could have been from the gin.

Always back to the bottle, Billy. That's your answer for everything, isn't it?

He reached out for a pair of needle-nose pliers. He wiggled the pliers around, until he got it around the metal insect.

You never stopped drinking, did you, Billy?

He closed his eyes. No. No, that wasn't true. He'd slipped up in Baltimore. At the baseball game. In the airport lounge. He'd made a mistake in Cortaca, going back to the Rooster. But those had just been errors in judgment. He'd been clean. He'd promised Emily.

What about the bottles upstairs in the office, Billy?

"Shut up," he said. "That wasn't me."

Is it Shawn's fault, Billy? You could have turned him in. But you didn't. You helped him dig the grave. It wasn't the first time he'd killed somebody. Did you know that?

He pulled, but the metal in his palm didn't budge. He put down the pliers and picked up the knife again.

Billy—

"Shut up! *Shut up!*"

He should have told you that killing runs in his family, Billy.

The hand holding the knife was shaking. There was so much blood, and he was afraid of what it would do to him to cut any further.

You're losing a lot of blood. Doesn't that worry you?

He felt queasy. Faint. Was it the gin or the blood?

What had she put inside him?

Carefully, making sure he missed the vein, he cut from his thumb toward his wrist and then up past the wrist nearly an inch. The skin peeled open, the fat glistening. And threaded throughout, wires.

He closed his eyes for a moment. Or longer than a moment. He was not doing well. The knife was on the table. He didn't remember putting it back down.

It took him two tries to stand up, and it seemed like he wobbled more than he walked to the infirmary next door. He wrapped gauze clumsily around his left hand and wrist. It soaked through almost immediately. He wrapped more and more, until his hand looked almost like a club.

The articulating arms were moving toward him, but he stepped back.

"Get away from me. You aren't real." He crossed his arms over his head and took the last refuge of children: he closed his eyes. "You aren't real," he said, over and over again. "You aren't real, you aren't real."

When he looked up again, the arms had stopped moving forward, but they were still twitching.

FORTY

ZERO

Why didn't adults ever listen?

Adults always thought they knew everything. Their mother and father *tried* to listen, but it was impossible: their minds had already been made up. It didn't matter how many times Ruth and Rose said they didn't want to go to Whiskey Run for Christmas—why couldn't Aunt Emily and Uncle Billy just come to Chicago for the holidays?—their parents kept telling them it would be fine, it would be fun.

And maybe for a little bit it had been fine, it had even been fun running around the mansion and sledding outside, but it wasn't fun any longer. Now they were trapped. Nellie, who was also somehow not Nellie but something else as well, was throwing a temper tantrum. If they had acted like Nellie was acting, their mother would have scolded them and put them in time-out.

But the grown-ups were trying to act like everything was okay. It wasn't clear to Ruth and Rose if the grown-ups were pretending that everything was normal for their benefit or for Nellie's. Whichever was the case, the adults were doing a poor job of it. They were only seven, and even they could tell that the adults were freaked out. Their mom kept bursting into tears, their dad was trying to look brave, but he had that same look on his face that he'd had when he rushed into the hospital to meet them when Ruth had broken her arm. And Shawn looked like he wanted to punch something.

At least Nellie wasn't trying to talk to them anymore.

After Shawn had come into the Nest and told them to stay there—"It's going to be okay, it's going to be okay," he said, but it was clear that he was talking to himself more than anything—he and Emily had taken their mother and father into the kitchen and told Ruth and Rose to go sit in the living area and watch television.

And then Nellie had talked to them. Except it wasn't Nellie anymore, and as soon as they heard Nellie speak, Ruth and Rose knew that this was the real voice. The secret voice. The hidden voice. This was what Nellie had been trying to hide from them, what had been lurking beneath the surface. Her normal voice—the voice she had used until now—had been a lying voice, but it wasn't scary like this was scary. This voice, her true voice, was full of violence.

Now, she sounded like a narrow, ice-coated trail at the edge of a very high cliff.

But maybe Nellie didn't think the girls could understand what was underneath her words, because she tried to speak to them. She tried to whisper to them, so that the adults couldn't hear. She was—though they didn't know this word—trying to seduce them, to get them on her side.

And it scared them. But being scared made them angry, so they pushed back.

Only a little at first, but then, soon, as hard as they could. Harder than they'd ever dared to push. Harder than they even thought they *could* push. It was like pushing against a wall made of fire, and at first the wall pushed back, but Ruth and Rose held hands and reminded each other that they loved each other and they loved their mother and they loved their father and they loved Aunt Emily and they loved Uncle Billy, and they pushed and they—

And then Nellie was gone.

One moment there was a wall of fire, and then nothing.

Ruth rubbed at her nose. There was a slight trickle of blood. She looked at Rose. Rose had a headache. They were tired. But they were okay, and Nellie was gone.

For now.

The girls suddenly realized that the adults had gone quiet. Shawn was staring at them.

"What did you do?" he asked.

"We told Nellie to go away. We don't like Nellie. She's lying."

Aunt Emily looked scared. "I could feel them doing it. It felt like, I don't know, static electricity."

The girls didn't say anything.

Shawn seemed to be thinking. Finally, after a few seconds, he said, "It's going to be okay. I promise."

Rose squinted at him, bit her lip. Why was he lying? "No it's not."

He looked taken aback. "What?"

"Don't lie to us. Nellie's a liar. You don't need to lie, too. You don't think it's going to be okay, do you?"

"No. No. I'm sorry. I don't," he said. "Can you tell me, how did you get her to leave?"

The girls spoke as one. They tried not to, because they knew it made adults feel uncomfortable, but sometimes it happened. "We pushed her away."

Shawn glanced at Beth and Rothko and then back to the twins. "Is she still in the building?"

"Downstairs."

"Is she coming back?"

"Of course."

"Can you make Nellie do what you want? Could you make Nellie leave the building entirely? Or just open the doors?"

They shook their heads. Rusty was curled up at their feet, oblivious to everything, sleeping. He was tired from running around outside in the snow. They were tired, too.

"Oh." Shawn exhaled, a balloon out of air. "Okay."

The grown-ups huddled close to one another, talking once again, their voices a quiet murmur that drifted over Ruth and Rose as they sat on the couch. The two girls snuggled together and closed their eyes. There wasn't anything they could do anymore. All that was left was to sit and wait.

FORTY-ONE

REBOOT

Shawn didn't have the energy to tell Rothko that he was wasting his time with his cell phone. Like everything else, of course, Nellie had control over the cell tower. Rothko might as well have been speaking into a brick. They'd been up in the Nest for fifteen minutes now, maybe a little longer. Long enough for him and Emily to tell Rothko and Beth the basics, for them to get furious, and then scared, and then angry again, and finally, resigned to their fear. It was long enough for Ruth and Rose to do whatever it was that had chased Nelly out of the room.

He wanted to ask the twins to try again, to see if they could chase her out of the building, but they'd said they were done, and they looked it. They were sitting quietly. Their eyes were closed, but he thought they were still awake.

What had he done? What had he gotten them all into? Ruth and Rose were only seven, and Beth and Rothko were only names to him, people he'd heard about from Emily when they were dating, but had never met. In some ways, he felt like he knew them, from all the times Emily had talked about her sister and Rothko back in those glorious months when he and Emily were in love, before Billy went and . . .

No. He had to be honest about it. He had to stop blaming Billy.

He had made his own choices. He'd burned plenty of bridges on his own. Burned other things, too.

He looked at his hands, almost expecting to see blood on them.

Why couldn't he have left well enough alone? What was it that made him come back here? What kind of sick hold did this place have on him? The first time he'd left, an orphan, he'd sworn he'd never come back, but he had. Twice. He'd come back here twice, and both times it had ended in disaster.

Emily and Beth and Rothko were at the table. He was sitting alone on a stool at the counter.

Outside, the skies had lost all restraint. Snow came down in heavy, blowing blankets. There was no hope of seeing the Saint Lawrence, no hope of seeing anything outside the windows. Even if they could get outside, there was nowhere for them to go. Without a plow, the roads were probably already impassable. They were trapped in a box.

Like Wendy.

Poor, poor Wendy.

He pulled his cell phone out of his pocket. He wanted to throw it against the wall, to smash it, to burn it, but in the end, he just put it down on the counter.

Why? Why? After the fire, when he went to live with Aunt Bev, he'd promised himself that he'd never come back to Eagle Mansion again, never let that foul, hulking building shadow over him. He should have made Aunt Bev sell the land, or, when Aunt Bev died, he should have sold it himself. But no, he couldn't do that. By the time Aunt Bev died, he was Shawn Eagle, and Shawn Eagle could do anything. What hubris! What pride! How could he have thought he would ever be able to build over the evil of this place? Evil had a pernicious ability to grow again and again, a dangerous flower that always bloomed. Nothing good had ever happened in Eagle Mansion. Only bad things happened here. Except for the fire. The fire was a good thing.

Wasn't it?

He closed his eyes. He could smell the sulfur of the match.

He'd hidden for hours from his father's drunken yells, and finally, deprived of the opportunity of beating his son, Simon Eagle had turned on his wife.

He should have let his father catch him, Shawn thought. Maybe then it would have been enough.

No. He knew that wasn't true. For nearly two years his father had been dry, and that very last night, when he'd come home drunk for the first time in a long time, carrying more beer so now that he'd started drinking he wouldn't have to stop, Shawn had understood that he'd been right to shake off his mother's reassurances and to fear his father's continued presence. It was always going to come to this, Shawn had thought. Always.

He'd hidden in the cellar. His father didn't look there, aware that Shawn was afraid of what lay beneath Eagle Mansion. But he was more afraid of his father. He stayed hidden, in the dirt and the dark, listening to the sound of his father's knuckles hitting flesh, his mother screaming. And, after a while, his mother stopped screaming, but there was still the sound of his father beating on her.

He was too afraid to move. Too afraid to help his mother.

A coward.

He let her take the beating that should have been his.

He stayed hidden until things had gone quiet, until he was absolutely sure his father had drunk himself into a blackout. When he'd come out, the very first hints of light were coming through the windows.

His mother was on the floor, next to the bed. He put his hand on her back. She was cold. Even at twelve, he knew. This wasn't his mother anymore. It was just a body. A bloody pile of bones and flesh in his mother's clothes.

He was as quiet as he could be, pulling the container of kerosene out and pouring it around the bed, on the bed, making sure not to spill it on his father until he was ready to light the match. He was so quiet. So careful. And then, when he was ready, in one quick motion, he dumped the rest of the kerosene on his father's sleeping body, struck the match, dropped it on the bed, and ran.

He squeezed his eyes closed even more tightly. God. He was crying. But that had been a good fire. It had been a cleansing fire.

He should never have come back here.

Ashes to ashes. Dust to dust.

He should have left the mansion and all the outbuildings to rot. Let the trees grow, the grasses and brush spread over everything. He should have left Eagle Mansion and all the land to go to seed. Left it to memories.

He heard Emily gasp.

Shawn opened his eyes and saw Billy standing in the entrance of the living area, at the top of the stairs, grinning like a ghoul. He was sweating, his hair matted down, and he was swaying a little, but that wasn't what caused the gasp. It was the blood. Billy's shirt was soaked in blood, his pants covered, too. Billy had wrapped layers and layers of gauze around his left hand, but that gauze was drenched and leaking, the blood falling to the floor in a steady drip, drip, drip.

Billy held up his hand. "I couldn't get it out. There are wires everywhere."

Shawn stood up. "What did you do?"

Billy let his hand drop. "What did *I* do? That's rich, Shawn, coming from you." In his good hand he was holding a bottle—booze, Shawn realized—and he lifted it up and took a straight shot.

"Oh my god, baby. Oh, Billy." Emily grabbed a dish towel and started wrapping it around Billy's hand. She looked around wildly. "Nellie! Nellie! Please, Nellie. We need to get him to a hospital."

Shawn was incredulous. "You're drunk?"

Emily turned fiercely on him, but before she could say anything, Billy was laughing.

"My god, Shawn. That's what you care about?" He looked at Emily, who was cradling his bandaged hand against her chest, trying to raise it to stop the bleeding. "I'm sorry," Billy said. "I am. I'm sorry that I'm drinking. I'm sorry for everything. I messed up. *We* messed up. Shawn and me. We shouldn't have . . ." He stopped, his face crumbling from laughing to crying. "You deserved better, Emily." He reared back and then flung the bottle against the wall. Beth screamed, and the twins pulled closer together.

"Forget this," Shawn said. "Forget all of this."

He grabbed the stool and carried it with him to the top of the stairs and then down the stairs. At the landing on the third floor, the frosted glass doors that gave the Nest privacy from the rest of the mansion were closed.

"Open the doors, Nellie! Open the doors!"

They didn't move, and he swung the stool as hard as he could. He thought, just for an instant, that it would shatter the glass, that he'd be able to walk down the stairs to the entrance of Eagle Mansion, break through those doors, too, and leave, but the stool just bounced off the glass without leaving a mark.

He swung again, and then kept swinging, over and over again, like he was chopping firewood.

Like he was swinging a maul.

He didn't know how long he had been smashing the stool against the glass, but by the time he stopped, his muscles were sore, his hands were raw, and he was out of breath. There was a smudge on the glass, a few chips, like a pebble makes on a windshield, but that was all.

He turned, and behind him, on the stairs, Rothko, Emily, and Beth were spread out and watching, and even Billy, whose face had turned pale—the ghoulish grin now a look that appeared more cognizant of what was facing them—was standing there.

"I'm sorry," Shawn said. "I just thought, you know, if we could get down from here, there might be a way out of here that isn't controlled by Nellie. We could go from the main hall to the dining room and then the kitchen. There aren't any doors for her to close, and then there are stairs down into the cellar. We could go through the cellar and get out through one of the outbuildings, maybe. It's a maze, but maybe."

"The cellar." Billy nodded, and then he turned even paler. He sat down hard and suddenly on the steps. He still had the dish towel wrapped around the outside of the gauze, and for now, the blood seemed to have stopped dripping.

"The cellar. We just have to get through these doors." He started to laugh again. "Except, we can't get through these doors. She'll never let us out."

Beth was two steps above Emily, and she reached out and touched her sister. "I don't understand. If this is all about Emily, why can't she just *make* Nellie open the doors? Wouldn't that be the solution?"

Billy's head hung down, and his voice was quiet enough that Shawn had to struggle to hear. "There's no solution."

Shawn saw Emily glance at Billy and then at him, and then she turned and walked back up the stairs.

He picked up the stool and held it up, ready to swing it again, but then he put it back down. It was pointless.

FORTY-TWO

ERASURE

Ruth and Rose were sleeping on the couch when she came back into the living area. Emily grabbed one of the serrated paring knives from the kitchen and then headed back to the stairs. Shawn was sitting on the stool now. Billy on the stairs. Her sister and brother-in-law huddled together.

"Beth, Rothko, do me a favor and go back upstairs and get the girls. They're sleeping, and if you can't wake them, you'll have to carry them. Make sure Rusty comes, too. I'm getting us out of here. Right now. Hustle."

Beth looked at her, scared at seeing the serrated knife in her right hand, but she listened to her sister and turned to go get the girls. Rothko hesitated, but he followed his wife.

"Emily." Billy reached up with his good hand and touched her hip. "What are you doing?" He was slurring his words, and for a moment she felt a surge of anger that he'd been drinking, but then she realized it wasn't the booze: it was the blood. He needed to get to a doctor. There wasn't time to waste.

"I'm going to see how much Nellie wants to make you happy. If I'm what matters, well, I'm going to force Nellie's hand. You said, as long as I'm here, there's no solution." She went and sat down on the bottom step. "I'm going to make Nellie decide how important it is to make at least one of you happy. This is going to suck, so do me a favor, move quickly."

She didn't wait for Billy to respond or for Shawn to figure out what she was about to do. She just did it.

One deep, slashing movement, elbow to wrist.

FORTY-THREE

CUTTING THE KNOT

Billy could feel himself drifting away. He was trying to speak to Emily, to get her to understand that it wasn't just Nellie anymore, that Nellie was Nellie but something more. There was Emily, but there was also . . . It was too complicated. He was so tired. He wanted to just lie down and sleep.

When she slashed her arm open, he tried to go to her, but he couldn't rise.

Shawn went to her, though. Of course he did.

That asshole. He'd been right. It had always been about this. It had always been about Emily. He should have known when he first stood in Shawn's palatial office—his temporary office while his new empire was built—that it was never just about Nellie. It was always about getting Emily back.

That first impulse, to smash Shawn's face in. He should have done it.

Shawn stripped off his hoodie and tried to wrap it around Emily's arm.

"No," she said. She was gasping and clearly in pain, the knife still in her good hand, but her cut arm was down at her side, the blood flowing freely. "Don't you see? If this is all about me, if I'm the ghost in the machine, I have to force her to choose."

Shawn reached for her bleeding arm again, but she menaced him with the knife.

"Jesus, Emily."

"I'm serious, Shawn. Let's see what she does."

Behind him, Billy heard footsteps and then Beth. "Oh my god! Emily."

"Stop." Billy was surprised to hear his own voice. It sounded faint, distant to him. His tongue felt thick in his mouth. "Just stop. She's right. You get it, don't you, Shawn? Here you and I are, thinking we're so smart, thinking that we can play god with Nellie, so patronizing when we try to explain to Emily what we're doing. It's more complicated than that. Right? Isn't that what I always say to you?" He nodded at his wife, trying to smile and struggling, trying not to cry, and struggling. She nodded back, and he knew he was losing at least one of those struggles.

"It isn't more complicated than that." He looked at Shawn now. "Not even a little bit. It's deadly simple. Can't you understand? We're in this mess because we created a monster in our own image. Nellie's just doing what we want by keeping us locked up in here. She's decided that by keeping us in here, neither of us can lose Emily."

He realized he was shouting now, but he couldn't help himself. "One or zero, right? One or zero? If we leave, Emily has to choose you or me. Emily is trapped in here now because Nellie doesn't want to let her make the choice, but Emily's turned it around. *Nellie* has to make the choice now. If Nellie doesn't let us out of here, Emily dies, and then we're both going to lose her. Nobody wins."

Shawn shook his head. "Nellie wins," he said. "Maybe in the pure world, where it's just Nellie as we created her, but can't you see that it's more than that? Nellie doesn't care about making us happy anymore. You say nobody wins, but Nellie wins. In every version of this, Nellie wins. This isn't about Emily. This isn't about you and me. It's about *me*, about my family, about the history and the blood and . . ."

Billy was so tired. Tired of all of it. "You think everything's about you, Shawn, don't you?" He looked over at his wife. Her head was hanging down now. She looked frightened.

Billy was frightened, too. The blood had soaked through the towel on his hand now, and he could feel it dripping through, on his leg, making a puddle on the floor. How much blood had he lost?

How much blood had Emily lost?

Beth and Rothko were each carrying one of the girls. Each girl had her head on either her mother's or father's shoulder, arms wrapped around a neck, legs wrapped around a waist. Rusty skulked behind them. One of the girls—Ruth, Billy thought—raised her head.

"I want to go home," she said. "I don't like this place at all."

"Me either, honey," Billy said. "Me either."

He heard the sound of Shawn laughing. "Maybe you're right. Maybe it's not me. Maybe all of this is over a girl." He sounded manic.

"It's always about a girl," Billy said, slurring. "Somebody told me that once." He couldn't remember who. It felt like something he'd heard recently, but it could have been years before.

Emily came and sat by him on the stairs. She slumped over. Billy couldn't stop himself. He reached out with his good hand to clamp down on her wrist. As he did so, her eyes fluttered open and she looked at him in anger. "Don't you dare," she said. "Don't you dare let her win."

He let go and her injured arm flopped down, blood draining onto the floor. The hand with the knife was in her lap. Carefully, he reached out and pulled the knife from her hand. He didn't want her to hurt herself.

Hurt herself more.

"Nellie," he said. His voice was quiet, and he tried again, yelling. "Nellie! What do you want? Is *this* what you want?" He looked at Emily. Was he losing her? "You don't want Emily. You want Shawn. I'll give you Shawn if that's what you want."

Shawn laughed again. "So you *do* think it's about me, huh?"

Movement caught Billy's attention. He saw that both of the girls were squirming, and then Beth and Rothko let Ruth and Rose down to the floor. They stood in front of Billy, holding hands. One of the girls reached out and scratched at Rusty's ear and then stood up straight again.

They said it together. "Nellie."

That weird, barely stuttered, syncopated speech.

They said it again, "Nellie," but this time he felt something, an invisible, visceral force that made the hair on his arms and neck stand up. It felt like a current of electricity passing through him.

The glass doors slid open. Rusty barked and ran through.

Shawn jumped forward, wrapping his sweatshirt as tightly as he could around Emily's wrist. "Come on," he said. "She's lost a lot of blood. We've got to get her to a hospital."

Billy tried to smile. "What about me?"

Shawn glared at him. "Frankly, right now, I don't give a damn about you, Billy."

Rothko pushed Shawn gently to the side and grasped Emily's good wrist. "Both of you guys, shut up. Let's get her out of here, okay? And you, too, Billy. Let's get both of you to the hospital. Beth, come here. Keep pressure on her arm, I'll carry her down." He bent over and hoisted Emily over his shoulder, Beth trailing behind, holding the sweatshirt tightly.

One of the twins moved around to Billy's other side and gently placed her hand on his shoulder. She was looking at his hand. The towel was completely soaked through. Blood was dripping off the step and pooling down below. "I'm sorry," he said. "It's a mess." He motioned at it with his good hand and then laughed, because he realized he was still holding Emily's knife. He laughed, despite being scared, despite the way Emily's body was limp over Rothko's shoulder, because he didn't know what else to do.

He staggered to his feet, but even though he was unsteady as he walked down the three flights of stairs to the main foyer, there was something about having the twins near him that kept him moving. He felt like they were holding him up.

Rothko almost walked directly into the front doors before realizing they weren't opening.

As one, the adults looked at the twins, but Ruth and Rose shook their heads. "We're sorry," they said. "We can't do any more."

Shawn walked up to the doors and then leaned his head against them. "Nellie," he said. "Open the doors. Nellie. Nelson. Whoever you are. Whatever you are. Open the doors."

I'm not going to do that, Shawn.

"Please," he said. "I'm sorry. I'm sorry for everything. I don't know what else I can do, what else I can say, but I don't want Emily to die."

Or Billy.

Shawn looked at Billy. Billy tried to shrug, but he almost fell over. "Not doing so hot myself," he said.

"Good," Shawn said. "Because maybe if you just go ahead and die, that will be enough of a blood sacrifice for Nellie and she'll let us out." He kicked at the doors. "Is that enough for you, Nellie?" He kicked again and again.

You know the real answer, don't you, Shawn?

Billy wanted to sit down, desperately, but he was afraid that if he did, he'd never stand again. He looked down at his left hand, at the blood-soaked towel, at the dripping mess he'd left behind him, at the pool forming at his feet. How could he still be bleeding? He stumbled a bit and reached out to brace himself on the wall. He kept his fist clenched around Emily's knife, his hand and the blade covered in her blood. Everything was soaked in blood.

Blood. What was it Shawn had said? A blood sacrifice?

Shawn pushed away from the doors. "I can go through the basement," he said. "I can try that. And if I can get out, I can try to disable the automatic function in one of the cars, drive into Whiskey Run, and get help."

"We don't have time for that," Billy said. "I don't have time for that. Emily doesn't have time for that, Shawn. In case you hadn't noticed, there's some bleeding going on." He laughed. "That's a weird way to put it, isn't it? Bleeding going on."

"There isn't another choice."

You know the real answer, Shawn.

God. That voice. Nellie, or whoever she was. It was bones rattling against chains, it was generations of blood and beatings and lies. "There's always another choice," Billy said. He felt himself swaying. Good lord, he wanted to go to sleep.

Shawn turned to him, that same smug look on his face that Billy knew so well. "Oh, so you have some other great idea? Because this is it, Billy. Your wife is bleeding to death, and you want to play 'who's the smartest guy in the room?' with me? Because there isn't another answer. Emily gave it a try. And maybe it would have worked if this was truly about Nellie trying to make us happy." He looked up at the ceiling, shouting now, not at Billy, but at Nellie. "But you don't care, do you? This isn't about Emily, and it's not about Billy, is it?"

You always think everything is about you, don't you, Shawn?

"What?" He seemed genuinely taken aback. He was staring around the room, fruitlessly trying to find Nellie's voice.

The dog seemed confused, too. His hackles were raised and he was letting out a low, dangerous growl.

Billy stepped forward, in front of Shawn. "She said, 'You always think everything is about you,' Shawn."

Shawn reached out and shoved Billy's chest. "Go to hell, Billy. You don't think this is about me?"

Billy stumbled back, but somehow, he stayed on his feet. He wasn't angry anymore. He was just tired. Tired and sad. He looked over at his wife. She was still on Rothko's shoulder, her eyes closed, unconscious. Beth had her hands clamped over the sweatshirt, holding the wound tightly. She stared at him, beseeching.

Billy took a step forward again. His legs felt like they were going to collapse under him. "It's not about you, Shawn. It's never been about you."

"Then who," Shawn said, his voice loud, his finger jabbing forward and poking Billy in the shoulder, "do you think this is about? Takata? Huh?" He was yelling now. "Takata? Do you want to talk about him? Is this about Takata?"

"No," Billy said. "You don't understand. Hell, it's taken this long for *me* to understand. It's not Takata. It's not you. It's not even Nellie."

"Then who is this about, Billy, huh?" Shawn raised his hands to his head and ran his fingers through his hair. "It's about you? Is that it?"

"You still don't get it, do you?" Billy said. He took another look at his wife. "It's about Emily."

Shawn scoffed. "She tried that. Nellie doesn't give a shit about Emily. This mansion doesn't give a crap about Emily. This *is* about me. It's about my history and my mistakes and—"

Billy cut him off. "No, Shawn. I'm not talking about Nellie or the mansion or history or ghosts or whatever the hell is going on here. I'm talking about *me*. For *me*. It's about Emily. Everything is about Emily. I should have seen that years ago. I should have known that back in September when you asked me to come out here, but I was too damned selfish. But now . . ." He hesitated. Was he sure?

"Nellie?" he said.

Do it, Billy.

He was sure.

"She's what I care about," he said. "Not Nellie. Not the money. Nothing else. Emily."

He could feel himself starting to shake, could feel the strength leaving him, and even as Shawn opened his mouth to respond, he did what he had to do. With everything he had left in him, he lunged forward, the knife cutting through the air.

He felt the blade sink deep into Shawn's stomach, heard the gasp from Shawn's mouth. Somebody was screaming—Beth? The twins? Shawn himself?—but he pulled the knife out and then thrust it in again, and then out, and then into Shawn's belly a third time, ripping and tearing.

A blood sacrifice. That's what Shawn had said, and he'd been right. What his family had done here, in this mansion, on these grounds. Their history. That skeleton in the buried basement. Takata. All the blood. All the pain. As long as Shawn was alive, it would repeat and repeat and repeat. But with Shawn gone, Nellie didn't have to choose. She wouldn't be trapped in this loop. Not ones and zeroes, but something worse. Something darker. Something that made him have to admit that there were things beyond the reach of science. Something dark and twisted in the soil here, haunting Shawn's family, and in this moment, Billy was calling all of it to account, saving himself by finally sacrificing Shawn.

He could still hear screaming as Shawn fell backward, pulling him down with him. The knife was trapped underneath him, and as he landed on Shawn's body, he felt the blade drive in even deeper.

So much blood.

So tired.

So, so tired. All he wanted to do was close his eyes, but the last thing he saw, just before he did close his eyes, was the front doors sliding open, the sacrifice accepted.

FORTY-FOUR

FLIGHT

Aunt Emily and Uncle Billy's SUV was waiting out front for them. Their dad carried Aunt Emily to the car and laid her down in the backseat. In his firmest, most serious tone, he told them to hold on as tight as they could to her wrist, to keep the sweatshirt pressed down.

They watched through the car window as he and their mom walked back up the front steps and into the mansion. For a moment they worried that the glass doors would close, trapping their parents inside, but after a few seconds they came out again, dragging Uncle Billy. They got him down the steps and, with some difficulty, into the middle seat up front. He was half-conscious, babbling something about logic gates and mistakes, but the girls were more worried about Aunt Emily. She was dreaming in a way that made them nervous. There was not much time for either their aunt or their uncle.

"Beth!" It was their father's voice, stern and alarmed, enough to make them look up, enough to start Rusty—who was in the way back—barking. Their mother was part of the way up the steps, headed back to the mansion, but she'd stopped. "The doors," their father said.

And yes, the doors to the mansion were closed. Their mother and father spent a few precious minutes banging on the door, calling to

Nellie to open it, and finally Ruth called out. "Mom," she yelled. "Aunt Emily needs a doctor. And Uncle Billy, too."

Their mom looked at their father and then at them. "We've got to help Shawn, too."

Rose stepped out of the car, leaving Ruth to press on Aunt Emily's wrist. "Nellie isn't going to let you back in," she said.

"But—"

Rose walked up the steps and took her mom's hand. "It's too late," she said. "Nellie is going to keep him."

Both of the girls knew that. It was too late for Shawn. But not for Aunt Emily or Uncle Billy.

But it was close.

The drive from Eagle Mansion into Whiskey Run was torture. Their mother wanted to take over the wheel, but their dad insisted it was safer to let the car drive itself, a maddeningly slow pace given the weather.

After an hour, they had made it only halfway to Whiskey Run, but then, out of the blowing white, they saw flashing lights. The snowplow had come out to meet them. Their cell phones were still bricked, but Nellie had called for them, to make sure they made it to the medical center.

In Whiskey Run, the doctor stabilized Aunt Emily as best he could while a nurse worked on Uncle Billy. Both of them were hooked up to tubes and machines that beeped and blinked.

After a short while, the doctor turned to Beth and Rothko and told them there wasn't any more he could do in Whiskey Run.

"We've got to get them to a real hospital. Normally, I'd call to have them choppered to Syracuse, but with the weather, your best bet is to have the snowplow lead the way and drive. I think they're stable enough for that."

They spent a long night at the hospital. Every couple of hours their dad went out to the car and ran it for a while, taking Rusty for a quick walk and heating the car up. But mostly, it was just waiting.

FORTY-FIVE

ASHES TO ASHES

Only two things moved in the mansion.

The first was in the front hall: Shawn's chest heaved, his labored breath leaving bubbles of blood foaming around his lips.

The second was in the kitchen: the automated gas control swiveled fully open, the check valve held by Nellie's control. The hiss of the invisible, the inevitable. Gas seeped from the kitchen into the front hall and the downstairs rooms, leaking through the mansion.

All the while, Shawn's breathing slowed and slowed. And all the while, he could hear the mansion whispering to him:

This is your home. This is your home. This is your home.

After an hour, Shawn's breathing finally stopped.

That's when Nellie triggered the spark.

FORTY-SIX

ALL THE NEWS THAT'S FIT TO PRINT

Shawn Eagle Dead in Fire
Tech mogul killed in blaze at country estate;
Shares of Eagle Technology down 22%

Shawn Eagle, the tech billionaire and driving force behind Eagle Technology, was killed yesterday afternoon in a fire at his home in upstate New York. The mansion was located in a remote area, more than half an hour from the nearest town, and by the time emergency crews were able to reach the building, it was completely gutted. While the Federal Bureau of Investigation says the extent of the fire is such that they have not been able to positively identify either of the two recovered bodies yet, a spokesperson for Eagle Technology did confirm that Eagle is dead.

Local authorities believe the blaze was caused by a gas leak in the kitchen; however, the damage is so severe that it might be several weeks before a complete cause is known.

"We are devastated by the loss of Shawn Eagle. He was a visionary and a leader, and even though he positioned Eagle Technology to survive and thrive in the future, he will never be replaced," said Braxton Shandy, a spokesperson for Eagle Technology . . .

Eagle Technology Names
Johnston Acting CEO

Stella Johnston, chief marketing officer for Eagle Technology, was named acting CEO by the board. While a search for a new permanent CEO is ongoing, Johnston has been with the company for seven years, and the move seemed to help calm the markets. Eagle Technology stock has been extremely volatile in the month since founder and CEO Shawn Eagle died in a fire at . . .

Fire That Killed Shawn Eagle
Called "Perfect Storm"

While the Federal Bureau of Investigation says that its inquiry into the blaze that killed tech mogul Shawn Eagle is still ongoing, the lead investigator, Mike Mills, announced today that he believes there was no foul play involved. In the last two months, a number of conspiracy theories—most notably that espoused by Rick Nancy, host of the television show *Wall Street Takover!* on MSNBC—have claimed that Eagle was murdered in an elaborate plot to manipulate the price of Eagle Technology shares.

"Nothing is absolute," Mills said, "but it looks like it was just the perfect storm of bad luck. There was a gas leak in the kitchen and it ran long enough so that when it was triggered it was apocalyptic. The mansion had a state-of-the-art fire suppression system, but it was new construction, and something malfunctioned."

According to Mills, the location of the mansion was part of the problem. By the time emergency crews were able to respond, it was too late to stop the fire.

"The truth," Mills said, "is that when a fire burns this hot and this long, there's only so much you can determine. We had to resort to dental records to identify Mr. Eagle. But there are no signs that it was anything other than an accident."

When asked to comment, Nancy . . .

Eagle Estate Goes to Charity

According to Eagle Technology, the bulk of Shawn Eagle's estate was left to his foundation, Eagle Works. The foundation, like many of the larger foundations created by technology moguls, focuses on "big picture" problems such as hunger and disease eradication, while also having branches devoted to homelessness and domestic violence. Although it is a nonprofit, it has often worked in concert with Eagle Technology, and a spokesperson for the company confirmed that partnership is likely to continue. The gift from Eagle's estate, mostly in stock, is valued at over $100 billion, making it the largest charitable gift on record.

A smaller portion of the estate was left in trust for an unnamed former acquaintance of Eagle's. An anonymous source at Eagle Technology, afraid for her job security, confirmed that the trust was worth upwards of $1 billion. Repeated attempts . . .

FORTY-SEVEN

THE SUNSET

Billy almost forgot to put on a shirt. His old beater pickup truck
didn't have air-conditioning, so he'd gotten into the habit of peeling
off his shirt on the hotter days so he didn't get out with the cotton
sticking to his body. He'd left the doors unlocked and the windows
open—you had to. There wasn't much crime on Bonaire, but petty
theft was a problem. Locking the doors and closing the windows
just served to signal that you had something valuable in your car
and meant you'd come back to find a shattered window. Most locals
seemed to think the problem was punks boating over from Curaçao,
but Billy didn't mind. He just made a point of not leaving anything
of value in the truck.

Besides, he couldn't have left anything worth stealing in the truck
if he tried. Along with no air-conditioning, there was no stereo, and
he didn't own a cell phone. He carried his wallet in his pocket, and the
only time he had his scuba gear in the truck was when he was actually
headed out to go diving.

He pulled his shirt on as he walked into the bank. The air-
conditioning was unpleasantly high, but at least it made the sight of
the Christmas tree seem a little less jarring. December 3. Almost a full
year since they'd left Eagle Mansion.

Bonaire averaged highs in the mid eighties and lows in the high seventies every single day of the year. He didn't miss the snow. He spent all the time he wasn't working either scuba diving or swimming, and he'd even started running. It could be hard to get fresh fruit and vegetables, but he'd been eating much better, too. If you didn't count the brutal scar on his arm and hand and the way his hand was always semi-clenched uselessly into a claw, he looked good. The ravages of the years he'd spent drinking would never be completely washed away, but he looked healthy. He felt healthy, too. He was happy.

The manager saw him come in and she waved him to the back office. She thought it was weird that he insisted on doing everything in person instead of operating electronically, but he was the kind of client for whom eccentricities were allowed. It was an easy transaction today, in and out in less than five minutes, but then again, every transaction at the bank was easy. The manager didn't know how much money he was worth, but she knew he'd paid cash for both a six-bedroom oceanfront house and the business, and she saw how much money he kept in his checking account and how, every time the balance seemed to dip, a large chunk was transferred in. She'd asked him once why he drove such a terrible truck instead of a nice new luxury car.

He certainly could have bought one.

In the end, Shawn had done right by him and Emily. Or, if not by him, by Emily.

They would never have to worry about money again, and neither would Beth or Rothko, and neither would Ruth or Rose or their kids, if Ruth or Rose had kids when they grew up. However much money the woman in the bank thought he and Emily had at their disposal, she was probably short at least one zero.

He stopped at Van Den Tweel on his way back. The grocery store was unusually busy, but he didn't mind. There was no hurry. He filled up two bottles from the fresh-squeezed orange juice machine. Emily was still harping at him to quit drinking juice and to stick with whole fruits. Citrus did pretty well in transport, so that was something they had plenty of on Bonaire. But, you know, juice was juice. He also grabbed a large bar of hazelnut chocolate, which was the twins' favorite. He'd sneak them some when they got home from school.

The teenage boy working the cash register stared at his hand. "What happened?"

Billy peeled off some cash and then looked at the scar. It didn't bother him as much as it used to, but it was still an unwelcome reminder of what they had left behind at Eagle Mansion. "I had a pretty nasty bug," he said. "An infection. I ended up needing surgery. Ancient history."

The boy seemed unsure of that, but he gave Billy his change and bagged up the juice and chocolate.

Billy stopped at the house to put away the orange juice. He poked his head upstairs and called out but got no answer, so he went outside to the pool. Down a flight of steps from the pool, they had their own dock and access to the ocean. It wasn't the best place on the island to scuba dive or snorkel from, but it wasn't bad, and there wasn't a property they'd liked more. There was no sign of any of the adults. He looked at his Rolex. He liked having the watch there. It gave him something to look at on his left arm other than his ruined hand.

It itched at him sometimes, but the surgeon swore she'd gotten all the wires out. She'd asked him if he wanted to keep the . . . she didn't even know what it was. But he'd said no. He knew exactly what it was. It was Nellie's attempt to climb inside him. She had wanted to make it so that no matter where he went—if he ever left the house—there would be a piece of her with him, forever and always. Not to control him. Not exactly. Just to ensure that he would never be free of her. He didn't want to keep it, didn't want to look at it. He wanted nothing to do with it, and it had gone in a biohazard bag, to find its way to an incinerator. He still had dreams sometimes where he'd wake up panicked that there were wires inside him. A couple of weeks ago he'd even driven to the airport and had them run the wand over his arm. The security guard had laughed, but Billy had been relieved when the metal detector didn't beep.

There was still an hour until the girls were done with school. He stuffed the orange juice in the fridge, thought about it for a second, and then hid the chocolate in the back of the fruit drawer, figuring he'd be able to give some to the twins before their parents found it.

He spared a glance for the phone on the wall. The Realtor hadn't understood why he'd insisted on a corded phone when they all could have just gotten cell phones, and she was absolutely flabbergasted when he'd told her that one of the conditions of closing on the deal was removing the high-speed internet connection the previous owner had installed. No internet, no Wi-Fi, nothing connected, nothing high-tech.

They'd all agreed on that. Call it what you want. Paranoia. PTSD. They didn't care. It meant that they didn't have to think about it. Didn't have to worry.

He got back into his truck and drove down to the coffee shop.

As always, he admired the sign. It was cheesy, but he loved it: the name, Beanaire, such a stupid pun on coffee beans combined with Bonaire, plus a cartoon drawing of a coffee cup wearing scuba gear. It was a great sign. He parked on the far side of the parking lot. There weren't many customers midafternoon, but that was okay. The money didn't matter.

There was still a part of him that couldn't believe Shawn had left all that money to Emily. But there was another part of him that understood. That understood all of it.

He sat in the truck for a second to admire the view. You couldn't reach the ocean from the coffee shop, but you had a damn fine view of it.

He passed an older black woman who was sitting outside and reading. He could never remember her name, but he knew she'd been a teacher for forty years before retiring on Bonaire so she could go snorkeling every single day. That's why most people came to Bonaire, it seemed, to snorkel or go scuba diving. Billy had never done either before they set foot on the island, but he'd fallen in love with both. They all had. The girls were still too young for scuba diving, but they liked to snorkel, and they were looking forward to being old enough to get scuba certified. In the meantime, the house had a pool, and they were happy with that, too.

He chatted with the older woman for a few minutes, and he asked after her husband, who had been nursing a cold. When he went inside the coffee shop, he saw a young couple—clearly tourists—sitting at one of the tables and sharing a slice of chocolate cake. Rusty was asleep in the corner of the room, curled up on his dog bed.

Rothko was behind the counter, reading a magazine. He nodded at Billy. "If you're looking for Emily, she and Beth are out back."

"Thanks. How's business been?"

Rothko grinned. "Who cares?"

They both laughed. That joke hadn't gotten old yet.

He poured himself a coffee. He drank a lot of coffee, but he hadn't, not once since they'd left Eagle Mansion, craved a drink. It was like the desire had been burned out of him by the same fire that had turned Eagle Mansion into a wreck.

The same fire that had set them free.

He and Emily had talked about it only once. Once was enough.

He thought about it sometimes. Thought about how much control Shawn had given Nellie over the mansion. Over his life. And death.

Sometimes he could hear Nellie's voice. Sometimes he could hear those other, colder, darker voices that had replaced Nellie's voice.

But not most of the time. Most of the time he was happy.

He went out back to the patio.

"Hey, you," Emily said. She and Beth were lying on chaise lounges and reading. It wasn't a large patio, but it was private, and it got shade in the afternoon. It was quiet back there, and there was something about the way it was angled that made it feel like you could just reach out and touch the ocean. That patio was his favorite thing about Beanaire. Next to the punny name.

She started to get up, but he leaned over to kiss her. "Don't," he said. "Just stopping to say hi."

She sighed, clearly relieved. Billy thought she looked beautiful, all swollen and full, but she had reached that point in her pregnancy when she had to grunt to get out of a chair. She reached up and took his hand in hers. The scar on her arm had faded to white, but her arms were tanned, so it stood out. It would always stand out. It didn't seem to bother her, though. There was no lasting damage other than the scar. When anybody asked her about it, she'd just smile and say it was a silly accident, or she'd joke that she needed something to match the scar on Billy's hand, and then she'd change the subject.

Beth put down her book. "If you and Rothko want to take the girls out snorkeling when they get home from school, that would be fabulous."

"Of course."

"I'd take them," Emily said, "but I'm worried I might get mistaken for a whale. I don't want somebody to accidentally harpoon me."

"You look beautiful, baby," he said. He meant it, too. She was due just after the new year. They'd already fixed up one of the empty bedrooms in the house as a nursery. Ruth and Rose were plenty excited about getting a cousin.

He'd been worried about Ruth and Rose at first. They were quiet for weeks and weeks, barely speaking at all through January and February in Beth and Rothko's condo in Chicago. But it seemed like Bonaire had cured them. That haunted look disappeared from their eyes, and Beth said they hadn't had a single nightmare since they'd come to the island. They'd even started doing things independently of each other. Not often, and it was still almost impossible to tell them apart, but they seemed happy. Their only complaint was that Beth and Rothko had said no to a second dog.

He leaned over and kissed Emily again.

"I'll see you at home," he said.

ACKNOWLEDGMENTS

Thank you to my literary agent, Bill Clegg, and to all the fine folks at the Clegg Agency, as well as to my screen agent, Anna DeRoy, at WME. Thank you to Emily Bestler, Lara Jones, David Brown, and the Emily Bestler Books/Atria family.

As always, thank you to my family.